www.hants.gov.uk/library
Hampshire
County Council
Love
YOUR LIBRARY
Tel: 0300 555 1387

ERIC VAN LUSTBADER

THE SUM OF ALL SHADOWS

First published in the UK by Head of Zeus in 2019

9 7 5 3 1 2 4 6 8

A catalogue record for this book is available from the British Library.

ISBN (HB): 9781838931889
ISBN (XTPB): 9781838931896
ISBN (E): 9781838931919

Printed and bound by CPI Group (UK) Ltd, Croydon, CR0 4YY

Head of Zeus Ltd
First Floor East
5–8 Hardwick Street
London EC1R 4RG
WWW.HEADOFZEUS.COM

For Victoria, who keeps me from floating off into the ether, the upper air beyond the clouds. Always and forever.

SHAW FAMILY TREE

LAST FIVE GENERATIONS

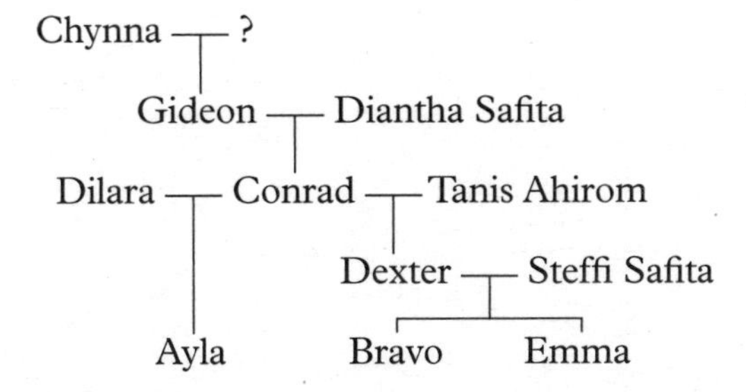

IN THE BEGINNING

In the 1500s, with the Franciscans at the height of their power and influence, the increasingly autocratic pope issued a verdict that would change the order forever. Worried that the Franciscan would soon rival his own Jesuits, Pope Leo X ordered the Franciscans to become Conventuals. This edict was in direct opposition to St. Francis's command to his followers when he formed the order. He told them to go out into the world to spread the word of God to the four corners of the earth. An intrepid group of Franciscan Observatines had traveled abroad over the Mediterranean to plant God's words in what seemed the fertile soil of the Levant, Constantinople, as Istanbul was then called, and beyond.

This was territory the pope had promised to the Jesuits, and so the edict called back these Observatine wanderers, called them back to Italy to work and study at home. In other words, to keep to themselves, while the pope's chosen order carried his increasingly bellicose word to the Muslim world. To ensure the Franciscans obeyed the edict, the pope had cause to form the Knights of St. Francis. But the group of Observatines already in the Levant refused to return home. They defied the pope's edict, even to calling themselves Gnostic Observatines, which poured salt on the wound they inflicted on the pope. They resisted the cohort of Knights the pope sent to take them home, by force if necessary. But it was the Knights who failed to return to Italy, their blood fertilizing the soil of the land the pope hoped to conquer.

The violent schism with Rome was accompanied by an equally angry break with the Franciscans who chose to obey the edict and become Conventuals. Over the years, decades, and centuries the enmity between the Gnostic Observatines and the Knights of St. Francis grew until they became the bitterest of enemies, even after Gideon Shaw, Bravo's great-grandfather, turned the Order further away from Romish doctrine in order to explore the more esoteric aspects of religion that the Vatican deemed anathema.

Today the Gnostic Observatines are more of a lay order, more powerful and influential than Leo X could ever have conceived, its reach extended into banks, industrial and tech corporations throughout the Americas, Western and even Eastern Europe, due mainly to the brilliance and uncanny business acumen of Bravo's grandfather, Conrad. And as for the Knights of St. Clement, their fate will be explained in due course.

PROLOGUE

Slight Return

THE MOON, BONE-WHITE AND BEAUTIFUL, HUNG LIKE A PAPER lantern in the sky, so close that Haya could almost reach out and touch it.

"It's time," her mother said. "Are you ready?"

Haya nodded as her mother bundled her into a black cotton jacket, then slipped on a quilted coat, also dyed black. Hand in hand, mother and daughter stepped off the porch of their house facing the beach on Arwad, and picked their way down to the shingle, where a small sailboat was waiting for them. Haya was lifted in, then her mother unwound the lines, pushed the boat out into the shallows, and kept its momentum going until she was waist deep before springing lithely aboard. She rowed a bit, then shipped the oars when deeper water opened up.

By the time they passed between the scimitar arms of the breakwater, the sail had gone up and had caught the offshore wind. She tacked starboard, coming around the outside of the southerly breakwater arm, until they were headed due west.

Moonlight fell upon the water like shards of ice. The stars sparked and twinkled. The water was pitch-black. Haya let her fingertips trail in the water. Her mother breathed deeply of the salt air and, for the first time in many years, felt the ecstatic brush of freedom against her cheek.

There were no boats about. She had placed them in an area free of both the fishing fleet and the shipping lanes. They were all alone in the night.

"Are you happy, my darling?" she said to Haya, though she could just as well have been talking to herself.

"Yes, Mama," her daughter answered. "Oh, very yes."

"Excited to meet your father?"

Haya screwed up her face. "I don't know my father."

"But, my darling, that's part of the excitement, isn't it?"

Haya, safe and secure in her mother's arms, allowed that it was.

The wind shifted and the sail needed tending to. A gust blew wide the open edges of Haya's jacket, lifted up her thin cotton shirt, exposing her belly to the moonlight. It was as smooth and unruffled as a porcelain vase. No navel indented or protruded from its perfect velvet surface.

Her mother, finished with her brief tacking maneuver, raised her eyes to the moon, noting its position in the sky. A shiver of presentiment passed through her as the last barrier to her freedom was left behind.

"He's coming, my darling." She held out one arm, gripping her daughter tighter with the other. Overhead, a flock of cormorants circled. "Your father is here."

Directly in front of their small boat loomed a darkness deeper than the night. As they closed with it, its six wings became apparent, then its massive upper body. For Haya's sake, the face was entirely angelic. No trace of the demonic was visible.

"Greetings, my husband." She put her hands on Haya's shoulders, presenting her. "Meet your daughter. Her name is Haya."

"How beautiful you are, Haya, just like your mother," Leviathan said. Then, he turned his gaze upon his beloved. "At last, Chynna. We are together again."

And with that, he scooped up the boat, gathering it and its passengers into his effulgent embrace.

PART ONE

DEATH BE NOT DEATH

1

BRAVO SHAW, HANDS ON HIPS, STOOD BENEATH THE brilliant Maltese sun. He was atop the highest point of the headland, the better to give him perspective on the site of the castle of the Knights of St. Clement. Of the castle itself, ancient and holiest of holies to the Knights, there was no longer the slightest sign. And, after the former head of the Knights' Circle Council, Lilith Swan, to prove her love for Bravo's sister, Emma, and her newfound loyalty to the Gnostic Observatines, had given Emma the electronic keys to the Knights' main server and thus the means to destroy them, the Knights themselves were scattered to the four winds, leaderless, penniless, without hope.

Over the protestations of some, Bravo had taken in a number of former Knights, after he and his sister Emma had vetted them properly. Currently, they were being used as guards, but in the longer run he felt their perspective could prove useful to the Gnostic Observatines in the war to come. One of those—a young woman he had newly recruited into the Knights—was Lilith's younger sister, Molly. He had initially sent Molly to Ethiopia, to learn as an assistant to one of the archivists working diligently on deciphering ancient codices, before summoning her to Malta. The two sisters hadn't seen each other for many years. Bravo did not know why: Lilith wouldn't speak of it, even to Emma, her lover. And as for Molly, she turned stony and nonresponsive when Bravo had queried her on the matter. At first, his motivation for bringing her aboard was simply to effect a reconciliation between them, but after vetting her he had begun to formulate another idea. In any event, Molly's presence had served only to infuriate Lilith. Molly was here now, helping him and Ayla supervise the construction of the Observatines' headquarters. As for Lilith, she was in

Addis Ababa, the Order's previous headquarters, directing the huge and complex move to this group of new buildings on the headland of Malta. Emma was scheduled to join her tomorrow.

In the months since the Order had taken over this acreage, the burned-down castle had been completely razed, the basement excavated and exorcised by giant machinery that broke the concrete apart, lifted the pieces, and ground them to a fine powder that was trucked away. A new basement had been designed and poured; the stones, bricks, steel beams, and wooden rafters brought in and erected. Belgian blocks were set, re-purposed wooden paneling scavenged from shipwrecks nailed in place, and winding staircases up to the second and third floors installed with Arabic filigreed balusters and newel posts, Moroccan tile risers, and pecan wood treads. The glazed tile roof shone green or blue depending on the angle of the sun. On clear nights, it glowed indigo beneath the full moon, and in storms it rippled like mercury unleashed.

There was still work being done on the western wing of the main building, as well as a number of the outbuildings that would house personnel, equipment, stores, and the like.

The largest of the outbuildings—quartering the staff soon to arrive from Addis Ababa, housing the various labs, study areas, seminar spaces for the newbies from the Knights, meeting rooms, and sheds to store maintenance equipment—were nearly finished.

Emma Shaw did not turn when Bravo came up beside her. She was staring beyond the cliff face, at the sea. The wind pulled her hair back from her face.

"About Lilith . . ." She turned to him. "She's very special."

"I believe you."

"I wouldn't have made it all the way to Arwad without her."

Bravo touched her shoulder. "Emma, you don't need my blessing."

"Need has nothing to do with it."

He nodded. "I know. I misspoke."

"It's true that she's been with the Knights of St. Clement, our erstwhile enemy, but she's proved herself by allowing us into their servers, by handing what's left of them to us on a silver platter. They're scattered, all but finished forever. Because of her. We could not have a better, more loyal ally. I very much want you to like her."

Bravo's heart melted. Why, he wondered, did it take a near-death experience for him to realize how precious she was to him? "I don't even know her." He stroked her arm, lightly. "But once I do I have no doubt I will."

That brought a smile to her face. "This is very important to me."

"Nothing could be more apparent, I assure you."

The moon, full and blazing with a cool, bluish light, highlighted her neck and cheeks, threw her eyes into shadow.

"So, Lilith aside, how are you doing?" he said softly. "Really."

She shrugged. "I wish I knew. This shameful episode in our family history . . . Great-great-grandmother, Chynna, mating with the Seraph, Leviathan." She turned her head away momentarily. "It's unspeakable."

Bravo let some time pass. "I meant you. Inside you. With all that's happened."

"I feel as if I've been hollowed out."

"How so?"

For some time, Emma stayed silent, staring out to sea, not meeting his gaze.

"Emma, what is it? Please tell me."

She sighed. "All right. If you really want to know I keep thinking about Beleth." She meant the Fallen angel who had invaded her.

Unconsciously, one hand stroked Beleth's talon. It hung around her neck by a gold chain she had purchased in Cyprus on their way across the eastern Mediterranean. She had bored a small hole near the top of the talon with a small bronze-bladed knife she had found where they had made their successful stand against the Fallen, deep within the bowels of the Arwad, the island off the coast of Syria. Nothing, not even diamond drill bits, could make a mark on the talon, but the Fallen were susceptible to bronze. The point of the blade punctured the talon without difficulty.

She shot him a sideways look. "It might sound strange, but in a way I miss him."

"That *is* strange." Bravo's brow furrowed. "And, frankly, worrisome."

Emma tossed her head. "I knew you'd react that way."

"Is there any other realistic way for me to react?"

"While Beleth was inside me, he changed." She rounded on him, her eyes flaring. "*I* changed him. *Me*. Not you, Bravo, but *me*, Emma Shaw."

"I thought we had hashed this all out."

"This power thing between us isn't so simple, Bravo." She tossed her head. "Sometimes I feel like a child around you."

"You're on the wrong track." Bravo shook his head. "Listen to me: It's your fixation on Beleth I object to. He wasn't your friend, Emma. Beleth was a Second Sphere Power. A warrior, in every sense of the word. Evil doesn't change. It's monolithic in its thinking."

"Now you're spouting Church doctrine." Sometimes searching his face was like looking at a rock wall. You saw the crevasses, but they didn't reveal the way forward. "Beleth wasn't evil, but I can see you don't believe me."

"I'd like to, Emma, but I can't."

"You mean you won't." She tossed her head. "You don't know. You *can't* know. He was inside me. I saw into his soul."

"Fallen angels don't have souls." The hint of a sardonic smile wreathed his lips. "Ah, yes, more Church doctrine."

"You have to trust me," Emma said firmly.

"Normally . . ." He shook his head. "Forgive me, but my concern is that with all you've been through your judgement might be a wee bit skewed—"

"So you *don't* trust me."

"Right now I don't trust your reaction to the trauma with Beleth. We stopped Leviathan from transforming you. By the skin of our teeth. You seem to have forgotten how close you came to being transformed by Beleth into one of them."

She laughed bitterly. "Nope. It was the other way around. You don't get it at all. But that's okay. I'm on my way to Lilith tomorrow morning, which means I don't have to see you for a while." The edge of sarcasm in her voice was unmistakable.

"Emma."

She shook off his offering as too little, too late. "I mean this family—our history." She shuddered. "In the bigger picture what you don't get is that no matter what we do or say, we're Shaws. We can't escape the fact that we have a Seraph's venom in our blood. We are steeped in ancient sin, murderous impulse, and treachery. We're damned, Bravo, and that's the truth of it."

Behind them the air was filled with shouts and the grinding of machinery as the Order's new headquarters was being constructed. Overhead gulls swooped and cried, skimming the air, then down the cliffside to the thrashing sea.

Bravo drew her to him. "Emma, believe me when I tell you that what we've just gone through has made us stronger. The past is the past. We can't change it, that's true enough. But what's important is how we handle things going forward."

She bristled: "It's too late, Bravo. You've said it over and over." She broke away from him. "A few chosen Fallen have already found their way into this realm through the Rift; and Leviathan's master must be close to opening the Rift completely. That will begin their final assault on Heaven, and surely our world's destruction."

"If you have a suggestion now's the time to voice it."

She stared at him for a long moment. Somewhere in the back of her mind a small voice was wondering why she had become so hostile. But a far louder voice, one she'd been holding down during years of frustration and resentment sent the small voice packing. "I'm going to find one of the Fallen, one like Beleth, cull it out of the group."

But Bravo was already shaking his head. "Absolutely out of the question."

"You didn't even hear me out."

"I don't have to. It's far too dangerous."

"Yes, of course. My judgement is a *wee bit skewed*."

"Put such suicide missions out of your mind, Emma. I need you in Addis Ababa, supervising the laboratory's move here."

"No, Bravo. You *want* me there."

"Parse it any way you want. The simple fact is I don't trust anyone else to do it." He raised a hand at her protest. "In any event, what you propose is too fraught with peril."

"But don't you see? I can get through to these demons."

"Just because you did it before, doesn't mean you can do it again."

"I can turn them, I know I can."

"I'm not going allow you to put yourself in harm's way again."

Her eyes blazed. "Your time of protecting me is over and done with. Besides, since I'm already damned what do I have to lose?"

Bravo looked at her skeptically. He seemed bewildered by her aggression. "Where do you even think you'd find one?" He shook his head. "No. I forbid it, and that's final."

"I will find one," she said, "and when I do, my blue fire will protect me, I'm sure of it."

"You can't be sure of it," Bravo said softly.

"If you say so." She dropped her head, made her voice small and weak. "And perhaps you're right. I'm unsure of so many things. We're not even Shaws. Shaw is a name Chynna made up."

"So we're Safita, Ahirom."

"And Sikar. Three of the four great families of ancient Phoenicia."

"And that makes us Shaws. All names are created by ancestors; ours is no exception." He looked at her levelly. "Grandfather Conrad somehow foresaw this outcome; Leviathan didn't."

"Sweet Jesus, I'm through arguing with you." Emma breathed. "Why wait for tomorrow? I'm taking the plane to Addis now, and that's the end of it."

Fat chance, she thought in the deepest fiery level of her mind. *I am the only one of us who has a chance to recruit another Fallen, the way I did Beleth. And I'm fairly certain I know where to start.* She smiled winningly at her brother. *Whether Bravo believes it or not.*

2

LONG AFTER HIS SISTER HAD DEPARTED, BRAVO REMAINED sunk in unsettling contemplation. He knew she was strong-willed, just as he knew that she did not yet understand the potential power locked deep inside her. The cold fire had unlocked the first door, but there were many more. And what wonders and terrors lay behind those doors Bravo couldn't impart to her, much as he would wish to in order that her maturation be accelerated. She was required to discover them on her own. Until that time, she needed protection, from herself, it now seemed, as well as from their enemies. He was convinced that something had happened to her while Beleth controlled her, something that had outlived the Fallen's demise. As soon as she returned with Lilith from Addis he resolved to keep a closer eye on her.

Turning his thoughts from Emma, he saw Molly. As usual, she was standing apart, and he went down to speak with her. She was smaller than her older sister, fair where Lilith was dark, but they had the same lurking intelligence. In the three months since he had recruited her Bravo had never seen Molly smile. She spoke very little. He meant to change that today.

She turned as she sensed his approach. Her gaze slid over him as if he were part of the landscape. She turned back to contemplating the platoons of workers swarming over the building, putting on the finishing touches to the outside and inside. The trucks filled with furniture were lined up, standing by.

"Everything going to your satisfaction?" Bravo asked.

"I imagine you find that amusing," she replied without altering the direction of her attention. "Seeing as how you've given me no sway here."

"Have a bit of patience," he told her. "Have you observed anything amiss?"

When she refused to respond to this, he decided to take another tack. "Why did you decide to join the Knights?"

"Didn't we go over this during my intake interrogation?"

"It wasn't an interrogation, Molly," Bravo said as quietly as he could over the noise of the various work crews.

"Call a turd a rose, if it assuages your conscience."

Bravo waited a moment before he said, "You're free to leave anytime you wish." He paused a beat to better drive home what he said next: "And yet you're still here."

Molly watched the progress with uncanny concentration. She pushed her hands into the pockets of the skin-tight jeans, which, along with black boots with thick soles, sleeveless shirts that limned her braless breasts, and a curious octagonal medallion she always wore around her neck, was basically her signature outfit. Bravo had asked her about it once, but her face had turned stony, and he had left the matter alone. Though her moods were mercurial, with him, she often played the flirt, but she came off as immature instead of sexy.

Her thin shoulders lifted and fell. "I've nowhere else to go."

"You have a home here," he said. "You know that."

She turned to him at last, looked up into his face with her intense, questing gaze. "Do you like me?"

And in that instant, Bravo got her, saw her underlying problem in a nutshell: Lilith was the accomplished one, the successful one, the mated one. Always measuring herself against her older sister, where did that leave her? Wanting on every front. Out in the cold. A homeless child, always acting out, never taken seriously.

"I might," he said, "if you allowed me to get to know you."

She gave him what seemed to him a dolphin smile or, because it was her, perhaps it wasn't a smile at all, but an expression he could not identify. "You might not like what you see."

"That would be up to me, wouldn't it?"

She appeared to consider this for a moment. "My father—Lilith's dad's brother—he and I lived with Lilith's family from the time I was a baby. Her mom was the only mom I ever knew. One day my father disappeared, and the next day, Lilith disappeared. Just like that, never came back."

"Without a word?"

"Without a word she abandoned us."

"Like your father, she abandoned *you*."

Molly's eyes slid away. "She did that, yes."

"Did you try to contact her?"

"I was eight." Molly glanced at him before gazing off into the hazy distance of memory. "It was a long time ago."

"So, what, you're still punishing her?"

"In that sense, I'm still eight," Molly said with startling self-insight. She looked up at Bravo. "That's what you'd say, isn't it?"

"What I'd say—or think—isn't important. It's not even relevant."

"Well, aren't you the charmer." She walked away, but soon enough returned. "I can be quite the shit, can't I? Well, I've been practicing almost my whole life."

"I think you need a new hobby." Bravo began to pick his way toward the series of driveways and gardens that had been marked out and were now being filled in. Somewhat to his surprise, Molly matched him step for step. "Have you ever asked Lilith why she left?"

Molly shook her head. "I don't want to know."

"I don't believe that."

"It might be too painful. I mean, what if it was because of me?"

He stopped so abruptly, she nearly stumbled over his feet, and it was only then that he realized how close she was. "Why would it be because of you?"

Molly shrugged. "I can think of a million different reasons."

"I wonder if she's aware of any of them."

"She'd have to be blind, deaf, and dumb not to be."

When he made no reply, she blurted out: "She left me!"

"And yet," Bravo said as gently as he could, "you joined the organization she was the head of."

"I—"

"Yes?"

"Nothing," she said, and this time when she stalked off she did not turn back.

"WHAT WAS that all about?" Ayla asked sometime later when she met up with Bravo in the building's entryway. The floors were in, the tile work finished, but the painting had yet to commence.

Bravo had met Ayla in Istanbul at the behest of her mother, who was an Ahirom, one of the founding Phoenician families of the Syrian island of Arwad. She had lost both parents to the Fallen. Together, they had traveled to Tannourine, in Lebanon, to the cave behind the Baatara Gorge falls. As a result of going through crucible after crucible against the Fallen. They were very close, and became even closer when she told Bravo that her mother had had an affair with Conrad Shaw, Bravo's grandfather. Conrad was her birth father. Like her mother before her, she was a Farsighter, someone who could often see future events.

"Molly being Molly."

She shook her head. "I don't know why you put up with her."

He sighed. "Sometimes, I don't either. But she's smart and she's detail-oriented: she often notices things others miss."

"But can she be trusted?"

His brow furrowed. "What are you really saying?"

"I think she's trying to play you. I think she wants to turn you against Lilith."

"If so, she's doing a remarkably poor job of it."

"Maybe she's still clumsy, feeling her way. She's still wet behind the ears."

"In many things, yes," Bravo said. *But in others, she's highly advanced,* he thought.

They moved farther into the building, into the two-story library, vast as a ballroom.

"As for whether she can be trusted," Bravo continued, "we'll just have to wait and see."

"That's likely to be a dangerous game."

He nodded. "I imagine it will be."

FOR THE Principal Resident, jealousy was the favorite of all transgressions. Jealousy had about it that delectable poisonous edge of schadenfreude—the desire to take pleasure in the misfortune of others—the Principal Resident found irresistible, basically because she found it in herself.

For at this moment, standing at the crystal window high up in the island tower where she had been imprisoned ever since the Fall, the Principal Resident had decided to be female. There was a certain flexibility of thinking that came as such a relief she became momentarily lost in giddiness. After all, Evil was a monolithic structure, with no option to retrace your steps or even branch off from the trunk. The inflexible solidity of the trunk was, in fact, its singular strength, the source of Evil's implacable power.

Though she stood at the window observing the masses of the army going through their last preparations for the final invasion of the realm of human beings, on their way to the assault of Heaven, her mind's eye was fixed firmly and lovingly on Emma.

She watched Emma boarding the Order's jet. Because of Beleth, Emma had a weak spot. Using the pathway that Beleth had created when he invaded Emma's mind, she again inserted the slenderest of poisonous threads into Emma's system to heighten her resentment. Seeing her twitch, she smiled, hugely satisfied with herself. The first strike of the wedge that would split the Shaws apart had been pounded home.

3

AS BRAVO AND AYLA MOVED THROUGH THE ROOMS, REDOLENT of exotic wood, stone, and plaster, Bravo was again lost in thought. It was Conrad whose echo lived on inside him, who had coached Emma, guided the blue flame conjured with a wave of her hand. Conrad did what no other human being had done and lived to tell about it: he made a deal with Lucifer, and then outfoxed him. But in so doing, the seam created by King Solomon's alchemists when they made his hoard of gold widened into a true breach between the realms of humans and the prison into which the Fallen had been cast down. The alchemists accomplished their otherwise impossible feat by siphoning dark sorcery through the seam. It took a long time, perhaps as much as eighteen months, for the seam was minuscule, the most their combined efforts could manage. It was certainly not wide enough to allow even a single Fallen angel to slip through, though some dispatched by Lucifer had tried. The breach expanded further when Ayla's mother, Dilara, brought her into the red tent of shadows in Tannourine, Lebanon, in order to trigger her child's extraordinary powers. Very possibly her Farsight had showed her the consequences of her actions. If so, it didn't matter; she knew what she was fated to do.

Ayla said, "I'm still unclear as to how Conrad is still alive."

"His friend, the poet Yeats, prophesied that I would be murdered before my time. Conrad did everything in his power to keep that from happening, but nothing worked. In desperation, he begged my grandmother, Tanis Ahirom, to summon Lucifer. Quite a power, Tanis was, in her time. In due course, Conrad struck a bargain with the Fallen Seraph: my father, Dexter, would be stripped of his powers and I—and by extension, Emma—would live."

Bravo chuckled. "What Conrad knew and Lucifer didn't was that my father would turn out to be useless to the Order. It was me—and Emma—who would be needed in the war to come."

"Conrad foresaw all this?" Ayla asked.

"With Yeats's help, yes."

"Go on."

"After his ruse became known to Lucifer, Grandfather was targeted. There was only one way he could escape the kind of death Lucifer had in mind for him. He secreted himself . . . well, even I don't know where."

"And so he survived, over the decades." She shook her head. "But in what form exactly?"

They were moving on, down a long winding hallway, which Bravo had had created, odd in any building of architecturally dictated right angles. For now, the walls were bare, but that would change soon enough. The custom lighting had been installed, soft, indirect, mimicking the flicker of rush torches from within stone niches.

"The ancient texts have a word for it: disincarnate."

"Conrad disincarnated himself? Am I using it correctly?"

"In our world, yes. Just before his corpus died, Conrad disincarnated himself."

They had come to a halt in front of a closed door. It looked like any other door in the building. In fact, it was anything but. Beneath the thin veneer of wood was three inches of reinforced steel. There was no lock visible, no knob either, just a titanium and polycarbonate iris-reader set into the wall to the right of the door frame.

Stepping up to the reader, Bravo looked directly into the glass-covered lens. A moment later the door popped open with a distinctive double click. As they entered the room, the lights came on automatically. The door closed silently behind them. The place felt like a vault, which, in many ways, it was. Windowless, set in the center of the building like a medieval castle keep, it nevertheless held the aspect of a monks' athenaeum with its weathered wooden desks, each with its own banker's lamp with a glass shade the color of a fly's thorax. The one concession to the modern world were the Aeron chairs set before each desk.

Here was housed the most precious of the Order's artifacts. Ayla was now familiar with all of them, save one: hanging on the rear wall was the painting they had found in the Knights' reliquary in a cave within the island of Arwad.

On first inspection, the painting seemed to be a study of *The Last Supper* by Leonardo da Vinci. Unlike all depictions painted before the fifteenth century, which portrayed the thirteen crowned with halos, this one, like da Vinci's, did not. It also showed those surrounding Christ in groups of three. In addition, unlike the earlier paintings, which presented the Last Supper from different perspectives, the placement and attitudes of the participants were identical to da Vinci's. However, the great artist's was a mural, while this one was smaller, residing inside a wooden frame as plain as the coffin of an indigent. Hence, the impression that it was a study. On closer inspection, though, it became clear that the painting wasn't by da Vinci at all, that it was far older than his or, for that matter, all of the earlier known paintings. The style was both cruder and more alive than da Vinci's, but it seemed clear that the master had had this in his possession at the time he was working on his own, because, as in da Vinci's masterwork, this Christ, these people surrounding him on either side of the long, food-laden table, appeared more like regular people than apostles and soon-to-be saints. They looked like they ate, drank, shat, and fucked just like everyone else.

In that respect, as well as others, it was a curious piece of work, more like an ancient tabloid illustration than a work of art that sought to commemorate for all time a holy and celestial moment.

They had brought it first to the Order's labs in Addis Ababa, but it had stubbornly refused to give up its secrets, including when, precisely, it was painted, and by whose hand. Neither the old-school forms of art identification nor—far more disturbingly—the most cutting-edge techniques, including X-ray analysis, microscopy, light refractography, infrared reflectography, and IR spectroscopic analysis yielded any answers at all. It was as if the painting had been locked away, as if it was completely resistant to any method of probing beneath the top layer of paint. And even the paint itself defied analysis. It was nothing any of the techs had ever encountered before, and they were experts at unraveling even the thorniest mysteries of the wide range of ancient texts that landed in their lab.

"A conundrum," they said, hands on hips.

"An enigma," they said, shaking their heads.

"Impossible," they said, throwing in the proverbial towel.

That was when Bravo knew. This was no ordinary artifact from the distant past. This was something exceptional. It had not been made by the hand of man. Or if perchance it had, it had been sealed by either an alchemist of the highest rank or, terrifyingly, something far worse.

MOLLY, HER palm and spread fingers pressed firmly against the reinforced steel door, listened intently to the dialogue between Bravo and Ayla via the vibrations transmitted through the air of the vaulted room, thence to the metal. These vibrations, though incredibly subtle, nevertheless came to her as if amplified by her splayed extremity, so that it was as if the room's occupants were standing beside her.

Ayla said, *"So what are we looking at?"*

"Exactly," Bravo answered.

Molly's lips curled upward in what could have been a smile. Or it could have been something else altogether.

4

IT WAS AN ILL WIND THAT BLEW NO ONE GOOD. ALMOST NO one. This vagabond wind raced across a barren sea, where red-eyed angels—foot soldiers of the Fallen—prepared for the final resurrection—day and night. Except that in this realm into which they had been hurled by an almighty hand there was no day—neither was there night. Only darkness, eternal and pitiless. This was as it should be, for these red-eyed angels required no pity. But rather scorned it as being beneath them. Which was, in its macabre way, amusing, since there was nothing and no one beneath them.

The liquid that was once held within the barren sea had burned away in an era before Time, before the Fall. The sole island, equally barren, equally bleak, had been waiting for the Principal Resident. The island stretched away from the barren sea, ending abruptly amid a jumble of steep, rocky cliffs at another ocean, so dark, so deep, so tempest-ridden even the Fallen were loath to set sail upon it. Over these inimical expanses dry gales blew almost constantly, each one taking to its bosom the shadow-webs it encountered, the vile emotions, the rancorous fulminations, until it arrived on the obsidian shores of what was the solitary island in this realm of ultimate desolation. On one side of this mass rose what might be termed a citadel, though it bore no resemblance to a human-made citadel. But then why should it? It was not made by the hand of woman or man; it was not made by any hand at all. Rather, it was a structure of what might be termed sorcery, but again, that was not quite correct. It was the product of its Principal Resident's will, made instantly manifest as he formed it in his mind. It sprang full-blown, as the goddess Pallas Athena was said to have sprung from the mind of Zeus. It looked like spun black-steel threads, or an incredibly intricate spider's web, and in some ethereal way it was alive, breathing to the beat of his invisible heart. There were three stories. The first was where the elite of the Fallen—the First Sphere Seraphs and Thrones, highest in the infernal hierarchy—dwelled, scheming and drinking Lucifer alone knew what foul ichor. The middle tier was where the Principal Resident held his periodic meetings. It was at these gatherings that the plans for the final insurrection, centuries in the making, were chewed over, endlessly debated, and, until recently, rejected by the Principal Resident. It was also from this one great room that the Principal Resident issued orders to members of his advance guard to venture up into the world of the humans, a place highly coveted by the Principal Resident, not only because it was, for now at least, forbidden to him, but also for being the first and last stepping stone to victory. This was prophesied by the Regent, the demon of fate, the Lord of Limbo, who, existing in his own world, answered to no one. It is said that he is the saddest of demons and the most bloody-minded, although no one, not even the Principal Resident, knows why. The Principal Resident had committed the Regent's prophecy to memory: *Only when the realm of men and women is conquered, when all humans are subjugated to Lucifer's will and eternal darkness everywhere falls, can the last stage of the assault on Heaven be launched.* This was his mantra, the daily curse he uttered, his singular goal.

And then came the third and highest level, the private quarters of the Principal Resident. Its topography was virtually unknown to those who dwelt below. Only rarely was one of them summoned Upstairs, as it was known among the elite of the Fallen, and then for short times only, and then that entity was forbidden to speak of the interview, if one could call it that. Inquisition was more likely.

Inside this pulsing, spun-citadel, its Principal Resident labored with an obsession that had, centuries ago, turned into mania. His incarceration was intolerable. Each moment, which, in a realm where time did not exist, he parsed out in his head. This millennia of helplessness at the hands of God fed his rage, his resentment, his humiliation, his thirst for vengeance. It was his food and his drink. A prison in and of itself, it kept him in a smoldering state of fury, rocking on the saw-toothed edge of rampage; in a form of madness that was his and his alone to bear. At times, it weighed him down, as if he were Atlas, carrying the world on his shoulders. But unlike Atlas's brawny shoulders, the Principal Resident's were thin, knife-edged. And they ached all the time where the six bloody stubs of his wings, excised at the moment of his defeat in Heaven, refused to heal. But at other times, it was a source of the most ecstatic elation, a consequence he was quite certain his nemesis could not have anticipated, despite his carefully constructed mythos of omniscience. Much as omniscience appeared to be a most satisfying goal, the Permanent Resident knew it for a seductive mirage, for to know everything all at once was to be insane. Insanity was the central thesis he voiced during the original failed uprising in Heaven, before he and all his minions were cast down into this abominable no-world.

During his endless incarceration, the Permanent Resident had touched madness, had once even tasted of its bitter flesh. But he had spit it out before it could enter him fully and poison him irrevocably. The small madness he held inside him was manageable, in some ways a comfort. Though daily others in the hierarchy of the Fallen came and went around him, spoke to him, received his orders, and on occasion voiced their dissenting opinions, it was his only true companion.

He sat in his study, on a woven silk-spun chair—at times of his greatest despair he thought of it as a throne, but really he was not that grandiose in his thinking; he was not a creature for whom physical things mattered in the least. He was created in the aether, and there he remained, even in his soiled prison, deathless. Without survival to occupy his mind, what was left to contemplate but all the things he had done wrong—the self-loathing?

A rattling at the crystal windows caused him to rise from behind his massive workbench-desk, laden with laboratory equipment, including racks of test tubes, lines of flasks and beakers, and a thick iron vessel, incised with glyphs, on a raised tripod above the same naphtha-fueled opalescent flames that lit the lamps. Naphtha and phosphor were the only fuels that worked in this God-forsaken prison. In the vessel a quicksilver liquid heaved like a sluggish sea whipped by an invisible tempest. The floor was the most peculiar element in the room. Made mostly of highly polished basalt sheets, it nevertheless featured a three-foot-wide dirt path, which ran straight as a spear from the massive door to the Principal Resident's workbench-desk. The path was as smooth as the basalt that guarded it on either side; not so much as a single footprint marred its surface.

Crossing the study, he threw open the windows to greet the tempest that had traveled far and wide to reach him. Feeling its touch, he threw his head back. His jaws hinged open, wide as those of a crocodile's. At once, he was filled with the prize Leviathan had sent through the Rift between realms. The Principal Resident vomited up the human, as real and alive as Peter Pan's shadow. It squirmed as he held it off the floor, long fingers curled around the back of its collared shirt, all six eyes fixed on the specimen.

The specimen took one look at the frightful creature before him and promptly passed out.

When the Principal Resident revived it, the specimen croaked: "Am I dead? I must be dead."

"If you were dead I'd have no use for you."

The specimen's hands shot to cover its ears, for the Principal Resident's utterance sounded no different than the screeching a penful of pigs make when they're slaughtered.

"Then where am I?" it managed. "Who . . . What are you?"

"You, insect, are a suicide. You have no say in your fate here."

As the Principal Resident examined his latest specimen, he wondered whether it would be the one to perfect the spike—a black shard perhaps eighteen inches long that he had painstakingly manufactured over the course of months, following ancient formulae long forbidden to mankind. In this same vein, he considered the Rift between realms, inadvertently caused by two incidents provoked by two generations of the accursed Shaw family. The irony of this never ceased to bring on a flush of pleasure—a gift that kept on giving! And still the Shaws were his nemesis, the only humans with the knowledge and power to defeat his purpose. Not that they knew the extent of their knowledge and power, and he meant to keep them in ignorance.

Dragging the specimen across the floor, he forced it to kneel beneath his workbench with head bowed while he positioned it correctly. Then, grabbing its hair, he pulled the head up through a hole, fixing it in place by means of a sturdy band around the neck. The specimen's mouth opened wide, doubtless about to utter pleas for mercy—for it was always thus with these specimens—when the Principal Resident touched its Adam's apple with the honed tip of the talon on his forefinger. The specimen was instantly rendered mute, which, of course, terrified it all the more. But the terror was just beginning.

The Principal Resident adjusted the specimen's head so that it turned upward. Now there was a clean path from mouth to throat, to esophagus, and below. Satisfied with the angle, he clamped a second band around the specimen's head. Then he inserted an implement that held open the specimen's jaws as wide as possible.

He smiled into the panicked face, and it was a terrible thing to behold. Tears welled in the specimen's eyes, overflowing, then running down its sunken, waxy cheeks.

Donning gloves of a peculiar woven metal, he picked up a pair of heavy-duty tongs, with which he gripped opposing sides of the vessel. He lifted it off the tripod, swung it until it was directly over the specimen's open mouth. Slowly and carefully, he tilted the vessel. The bubbling contents entered the opening in a thin stream. The specimen's body spasmed, the fists slammed against the underside of the workbench, the legs trying and failing to kick out. But the head remained securely vised.

The Principal Resident kept up the steady stream until the thick, heavy liquid reached the level of the specimen's guts, at which time he returned the vessel to its tripod, set the tongs back down on the workbench, and turned off the naphtha flame. The specimen was now dead, really dead this time, as opposed to being pulled along the life-death threshold by the sentient wind. In any event, it had served its purpose. It was nothing more than a husk, an empty vessel itself.

The Principal Resident stretched as he stood. He strolled to the tiers of shelves filled with ancient tomes, medieval scrolls, and rolled skeins of papyrus on which were written Egyptian hieroglyphics and other writings of the civilizations of prehistory. Selecting one of the scrolls, he unraveled it, held it under a naphtha reading lamp.

He scanned paragraphs of densely packed Tifinagh script. Tifinagh was the world's oldest language. It was from Tifinagh that the Phoenician language was born, and from Phoenician, Latin. The glyphs were interrupted by a meticulous drawing of what appeared to be a long black object eighteen inches in length, the precise duplicate of the one he had created. The drawing was annotated as if it were an architectural blueprint, detailing composition, length, width, and taper. He studied this drawing and its annotations as if he had never seen them before, though in fact he had committed them to memory the very day he had acquired the scroll with great excitement and anticipation some time ago.

Rerolling the scroll, he placed it reverently back on the shelf that was reserved for his most revered writings. Returning to the window, feeling the ill wind brushing up against his cheekbones, he murmured to it under his breath, sensed its immediate response. He smiled, staring for a moment out at the nothingness of the barren sea, at a sky without sun, moon, stars, or clouds. An unchanging dome that might well be made of stone for all he knew, just as he knew that, though he could send a few minions at a time through the Rift, he himself could not make the longed-for journey. But if all worked as planned that would change soon enough. And again, irony of ironies, it would be one of the Shaws who would usher him through the gateway into the world of humans and, thence, his assault on Heaven.

With that prospect a Xanadu in his mind, he turned back to his workbench. The molten material inside the specimen had now settled itself around the black spike. Creating, in effect, an armor plating impervious to any and all psychic or alchemical assault. Taking up a smaller pair of tongs, he slowly grasped the top of the spike. Its teeth had melted, the enamel lending the top a pleasing opalescent luster.

He lifted it up; it emerged anew as if from the womb. It was made of a crystalline substance of an astonishingly complex composition. It appeared to absorb light, turning it into shadows that seemed to move as if alive. Indeed, there was something moving inside the spike—his principal nemesis trapped inside this very special prison, though by its very nature temporary, as these crystals broke down too quickly to use the spike for permanent incarceration.

Now he held the spike up to the naphtha lamplight, polishing the facets as if he were a carver smoothing off the rough edges of his artwork. He worked slowly and methodically, and if he were another kind of creature—human, for instance—he would have whistled. If he were another kind of creature—human, for instance—he would have been happy. But he did not understand happiness, let alone have the ability to feel it.

When he was finished it was blacker even than the shadows it threw off, as a lamp throws off light.

Now he began an incantation that, had anyone else been in the vicinity, would have sounded like talons scraping across rough rock. Sparks flew up, swirling into a funnel shape not unlike a whirlwind. Each spark was a rune, each rune a word created in the Principal Resident's mind, shaped by his larynx, uttered by his half-open mouth. Faster and faster the incantation went, faster and faster the spike moved, describing complicated geometrical forms known only to a few of the ancient alchemists in the employ of King Solomon. Sparks pinwheeled off it.

A shudder rippled outward from it, set all of the room's loose items shaking and quivering. The panes of glass rattled in their frames, bowing out slightly as if from percussive noise.

Then all was stillness. An unnatural silence.

The Principal Resident took several breaths. The incantation and its result had taken a lot out of him, and he waited, patient as Job for his power to flow fully back to him. Then, and only then, did he hold it up in front of his face and with all six eyes stared into its faceted surface. Nothing. The inside was empty, as it should be. And yet, it showed him what he needed to see: the permanent prison it and he had incanted into being.

With a great upwelling of satisfaction, the Principal Resident saw the image of Conrad Shaw staring out at him in rage, frustration, and—could it be?—a bit of fear.

Yes. Yes, he believed it was fear. And why not? The unholy spike created the perfect cage to house the essence of Conrad Shaw. His prison blocked any connection, ethereal or otherwise, between him and his accursed grandson, Bravo Shaw.

5

HAYA DESPISED LEVIATHAN, BUT SHE WAS A CLEVER CHILD, and she knew not to show her dislike or even think it in his presence. She hated him not only because he came between her and her mother but also for himself; every time she saw him there was a vile taste in her mouth, like biting into a peach gone rotten.

Surprisingly, of this was Leviathan unaware. Haya had had enough practice concealing her feelings from the man who had raised her—the man who she had thought of as her father until her mother, Kamar, had informed her that Leviathan had sired her. Of course, her mother hadn't told her that Leviathan was a Fallen Seraph; she hadn't told Haya anything about Leviathan other than that he was her biological father.

For his part, Leviathan always took the form of a human male when he was with Haya. But one night when the two adults thought she was asleep, Haya slipped out of her bed, crept down the stairs of the house that had been awaiting them after Leviathan had swept them up into the spangled night high above the coast of Arwad.

She spied the two of them silhouetted by a ghostly light whose source she could neither find nor name. Neither her mother nor Leviathan was recognizable to her, though there was no doubt in her mind that that's who they were.

Her mother was taller, slimmer. Her nose was sharper, her lips wider, her cheekbones more prominent, and her eyes had an upswept tilt at their outer corners. Her hair was red instead of black, and her skin was as pale as porcelain.

Leviathan was something out of a lunatic's nightmare: a six-winged beast with red and gold eyes, a bestial snout, and ears like a bat's wings.

She shuddered and, just as she did so, she sensed his head turning in her direction, as if he somehow scented her, and she ducked back below the window through which she had glimpsed them. Down on all fours, she slithered like a snake across the floor until she reached the bottom of the stairs, which were out of view from outside. Then she sprang up and beat a silent tattoo on the treads up to her bedroom, hurling herself beneath the covers. She worked then to slow her breathing, while her heart hammered against her ribs.

Blue water, she thought. *You're sailing along the river, alone, safe. Safe!*

Moments later, Leviathan's human-shaped shadow fell across her bedspread like the contents of a spilled inkwell.

IN DEFENSE, Haya cast her mind as a fisher will cast her line, far off into the depths . . .

Where had Leviathan taken his inamorata and Haya? The house he had caused to be built for them sat on a ridge, the highest point in a valley slung like a hammock between twin mountains, craggy and pointed as a carnivore's teeth. These mountains scraped the slate-gray sunless sky, blocked out stars—if there were any stars. Down below, a darkly glistening river wound its way out of sight. This strange and unsettling land was so unlike Haya's home she might have been dreaming or at the bottom of the sea. It was impossible to tell whether there was anything at all beyond the mountains; the house and its surrounds seemed to Haya to have been created as a self-contained unit, as if this was the best Leviathan could do with world-building. And so, being clever way beyond her tender years, she had come to the conclusion that powerful though Leviathan might be, he also had his limits. A useful bit of information she filed away for future reference.

The interior of the house was most passing strange, seeming to change every time she attempted to explore it. One thing remained true, however: the interior was ever so much larger than the exterior. How this could be so, Haya had no idea. But she meant to find out. She was an incurably curious child. To her, learning was the most important thing in her life—in fact, in many respects, it *was* her life. It gave life meaning, and she was constantly on the lookout for more and more difficult puzzles to solve. Which was why the amorphous interior of the house fascinated her. Also, where did the food and liquids they ate and drank come from? There were no deliveries. She never saw either of the adults laden down with shopping bags. In fact, the notion of Leviathan carrying a shopping bag gave her fits of the giggles. But there was real terror hidden inside those giggles, like the horrid taste of soap bubbles.

Thinking of Leviathan and food, Haya realized that she never saw him eat a bite of anything she and her mother consumed. For her part, her mother never seemed to care for her food. Had she always been like this? Haya put a hand to her temple. She couldn't remember. There were many things from when she was younger that seemed hazy to her, as if they belonged to someone else, or hadn't existed at all. But this, like her mother's lost appetite, she laid at the feet of being in this awful netherworld.

Leviathan had an enormous tankard that sat empty—she had checked—until mealtime when, magically, it was filled with a thick, dark liquid he drank in great gulps, as if ravenous. He never seemed to sleep, either, but he always seemed ready to part her mother's legs and take her into their private room.

"For the child's sake," she had overhead her mother tell him.

Another puzzle for her restless mind to turn over and over: why did her mother call her "the child" and not "Haya" or even "my daughter"? *The child* sounded so cold and unfeeling, as if Kamar had adopted her instead of bearing her from her own loins.

WHERE, IN fact, Leviathan had situated Haya and Kamar was neither in the world of mankind nor in the ancient prison inhabited by the Principal Resident and the vast majority of the Fallen, those who still could not as yet worm their way through the Rift between realms, the way some could, singly. As Haya would discover in due course, Leviathan had taken her and her mother to an area of the Hollow Lands, long disused, long forgotten, hidden away like a sylvan glade in the midst of a dense forest. Except, so far as Haya was concerned, there was nothing sylvan about where they were. What her mother felt about it she had no idea. The instant Leviathan had appeared to them out of the eastern Mediterranean, Kamar had ceased to be so much her mother as Leviathan's plaything. That was not a word most children of her age—she had just reached her sixth birthday—would normally be acquainted with, however there was nothing normal about Haya. She had come across the word *chatelaine* in one of her mother's books she clandestinely read back on Arwad. It had a number of meanings, including the mistress of a large house, but she was quite certain this was not the meaning she would ascribe to her mother in this instance. She was Leviathan's lover, his mistress, his love-slave.

Sunless, moonless, starless here, there were no books but Leviathan's books and they were forbidden to her. With good reason, as it turned out. The one time Haya had tried to open one it had burned her fingertips.

AS THE shadow rippled over her bedspread like black water, Haya's mind momentarily returned from the faraway depths into which she had cast it. She was careful to continue breathing in long, deep, rhythmic breaths, just as she would if she were asleep; asleep was what she needed to appear to Leviathan.

His shadow loomed large and stupefying, and she sent her mind off again, this time into the recent past. Could it have been only months ago when she had loved crawling into her mother's lap, falling asleep to her mother's singing and, when starting awake with night terrors, being cradled against her warmth? It seemed to her that in the space of those months she had grown into an adult; her body was still that of a six-year-old, but her awareness of the world and its boundless possibilities had been irrevocably altered. The advent of Leviathan in their life had ripped away the protective veil of childhood her mother had provided; it had, with her mother's silent acquiescence, violated her childhood, stolen it from her like a thief in the night. This she would neither forget nor forgive.

But by far the most puzzling thing to her was how—and why—her mother would cede control of their lives to this, well, this monster.

She felt him close now—very close. His scent was pungent, like a fire of terrible things long burnt out but still, in some way, active. His head was close, his nostrils hoovering up the air around her, smelling her, *tasting* her in a way she found as horribly intimate as if he had stuck his nose between her legs. It was all she could do not to shudder, but she shut down that instinct with the iron control of an adult. She was indeed, in so many ways, an adult. A profound sadness pervaded her, for a moment paralyzing her thoughts.

This extreme manifestation of her sorrow turned out to be her savior. Leviathan was about to touch her, about, she was sure, to find out all her secret thoughts, but her paralysis stopped him. Something she had unconsciously done had halted him dead in his tracks.

And then she heard her mother's voice: "What are you doing?"

Leviathan's swift withdrawal. "Simply checking on her, dearest." His voice was like nothing Haya had ever heard before. It was as if many voices were talking at once, the one overlapping the next, like the wheezing start-up of an immense calliope—another word she had found in one of her mother's books. She had never heard a calliope, of course, but she imagined this was what it must sound like. If so, she couldn't understand how its music would bring children flocking to it. She was certain that Leviathan's voice would have the opposite effect, that it would send them screaming in all directions.

"I can do that," Kamar said. "It's a mother's prerogative."

"But I am here now," Leviathan said. "To watch over and protect both of you."

It was all Haya could do not to let out a moan of despair.

6

WITHIN MOMENTS OF ARRIVING IN ADDIS ABABA, THE STIF-ling heat was already getting to Emma. Blazing sun, blue skies throbbing like an ancient heart. The breathless morning verged on the unbearable; what would the afternoon be like? She longed for clouds to give her a modicum of relief. Fortunately, she didn't have to suffer for long. Lilith Swan was there to meet her and take her to the old compound that for years had held the Order's headquarters. Lilith herself had arrived just two days earlier, after three days spent at the GO's data center in Gibraltar, though there were redundancies in Reykjavik and the fringes of the Atacama Desert in Chile. There, Lilith had directed the siphoning of the deepest layers of the Knights' servers into the Order's hands. All the Knights' various bank accounts had been drained, all their contacts severed, bringing about the total collapse of the Knights' infrastructure.

Once inside the headquarters' blessedly air-conditioned labs, supervising the last of the packing and shipping of all the delicately calibrated equipment, Emma felt more herself—the person who was planning her escape; she'd had enough of being pinned under her brother's powerful thumb. She had power in her own right now.

The books and manuals and such were already on their way to Malta. Now the last of the double-lined crates were being trucked to the coast, where freighters were waiting to take the Gnostic Observatine paraphernalia on its last leg to its new home. The last of the scientists, historians, and techs were on flights to Malta. The bulk of the archeologists had been reassigned to Order digs in Jordan, the Sinai, Tuscany, and Crete, while a small group were staying on here temporarily in an outbuilding to complete their current project.

With Gnostic Observatine money the compound's buildings were being converted to schools for the local populace, some of the labs being repurposed for younger minds. Bravo had seen fit to put the supervision of the conversion into the hands of the local leaders he knew and trusted. Every dollar the Order spent would go to help the children and not to line the pockets of politicians. And so, by day's end, while the former headquarters was swarming with workers, trucks filled with desks, chairs, and the like being unloaded, Emma and Lilith had nothing left to do. All their heavy lifting was finished and the most precious of the laboratories' secrets were safely packed, crated, and on their way.

It was only then that Emma and Lilith were finally able to talk for the first time since Emma had flown in. Having had enough of the building site, Emma took Lilith's hand and guided them away from it, picking her way along the road, turning abruptly to the right, where a path led down to a stream, shaded by a large copse of acacia trees, their tops spreading like umbrellas, giving immediate relief from the burning sunlight. Inside the copse the shadows were stark, so absolute it took several moments for their eyes to adjust.

Sighing, Emma sat down on the ground, a cloud of ruddy dust rising to envelop them both. Side by side, they remained silent for some time. The topography muted the man-made sounds from the building site. The buzzing of saws, the rhythmic thwack of hammers, the occasional shouted order, and the gunning or truck engines seemed like a swarm of faraway insects.

Emma could still feel the pain of the wings that had begun to grow from the place just beneath her shoulder blades. And at night, terrifyingly, she thought she could glimpse them fully formed, shivering the shadows around her, even after Lilith, arms wrapped around her, assured her that all was well, that no trace of the wings remained, not even discolorations on her back. Still, she avoided the deepest shadows by day, constantly scrutinized her own shadow, fearful that they were, in fact, there, it was just that Lilith couldn't see them. Fear rode her like a beast, comingling terror and helplessness. Lilith said she might be suffering from PTSD, which was all too likely.

"I'm tired," Emma said now, resting her head on Lilith's shoulder.

"Didn't you sleep on the plane?"

"Too much to do."

"You go on like this," Lilith said, "you won't get anything done at all."

Emma stared out at the purling water, muddy-brown beneath the acacias, a blinding electric green where the sunlight struck it. She wondered what she was doing. It wasn't so long ago that she had allowed Bravo to talk her out of walking away from all this—the accursed Shaw legacy.

"I don't want any part of the fate of all the Shaws," she said now.

"Do you really think you have a choice?"

"Of course I have a choice!" she said a little too quickly, a little too loudly.

"In that case, why not just walk away?" Lilith waited a beat. "If you do, you must know I'll go with you."

What have I done? Emma thought. *What am I doing? I can't tell her where I'm going or why. She won't let me go alone, and this is something I have to do on my own.* Silence grew between them like the weeds on the shoreline.

"But I don't want to," Emma said at length. "Not really."

Lilith turned Emma's head toward her, looked at her full in the face. "Tell me," she said. "Tell me the truth."

"Always," Emma said, preparing to lie. "Always."

"Then what's gotten into you? Ever since I picked you up this morning you've been different."

"How different?" Heart in throat. How could she be so transparent to Lilith? Was that part and parcel of love? If so, she didn't care for being so exposed.

Lilith took a breath, let it out slowly. "I don't know . . . distant, preoccupied. And you're frowning all the time, like you're trying to work out a problem. Is that it? Because I can help, no matter what it is."

"Shut up," Emma said, not unkindly. "Please."

She caught a glimpse of Lilith's perplexed expression just before she turned away, ostensibly to contemplate the stream. Water-spiders climbed across its surface. A bullfrog lifted its head, then remained still as a stone until a mosquito came within range. Then *thwap*! And in the blink of an eye the mosquito was gone.

"A tongue that can kill," Lilith said with a small laugh. "Just like some humans, yes?"

"Yes," Emma said, and laughed too.

The frog, in the midst of its lunch, continued to ignore them.

LATE AT night, a cicada sang its sad rhythms in a twenty-foot Wanza tree outside their window. Over the bed, a mosquito net veiled them against the occasional whine. The room was shrouded in shadow, but blue-white bars from one of the perimeter security lights striped the lower third of their bare legs, twined like the vines creeping up the Wanza's trunk. Legs still entwined, they had finished making love: at first blush frantic with need, then, later, languorous with want. Now the night itself seemed to breathe in and out along with their own slow rhythm.

"I know you're worried about being vulnerable to transposition," Lilith said softly. "But just because Beleth was able to do it, doesn't mean it will be easier for another member of the Fallen to do it."

It's ironic, Emma thought, *but she's got it the wrong way around.* Lying on her bare chest, Beleth's talon rising and falling with her slow, relaxed breathing.

"You're on your guard now. Plus . . ." Lilith took Emma's right hand, turned it palm upward. "Say it."

Emma looked into her eyes.

"Say it, darling."

Emma closed her eyes for a moment, focusing her mind. *"Et ignis ibi est!"* she intoned. *Let there be fire!*

At once, a blue flame, cool and crisp as an autumn morning, sprang up from the center of her palm.

"The cold fire," Lilith said.

Emma closed her fingers, extinguishing the flame. "The thing is, I wish I could have saved Beleth."

"Because he changed."

"Because I saw inside him. He liked us, Lilith."

"And I think he learned to love you."

"I don't think he would have harmed me. Even from the first."

"Yeah? He scared the hell out of me. You, too." She eyed Emma. "If I'm not mistaken."

Emma smiled. "No, you're not."

"But, hell, Emma, he was *inside* your mind. Too creepy."

"But—and here's the important part, the part I didn't tell even Bravo—I was able to wall the most private part of myself from him."

Lilith took Emma's hand again. "So deep down you were still you."

Emma's eyes glowed, as if with the cold fire she wielded. "Always and forever."

Lilith kissed her. "And now I believe you could wall off all of your mind, if there was a need to."

Emma ducked her head, rested her cheek against Lilith's breast. For some time they lay like that, silent, listening to the cicada in the Wanza tree, the sound of their own breathing, and, for Emma, Lilith's heartbeat. The mosquitos in the netting were silent, possibly dead.

"Emma, I've something to tell you."

Emma felt Lilith tense, and she stroked her arm as she would a child, to soothe her. "You can tell me anything."

"I know." Lilith voice had dropped to a whisper. "But this . . ." She paused, licking her lips. "Molly hates me because I abandoned her."

"She's made that abundantly clear."

"Well, she doesn't know the truth." Lilith stopped there, seeming to have run out of breath.

Emma, intuiting she needed some help, said, "When I was eleven, I did something that made my father so angry he didn't talk to me for months."

"What did you do?" The relief in Lilith's voice was palpable.

"I followed him once, sneaked into the training facility he had set up for Bravo. See, it was secret. Mother knew nothing about it; if she had, she would've raised hell with Dad for possibly putting Bravo in harm's way."

"Training for what?"

"For what he has become, what he is now. And you know how close he's come to death."

"So have you."

"Well, that's the point. Why my father was so angry with me. He was bound and determined to keep me safe at all costs. The thought of losing us both was intolerable to him. I'm dead certain that if Mother knew she would have left him and taken us with her."

Emma sighed. "I know I shouldn't've been sneaking around like that, but I needed to know. I couldn't live without knowing, and you can be sure Bravo wouldn't say a word."

"It must have been bad, your father freezing you out."

"Those were among the worst months of my life. The time seemed to go on forever. And, of course I couldn't tell Mother anything. I was alone. Utterly alone."

"Did Bravo know?"

"Probably not. We weren't the best of friends then. Plus, I was all but invisible to him. He was too focused on his training and I was too young."

"It's awful being utterly alone."

"You sound as if you're speaking from experience."

And that's how Emma gentled Lilith over the last barrier of her reluctance. She spoke to Emma in a voice softened with grief, but also steely with rage. When she had finished, the room was very still. Everything held its breath. Even the cicada was shocked into silence.

"I know, right?"

Emma held her lover tighter, filled the hollow above her shoulder blade.

"So now you're left with the ashes of your relationship with Molly."

"And the waiting."

"Waiting for what?"

"My punishment."

"God is not going to punish you, Lilith."

"I don't believe in God."

"And yet you joined the Knights of St. Clement."

"They didn't believe in God; they believed in money."

"The universe doesn't hate you." She cupped Lilith's face in her hands, kissed her forehead, her cheeks, her neck, her lips. "I would say, judging by the last six months, it's just the opposite."

But Lilith didn't respond to her half-teasing. Silence again, until the cicada started up, as if, having overheard the conversation, it was offering its opinion.

"Emma, did I do the right thing?"

"I think that's for you to come to terms with."

She looked at Emma closely. "But what I'm asking is . . . if you had been in my shoes . . . if it had been you and Bravo."

Emma said nothing for the longest time. They both listened to the cicada, as if it spoke for the universe.

"Emma?"

"If I'd had no other choice—"

"I didn't, so . . ."

"Lilith, you know I can't absolve you."

"I know."

"Only you can do that."

"I know that too. Otherwise, I wouldn't have told you."

Emma sighed. "If it ever comes down to it," she said, "I would do anything to protect Bravo. Anything."

She wasn't only speaking of her brother. She'd do anything to protect Lilith, as well. And as much as Lilith's intimate confession lent urgency to her to make her own confession about what she was planning to embark upon, good sense prevailed. Lilith had no tools, no weapons to safeguard herself against the Fallen. To lie to Lilith now was to protect her from an almost certain death.

7

"I WANT TO SEE THE HOLLOW LANDS."

Bravo turned from taking books out of crates, putting them in order on the shelves of the library. Ayla was in another part of the building, taking a shower, or eating a cold dinner perhaps. They'd all been too busy to scarf down anything but pickup meals.

He studied Molly, trying and failing to find something of Lilith in the young woman's face. "I don't think that would be a good idea."

"Why not? I want to be of use to you."

Bravo shoved the books he was holding onto the shelf, aligned their spines. "You are of use to me."

She shook her head. "I don't mean logistics."

"Logistics are what I need. It's what you're good at."

She cocked her head, hands on hips. "Are you being deliberately dense? Or d'you take me for a fool?"

Bravo, who had been about to reach down for another couple of books, straightened up and turned to face her. "Neither."

"What then?"

They stood regarding each other for some minutes, not with hostility, but not friendly either. "You're not ready."

"Now you're being condescending." She shook her head. "You don't know enough about me to make that judgement."

He went back to transferring the books from crate to shelf, keeping them in order.

"What do I have to do to prove myself?"

"Stop acting like a spoiled child, for one." Bravo dusted off his hands.

"Emma and your sister are due to arrive back from Addis Ababa tomorrow. I want you to normalize relations with her."

"I can't do that."

"Then you're of no use to me. I have enough to worry about without having feuds going on around me. War is coming. Everyone has to pull together, no ifs, ands, or buts."

Molly took a breath. "If I find a way to have rapprochement with Lilith will you take me down to the Hollow Lands?"

Bravo's expression hardened. "I don't make deals."

"Everyone makes deals; it's human nature," she said. "Unless what some people say about you is true: that you're not really human." Seeing the look on his face, she tried to walk back her words. "I didn't mean . . ." She lowered her head. "That was . . . I'm sorry." She turned and fled.

LATE IN the night, Bravo was awoken by a familiar whispering in his ear. He opened his eyes. A wedge of light from the hallway intruded onto the bare stone floor of his bedroom. A moment later, it became a flame of wavering silver as a slim shape slipped through, occluding the illumination.

He knew who it was before he saw her face. She was preceded into the room by her scent, subtle but unmistakable. He could not tell whether she was clothed or naked. Not that it mattered; he knew why she was here. Nevertheless, he said nothing, watched her step slowly toward him, like a dancer placing one bare foot in front of the other. He noted with interest that she made no sound whatsoever.

She approached his bed, focused on him and him alone. From the partially open door shards of light fell back to the floor, as if she had brought with her incorporeal sentinels.

She was almost close enough to reach out and touch him when he said, "Molly."

She started as if touched with a cattle prod, froze in place.

And he said quietly but distinctly: "No."

It was a moment before she found her voice. "No what?" she said.

"There's no point in stating the obvious."

"I don't see anything obvious about—"

"You're not going to share my bed."

"Flattering," she replied in a tone he could not identify. "But first there's something you need to see. Downstairs."

He was up and out of bed in a heartbeat. "What is it?"

"Come. Come, Bravo. Now."

He drew on a pair of jeans, dropped a T-shirt over his head. He grabbed an LED flashlight from his bedside table, but he didn't bother with shoes. She hadn't, he noticed: in a hurry or wanting to move silently?

She led him out of his bedroom, along the hall, down the stairs. The building smelled new, antiseptic, unlived-in. It had not yet been imbued with the lives of its inhabitants. The techs, scientists, and archeologists, newly arrived from Addis Ababa, had been permanently installed in the most spacious of the outbuildings. Apart from the two of them, the compound was wrapped in slumber. Now and again as she hurried them down twisting hallways he could glimpse starlight coming in through narrow windows, lying blue and bruised on the bare floors.

He knew where she was taking him long before they reached their destination. He couldn't believe it. What did she know of—?

"There," she said pointing. She had led him to the vault that housed the prototype painting of *The Last Supper* they had discovered in the Knights' reliquary.

And then more forcefully: "There! Look!"

Bravo switched on the flashlight, played the beam along the bottom of the door, where a thick liquid was seeping out onto the floor. It glistened black as oil in the harsh light, but it wasn't oil.

It was blood.

8

THE FOUR THRONES WERE DEAD. IMPROBABLY. STARTLINGLY. Alarmingly.

Dead.

This was an unpalatable fact the Principal Resident had to deal with. Murmur, the Mesmerist; Phenex, the Scryer; Raum, the Declaimer; Verrine, the Reaver. His Four Horses of the Apocalypse. Dead at the hands of the Shaw family, led by the accursed Bravo Shaw.

High in his citadel, the Principal Resident pondered the question of who should replace them. Demons who could succeed where the Four Thrones had failed. True, they had managed to kill Phaedos, one of the Four Sphinxes of Dawn, but in the process the Thrones had been ground to cinders. There were other First Sphere Thrones, of course—eight, to be exact. But what was the point of sending them through the Rift between realms? Chances were high the accursed Bravo Shaw would ensure that they suffered the same fate as the Four.

The Principal Resident was rarely enraged; the long eons of his imprisonment had taught him the futility of rage. But Bravo Shaw caused him to loose his reins. Rage flooded him, and not only for Bravo Shaw, but his grandfather, the accursed Conrad, as well. It was Conrad who had outmaneuvered him, tricking him into a bargain for Bravo's life in exchange for the gelding of Dexter Shaw, Conrad's son, Bravo's father. The Principal Resident had foreseen that hobbling Dexter would cause the end of the Gnostic Observatines. But even though he lent his weight to the Knights of St. Clement, the Observatines' mortal enemies, even though he helped them kill Dexter, the Order had not been destroyed. In point of fact, it hadn't even faltered. And all because of Bravo and Conrad.

So what to do?

The answer arrived momentarily. A rapping on the door, to which the Principal Resident responded: "Come!" That single word, spoken in that tone would have shredded his subject's eardrums had he been alive to hear it.

The door opened inward, silently as an owl's flight, to reveal a hideous figure, bent over with its hindquarters facing the study.

"Good dog," the Principal Resident said with not a hint of irony in his voice.

The figure rose to its feet, began to walk backward into the study. As it did so, it used a special broom-like metal utensil that hung from a hook outside the door to the study to erase its footprints as it went. It was only when the figure reached the workbench-desk that it turned around, set its myriad eyes on the Principal Resident. As a sign of fealty and submission its six pairs of wings were folded in on themselves. There was no sign of how it had entered the study; it had obliterated its final path to its Lord and Master.

"Kill those fucking flies," the Principal Resident said.

The figure who was Leviathan lifted his left hand, turned his palm up to palm down, and the army of flies rising and falling above his wings was instantly incinerated. The First Sphere Seraph had no need of a human body here. Its skin, looking slippery and shiny as an eel, was rubicund, its eyes flame-ridden. A single horn protruded from the center of its sloped forehead. A serpent's tail, thick and powerful, rose up behind it, for the ancient Jews were correct in interpreting the word *seraph* as *serpent*.

"I hate flies," the Principal Resident muttered. "I hate insects, period."

"You hate everyone and everything, Master, if I may be so bold."

The Principal Resident impaled Leviathan's gruesome face on the twin forks of his implacable gaze. "So. How is your Lady Love?" The Principal Resident spoke certain words with a certain emphasis, as if their first letters were capitalized.

"Passing well," Leviathan said.

"And the Abode you have built?"

"It fits."

"Big enough for the Four of you, is it?"

The Principal Resident's eyes flashed when he said this, setting a warning bell reverberating deep inside Leviathan.

"Is there a problem?" Leviathan asked.

"Of course, there's a Problem." The Principal Resident locked his wrists at the small of his back, like a university professor about to begin his lecture. "The Child is the Problem."

"Her name is Haya."

"She has no name here, Leviathan," the Principal Resident corrected. "It is wrong of you to believe otherwise. The Child is an insect, just like her Mother."

"Half-insect," Leviathan said. "She is half mine."

The Principal Resident shook his head. "You have many eyes, Leviathan, and yet you do not see the Problem. There is good reason why Miscegenation is not allowed. It leads to all sorts of Mischief of the mind, the Principal One being that you come to think of the progeny as anything But an insect." The Principal Resident paused, possibly to weigh the effect his words were having. Not enough, he must have concluded. "I despise them, Leviathan. The two of them are an Abomination. Make no mistake, the only reason I tolerate them is you, my Strong Right Hand. I have granted you this Leeway, but the Leash goes only So Far and no more. I have only to jerk on it once and you are back at my flank, alone again."

A drumbeat of rebellion briefly thrummed in Leviathan's breast, only to be abruptly quelled by the piercing gaze of the Principal Resident.

"No, no, Leviathan, we'll have None of That."

Unable to tolerate the scrutiny an instant longer, Leviathan lowered his head. Silence for a time. Leviathan could sense the clockwork apparatus of his Lord and Master's mind ticking like a bomb about to detonate, and was briefly afraid. Not for himself; he did not have that in him. But fear for Chynna. Haya—the Child—as well.

"And because your Unsavory Attachments worry me, I want you to leave them for a time. I want you to find replacements for the Four."

Leviathan, who was about to say, *That's easy, there are a number of other Thrones to choose from,* cannily bit that idea back. His Lord and Master would hardly set him such an easy task—one he himself would be better at. No, he sensed another hoof about to drop, and he was gripped with a sense of foreboding.

"That is your Reward for accomplishing the Task I am setting you. You will find the Regent."

Leviathan shuddered inwardly. There were few creatures he found unpalatable, but the Regent was one of them. The Regent was the demon of fate, the Lord of Limbo. He answered to no one, neither to the Principal Resident nor to God. He was a denizen of neither the aether nor the world of humans nor the underworld. It was said that he existed between realms, in an airless, lightless place where even the laws of the known universe did not extend. Perhaps because of this, he was the saddest of demons. And the most bloody-minded.

"You will find the Regent and with your Unparalleled Glamour you will convince him to Join with us as we make our Final Assault upon Heaven."

Leviathan was astonished. Tapping the Regent's shoulder was a breathtaking maneuver; one never tried before. And with good reason. The Regent was not to be trifled with: never, never, never. "Even if I find hi—"

"You *will* find him, Leviathan." The Principal Resident's voice was like the discharge from ten thousand thunderclaps, rocking even Leviathan back on his heels, making him grit his fangs so hard their tips punctured his black lips.

"He may not agree," Leviathan said, trusting that the trepidation he felt did not leak into his voice.

"I trust that with your Silver Tongue you will know just how to Woo him to our Cause."

The Principal Resident moved out from behind his workbench-desk. He carried in his right hand a curious-looking spike that threw off darkness the way his naphtha lamps threw off light.

Something about the spike and the absolute darkness which surrounded it made Leviathan uneasy.

"What is that?" he asked, before he could stop himself.

"This?" The Principal Resident lifted the spike. "Just a little Something I've Conjured up in my study here." His black lips curved just slightly at their outer edges, hinting of what was inside his mouth. Even for Leviathan it was not a palatable sight. "This is the Antidote to a venom that has been running through us like a fever."

His hand swept away any more talk along this line. "My Bet is my Bet, Leviathan. It cannot, it will not be Rescinded. But be Warned. If perchance you Fail me . . ."

Leviathan stood very still, what passed for his heart hurling itself against its cage of bones. "Then what?" he managed to get out.

That ghoulish half-smile again. "You will face the Consequences: you will witness the Eternal Agony I will visit upon your misbegotten Family."

He twisted the spike through the naphtha lamplight. Where it moved, darkness fell. "First, isolate the venom," he said in an incantatory tone, his eyes glowing with an unfathomable light, "then Neutralize it."

Then his eyes cleared and his tone returned to that familiar to his right-hand Seraph. "Go now, Leviathan," he said briskly. "And take Heart. For Lucifer is with you. Always."

DOWN THE rather steep hill, the river wended its way through the valley, curving like a serpent to her left and right—she had no sense of north, south, east, or west—vanishing into what might be mist or even smoke filled with shadows and secrets. Every so often, Haya was allowed down to the riverbank. The water rippled and burbled, its current swift and sure. Otherwise, everything around her was still as death. There were no animals evident, no birdsong, and no insects. But she was constantly on the lookout for the flies. Leviathan's spies—large and seemingly armored, their green-blue bodies gleaming evilly.

There were times when she felt panic rising in her like an amphibian squirming up through her guts. No sun, no clouds, no moon, no day or night. Only disorientation. And it was particularly these times, feeling overwhelmed, that she begged to be allowed to be released to the riverside.

It was an eerie place: trees vanished like wisps of smoke the moment she got close to them. Other, lower foliage crumbled to dust when she touched them. But the river—the river was real enough. There she crouched, dipping her fingers into the dark water, paddling her hands, watching the eddies and tiny whirlpools she made. With loose stones, she created jetties and harbors, shimmering crescents into which her imaginary sailors could put in, safe from the current. There was nothing to make a bit of a boat out of, nothing that would float. The sense of constant motion of the water, of it being here, then there, then rushing onward, which she longed to do, grounded her. The power of the river, which seemed to her in direct opposition to Leviathan's power, calmed her. She made the river her friend, whispered to it, nodded in assent as it replied in its secret language only she could fathom. Pale simulation of day into night, but beggars, she thought, could not be choosers, and she thanked whatever force guided the universe—not God, she didn't believe in either God or religion—for this water that ran through her hands, whispering its secrets, gifting her with something she—freak that she was—had never had: a childhood. She reveled in her time with the river, and for this period, she stuffed all her cares and fears into a trunk, locked that trunk, consigning it to the deepest, darkest corner of her mind's dusty attic.

Every once in a while, if she squinted hard enough, she could convince herself that she saw a boat upriver, not unlike the one she and her mother had used to shove off from Arwad—small, wooden, single-masted, with a canvas lateen sail. But when she looked again it was gone. Most likely it had never been there at all. Could this place be like the desert where, she had read, wanderers were lured to their death by mirages, images from their most secret desires, made seemingly manifest by their imaginations, their need for the visions to exist? Each time, though, she remained alone beside the river with no fish, no water-spiders. And thank Astarte—her guiding figure—none of Leviathan's disgusting flies.

She had been on the riverbank for some time when she was distracted by a large leaf spinning into view. Swirled by the eddies, it fetched up against her upriver jetty. Plucking it out of the water, she set it in the harbor she had constructed, but the stem made it back-heavy and it would not float as she wanted it to. She bit off the thick brown stem, relaunched the leaf-boat into the harbor, where it obediently sat up, waiting to take on its load of seeds and tiny passengers. She fervently wished herself to be small enough to board her leaf-boat, journey downriver, away from this beastly place, wherever or whatever it was. While imagining this, she chewed absently on the stem. It had a peculiar sweet-sour taste that was not unpleasant, and she kept chewing, now savoring the taste.

Whatever caused her to glance back over her shoulder at the house on the hill she could never say, but she saw that moment in time just before the downstairs naphtha lights were switched on. By the time the cold and baleful illumination leaked out from behind the curtains, a lacework that looked to her like the handiwork of spiders, she was standing behind a tree, hidden.

She took a path she had discovered that wound up the hill, the longest one up to the top.

9

"GO BACK TO BED," BRAVO SAID.

"Like hell I will."

Bravo, who was crouched down beside the tiny lake to confirm that the liquid was, indeed, blood, rose, turning on her.

"What were you doing here?"

"There's fresh blood coming out of that room," Molly fired back, "and you want to know what I was doing here?"

"In the middle of the night."

"Well, to answer your second question first, I couldn't sleep. And, as for why I was here, I saw you and Ayla go in here this afternoon."

Bravo stared at her. "And that made you curious."

"Aren't you worried that someone may be lying on the floor, dying in there?"

"There's no one in there, Molly."

"Then where—?"

"Answer the question," he thundered. In truth, he was itching to get into the vault, to find out what was going on inside it.

She sighed. "Fine, whatever." She fluttered a hand back and forth. "What really piqued my curiosity was the conversation the two of you had in there. About the painting."

Bravo frowned. "Beneath the wooden façade this door is solid steel. How could you hear anything?"

Stepping around him, making certain to keep wide of the blood, Molly placed her fingertips against the door. "That's how," she said, taking her hand away from the door.

"That's impossible," Bravo said, even though he knew from experience that if something seemed impossible, it wasn't.

"So's this blood," she pointed out. "Are we going to find out what's going on?"

"We?"

"I discovered it. I brought you down here."

Bravo knew that she was about to say, *I deserve to see.* She would have earlier in the day, but something about her had changed. Had she taken his advice to heart? Whether or not this was so he decided it would be far too much trouble to get her to go back upstairs. And, belatedly, he realized, that stubbornness, that strength was something he admired in her. More than that, he liked it.

"Fine," he said.

Turning back to the door, he repeated the procedure, unlocking it. The moment it swung open Molly made a move to step over the threshold. But Bravo held her back.

"This is human blood."

"How can you be sure?"

"I can smell the difference between human and animal blood."

"Okay, I suppose I could believe that. But you said no one's in there." She cocked her head. "Could someone get in there without you knowing?"

So far as he could tell her question was asked in all seriousness. He played the flashlight beam around the inside of the vault, followed the near-black line, reflecting like a diamond-encrusted serpent, along the floor, all the way back to the painting on the far wall, bleeding like a gutted animal.

"What the fuck!" Molly blinked hard, then passed a hand across her eyes. "Am I waved?" She meant was she high.

"Go back upstairs and fetch Ayla for me, will you?"

She hesitated a moment before saying, "Okay, sure. We're a team, right?"

Bravo, still searching for a hint of snarkiness in her voice, and finding none, said, "Half-right. We're also a family."

WHILE HE waited, Bravo entered the vault. He did so with the utmost caution, for though the blood was indeed human, there was a sour edge to it that perplexed and worried him. He listened for any words of wisdom from his grandfather, but nothing swam up into his consciousness. Still at the periphery of the vault, he turned on the desk lamps from a wall switch. Their light was warmer, softer than the LED beam of his flashlight. He squatted beside the winding stream. Leaning forward, he sniffed deeply, then almost immediately reared back as the unmistakable stench of rotting corpses, human ash, and open graves tangled in the usual sweetish, coppery smell.

He stood, picked his way along the stream until he reached the back wall. There, he peered at the painting. As in da Vinci's immortal work, this progenitor showed the same thirteen figures with Christ virtually dead center. Also as in da Vinci's depiction, there was a blank space at Christ's right-hand side, as the youngest apostle, a pasty-faced John, leans away from Christ. It was from this empty space at the table, which da Vinci specialists and religious scholars alike entirely elided, intent as they were on arguing over whether or not da Vinci had painted men or saints, that the blood was coming.

That space was bleeding. *As if someone had once been there,* but was now missing.

This was the first thing he pointed out to Ayla and Molly when they joined him in the vault.

"As I told Molly," he said, "the blood is human."

"Explanation?" Ayla asked, examining it closely.

And Molly said: "It's a freaking miracle."

"Is that a joke?" Ayla said.

"Of course it is. This thing freaks me out as much as it does you. Joking is my way of coping. Would you rather I panic?"

Ayla turned away.

"What?" Molly said. "Are you embarrassed by me?"

"I was wondering how long you were in Bravo's bedroom before you told him about the blood."

"Jesus!" Molly exploded. "Really?"

"You've only to take one look at how provocatively you dress, like you're inviting Bravo to fuck you."

"All right, you two." Bravo stepped between them. "Enough."

"I don't like her," Ayla spat, keeping her eyes on Molly.

"Back atcha, skank," Molly retorted. She was fairly shaking with rage.

"What did I just say?" Bravo pointed. "With all this spitfire the two of you have missed the fact that the painting has stopped bleeding."

"That's because it's achieved its purpose."

Bravo and Ayla looked at Molly. "What d'you mean?" he asked.

"We're here; the bleeding's stopped," she said with youth's ability to cut right to the quick. "Ergo, it got what it wanted."

"Which is?" Ayla challenged.

"Our attention," Molly replied.

Ayla snorted. She was annoyed with herself for letting Molly get under her skin. "Okay, then, smart ass. Now what?"

"Bravo knows," Molly said, eyeing him. "Don't you?"

"In fact, I do." His voice was heavy with foreboding. "It's time to see Oq Ajdar."

IN THE dead of night, Emma moved with the stealth of a jungle cat. Her time blinded by the explosion that had killed Dexter Shaw had inured her to the dark. Even better, it allowed her to navigate without the help of a light source.

After an extended bout of lovemaking, Lilith always slept like she was drugged. Emma took advantage of her lover's insensate state to slip out of bed, take her clothes to dress in the adjacent room, and leave the old fortress.

At the airstrip the Order had had built to accommodate jets, she boarded. She had given orders to the pilot to refuel and keep the crew at the ready for a split-second takeoff. He was used to such orders, and complied without comment.

Now safely aboard, she told him and the navigator where they needed to take her. Moments later, she was buckled into her seat. The engines started up, and the jet rolled out onto the end of the runway. It held fast for a moment, while last checks were made. Emma could feel the engines thrum, as if she were riding a horse held tense and ready at the starting gate.

Then the brakes came off and they shot forward, faster and faster until the wings grabbed the night air and they lifted into the star-spangled night.

Down below, Lilith, innocent of the enormous risk her beloved was taking, slept on in the quiet of the Addis Ababa night.

Forgive me, my dearest darling. A singular task lies ahead, and I'm the only one who can do it.

Kisses. Always,

Your Love

10

"IS THIS WISE?" AYLA ASKED. "BRINGING HER DOWN TO THE Hollow Lands with us?"

"She's earned it," Bravo said.

To her credit, Molly didn't smirk. Now that they were on their way down to the Hollow Lands—the place she seemed so eager to go—she was all business, sober as a judge. The Hollow Lands had an access point beneath the old Knights' castle, below the lowest level of the new foundation the Order had built. Bravo had replaced the crumbling upper half of the stone staircase with a new stainless-steel spiral staircase connecting to the lower half, where the stone treads were in better shape. It was a long way down, the vertical shaft lit by reed torches set into niches along the outer wall, which Bravo lit as they went. Clearly the shaft was hand-hewn, impossibly ancient, carved with tools that had been long forgotten by the collective memories of human history.

"This feels as if we're following Orpheus's journey to the Underworld," Molly said, in a tone that held a note of awe.

"There's more than a little truth to that," Bravo said.

Ayla had lapsed into an inscrutable silence; her expression gave away nothing of her current mood.

They were halfway down, having just transferred to the old stone steps from the spiral stainless-steel treads, when Molly said, "You said that hearing what you and Ayla said through the vault door was impossible."

"If I've learned anything since my father's murder it's that nothing is impossible," Bravo replied.

"You did *what*?" Ayla said almost at the same time.

He stopped their descent, turned back to stare at Molly. "Can you explain to me how you were able to hear that conversation through a door?"

"I can't. It's just something I've always been able to do," Molly replied truthfully.

Bravo's gaze did not waver. "Then what is it you want to tell me?"

"I know what you're thinking," she said.

"Tell me."

"A wasp in the nest. I'm not. I promise I won't be."

She said this last to the both of them, and Bravo was relieved that she had included Ayla.

"I want to be of help. Honestly, I do."

"What do you know of the Hollow Lands?" Bravo said.

"Next to nothing," she admitted.

"Well, you'll find out fast. Keep your eyes and ears open. Remember everything."

Molly nodded.

Bravo returned to leading the way, lighting the torches. It was some time before Molly, glancing backward not for the first time, realized that the torches were not burning down. They simply gave off flames, remaining intact, like the sacred Burning Bush of God.

Nothing more was said, but Molly was acutely aware of Ayla watching her from behind, as if she expected Molly to suddenly turn on them, knife raised, teeth bared, or turn tail and run. A shiver went through her at the thought. She felt herself to be in some kind of limbo—with the family, yet not a member of it. No matter if she stood next to them, she was still apart, not accepted into the fold. She wondered what it would take; she wondered whether she would ever be accepted. She was a sad clown, out in the cold with her nose pressed against a windowpane, watching a family gathering in the fireside warmth, toasting one another, praising one another, loving one another. Making promises to each other they had no intention of keeping . . . and just like that her fantasy evaporated, leaving her more certain than ever that she belonged nowhere.

At length, Bravo plucked the torch at his level from its niche, carried it aloft the final few steps to the rock surface upon which the staircase ended.

They were in the Hollow Lands. Molly felt her heartbeat accelerate until the thrumming of her blood in her ears became almost unbearable. A surge of electricity bolted through her like a runaway train. Something deep inside her was thrilled, another part of her she had never tapped. It was like a lodestone drawing her onward, as if this journey was meant to be.

Now we go forward, she thought. *Now we go to meet Oq Ajdar.*

"The Hollow Lands are accessed from four locations," Bravo said. "Malta; Arwad; Lalibela, Ethiopia; and Alexandria, Egypt." He picked his way slowly, deliberately, carefully. His tread was as light as the aether they breathed.

"But Oq Ajdar is in none of these places. She dwells in Another Place, another part of the Hollow Lands entirely." He paused to glance at the two women. "It's a place I have never been."

"Has Conrad?" Ayla asked.

"If so, he hasn't told me." Bravo's brow furrowed. "Which reminds me that he's been strangely quiet of late. I've tried to speak with him but he doesn't answer."

"Is that unusual?" Molly asked.

Bravo smiled. "When it comes to my grandfather everything is unusual."

But to Molly that smile was strained, thin as a coat of lacquer. She wondered whether she should be worried before realizing that she didn't know these people well enough to make a judgement. Still, something nagged at the back of her mind, wouldn't allow her thoughts to settle, but kept them scattered like dry leaves in an autumn wind.

They moved on, but gradually Molly sensed that they were going in a circle. She was about to point out that maybe Bravo had lost his way when she saw that their path was deliberate. Bravo was leading them in smaller and smaller concentric circles. Too, he had slowed the pace considerably. Nevertheless, she found herself growing dizzy. A softly spoken incantation wafted over her. Ayla's lips were moving, the breath she emitted was dark as smoke, thick as fog. The space around the three of them grew shadowy and disturbed, as if roiled by invisible currents. An eerie whistling came to her, like wind caught in the cracks of an old, abandoned house on Halloween. Her skin crawled with goose bumps.

It seemed to her that midnight was fast approaching, though why she thought that she couldn't say. Perhaps because the darkness was increasing along with her vertigo. She staggered, felt that she might topple over at any moment. She tried to lift her arms to balance herself, but some force pinned them to her sides. She attempted to cry out, but that same force squeezed her voice box tight. She felt as if she were in the middle of a nightmare.

It was then that she began blanking out, at first for only seconds at a time, then for longer and longer periods, until at length she passed fully into unconsciousness.

11

"WHERE ARE WE?"

Molly heard her own voice, wobbly and feeble, as if it were coming from a faraway chamber filled with water.

"In Another Place."

It was a familiar voice, warm and intimate, and she turned her head to see Bravo watching her. Ayla was gauging her reaction. Judging how fast she would come to her senses. She decided she didn't like Ayla, not one bit.

But she did like Bravo. She liked him a lot. Better still, and much to her astonishment, she trusted him. She didn't understand why. But then, from the moment she met him—and the rest of his family—in the absence of hard evidence she had been going on instinct, allowing a deeper part of herself, one she had never before dared access, room to make itself felt.

"We're in Another Place."

Ayla repeated what Bravo had said, and whether the sharp edge of condescension Molly heard in Ayla's tone was real or imagined, either way, it reinforced her antipathy toward the other woman. That Molly was both peculiar and prickly was beyond doubt. By the same token, she felt the girl's intense curiosity like a ghost under that reflective shell.

Molly considered and rejected a number of responses, all within a matter of the blink of an eye. "Have you been here before?" she asked Ayla.

Instead of replying, Ayla looked to Bravo. "Where to now?"

But despite Ayla seemingly ignoring her, Molly understood that Ayla had replied to her, or at least betrayed that, no, she hadn't been here before.

"This way," Bravo said.

The reed torch he had been carrying had vanished. There was no need of it here in Another Place. Light emitted by unseen and unknown sources illuminated the space adequately. But this space was so high, so immense, that the light faded out into a charcoal gloom in all directions.

At Bravo's order, they continued on single-file, Molly still in the middle. She did not care for Ayla at her back, but there was no help for it. To speak up would be to admit to the kind of immaturity Bravo had accused her of.

How long they trekked she couldn't say; as in the Hollow Lands, all sense of time was AWOL. Actually time *and* space. They could be on Earth or light-years away. This sense of disorientation exacerbated her light-headedness, and she had to consciously slow down her breathing to keep an anxiety she had never known before at bay.

"Not long now," Bravo said from just ahead of her.

Molly, peering ahead over his shoulder, saw what she at first took to be a wall in front of them. But as they drew nearer she saw that it was in fact a mist so thick it had tricked her into believing it was solid.

As they stood before it, the mist swirled, coruscating with an opalescent light. At length, a dark patch seemed to form in its midst. The darkness grew larger at an alarming speed. Then it vanished, and from out of the mist stepped a creature of such immense proportions it took Molly's breath away. And this while it was still half inside the mist.

"What is that?" she heard someone whisper. She herself.

"Oq Ajdar," Ayla breathed, though it was clear she had never before set eyes on it.

A sound emanated from the creature so terrible that it all but curdled the two women's blood. It made their bones ache deep in the marrow.

Bravo seemed unaffected. He made no move, instead saying, *"Djat had'ar." He is present,* in the most ancient language of Tamazight.

The creature advanced all the way out of the mist so that they could see her for what she was: a white dragon. But then in the blink of an eye she became a sea serpent with metallic scales. Another blink and she was an enormous eagle.

Blink, blink, blink.

The creature—Oq Ajdar—was a chimera.

Behind her fluid shape-shifting, and through a mist that shimmered like metal, Molly glimpsed the sheen of a river as it wound between two seemingly identical peaks. On a hillock in the valley between was a building—a house, maybe? The image was smeared, indistinct with haze and distance. And then Molly saw—or thought she saw—a tiny figure emerge from the house—Molly had decided to call it a house—and run down an embankment to the riverside.

There might have been more—or the entire vision may have been a mirage caused by the mist—except that the dark medallion now began to tingle as if charged with electricity. It had belonged to the mother she'd never known; it was precious to her, all she had left of the unknown woman who had birthed her. But she had no more time to contemplate this exciting and terrifying experience. Oq Ajdar began to speak to Bravo.

"It is dangerous for you to be here," the chimera said in a burst of overlapping echoes and voices, ranging from soprano to basso profundo. "It is not written. You understand."

"I think that's the point, if I read you correctly," Bravo said. "The painting is bleeding."

Oq Ajdar nodded. "Ah, *The Last Supper.* The original painting."

And now it seemed to Molly that a shudder passed through the chimera's body like an icy wind. Her body melted again, reforming into that of a breathtaking female human—long blond hair flowing, huge sea-green eyes, wide lips naturally pink. She stood naked in front of them, without shame, oblivious to their various reactions.

"So you found me. It is as it should be," Oq Ajdar said in a voice that approached but did not quite condescend to being human. "We are on the cusp of something unprecedented since before the Fall, Little Shaw. Terrible. Dreadful."

Then an odd thing happened. The chimera's attention shifted, and Molly felt the creature's gaze drop upon her like a hundred bombs. Something detonated deep inside her, and her surroundings began to swirl around her. Stumbling, she almost lost her balance, but righted herself. *Breathe,* she told herself. *Breathe, Molly.*

It took several moments for her to realize that the sound emanating from the chimera was a laugh—or as close as the chimera could come to it. But it was a laugh devoid of all merriment, a bitter, sharp-edged laugh bleaker than a human's curse. She should have been offended, but for some mysterious reason she wasn't.

A heartbeat later the chimera's attention returned to Bravo, as though nothing had happened. Molly's relief was tinged with sorrow.

"Oh-oh-oh-oh. The End Times, Little Shaw," Oq Ajdar intoned in her oddly formal manner. "As was foretold in the *Nihilus Inusitatus*. The End Times are upon us." Oq Ajdar reshaped its corpus into the sea serpent, its glistening coils rising upward in a kind of rounded ziggurat, lending it even more of an ancient aspect. The beautiful human head remained. "So soon. So soon."

"What, precisely, does the bleeding painting signify?" Bravo asked.

The chimera morphed back into her human form. "Your grandfather has of course told you about the fissure between Spheres. This fissure is unlike the membranes which allow you to move between your Sphere, the Hollow Lands, and here. The membranes can be breached, as you know, by certain creatures, you Shaws among them. The membranes have stood since the beginning of time, when the earth was a fiery molten ball, before life was established there."

"Will you help us, Oq Ajdar?"

The chimera reared back; possibly she was offended. "Little Shaw, I brought you here. We are speaking together." She frowned. "But know that even this meeting should not be happening."

"But here we are, you and I. And you know that the Shaws are fated to try to save humankind or die in the attempt."

"Humankind!" Oq Ajdar turned scarlet, the color of blood as it hits the air. "You humans think so much of yourselves. You believe you are more important than anything or anyone. Sometimes I wonder whether you deserve to keep living."

"Oq Ajdar, I know it may appear that way, but I assure you there are humans who do not feel that way. Besides, we Shaws know the truth. As humans, we are nothing. But as Shaws, we are all that stand between Lucifer and his coming assault on God in Heaven."

"You know what you ask of me, Little Shaw. I am Medius. Bound to neutrality. Like my sister, Surah. Like my brothers, the Regent and Ayel-eye. We are all related by blood. Bound by Fate. Would you have me sever a millennia of trust?"

"As you said yourself, Oq Ajdar, we are at the End Times. All who oppose the rule of Evil must now take up arms. There is no other choice. Unless you wish to stand back and watch the darkness spread like a virus from hell to Heaven and everywhere in between."

The chimera appeared to ignore this outburst. "You are the djinn that

lights the way. Only you, Little Shaw, can gather the forces to stop the End Times from annihilating everything we know and hold dear. Only you can defeat he who is coming. He is already alight in his prison realm with the fervor of war. Gathering vital information brought to him through the breach. This too is foretold in the *Nihilus Inusitatus*. Your grandfather understood this. He has protected you, even from the afterlife.

"*You* must heal the Rift. It is written, Little Shaw. But know that he is even now moving hell and Earth to stop you." Oq Ajdar eyed Bravo. "You know him, Little Shaw. You have felt his shade brush against you, from time to time. And you know his name. He is the Sum of All Shadows."

Oq Ajdar was right. Bravo had brushed up against at least the whisper of Lucifer, though he hadn't known it then. On the day he had helped bury Conrad beneath the old apple tree where, as an elderly gent, confined to a wheelchair, he had tutored Bravo, against Dexter Shaw's express wishes. But then neither Dexter's father nor Dexter's son were in the business of conforming to rules and regulations, even those laid down by the Gnostic Observatines themselves.

"What must I do to close the Rift?"

The chimera took an alarming step forward, so that she was face-to-face with Bravo. "Little Shaw, hear me first. You must think of it as a wound. It was never meant to exist." The sea-green eyes had turned a blazing cobalt. "Never. Never. Never."

Bravo, feeling as if he had been struck square in the chest, rocked back on his heels. Such was the anger generated by Oq Ajdar.

The chimera's eyes changed back to sea-green and, as if shaking off her fit of ire, she said in a calmer state, "Conrad committed the gravest sin, which is why the fissure that is now a rift opened. The Sum of All Shadows outmaneuvered him. Despite his mother's pleas, he went too far in an attempt to save her. He failed. But his forbidden act cracked open a fissure. No one could have done that, save Conrad. The Sum of All Shadows knew that. Of course he did."

"And?" With a terrible foreshadowing, Bravo knew what was coming next.

"And," Oq Ajdar said, "since your grandfather opened the original breach, he is the only one who can heal the wound between Spheres."

"But you said that I was the one who needed to heal the Rift."

When Oq Ajdar did not respond, Bravo passed a hand across his brow. "The trouble is, my grandfather hasn't contacted me in some time."

The chimera's shape changed into that of a terrible bird of prey. Her marble-black eyes burned, her feathers gleamed iridescent. "Little Shaw. He is imprisoned. You must find him."

"Will you—?"

"Allies, Little Shaw. You have only to find them."

"But will *you* help me, Oq Ajdar?"

Bravo felt the force of Oq Ajdar's final statement: "I already have," and disturbingly felt the chimera's regret as his own.

12

THE CLIMB UP TO THE BAATARA GORGE WATERFALL WAS steep but hardly perilous. It was well-worn, but not by tourists: there were no telltale signs of discarded crushed beer cans, knots of urine-sodden tissues, and the like. No, whoever used this path that wound dizzyingly above the Lebanese town of Tannourine were professionals, trained to leave not even the minutest bit of evidence that they had made this climb. Whether these professionals were science-minded spelunkers or one of the cadres of hard-line, harder-line, or hardest-line Islamic terrorists who created, curated, and fueled the sectarian war in Lebanon was impossible to say.

The flight from Addis to the airstrip outside Tannourine had been a short one, nevertheless Emma had used her time in the air wisely. As she slept, she dreamed, and when she awoke just as the plane started its descent, she knew precisely what to do and how to go about doing it.

She had been to Tannourine before, following Lilith when they were still from enemy Orders. The small but well-equipped hiking outfitters was still there, manned by the same grizzled Lebanese owner. Such was the dearth of customers that the old man recognized her. All his equipment was high-end and state-of-the-art. He charged outrageous prices for the already expensive inventory, so he didn't need many clients. Emma bought sturdy hiking boots; a vest and trousers of a thousand pockets; a backpack into which she put a small but powerful LED flashlight; a short-handled pickax; a pair of WWII grenades, in perfect working order; and a half-dozen protein bars. Delighted, she bought a pair of binoculars that fit on the bridge of her nose like glasses; two knives, one thick-bladed with a serrated edge, the other a gravity knife with a wicked blade almost as thin as an épée; and a filled polycarbonate water bottle for each hip. She paid in cash; left no traces, like a good professional.

"Allah-Ma'ak." Go with God, the old man said.

"And with you," she replied in the same Lebanese dialect of Arabic.

Two-thirds of the way up, she began to hear the rush of the cataract, and just above, where the path turned inward to the right, she came upon an outcropping of rock, flat as a tabletop. Crawling out onto it, she stuck her head past the lip, adjusted her binoculars over her eyes. They were quite powerful: she could see clearly into the pool at the cataract's base. A bit farther out, where the churning water turned transparent, she peered through the shreds of sunlight coming through the trees.

Bones, rippling beneath the surface, like the banners of a defeated army. Human bones, stripped bare by carnivorous fish. She knew those bones, some of them at least.

Wriggling back onto the trail, she completed her ascent. Though the way became steeper and rockier, her boots held her and her knowledge of the path guided her.

She was drawn to the cavern behind the cataract as surely as a compass needle is drawn to true north. Perhaps the same principle—magnetism—was at work inside her body. It was here at the cavern's maw that she had been with Lilith. It was here that she had been with Beleth, Power of the Second Sphere. It was somewhere inside this cavern that the first of the Fallen to come through the Rift had lurked. It was a better place than any other she could think of.

The sound of the cascade was deafening. Water droplets filled the air like spray from a lawn sprinkler. She stood for a moment, transfixed, not yet looking at the yawning mouth of the cavern behind her. Through the multitude of tiny rainbows the cataract made of the sunlight, she saw the past in bright flashes. She turned away, disappointed. What she had wanted to see was the future. But that was for Conrad, not for her. Not for Bravo either, though there were times when she would swear he had inherited at least a fraction of their grandfather's Farsight.

Now she turned to face the darkness looming above her and, without another thought, plunged into it. The light motes that made it through the waterfall should have illuminated the forecourt of the cavern, but some peculiar quality of the place seemed to swallow the light from outside whole. Soon enough, she was surrounded by pitch blackness.

She smelled the mineral qualities of the rock, but also, oddly, the tang of sea salt. As she moved forward, the way pitched downward. It became far colder than she had anticipated, and she shivered.

She moved by her own enhanced sight, though, of course, she couldn't see every detail. She felt it wisest to acclimate herself to the darkness before she resorted to her flashlight, but soon enough the ground rose briefly and then fell away so sharply she felt it prudent to flick on the powerful LED. She could see where she was clearly now. Though it was made of solid rock, she had the eerie feeling that the cavern was organic, that she was moving down its throat into the innards of some fantastic, unimaginably immense beast.

She continued for some time, playing the beam of light back and forth as she moved from chamber to chamber. They varied in size, but in all other respects they were more or less identical: rock and more rock, each chamber oddly symmetrical, as if they weren't natural formations at all. But then what ancient civilization had the tools to cut through yards of solid igneous rock? Clearly, another intelligence was at work here.

Emma drank some water, tore the top of the wrapper off a power bar, and ate it slowly and thoughtfully. Finished, she crumpled the wrapper, stashed it in one of her vest's many pockets. At length, she arrived at a chamber far vaster than any she had yet passed through. It was illuminated by some form of bioluminescence that was part of the chamber itself, and she immediately switched off her flashlight.

Passing a hand over the rock, she determined that the most obvious source of bioluminescence—a lichen—was absent. To the naked eye, at least, the rock seemed the same as it was farther up. Where, then, was the illumination coming from? The rock itself? How was that possible? But she hadn't come here to explore the possible, rather to find the impossible. And now that she had found one form of it, she—

A sudden sound froze her. She felt her heart rate ramp up as adrenaline was released throughout her body. There it was again, coming from behind her: a kind of scraping, mixed with a moaning sound that, she was sure, emanated from no human throat.

She turned on her heel. Her eyes opened wide, and she cried: *"Et ignis ibi est!"* Let there be fire!

At once, a cold, blue flame sprang from the palm of her outstretched hand, flickering greedily at the intense darkness before her.

"'**IN THE** Judeo-Christian tradition,'" Lilith read, "'the Grigori are the Watchers, the mysterious Eighth Order of Angels God created to be mankind's shepherds.'" She read this out loud even though she was the only one to hear it.

Nevertheless, she could hear Emma's laughter and her voice: *Don't believe everything you read—especially when it comes to religion. More often than not, the scriveners dreamed these things up when it suited their purposes.*

Lilith rubbed her temple with her thumb. But she knew Grigori existed: one of the Grigori was a progenitor of the Shaws. And this was why, in the absence of her beloved, she was reading the closely held history of the Shaws, a slim volume Emma had left for her under the note. It was clearly old, hand-bound, covered in the cured skin of a creature vaguely reptilian but which she could not immediately identify.

She sat at the last desk remaining in the all but abandoned Addis Ababa headquarters, wondering whether the same could be said for her relationship with Emma. She had awakened at dawn with a catch in her gut, the sense that something was wrong. And so it was. Emma wasn't lying beside her. Worse, the imprint of her body, the hull of a ship in which she had happily sailed for many nights over the past months, was cold; Emma hadn't been in bed for some time.

Pulling on some clothes, she did a quick but thorough tour of the complex, progressing through room after room. It wasn't until she had ascertained that Emma wasn't anywhere in the vicinity, let alone the building, that she returned to the last usable bedroom, furnished only with a futon and a starkly serviceable dresser, nothing more, not even a mirror.

She had opened the note with trembling hands, read it through three times before collapsing onto her knees, like a penitent pleading for the power of Christ. Tears stained the note when she picked it up again off the futon. That's when she saw the slim book, waiting for her as if they had had a long-standing appointment.

"'First, we must describe the Grigori,'" she continued reading now. Her voice sounded a tremulous echo through the hollow shell of what once had been the scriptorium. By her elbow was a bowl of cold cereal; she'd had to use water, as there was no milk. It was half-eaten; she had abandoned it, disgusted, in midmouthful. "'They are members of the Fallen who, against strict prohibitions, take on human form, seek out human females, and fornicate with them over and over, for the Grigori have a prodigious appetite for the carnal. It is not difficult. The Grigori have a glamour about them that makes them virtually irresistible. But though they can bring human females to heretofore unknown heights of ecstasy, they themselves will experience no satisfaction. To boil it down to its essence, the Grigori have a mighty itch they cannot scratch.'

"At least they don't manifest themselves as swans," Lilith said to herself as she paused in her reading. At any other time, that wry comment would have brought a smile to her face, but only because it would have been a reflection of Emma's laugh. And Emma was gone.

"'The Greek god, Zeus, took the form of a swan and raped Leda. The result was their blindingly beautiful daughter, who grew up to become Helen of Troy, over whom the Greeks and the Trojans fought a decade-long war at the siege of Troy where so much blood was spilled, or so the myth goes.'" And this passage, like every paragraph in this book, reminded her of Emma, who could never pass up the opportunity to talk of myths, legends, and, especially, Catholic heresy. To separate fact from fiction peppered throughout the annals of ancient history. It was from her being reared in the bosom of the Gnostic Observatines, Lilith knew, and the thought made her weep anew.

Wiping her eyes with the back of her hand, she resumed her reading: "'The truth is this: Leda did, in fact, exist, and she was uncommonly beautiful: pale of skin, with a swan's long, graceful neck. The further truth is this: she was impregnated, not by Zeus, who was nothing more than a god created by the mind of humans. She was impregnated by a Grigori.'"

Lilith paused for a moment to catch her breath and also to take stock of what she was reading. A moment later, she resumed:

"'Leviathan, a Seraph of the First Sphere—the second most powerful of the Fallen—became a Grigori to seduce Bravo and Emma's great-great-grandmother, Chynna. Chynna named their child Gideon—a Nephilim. Gideon married the great and powerful Diantha, Conrad Shaw's mother.'"

Lilith looked up from her reading. "So," she whispered to herself, "if their great-grandfather was a Nephilim—progeny of a Fallen angel and a human woman—that must mean that Emma and Bravo are Nephilim, too."

But according to the Shaw history, they were not. Nephilim only pertained to the one generation following. Emma and Bravo were something altogether different. But if Conrad Shaw knew what that was, he kept that knowledge to himself. Perhaps even he didn't know, Lilith mused.

Here the history seemed to end. But when Lilith turned the page she discovered more writing, and in Emma's own hand, accompanied by bits of what appeared to be an ancient text affixed to the page. The text was in the form of primitive runes so odd they almost seemed like an alien language.

Lilith frowned in concentration.

Almost. The runes were Tamazight, arguably the oldest known written language and one of the precursors of Arabic, Greek, Phoenician, and Farsi. Lilith's forefinger hovered over the runes one by one. Here the runes referenced "The Protectors." And here, "The chosen of God's warriors against the Darkness-to-Come." And here, "The-Sum-of-All-Shadows."

She kept coming back to the one rune that Emma had copied in her own hand.

Aqqibar, Emma had written. *If I'm reading this correctly, that's who I am, who Bravo is, who Ayla is. That's why everything we do seems fated to happen. We're Aqqibari: the Protectors against the Darkness to Come. God's defense against the Sum of All Shadows.*"

"Aqqibari." Lilith tried the word out on her tongue. "Aqqibari."

She put her head down, continued to read: *That word sounds vaguely Arabic, and so it should. I know that you've read Frank Herbert's* Dune, *Lilith.*

Lilith sucked in her breath. Emma not only left this history for her, she had written it for her.

You remember that Paul Atreides came to be called Muad'Dib. *Well, I believe that Herbert appropriated that word from the Arabic* "al-mu'aqqibat," *the singular of which is* "mu'aqqib"*—literally "one who follows." But the actual meaning is a form of angel who provides protection for every human in life, sleep, and death. Even in resurrection. In other words, an Aqqibari.*

THE HOUSE was so large, its hallways so winding, its chambers so incomprehensible that Haya could not stop herself from exploring, despite admonitions to the contrary. In truth, the forbidden, clandestine nature of her forays, penetrating deeper and deeper into the labyrinth, was one of the major attractions for Haya. Which was curious, as she had never been a disobedient child; if anything, just the opposite. But something irreversible had happened to her when Leviathan had appeared in the night to take them off their small watercraft to this place of no sun-no moon-no stars, this Elsewhere, as Haya thought of it.

She invariably began her forays a half hour after breakfast, by her reckoning, anyway, since the house had no clocks, watches, or timers, even in the expansive kitchen. Here, time was as immobile as a stele of granite, carved with her name upon its sleek surface.

By her count at the thirty-minute mark following breakfast, during which Leviathan stood, arms crossed over his massive chest, watching them eat with indifferent eyes like a bored headmaster observing test-takers, her mother and Leviathan departed without a word to her. Where they went she had no idea. Once, she'd had a notion to shadow them, but she hadn't followed that up with action, and now discovered that she didn't much care where they went or dwell on what they did there.

Besides, ever since the advent of Leviathan she had come to look forward to her time alone with a bittersweet ache. She missed everything about her world—sun, sand, wind, birds, the sea tides, the scents of sea wrack, the laughter of the boatbuilders, the bawdy stories of the fishermen and seafarers upon their return home. On the other hand, neither Leviathan nor her mother were around to keep track of her. These periods when she was left on her own were all too short and, therefore, became precious.

The problem was that her wanderings produced nothing at all. Despite the house's enormous size, its rooms, so far as she had explored, contained nothing: no furniture, no rugs or carpets, no fixtures or electrical outlets, and, certainly, no living thing. After seven cycles of breakfasts (counting them being her only method of marking the passing of days) she had visited more than a score of chambers without finding even a speck of dust. It was as if the rest of the house, apart from the chambers where they lived, ate, and slept, did not actually exist, but was a mere sketch, there for appearance and nothing more.

Until the morning when she discovered—well, at first she didn't quite know what it was. Then, as she moved cautiously into the chamber, her path describing a shallow arc from the door to the object, she saw that it was a chair—but one unlike any she had seen before, or even imagined. For one thing, it was colossal; its back rose a good eight feet from the base of the seat. For another, the back itself was oddly shaped: two vertical spindles rising in tandem from the center of the seat only inches apart, they curved at the apex, making an attenuated U.

Haya stepped around it, constantly glancing over her shoulder at the open doorway, her keen ears attuned for the slightest ghost of a footfall. To be caught exploring by Leviathan would trigger a terrible consequence, the mere thought of which turned her marrow to jelly.

And yet she continued on, could not help herself, her curiosity growing exponentially the more she saw. For beyond the strange chair was a wooden table—old, scarred, stained black by countless layers of a substance she could not name. It looked to her like nothing so much as a butcher's table, on which animal carcasses were hacked apart. Blood turned wood black over time, she knew that, had seen it on her father's ship, the decks dark "with fish blood," he'd told her, but she was very clever; she'd guessed the truth—that the "fish blood" was actually the blood of humans.

So, this table: what was its purpose, set so close to the chair? And then, because she kept moving in that arc she had begun, she came upon the metal bucket, as outsized in its way as the chair. The bucket was stuffed to overflowing.

Her heart hammered hard inside her chest, her breathing came quick and fast. As she moved closer, she recognized the contents of the bucket: bones. And not just any bones—human bones. Her mother had taught her human anatomy as part of her homeschool education. And now that she was side-on to the chair and table, she saw what lay underneath the table: bones cracked open, gnawed through, the marrow sucked out, before parts of the bones themselves were crunched into slender shards.

She stared at this tableau for what, later, seemed a very long time. At the moment however, the seconds raced by her, chasing each other, as if they could no longer bear to remain in this chamber.

And abruptly, neither could she. Awakened suddenly from her trance-like stasis, she turned and bolted through the door. The moment she did so, she heard voices—her mother's and Leviathan's—raised in querulous argument. The acoustics of the house were such that she could not tell whether the two were near her or far off. Dread suffused her. Clinging to one wall, she crept along, knees bent to reduce her presence further. The voices rose and fell tidally as emotions ebbed and flowed, but they did not seem to grow closer, or grow more distant, for that matter. What were they fighting about? she wondered. It seemed that lately they were always at each other's throats, like a pair of wild animals. She no longer recognized her mother. It was as if Leviathan had drawn something out of her, a personality long hidden, which she didn't like, which made her afraid. To be afraid of your own mother was a hellish thing. It violated some cosmic balance she sensed but did not understand. But there could be no doubt of the wrongness of her current situation; it was absolute.

She kept going, silently placing one foot in front of the other, while she told herself over and over that she was safe, that no one would discover where she had been or what she had stumbled upon. The way back stretched out before her interminably, and yet her steps were unerring. She possessed an uncanny sense of direction. Even in the dark, a path once taken was indelibly etched in her mind. Even in this bewildering labyrinth of twisting halls and chambers, the one virtually indistinguishable from the next, she never lost her way.

Once, thinking she heard a sound, she paused to listen. She was beside a window, and peering through it the sky looked brittle, like the inside of an eggshell after all the nutrition had been sucked out of it.

Silence lapped at her ears, so complete it almost hurt. Like a pressure against her skull.

She kept going. Down the last hallway that debouched onto the bedrooms she crept, until she was no longer in *terra vetitum*—forbidden territory. Her narrow shoulders, which had been up around her ears in tension, relaxed, and her heartbeat slowly returned to a semblance of normality as the adrenaline leached out of her system. Her eyelids grew heavy.

Turning in to her room, she flung herself onto the bed. She could no longer hear the voices, but it didn't matter much, for two breaths later she was deeply asleep.

13

"THE BEACH HAS WIDENED," AYLA SAID. "THIS IS WHAT THE chimera, Oq Ajdar, told us."

"And to close it we must find your grandfather Conrad," Molly added. "Only correct me if I'm wrong, but Conrad Shaw died some years ago."

Bravo, Ayla, and Molly were back in Malta, sitting at the table in the main building's vast kitchen eating breakfast. It was just past dawn. None of them had slept well following their time with the chimera. Apparently, she had that effect on humans. Ayla had dreamed of the time her mother had taken her into the red tent of shadows, reliving her terror, and the fire she had somehow manifested in order to protect them both from the thing that reigned there. Molly had found herself in that place she had glimpsed behind Oq Ajdar, sylvan yet at the same time malevolent: the house on the hill, the shivering water below it, and, what drew her most of all, the small figure running down the slope to join the snaking river, as if they were best friends. As for Bravo, he dreamed not at all. Instead, his unconscious mind, freed of the restraints the waking world put on it, had gone searching, searching for Bravo's beloved grandfather Conrad. But every time he sensed that he was getting close he felt a vault door slam in his face.

"His *body* expired," Ayla replied, "but when you get to know this family better you'll understand that they have a different concept of death than you do."

Molly cocked her head quizzically, and Ayla said: "Bravo, I think you should do the honors."

But Bravo was lost in thought. Emma and Lilith were due back in Malta by day's end. He was looking forward to that. He hadn't cared for how he and Emma had parted and he wanted to apologize. Also, he was holding out hope that since she had acquired the cold fire, she might succeed at contacting Conrad where he had failed. He had heard Conrad speak *Et ignis ibi est!* If he had communicated with her in this way, perhaps she could speak with him using the cold fire.

Ayla reached for a slice of fresh-baked bread, slathered it with strawberry preserves, then dipped it in her thick, bitter, Turkish coffee. She took a bite, chewed thoughtfully as she watched Bravo not responding. "*The Last Supper* we took from the reliquary on Arwad began to bleed," she said slowly and carefully, as if speaking to someone hard of hearing. "Apparently, that was the sign that the breach is widening."

"Which means more of the Fallen will be entering our realm," Molly said.

The mention of the Fallen appeared to rouse Bravo from his ruminations. "Precisely so." He pushed his plate away without having eaten much of anything. Molly plucked a strip of bacon off his plate and, ignoring Ayla's glare, put it in her mouth in a way that seemed, as she leaned toward Bravo, salacious.

Ayla's brows knit in a frown. "But who sent the warning? Who would have that kind of power?"

"Isn't it obvious?" Molly said, popping the last bit of bacon into her mouth and chewing contentedly. When she had swallowed, she added: "It was the chimera herself."

"Excellent point." Bravo nodded his approval.

"But this breach . . ." Molly began.

Bravo said: "If it is allowed to widen or, God help us, crack open entirely, Lucifer and his infernal army of Fallen angels will pour through into our realm. He and his army will conquer and enslave us, to assist in his assault on Heaven."

"Hell on earth," Ayla said. Molly stared openmouthed.

Bravo nodded again. "Quite literally."

"But if the chimera is so powerful, why doesn't she know where Conrad is?" Molly said pointedly.

"You heard her," Ayla said. "She is a Medius. It's her fate to remain neutral."

"But Oq Ajdar said she had already helped you," Molly said. "And I don't understand that. I didn't catch any hint of help in anything she said."

"Allies," Ayla told her. "She said we have allies."

"But she didn't tell us where to find them," Molly protested.

"That's because you have no experience with her," Bravo said. "The chimera likes visual puzzles—it's a key component of her nature, being a shape-shifter. And in that regard, recall the creature she became when she told me that she had already helped me."

"A bird of prey," Ayla said.

"But how does that help us?" Molly asked.

"I believe I know who the chimera was referring to," Bravo told them. "To find out for certain we'll journey back to the Library at Alexandria."

Molly's face lit up. "Egypt!" She was so excited by this prospect that she forgot to flirt with Bravo. "When do we leave?"

"This evening. As soon as Emma and Lilith get back. I want Emma with us," he said. "In the meantime, I have some research to dig into."

"Then I've got plenty of time to get ready," Molly said.

Bravo rose. "Molly, you'll stay behind with your sister."

"What?" Molly looked like she was going to jump out of her skin. "But you can't . . . I mean, this is too important. I don't want to miss—"

"What's most important right now," Bravo said levelly, "is for you and Lilith to get to know each other all over again. You're both different people now. You will find a way to love each other again."

Molly crossed her arms over her chest. "This isn't fair."

"Fair has nothing to do with it," Bravo told her. "It's what's necessary."

She pulled an unhappy face. "Is that an order, Boss?"

Bravo laughed. "What do you think?"

THAT AFTERNOON, an exhausted Bravo fell asleep the moment he lay down—just for a moment, or so he told himself. During that time, he was subjected to an unhappy and enigmatic dream. He is adrift in a boat, a dinghy, a lifeboat without either sail or oars. He has the distinct impression that he is the sole survivor of a horrific catastrophe, all hands lost. The sky is obscured by clouds, the horizon by a fog bank. The sea is gray-green, opaque. The boat lifts and falls dangerously as it is tossed from crest to trough.

He becomes aware that he is barefoot, standing in liquid. It occurs to him that he should begin bailing, but it's not water in the bottom of the boat; it's blood. The blood of a man lying at his feet. The man's face is obscured by a decorative, hand-painted skull mask like the ones used in the Mexican Day of the Dead.

As Bravo stares down at him, the man says quite clearly, *"Misericordia." Mercy.*

And Bravo awoke thinking of the bleeding of *The Last Supper.*

14

FOR THE NEXT SEVERAL SLEEP CYCLES HAYA DID NOTHING untoward. She kept close to the house, not even venturing down to her beloved river, though she often stood at one of the windows overlooking the snaking water. From time to time she would be racked with shivers, as if she had a high fever. She spoke little, and only when she was spoken to. As a symptom of her mother's new personality, Kamar never inquired of Haya whether something was wrong. She appeared oblivious, treating Haya as if she were another piece of furniture. She only had eyes for Leviathan.

And it was not lost on Haya that she, herself, had changed since the advent of he who purported to be her father (she did not believe it; she refused to believe it). When she and her mother had set sail from the shore of Arwad that fateful night she had been a little girl, clinging wide-eyed to her mother's hip. But since then something strange—some alchemical process—had worked its magic on her. She leapfrogged childhood, sped past prepubescence, engaging with adolescence without many of the requisite tools time provided. Time had ceased to exist for her. For better or for worse, she was now as different a person as her mother.

During this period Haya slept fitfully or not at all. When she did sleep she found herself back in the Bone Chamber, staring at the colossal chair that in her dream was made of human bones, slimed with human marrow. She would startle awake, her body drenched in sweat, which, in the terror-hangover from her nightmare, she at first took to be the same marrow that dripped off the chair. Unable to tolerate her bed a moment longer, she would throw off the covers and catapult out, only to find herself roaming the hallway between her room and that of the adults at odd hours. From behind the wide door to their bedroom she'd hear grunts and groans that both drew her and repelled her. She'd sit, back against the door, knees drawn up to her bony chest, listening, hating herself, but hating them more. Images of the chair and table, the bucket of bones, and the discarded waste pulsed in her head. A pressure continued to build inside her, roiling her insides.

There came a morning, following a breakfast she could not get down, when the pressure reached a point that she feared would break her unless she found a way to release it. There was only one way, she knew that instinctively. She needed to revisit the Bone Chamber.

The road map was clear in her head, visions of her goal coming in disturbing flashes, like glimpses into someone else's mind. Along and around she went, drawing ever closer. And at last it waited for her around one last left turn. She paused, her heartbeat hammering so fast she could scarcely catch her breath. Lurching around the corner, she approached the Bone Chamber. The door was open.

She froze; sounds came to her from within: a low humming, almost snatches of a song, along with a rhythmic crunching. Like a somnambulist, she moved forward, impelled by the same kind of magnetizing force she felt in the hallway outside the adults' bedroom. Drawn on and repelled at the same time.

At the threshold, she stopped dead in her tracks. The colossal chair was occupied, and now she understood its odd construction, for the thing sitting in it possessed three pairs of bat-like wings. It was Leviathan, in his real form, chowing down on his own food—human bones.

His armada of flies rose and fell like a dark shadow along the bony cartilage of his uppermost pair of wings.

She stared and stared, scarcely able to draw breath. And then Leviathan dropped the bone he was slowly and with great relish annihilating. The chair creaked as he began to turn. Spinning on her heel, heart in her throat, Haya tore back down the hall, so terrified that tears overflowed her eyes, ran down her cheeks.

She ran and ran, frantic to get back to the relative safety of home base. But she was betrayed by her abject terror. For the first time in her young life, she lost her way. She could not think straight, running willy-nilly, her only objective to get as far away from the monstrous Bone Chamber as she could.

When finally she realized that she was lost, she stopped, listening for what might be coming after her, but she heard nothing. Trying to calm herself and orient her mind at the same time, she stepped into a chamber she had never visited before. Like the Bone Chamber, it wasn't empty.

Something . . .

It might have been her own reflection in a large oval mirror which stood against the back wall of the chamber. But then, probably not, because the shape shifted like smoke rising out of a chimney. Also—and this was odder still—the mirror, if that's what it was, was the color of twilight, of the moment after the lunula of the sun slipped below the horizon but before the stars had appeared.

"Hello?" Haya whispered, and, then, feeling utterly foolish, clapped her hand over her mouth.

STARTLED BY her daughter's voice, Chynna stopped in her tracks. She had decided to follow Haya after cutting short another erotic session with Leviathan, which had devolved from tiresome to outright repulsive. Odd, after all this time of being wedded to him, of being addicted to his sexual prowess, his sheer power. But something had changed her in this place. Had he always treated Haya so badly? She had been so certain that he would come to love her the way she loved her, but the opposite was true. He ignored her completely, never spoke her name, was openly disdainful when she reminded him that it was three of them in the house, not two. Gradually, she came to see him through Haya's eyes, how they left her every day after breakfast for hours at a time, and when they did return to the house he walked by her as if she didn't exist.

And then there was this, something—and how could she have ignored it all this time?—that now filled her with nausea even though there was nothing in her stomach and never would be again. He was invariably famished after their energetic coupling. Once, and only once, she had stayed, watching in mounting horror as he drew humans to him with his charisma and his sorcery, rending them limb from limb with fangs and claws while they bellowed their agony and terror. He stripped the bones of flesh and sinew, licked them clean with the same tongue he had employed to such orgasmic effect on her. While he gathered the shining white bones she had turned away, nauseated and sick at heart. That was the first time, and the last.

She knew better than anyone the nature of her daughter—her insatiable curiosity, the cynicism she sometimes displayed that was incomprehensibly adultlike. She also knew better than anyone Haya's unerring nose for getting to the heart of matters. Now, too, Chynna felt that her daughter was leading her toward something that sat at the crux of this vile house she knew to be part real and part dream-stuff.

But when she stuck her head around the door frame to the room Haya had entered, when she saw what was drawing her daughter toward it, she snapped her head back. Heart pounding in her throat, she turned on her heel and ran.

HAYA APPROACHED the mirror, or whatever it was, crossing over a floor of uncovered polished stone, like the floors in all the chambers she had visited. As she drew nearer, she could see a specific shape, though it kept morphing. One moment it was animal-like, the next, reptilian, and then, some sort of sea creature with a wide, flowing tail. Oddly, the face never changed, or, more accurately, the eyes, which watched her with such disturbing intensity that her eyes opened wide.

She continued to move closer until her nose was almost pressed up against the surface of what might be a mirror or something else entirely.

She thought she heard her name, and she whirled, terrified, but apart from the chamber with its empty doorway there was nothing behind her. She heard her name being called as if from a great distance or through the depths of an ocean, and she turned back to engage again with the searching eyes. Reaching out with her right hand, she was about to touch the dark surface, but in a lightning flash, the eyes vanished, taking the coruscating shape with them.

Before she could react, something grabbed her roughly by the back of the collar, lifted her off the floor, turned her slowly around. She was face-to-face with Leviathan. He was in his human form, but no less terrible for it. Her mind sketched in the three sets of wings, the tidal shadow of his armada of flies.

"What did I tell you?" he thundered.

She stared at him, unblinking, her expression a mixture of paralysis and defiance. Enraged, he hurled her across the chamber. Her back crashed against the wall, and she fell, her lungs emptied of breath. Before she knew what was happening, he grabbed her again with one hand, while the other slowly closed into a fist. As it did so, she felt as if he were gripping her heart, squeezing it in his fist to the point where, at any moment, it would cease to beat, her blood would refuse to flow through her, her empty lungs would collapse upon themselves.

His eyes were bloodred; she heard the buzzing of flies in her ears, she smelled the stench of death, which she had smelled many times on her island home, an odor so common it was tumbled up in her mind with the salt-scent of the sea and of blood. She felt herself descending into a pit of fire. It was a living thing, this fire, wrapping her in its leathery wings, crushing the soul out of her. She tried to cry out, but as in a nightmare no sound emerged, not even the feeblest peep. She was cocooned in the flames, consumed by them. Terror ran through her like a live wire, building and building until, like a tsunami, it crashed against the shore of her mind, obliterating everything in its path,

She ceased to think, ceased to imagine, ceased even to try to find an escape. There was no escape; there was only the terror, which overran her nerves, ripped apart every fiber of her being. And every time she was on the verge of passing out, something cold and clammy, like the underside of a many-legged insect, brought her back from the brink, drove the terror deeper into her like a hot poker, twisting and turning, until there was nothing left of her but disconnected bones in a ravaged shell.

15

"GONE?" BRAVO'S VISAGE GREW DARK AND HIS VOICE DEEPened. "What do you mean, gone?"

"Emma left Addis without telling me. In the middle of the night."

"Where did she go?"

Lilith shook her head. "I have no idea."

Unfortunately, Bravo thought he did.

When the plane landed Bravo had greeted Lilith warmly but had almost immediately looked beyond her, into the empty doorway at the top of the short stairway, eager to talk to Emma. When she hadn't appeared, he'd turned to Lilith and started querying her. But truthfully, he'd known something was amiss the moment the plane came into view; he could sense his sister's absence, like the scent of an unknown flower. Lilith subsequently explained to him Emma had had to hire a plane to get her off Addis.

There was nothing else she could tell him, or, he wondered briefly, was there nothing else she was willing to tell him? He knew how close the two women had grown, how deep their love was. It was altogether possible that Emma had asked Lilith to cover for her absence.

Keenly attuned to his intense scrutiny and intuiting what he must be thinking, Lilith added: "Honestly, Bravo, she didn't tell me that she was leaving, let alone clue me in on where she was headed."

He left the topic there as they made the short walk from the private airfield to the Order's new main building, asking her instead about the last of the move. The final stages of construction were, here and there, in evidence, but overall, the din was more subdued and sporadic now that the outside work was all but complete.

Inside, Ayla was waiting for them. She and Lilith embraced, but when her brow furrowed quizzically, Bravo brought her up to date on Emma's AWOL status.

"Where's Molly?" Bravo asked as he led the way into one of the rooms that was fully furnished.

Ayla shrugged. "Sulking in her tent like Achilles, I expect." She explained to Lilith Bravo's order for her to stay here with Lilith while she and Bravo flew to Alexandria to start their search for Conrad Shaw.

They sat on facing sofas while Bravo filled Lilith in on the bleeding painting of *The Last Supper* and their subsequent interview with the chimera Oq Ajdar. Giving Lilith no time to digest the momentous events she had missed, he said, "Do you mean to tell me that Emma didn't leave you a note?"

After a moment's hesitation, Lilith replied, "Well, yes, she did, as a matter of fact. But it was entirely personal—and intimate." Nevertheless, she dug it out, showed it to Bravo. Watching him read it over three times she tried and failed to divine his expression. "As you can see, the note gave me no idea where she had gone. But there seems little doubt that wherever it is, whatever she's doing, it entails a great deal of danger. She must have given the decision to leave a tremendous amount of thought." She took the note back from Bravo, folded it carefully, almost reverently, secreted it away on her person. "Personally, I think she didn't tell me where she was going because she knew I'd insist on accompanying her. And she was absolutely correct. The only way to keep me out of whatever she was about to do was to leave while I was sleeping."

Ayla turned to Bravo. "I think Lilith's right. That sounds like Emma all over." She leaned toward him. "Did she say nothing to you before she left for Addis? Do you not have a clue where she went, or why?"

Bravo shook his head. It was telling that Emma had gone to the trouble to hire a plane when she could have used the Order's jet. But, of course, he could track and follow the Order's jet; he had no such means to do that with a private plane. Now, after it was too late, he knew that she was more determined to contact another member of the Fallen than he had realized. When, he wondered, had his sister become so impetuous, so reckless? These were traits he associated with Lilith. Had they rubbed off on his sister? None of this speculation did he share with Lilith, choosing to keep his own counsel in the matter until events proved him right.

Without saying anything further, he left the women and went back to work packing for his own trip to the Great Library at Alexandria. There was still much to do and though the night stretched on before him, dawn—wheels up time—would be here all too soon.

"MOLLY, I'M worried about you."

"Now?" Molly was showering when Lilith stepped through the open doorway into the bathroom. She turned her back on her sister, as if she were afraid to be seen without her clothes on. "Get out of here."

"This is the only time we'll get to talk."

"Lilith, I swear to God—"

"The sooner the better." Lilith was determined to stand her ground, both literally and figuratively.

Molly made an exasperated sound through her nostrils. "Now you're worried about me? After all these years?"

"Yes. After . . ." Lilith felt her throat drying up. "That was then. This is now."

"Fuck you!"

Whipping a bath towel off a pile, Molly stepped out of the shower. The towel was half-soaked, but she wrapped it around herself anyway, seemingly not minding. Wiping her face down with her hand, she tried to get past her sister. But Lilith stayed where she was, squarely in Molly's path.

"Don't talk to me like that."

"Who died and made you boss?"

Molly slammed her open hand into her sister's chest. But Lilith grabbed her wrist, swiveling her upper torso, upsetting Molly's balance. Her feet went out from under her and Lilith forced Molly down to the floor, onto her back, and knelt over her on one knee. Molly tried to fight back, but Lilith slapped her down. Molly feinted with her right hand, clawed her sister's cheek with the nails on her left. This brought the two sisters nose to nose as Lilith closed her hand over Molly's throat.

Lilith's eyes blazed. "I ought to—"

"Ought to what?" Molly sneered. "Leave? Like you did before?"

"Shut up!" Lilith's fingers closed to a tighter grip, and Molly gurgled. Her bloodshot eyes bulged.

"Go ahead. Leave," Molly managed in a strangled voice. "You do it so well."

"I said shut the hell—" A wave of vertigo swamped her, and without being aware of it she released her grip on her sister.

Rolling out from under Lilith, Molly coughed and choked, her own hand stroking her reddened throat. The ends of her towel had come apart, and she hastily rewrapped it.

"The truth, Lilith. Finally. You left me, you abandoned me. Why? Why would you do that?" She paused, gathering her breath as well as her thoughts. Her eyes were dull, darkened by memories. All the fight seemed to have gone out of her.

"Stop! Please stop!"

Molly did, hesitant or fearful of continuing. Neither of them said a word. Their gazes touched, recoiled, only to return, hesitant as rabbits to an outstretched carrot. Rising, Molly went to her backpack, pulled out underwear, a shirt, a pair of tube socks, and skin-tight jeans.

"So." Another pause. Molly swallowed hard as she dressed. Every few seconds, she rubbed her neck. "Here's the deal: I'm the result of one of my father's affairs."

"What?" Lilith shook her head. "My God, so that's where you came from," she said when she had recovered from her shock. "I never knew; no one would tell me. I assumed Uncle's wife had died and so he came to us with you in his arms."

"No, there was no wife. And apparently, this affair was different. The woman was weird, or nuts, or something, and he took me away and we came to live with your family."

"How did you find out? Did your father tell you?"

Molly's face screwed up and for a moment it seemed as if she would resume weeping. Instead, she bit her lower lip. "He didn't *tell* me, per se. I overheard a whispered conversation between him and your father when they thought I was asleep. We had just celebrated my sixth birthday. I was in shock; my whole world ripped apart. I didn't know what to think. I snuck back to my room and tried to sleep, but of course that was out of the question. Around dawn I must have finally dozed off because I dreamt I was alone on an unknown sea, surrounded by fog. No land in sight, no idea where I had come from or where I was going. I woke up terrified. I didn't know whether to be grateful to my father for taking me away from my mother or angry at him for taking me away, and your father for accepting it all."

She shook her head, a frown on her face. "But adults do that, don't they? Tell you vague nothings or outright lies, and assume you'll believe them, take them as gospel, or else just forget about it, that it won't matter."

"But the opposite is true."

Molly nodded. "That's right. Being lied to as a kid is a big deal, and gets bigger when you have to try to figure out what's a lie and what's the truth and why they're lying to you all on your own."

"Kids shouldn't have to do that," Lilith opined.

"No. No, they shouldn't." Molly looked Lilith square in the face. "My father was a good guy. He must have been; he took me away from a bad situation, right? That must be it—at least that's the story I told myself then. I wanted to ask him, ached to do it, but I was just too scared—scared that he'd lie to me, that the truth was something he thought I wouldn't be able to handle. And then he was dead and you were gone, and I was alone."

Lilith felt shell-shocked. The floor canted queasily beneath her, and she put a hand out as if to steady herself. She licked her lips. Her mouth felt dry and raw. "You don't understand," she whispered.

Fists on hips, Molly replied, "I don't understand what, exactly?"

"Why I left."

Molly's eyes blazed, her hands gripping her backpack—her property—with white knuckles. "Abandoned me."

Lilith blinked; she was on the verge of tears. "He came to me every night, Molly."

Molly's eyes opened wide. "He? Who?"

"Which is why I never told you."

Molly shook her head. The high color in her face was proof she was working up quite a head of steam. "What the fuck are you talking about?"

"The truth," Lilith said with a great exhalation of breath. "The truth is my uncle—your father—physically abused me."

"What?" Molly gaped at her.

Lilith sat herself on the edge of Molly's bed. "Every night he'd steal into my bed and, well . . ." Her voice faded out. "At first, I was terrified, then so ashamed. I thought about cutting myself, but didn't. You would see and ask questions I wasn't prepared to answer. Anyway, Uncle swore me to secrecy, and I complied. I was his nighttime slave. Until the day I outgrew his tastes, the day he started looking at you the way he used to look at me."

Molly recoiled.

This was so hard, but Lilith knew that having started she needed to see this humiliating confession through to the end. "At that moment," she continued, "something snapped inside me. I knew I couldn't allow him to do to you what he'd done to me, and he surely would have if, if . . ."

"If what?" Molly's voice was like a lone songbird amid winter snow.

Lilith took a long breath, let it out slowly. "If I hadn't killed him."

"Oh Jesus." Tears welled in Molly's eyes. "Oh God."

Lilith's gaze bored into Molly, and there was no mistaking the truth. "Every fucking night. He didn't even have to swear me to secrecy, I was so ashamed, so guilty, so . . . diminished, I never would have said a word. But then you were coming of age, and I was so terrified he'd go after you, and I promised myself I wouldn't let that happen.

"I couldn't go to my mom and dad; they loved him, they'd have thought I was making it all up. And then there was . . . he . . . I mean, he had a handgun; I saw it once. It was in his closet, on the top shelf in a shoebox, fully loaded. He showed it to me, as a warning, I guess. If your birth mother was difficult, I imagine now that's how he was able to get you back so easily. He threatened her.

"And after I'd got him into the nearby lake, filled his pockets with the heaviest stones I could find, and watched him sink out of sight, I high-tailed it out of there. So in that sense you were right. I chose to leave you rather than stick around to talk to the police, to get sucked into an investigation."

An interval of quietus arose around them, but strangely, and to Lilith's relief, not between them. At length, Molly said, "It's going to take quite some time to absorb everything you've told me."

"That's only natural." Lilith did not know what else to say. All she wanted to do was grab her sister and hold her close, but their evolving relationship was still fragile, and she was afraid to do anything that might crack it open. Until they were on firmer ground, she would have to content herself with silently rededicating herself to never allowing anything to happen to Molly, no matter what.

Molly glanced away for a moment. "I'd . . . I'd like to know something." Her eyes cut back to Lilith. "You'd gone missing, why didn't suspicion fall on you?"

Lilith nodded. "Excellent question." Perhaps a question of pure logic was how they might take the first real steps to rapprochement. "Well, I had done some research. Snooping around about him, really. Uncle was up to his ear bones in gambling debt. I used that. I shot him once in the back of the head with his own gun. Mob style. When the body was found, the police were convinced the people he owed money to had taken their two hundred pounds of flesh. For them, easy-peasy, and they moved on."

Molly sat back, her expression slack. "I can't believe that you'd . . . that you'd do that for me. That you *did* that."

Molly, head in hands, broke down, great sobs shaking her shoulders, tears leaking through the gaps in her fingers, until Lilith gathered her in her arms and, kissing the top of her head, rocked her like an injured child.

"It's all right," she whispered as much to herself as to Molly. "It's all right now."

"Oh, Lilith. I should be consoling you." Her voice was as small and disconsolate as a creature that had lost its ability to find its way home. "What you went through, night after night. And then to protect me from the same fate . . ."

"Molly, we grew up together, comforted and loved by the same mother. You're my sister, not my cousin. I'd move Heaven and Earth to protect you."

Molly, sobbing uncontrollably, nose running, snuggled closer to her sister, kissed the side of her neck over and over. "I'm so . . . lost." She hiccupped though her sobs.

Lilith, laying her cheek against the top of her sister's head, said, "We both are." And realized with a jolt just how true that was.

A silence enveloped them, a warm blanket, a shared intimacy they had never experienced before and was, therefore, infinitely precious to both of them. At length, as if by unspoken mutual consent, they broke apart.

"The morning after I found out, after I'd cried myself to sleep, I went to Auntie, but of course I always called her Mom, as she wanted me to. She was so upset for me that I had found out—the *way* I found out. She pulled me to her, wrapped her arms around me, rocked me like a baby. When, at last, she released me, she got up and came back with this." She fished in her backpack, brought out a small black object on a thin silver chain. "She told me it was from my birth mother. It was our secret, her way, I think, of trying to bind me to her because, later on, it seemed to me she was afraid that as soon as I knew anything about my birth mother, I'd run away, try to find her.

"All she said to me was, 'Uncle said she was a Sikar.' That was it."

Lilith made a little sound in the back of her throat. "Like Chynna, Bravo's great-grandmother. She changed her name from Sikar to Shaw in order to escape the family on Arwad she stole from."

"You know something about the Sikars?"

"I know this much through Emma," Lilith said. "Safita, Ahirom, Sikar were three of the four major Phoenician families that founded the island of Arwad, off the coast of Syria."

"Where you found the painting of *The Last Supper* that's now begun to bleed."

Lilith nodded. "All the families possessed unearthly powers passed down through the generations. The Sikars were the wildest, most aggressive, most immoral of the Arwad Phoenician families."

"So," Molly said, the dread in her tearful eyes pulling on Lilith's heartstrings, "what does that make me?"

"My sister," Lilith said.

"Cousin, technically."

"I told you, that's not what you are to me, Molly," Lilith said evenly. "You are my sister, and that's how I'll always think of you, even if you don't."

"Really?" Molly shook her head. "Wild, aggressive, immoral—that's how you just described me."

"That's the line on the Sikars, not you."

Molly drew her knees up to her chest, wrapped her arms around her shins. "But I'm a Sikar."

"They're not all like that."

Molly regarded her reproachfully. "You can't know that."

"Let's say it's a safe bet. Besides, Uncle was an inveterate liar. Who knows if he told Mom the truth?"

"Even worse." Sucking in her breath, Molly shivered. "I don't feel safe."

Lilith reached out, placed her hand on top of her sister's. "I'm here with you now."

Tears spilled out of Molly's eyes. "It's not enough." Once her hard armor had been pierced she appeared to be falling apart.

"What would make you feel safe, honey?" Lilith said softly. "What would reassure you?"

Molly looked away for a moment. When her gaze returned to her sister, she said, "There is something, actually."

Lilith leaned closer. "What?"

"I could tell you, but . . ." She took a deep, shuddering breath, let it out slowly, raggedly. "Will you help me?"

"Of course, I—"

"Promise me."

Lilith hesitated only a moment. Driven by her own guilt, she could not resist. "I promise."

"Is that for real?"

"Molly!"

"All right, but I'm so afraid . . ."

"Afraid of what?"

"Of being a Sikar, of being all the things you said. Of not knowing where I came from."

"You're the master of your own fate." But even as she said it, Lilith knew, having been in the company of Emma and Bravo, that this was a lie. Their fates were all tied together somehow. If she was sure of anything in this crazy world it was that.

"You think?"

"Absolutely," she said with all the conviction at her command. She wouldn't allow the one spark of hope flaring inside her little sister to be snuffed out. She knew what it meant to be drowning in darkness.

"Okay." Molly took another breath. "I need to find my birth mother."

"What?"

"You see, I knew . . ." Her eyes were dark with fear. "Lilith, it's the only way I can find out the truth—if I am a Sikar, if my mother was crazy or mean, if my father told the truth about anything. Lilith, I have to know."

"But how on earth will you—how will *we* find her?"

For the first time, the hint of a smile played across Molly's lips. "Ah, well, there I do have an idea."

She held up the medallion. It was octagonal in shape. Each edge was inscribed with a triangle—at least that's what she thought they were. In truth, it was difficult to focus on them; the medallion was made of a material that appeared to absorb light, rather than reflect it.

Molly's eyes sparked. "I think it's a way for me to find her."

Lilith shook her head. "If that's the case, you could have found her long ago."

"No." Molly shook her head. "I didn't know what it was until Bravo took me down below the Hollow Lands. It was there the medallion grew warm as it began to vibrate." She raised a forefinger. "But only at the instant I glimpsed a house on a hill overlooking a river. I don't think anyone else saw it; they were too busy staring at the chimera, Oq Ajdar."

Her eyes searched her sister's face. "You promised you'd help me."

"And I will."

"Then you'll go with me."

"Go where?"

"We start in the Hollow Lands, then go below that. To the place beyond. The one I saw when Bravo took us to meet Oq Ajdar." She squeezed her sister's arms. "I'm convinced that's where my mother is."

16

"WHERE IS SHE?"

"Where is who?"

Chynna Sikar—the moment Leviathan had appeared she had abandoned her Kamar Ahirom identity—whirled on the Seraph. "You know precisely who I mean. Haya."

Leviathan's human face was all but expressionless. "The girl—"

"The girl!" Chynna's face was livid. "Haya's our *daughter*!"

"She's not *my* daughter," Leviathan said without a change in expression.

Chynna kept her composure. "What are you saying?"

"You know very well what I'm saying." Leviathan took a step toward her, backing her up against the front wall of the living room. "The girl is from your womb, but my seed did not plant her there."

"How can you say—?"

"She's not of my line; she's a Sikar through and through." He stuck his face in hers. "How you managed to lie is still perplexing me, but I mean to find out."

"Is that a threat? There is nothing to find out."

His right arm swept out and, in a blur, the back of his hand slammed into her face so hard, she staggered, then fell over, sliding down the wall. Her cheek burned, and pain bloomed like a nasty weed at the hinge of her jaw. Her eyes watered, but she refused to put a hand up to her face. Instead she regarded him levelly. "Go on. Keep hitting me." Her voice was low and guttural, a small smile played across her lips. "The more you hurt me, the stronger I become."

He grabbed her by her shirt front and lifted her off her feet. "More lies."

"Try me. Be my guest."

He struck her again and again. She felt the pain transmogrifying into pleasure, the pleasure morphing into a power that coursed through her like fire. Her smile broadened. "Keep going. Please."

With a disgusted sound, Leviathan let her go, and she held herself up by pressing her palms against the wall. "You won't be having so much fun when you see what I've done to the girl."

Chynna's heart threatened to rise up into her throat. Her knees turned to water, and a crushing wave of vertigo pinned her to the floor. She fought against all this, fought with all her might, tapping into the increased power the pain dealt by Leviathan had brought her.

"Where is she? Where is Haya?"

"Let's see." Leviathan crossed to the window, made as if to look out. "Is she down by the river? No, she isn't. Is she up in her room? No, she isn't. Is she on the toilet? No, she isn't." A malignant twinkle in his eyes. "Though, now I think about it, it's highly likely she wished she was in any of those places."

Chynna's hands curled into fists; cords stood out on either side of her neck. "What have you done with her?" she said in a strained voice.

"Ah, now I have your full attention." The Seraph held out his hand. "Come, I will gladly show you."

She hesitated, calculating her options. In truth, she had only one. But the moment she placed her hand in his, he transformed into his natural demonic state. And, as if responding to a silent signal, the flies gathered along the uppermost ribs of his top wings. Chynna ignored them, felt the strength of him as he pulled her along, out of the living room, down the hallway, around corners and bends she had never known existed, let alone explored.

The trek went on and on, until Chynna was forced to wonder where they were. It didn't seem possible that they were still in the same house, but rather in a colossal cavern hewn out of the bedrock of one of the twin mountains on either side of the river valley in which the house was set. And yet, she could sense no connecting tunnel, just more rooms they passed on either side. Some had open doors through which she glimpsed a whole bunch of nothing, others had their doors firmly shut. These appeared cobwebbed, as if they hadn't been opened, their contents inventoried in a very long time—whatever time might mean in this place.

Finally, they entered a semicircular passageway containing a single door at its apex. The door was double-width, made of a curious material that was neither wood nor stone, but shone like metal. Leviathan manipulated a complex locking mechanism, keeping his body between it and her. After multiple clicks, the door opened. He stepped aside and gestured for her to precede him.

Steeling herself, Chynna moved across the threshold, entering a room shaped like an egg, illuminated by a hidden low light source. At first it appear that the room, white and glistening as the inside of an eggshell, was empty. Then, as she picked her way across the floor, a kind of chair materialized out of the gloom.

Nothing could have prepared Chynna for what she beheld. She opened her mouth to scream, but a merciful blackness engulfed her. Leviathan had plenty of time to catch her as she collapsed, but he didn't bother.

17

HOW MUCH TIME HAD PASSED BEFORE HAYA RETURNED TO consciousness was impossible for her to know. She awoke disoriented, every nerve ending in her body seemingly on fire. Fire without smoke. She thought she had heard something about that, when she was little—a story her father had told her, perhaps? But then it slipped away into the quicksand in which she found her mind.

For long moments she did nothing but stare vacantly at the ceiling, like the victim of a mesmerist, or a mental patient returning from shock therapy. Her eyes, clouded with the aftermath of inexpressible agony, scarcely blinked.

Gradually, the gray veils disintegrated, leaving her breathless and more alone than she had ever been in her life. At length, she turned her head, saw that she was in a space with translucent walls, smooth and curved, like the inside of an eggshell.

Rising unsteadily to her feet, she staggered to the wall, put her hands on it. It was neither hot nor cold, neither light nor dark, neither soft nor hard. She pushed on it without effect. Moving always to her right she went completely around the shell, testing it for weak spots, finding none. She pounded on the wall with her fists, shouted, then screamed.

Nothing. Nothing at all.

Leviathan! The monster had put her here somehow. Was her mother aware of what had happened to her, where she was? She had no way of knowing.

Despairing, she let her head drop until her forehead rested against the wall. Abruptly, exhausted by her mental and physical efforts, she slid down onto her knees and wept.

KAMAR OPENED her eyes. Looking up, she saw Leviathan looming over her. Her head felt muzzy, her thoughts unclear, she tried to raise herself, but her limbs seemed paralyzed. Then she remembered everything and she gave a quick cry. She could feel him, could hear the flies that buzzed around his wings, but perhaps that was her imagination for once again he had resumed his human guise. And then, as she looked past him, she saw Haya inside the cell.

Scuttling like a crab was all she could muster at the moment. She peered through the translucence at Haya. She screamed. Her splayed hands slammed against the wall, over and over.

Haya wanted to run to her, to put her hands against her mother's with only the thin membrane of the wall between, but two things stopped her. First, she knew this was precisely what Leviathan wanted, to see the agony and terror on both mother and daughter's face at once. Well, she was damned if she was going to give the arch-demon the satisfaction. Then she laughed out loud at that thought—since so far as she could tell both she and her mother, consorting with the champion of Fallen angels, were already damned. And another thing: her little heart had already begun to harden against her mother. It was Kamar's fault they were in this situation. Whatever befell her now she wouldn't lay only at Leviathan's feet but her mother's also. How could Kamar love this nightmarish creature, this monstrosity that belonged in the deepest pits of hell? Had some of its evil seeped into her when they were—but Haya turned her mind away. She couldn't countenance the thought of her mother and the *thing* coupling.

So she stayed were she was, curled, knees drawn up to her bony chest, watching out of unblinking eyes as Leviathan locked a metal collar around Kamar's, who was too busy weeping for the child she had lost. Staring back at Haya, Leviathan affixed a leash made of chain metal to the collar and, jerking hard at the end of it, forced Kamar away from the cell. He led her out the door, but the door did not close, and Haya's stomach dropped. Somewhere deep inside her she had an inkling of what was coming, though not its shape.

And sure enough, Leviathan returned to the room, alone this time. He advanced toward her, came through the translucent wall of her cell as if it did not exist, which, she supposed, for him it didn't. She quailed.

He stood over her for a moment, but only for a moment. Then, to her astonishment, he crouched down in front of her. He smiled, but even in his human form, it was so awful she felt her gorge rise.

"Tell me, Haya," he said softly, gently, "are you bored here? Do I not provide enough for you? Do you want for anything?"

A playmate, she answered in her mind, knowing it was dangerous, but unable to help herself nevertheless. *Freedom.*

"Ah! I see." Because he had heard her answer. He sat back on his haunches. "Pity." When he assumed his human form he never looked quite right, like a merchant in an outfit as ill-fitting as it was expensive; you knew right away he couldn't possibly be human. And this made her curious about the true extent of his powers.

"Do you recall that I told you expressly not to go off wandering through the house?"

"Yes." Her voice was that of a mouse confronted by a ravenous lion.

"And yet," Leviathan said, an unmistakable sadness tinging his voice, "you did so anyway."

"I did."

"Please tell me why."

She wanted to think, *I was curious,* but she immediately tamped down on that, said, "I was just playing."

"So you were bored."

She shrugged. "I guess."

"No. I think you were curious." He stared at her for a long time, his gaze growing more and more baleful until she shivered despite herself. "You may not fully understand this but you are a remarkable creature. Here you are, a mere slip of a thing and yet you have the mind, the reasoning ability, of an adult." He cocked his head. "How to explain it?"

Silence, except for her heart trying to gallop itself away from here, except for her breathing, which was shallow and short.

"Well, so much for the preliminaries." He slapped his thighs and rose, unfolding like a praying mantis, looming over her. She was engulfed in Leviathan's shadow. And from that shadow his armada of flies rose, buzzing angrily, as if starved for food. He flicked his hand, just the slightest of moves, and they were upon her.

She cried out. Her skin began to itch, then to feel as if it were on fire, the insects crawling all over her pinching, biting, drawing blood. She tried to scramble away but the flies only moved with her. She could not escape from them or their predations.

"Tell me, Haya, what did you see in that last chamber you entered?"

"N-Nothing." Her eyes were closed; she could feel the flies clambering over her lids, scrabbling to get in. "I saw nothing."

"I have a different opinion, and that opinion is based on fact." His voice, booming off the wall, made her cringe. "I saw you in front of the mirror. I saw you staring into it. You were transfixed."

"I—"

"What did you see? What so fascinated you?"

Haya clamped down on the image of the thing that kept changing shape, which had stared at her with such familiar eyes. "I saw my own reflection, which I will say scared me. I looked so thin and pale."

"And then?"

"And then I saw a shadow behind me—your shadow."

"And that's all?"

"That's all."

She could feel the flies, each an extension of him, trying to burrow beneath her skin, through her skull, to reach her thoughts. But she held fast, and they found nothing but an echo of the words she had just uttered. She had no way of knowing, of course, but her ability to construct this psychic wall against Leviathan was the same ability that Emma had used against the demons who had possessed her. And Haya's ability was on a higher plane even than Emma's; she was resisting Leviathan himself. But she could not block the pain the armada of flies caused. It mounted to what seemed an endless crescendo, and then, abruptly, was gone.

She shook herself like a dog coming in from a storm and risked opening her eyes. That was a mistake. A blinding light struck her such a blow that she had no time to scream before she was pitched headlong into oblivion.

IT TOOK her another uncounted time to regain her sense of equilibrium, or as much of it as her rendition at Leviathan's hands had left her. She was in dire straits, no question. She might be young but she was far from ignorant—or innocent. He knew that she had transgressed, not only by exploring the hidden depths of the house, but by discovering that thing—whatever it was—in the mirror. She knew her best chance—probably her only chance—at survival was to lay low. Play possum. She'd seen plenty of possums as illustrations and photos in books. There were none on Arwad, which was pretty much devoid of mammalian life. Plenty of bugs and birds, but no possums. No loss, she'd thought. Possums were ugly creatures, with nothing to recommend them save their habit of playing dead when danger was near.

This is what Haya did now. She tried to judge the passing of time by monitoring the workings of her body clock: Was she hungry, sleepy (No! Astarte keep her, no!), grimy? She was aware that she was seated, but just barely. Her entire body seemed encased in an exoskeleton of agony. Even inside . . . her heart hurt with every double-pump, sending deep wincing pulses through her.

But there was silence, blessed silence.

Crossing to the center of her cell, she sat down cross-legged and closed her eyes. And, though her skin still crawled in the aftermath of the fly armada's attack, though she still felt sick to her stomach at their attempt to breach her psychic defenses, she began slowly and surely to redirect her thoughts into the silence, until she was plumbing its depths.

The strange sweet-sour taste of the leaf stem was in her mouth; it had never left her, but had continued to change, mutate, revealing tastes more subtle, less recognizable. She had eaten that stem, had felt strangely compelled to by the secret language of the river as it continued to murmur to her, a crooning, almost, like a song or a lullaby. An oddly familiar lullaby, though she felt sure her mother had never sang it to her. But where else would she have heard it?

There was complete and utter silence now—not the silence of death that encompassed Leviathan's house, but a stillness so profound that Haya could no longer even hear herself breathing.

And then a darkness began forming around her, like a cocoon, and as the darkness grew she felt the leaf stem in her mouth again, though she was certain that she had totally chewed it up and swallowed it. But there it was, whole, resurrected. Haya rolled it around her tongue, and, as she did so, she began to deliquesce. Her skin seemed to vanish and her flesh lose its shape. Her bones were gone, evaporating. She could see one last sliver radiating a mephitic life of its own. Then all was darkness, her transformation into liquid complete.

She was falling, or, more accurately, being drawn down, as if through drains and pipes, vertical connections and right-angled elbows, then on a long, horizontal journey until she was spat out the other side of the darkness.

The river burbled. She was kneeling beside her stone jetty with its leaf-boat still taking on cargo and passengers. She was in the same spot where she had broken off the leaf's stem and eaten it. She looked around, then down at her extremities. They appeared the same as they always did—ten fingers, ten toes. She wiggled them all. She pinched her cheek, was relieved to feel it. She drew breath, let it out, heard it, along with the gentle soughing of the wind. Commanding the hill behind her: Leviathan's house, which she had proved with the explorations was far more than what it appeared to be. But then so was its master. Far more. Thinking of him, she shuddered, checked the immediate vicinity for flies—his spies—saw none. Only then did she return her attention to the harbor she had built.

Reaching out, she placed the flat of her hand against the surface of the water. Why she did this, she could not say, though afterward she formed an opinion. At first, there was nothing, simply the wetness, the coolness. Then the edge of the leaf rippled against her and she felt a pulse so strong that she immediately snatched her hand away. Nevertheless, it raced along, echoing through her entire body. When it reached her brain, the fine blond hairs on her arms stood up, trembling.

After a long moment of deep breathing, she slowly replaced her hand on the skin of the river. This time, the pulse reversed itself, racing outward along the dully reflective surface of the river, where it could be glimpsed through the low mist that hung over the water like a mantle.

And when, at length, she looked up, she saw the sailboat she had glimpsed like a dream before. This time, there was someone manning it.

THE BLUE flame flickered and cracked its warning. Emma stood her ground, staring at the grotesque thing before her. Bent and twisted as a tree on a seaward hilltop, shadows swirled around it like morning fog, like a hooded cloak. It was not tall; neither was it short. By the blue light, Emma saw that it was chained to the rock wall. Was it a prisoner or a sentinel? Possibly it was both.

It spoke to her in an incomprehensible language that sounded like sleet rattling a windowpane. It repeated itself, more slowly, and this time the sounds arranged themselves into words, the words into a sentence: "State your business or be gone."

The creature—whatever it might be—was speaking Tamazight.

Emma knew how to deal with this thing. She stepped forward and, in the same language, said: *"Djat had'ar."* He is present.

The sacred words she had learned from Conrad that had saved her once, saved her again. The figure reared up to a frightening nine feet, then stumbled backward until halted by the full length of the chain that bound it.

"Who . . . ?" Its voice cracked like a dropped glass. "*What* are you?" And turned sharp as a shard. And now the shadows around it began to part, to brush back, to vanish as if sucked into the wall behind him.

He—for he was male—was thin to the point of emaciation. His fingers were too long and too thin, with claws instead of nails. Eyes like nuggets of coal were fairly lost within the recesses below a beetling brow; deep circles, like purple bruises surrounded them. No nose to speak of, just a pair of oval nostrils. A knife-slash of a lipless mouth completed his unpleasant visage. He wore a shapeless shift, colorless and ill-fitting, and his feet were bare, misshapen, with the appearance of cloven hooves, like a goat.

The creature, hairless save for a silver topknot that had the appearance of a horse's tail, felt to Emma like a source of pity rather than fear. He appeared mesmerized by the blue flame flickering at the center of her outstretched palm.

She took another step toward him, almost stumbled on a bone. Lowering her hand, she saw around him what she had mistaken for rocks. In fact, they were bones. Human bones. The explorers or, possibly, plunderers, who had come here to gather fame and fortune. "My name is Emma," she said. "What's yours?"

"What? No one's asked me that before." He appeared taken aback by the question. "I . . . I don't know."

"How could you not know?"

Another step toward him, and now she could dimly make out the outline of a door directly behind the creature. It was locked with a large iron lock that looked like those used in the Middle Ages to secure cell doors.

"Well," the creature began uncertainly, "I was never given one."

Emma stared at him. "Even when you were born?"

"Born?" His face screwed up. "Only in a sense." What emotion it bore was a mystery. "I was made."

Emma let out a breath. "So you have no name."

"I do not."

"All creatures great and small must have a name. I told you that mine is Emma." She tapped her lips with a forefinger as she studied him. As she took another step forward, she raised her flashlight. When he cringed back, eyes glued to her blue flame, she smiled, extinguished it. "I mean you no harm."

He looked into her face. "But you must. You have penetrated this deep into the cavern, which means you must want to go deeper."

And you're here to prevent that, Emma thought. *Well, we'll see about that.* "You have no reason to fear me," she said. "Just the opposite, in fact."

The creature stared at her with wide-open eyes. "The opposite of fear? What is that?"

"Just watch." Using the end of the flashlight, she tapped him gently on one bony shoulder, then the other, before tapping the crown of his skull. "I now name you Omega."

Omega's eyes almost popped out of his skull as Emma knelt, studying the chains that bound him to the wall. They were also of iron, as ancient as the lock on the door he had guarded for God alone knew how many millennia.

Extracting the pickax from her backpack, she swung it down once, twice. The chain parted. She performed the same action on the chain binding Omega's other ankle.

"You're free now, Omega," she said into his bewildered face.

"I was told . . ." He swallowed, looked down as he stamped first one foot then the other. "I was told the chains were unbreakable."

"And so they were," she said, stowing away the pickax, "in your mind. That's all that mattered."

Omega lifted one leg, rubbed his ankle with both hands. "I don't understand."

"You were lied to, Omega." Emma stood up. "Whoever chained you here lied to you."

"I was assigned to guard this door by the Creator. Why would the Creator lie?"

Emma pulled a power bar from her pack, opened it, and offered it to Omega. "You must be hungry."

"I don't eat or drink," Omega said, eyeing the power bar with distaste. "I wasn't made that way."

Emma's eyes narrowed. "How were you made? Who made you?"

"I already told you. The Creator made me," Omega said, bewildered, as if everyone who darkened his doorstep should know who that was.

Keeping her patience, Emma said, "Does the Creator have another name, Omega?"

"He who has Fallen the most."

A chill raced down her spine. "Lucifer?"

Omega nodded. "None other."

Emma took an involuntary step back.

The ends of Omega's lips turned up, a ghastly thing. "Now you're as afraid of me as I am of you." He leaned back against the wall that had been the main part of his cage. He gestured with his claws. "You see what happened to everyone else who came looking for . . . what is behind me."

"Except me."

Lucifer's creature nodded. "You have the blue fire. You know the incantation. I have no defense against either."

Emma thought about this for some time. "You're free now, Omega. What will you do?"

He shrugged his skeletal shoulders. "I will help you, Emma."

Her brows knit together. "Why would you do that?"

"Two reasons." Omega came away from the wall. "First, you have ended my eons-long torment. Second, it will not be long before the Creator knows that I am free. Then he will kill me."

Emma conjured the blue fire, the flames leaping from her palm. "I won't let him."

That ghastly grimace again, before Omega turned and, inserting the middle claw of his left hand into the key slot in the iron lock, opened it.

As he threw it aside and opened the door, he said, "You must not try, Emma. You will die with me."

As she followed him across the threshold, she said, "I swear to protect you, Omega."

His laugh was like the rattling of a handful of beetle shells. "I do not need protecting, Emma. The pleasure of death is all that's left for me."

18

JUST STEP ON THE BOAT, **THE FIGURE SAID IN HER MIND.**

"Your boat is too far away," Haya whispered.

The leaf-boat, my dear.

"But it's so small!"

Haya, my dear, it's as small or as large as you make it.

"What? Really?"

You have only to conceive of it and it will be so.

"How is that possible?"

You are an extraordinary human. More than you know.

Haya squinted into the distance. The figure in the boat was tall and slender, but the face was still shrouded in mist and shadow.

"How d'you know my name?"

Trust me, Haya.

"Trust requires a leap of faith," she whispered just as if she were at death's door. "I have no faith."

You do not believe in God.

"No."

Likewise, you do not believe in the devil.

"That's right."

But you do believe in demons, since one is holding you and your mother hostage.

Haya was abruptly indignant. "We're not hostages. We came willingly. Mother loves him."

Please reconsider what you have said.

Color flamed in Haya's cheeks. "What does that mean?"

Just this, my dear. Demons possess a certain glamour. In fact, they're infamous for it.

"Glamour?" There was a word she didn't know.

Think of it as being able to cast a spell on, especially, but not limited to, human females.

"Well, he hasn't cast any spell over me," Haya said indignantly. "I hate him."

As I mentioned, you are extraordinary—one of a kind, really. Here is an example: you are immune to a demon's glamour. And what a demon! As a Seraph of the First Sphere, he is the Right Hand of the devil you don't believe in.

The figure was silent for the space of several heartbeats. Then: *What's the worst that could happen?*

"I'll get wet."

Considering your situation here, is that anything to be afraid of?

It wasn't. Of course it wasn't. Haya, unmoving, considered this for some time. It was totally, insanely true that Leviathan—who, this figure quite deliberately would not name (and why was that?)—was most obviously not human. Then what was he? Was he, in fact, a demon—a Seraph of the First Sphere, as the figure claimed? One of the books in her mother's collection had described the Fall, had traced out the hierarchy of angels and Fallen angels, who had been at war just before God had cast the insurgents, led by Lucifer, out of Heaven, so she was familiar both with the term *Seraph,* the highest of the high, the lowest of the low, save one, of course. But she considered the very nature of the so-called history so outlandish that she dismissed it out of hand. Now she seemed confronted with the opposite of her negation. If Leviathan wasn't a Seraph, a leading member of the Fallen, she had no idea what he might be, or even *how* he came to be. She cocked her head. Could the figure be right? Could Leviathan, indeed, be the right hand of the devil? But she had never seen any evidence that God existed, and if there was no God how could the devil exist? This conundrum had her totally flummoxed. What was she to do?

Step off the shore and onto her leaf-boat, of course. The logic of this illogical action was as inescapable as the illogical world to which Leviathan had whisked her and her mother.

Have faith, Haya. She took her leave of the shore, stepping off into space. The air hummed, a minuscule vibration that she nevertheless picked up. And then down onto the leaf-boat. At the first touch of her slipper, the leaf expanded to accommodate not only that foot but the other one, as well. The leaf continued to grow, easily holding her weight. Then the sides curled up, along with the tip, which became the prow. Recalling the pulse her hands had created, Haya placed them on the water to either side of the boat. The leaf-boat moved away from the shore, heading toward the sailboat and its occupant, who stood in the prow, awaiting her arrival.

She wondered why the figure hadn't sailed the boat to her, which surely would have been easier, and this was the first question she asked him. The figure was a man, and a striking one at that.

The short answer is I cannot, he said. *It took all of my powers to summon up this ghost vessel.*

"Ghost vessel?" Haya screwed up her face in puzzlement. But then, looking more carefully, she saw the shimmer of the river through the boat. And come to that the same insubstantiality as its captain.

Haya gave him a piercing look. "Where are you, really?"

You recall seeing me in the house above us.

"You mean the creature in the bronze mirror?"

That's not a mirror, Haya. It's the prison in which Lucifer has me caged.

Haya's eyes opened wide. "He is part of it, part of the house??"

There was a pause while the boatman allowed Haya to answer her own question.

There seemed to be so much rushing at her at once. How to make sense of it all? *Start at the beginning,* a little voice in her head offered—her voice, or his?

Her eyes narrowed. "How do you know my name?"

My name is Conrad. Conrad Shaw. And I know many things.

"How did you get to know so many things, including my name?" Haya asked, in the way of a child who instinctively cuts through the adult fancy-dancing to get to the nub of the matter.

Ah, that, Conrad said with a gentle smile. *Well, you see, it's because I'm dead.*

AROUND AND around they went, Molly chanting the words she had memorized as Bravo spoke them, but which were incomprehensible to her. She had descended, retracing her own footsteps. Lilith, following, following. It was a curious experience for Molly to be the leader, to have more information than her older sister. But this was a new world for her, a new reality. Her talk with Lilith had turned the past on its head. Everything she had believed, the bitter emotions she had hoarded like a miser her gold, were false, based on fallacies she had concocted in the absence of solid evidence. Like a child denied the facts, she had assumed the worst.

Over her shoulder, she said, "Don't worry if you lose consciousness," just before they both lost consciousness.

THE FIRST thing Molly became aware of after awakening in the place where they had encountered Oq Ajdar was holding her sister's hand. This experience was so extraordinary that she felt her eyes welling with tears, and she turned her head away so Lilith couldn't see her weak and vulnerable.

The chimera was nowhere in evidence. This did not surprise her; after all it was her belief that they had come upon Oq Ajdar because she had summoned Bravo, bleeding out *The Last Supper* painting. But why, Molly wondered, had the painting bled in the place next to Jesus, where there was no one sitting, rather than from one of the figures—Judas, for instance. That, at least, would have made sense.

But her ruminations on the painting were short-lived. They had come up against the membrane behind which the chimera had spoken to Bravo.

"Where are we?" Lilith asked.

"No idea. Just follow my lead." Molly was disconcerted at not being able to see the tableau of the house on the hill, the winding river below as she had before. She had a stab of panic then, wondering if the tableau was merely a backdrop, a mirage painted by the chimera as an artful background, as in a stage play. But then she recalled the intense magnetism of the place. How it drew her, as if it was somehow calling her home. And with a grunt of resignation, she put her right hand out, pressed it against the membrane. She felt a slight pain, like a tugging at her heart, and then she was through, pulling Lilith along after her. *Now who's the child?* she thought.

Much to her surprise, she found they were in a narrow band of neither light nor dark. And beyond was the tableau she already thought of as beloved: the house on the hill between the twin mountain peaks, the steep verdant pitch down to the river.

"Come," she said to her sister as she pushed through the second membrane and breathed the air that was at once strange and familiar. "We're almost there."

"Where?" Lilith asked.

Home, Molly thought. *Home.*

19

HAYA'S BROW FURROWED MIGHTILY. "IF YOU'RE DEAD HOW can you be talking to me? You're not even here. Also, you said you're the creature in the bronze mirror—"

"Prison cell."

She startled, almost losing her balance. "You spoke!"

That was just to focus you. I'm taking a risk projecting myself; it's terribly draining. So now you must listen to me.

"I don't want to listen to you," Haya said. "I want to get out of here, and I'm going to use this leaf-boat to do just that. I'll sail upstream to the far end of the river if I have to."

And leave your mother behind?

"I don't care about her. Look what she's done to me!"

To both of you. Both of you are his prisoners. And, Haya, I'll remind you that it's not her fault.

"She's not blameless!" Special as she might be, she was still at heart a child, and sometimes her emotions overwhelmed her. "She can't be!" She stamped her foot so hard her leaf-boat rocked this way and that. She seemed not to notice or, if she did, not to care. "I know she isn't! No one can tell me different!"

I wouldn't dare. Not now, Conrad said. *But I will tell you a story about your mother, Haya, and I trust you to listen with both your ears and all of your heart.*

Haya felt an angry retort bubbling up inside her, but another calmer part of herself held it back. That part of her wanted to hear what this ghostly presence had to say about her mother, who had always been a bit of a mystery to her. Certainly she wasn't like any other mother Haya had come across on Arwad. So she kept her mouth shut, but as a concession to her still boiling anger, crossed her arms over her chest and defiantly thrust out her lower lip.

You know your mother as Kamar Ahirom, but the truth is she's taken many names in her long, long life.

"What does that mean, 'long, long life'?"

Your mother is ancient, Haya. Her birth name is Chynna Sikar. She changed her name to Shaw after she was forced to flee Arwad, the island where both you and she were born.

Haya's frown deepened. "You said *your* name is Shaw."

Conrad gave her a wraithlike smile. *As Chynna Shaw, your mother founded a dynasty of remarkable offspring. Her first child, Gideon, was my father.*

Haya's remarkable adult brain had started up again. "Who was her lover?"

He who has imprisoned you and your mother.

She almost lost her balance. "Leviathan?" The name escaped her like a hiss of steam.

The very same demon.

Legs turned to jelly, Haya had to sit down. She drew her knees up to her chest, wrapping her arms around her shins. She felt very cold, indeed. "So . . ." Her voice trailed off for a moment. "So you and I are related?"

Across the generations, yes. Part of me is inside you.

"Is that what makes me . . . different?"

That and so much more. The sailboat was wavering, and Conrad with it. *Quickly now, Haya, for I cannot hold this image much longer.* He reached out an arm toward her. *Take my hand.*

"I want to leave here. I *will* leave here."

No! Conrad fairly shouted this, even though he and his craft were slowly fading into the mist. *If you do, Leviathan will find you, and his punishment will be as swift as it will be terrible. Please. Take my hand now.*

"But—"

Now you must trust in me, really and truly. Haya, I swear that I will not betray you.

Her mind made up at last, she took his proffered hand in hers. She felt nothing, or did she? Difficult to tell. She felt slightly dizzy, and her head was ringing, as if she had been standing too close to a carillon striking the hour. The world around her seemed to go in and out of focus. Then everything appeared to her as it had been.

"What—?"

But Conrad and the ghost boat were nothing but a wisp of smoke, mingling with the river mist.

"How will I get free?"

Conrad Shaw was gone, the mist mirrored the eddies of the river. He might never have appeared at all, save for the fact that inside her remained the echo of him: *Trust in me.*

BRAVO AND Ayla were on the Observatine jet that had brought Lilith from Addis. Bravo had had the crew refuel at the Observatine airstrip and had bunked them overnight in comfortable quarters, so they could eat well, sleep well, shower, be prepared for whatever their boss asked of them by the time he and Ayla climbed aboard at first light the next day.

Bravo went up to the cockpit to tell the pilot and navigator their destination: Alexandria, Egypt. Ayla double-checked the contents of the backpacks they had brought with them to make sure everything Bravo had asked for was there. The two-foot bronze-and-copper tube was the first thing she looked for, but she did not open it. She had no idea what was inside, but she was disinclined to look until Bravo gave his permission to do so.

Later, high over the Mediterranean, they both slept. They had been up all night planning, searching, and packing. Bravo closed his eyes after Ayla did, but he was the first one to fall into slumber.

HE STRUGGLES out of a drugged sleep. He opens his eyes, but he cannot move. He is immobilized by an unknown force against which he is helpless. His mouth tastes of blood. He is well acquainted with the stench of death, and his nose is clogged with it. So much is slipping away; his world disappearing, sliding down the side of the Great Pyramid. Sand, heat, blinding sun. He is in Another Place.

He tries to move, but his muscles are encased in cement.

He sees Lucifer. His yellow talons turn bloodred. Buzzing and hovering along the upper cartilage of his bat-like wings, wasps slavishly cling in hopes of feasting of the flesh of the dead and dying. Wasps love eyes—especially the vitreous.

Lucifer stalks silent as a serpent toward Emma. She is turned away from him, and is apparently unaware of his presence, let alone his proximity to her. Filled with horror, Bravo tries to cry out, to warn her, but his voice lies dormant somewhere beyond his reach.

Turning his head to look at Bravo, Lucifer curls his fingers, gesturing. "That's right. Watch me now."

He is only a small step behind Emma. For some reason, she is completely unaware of him. Bravo, frantic, bends his mind to voicing his fear, willing his limbs to move. All to no avail. The force has splintered his thoughts, cut himself off from his impulses, his needs, his body.

"She can't hear me because of the venom in her blood."

Lucifer buries his talons in the small of Emma's back. She arches. Bravo imagines he hears a small cry from her. Blood begins to leak out from the deep wounds.

"Watch what happens."

Lucifer draws his buried fingers inward, making a fist. Again, Emma arches back, and now Bravo is certain he hears her panting. Lucifer draws out a handful of Emma's viscera, nerves, bones, flesh. He puts them all into his gaping jaws, and Emma collapses, like a marionette whose strings have been cut. She lies at Lucifer's feet, amid a widening pool of her blood, unmoving. As Lucifer feasts on her, his armada of wasps attack her eyes, swarming, a black mass, moving, crowding shuddering.

And Lucifer, his face smeared with Emma's blood and viscera, turns to Bravo. "Dead, Bravo. Despite all your efforts, your sister is dead . . ."

PART TWO

VENOM IN THE BLOOD

20

HAYA MUST HAVE FALLEN ASLEEP, FOR WHEN SHE OPENED her eyes she was back in her egg-shaped prison. She blinked several times. When she tried to invoke the portal through which she'd been magically transported to the riverbank, she could not, and now she began to wonder whether she had been there at all, whether it was, instead, a dream. Her fingers, her slippers, the hem of her dress were all dry as bone. There was no evidence whatsoever that she had ever left her prison cell. Which meant there was no way out. With that, she started to weep, silent tears overflowing her eyes, running down her cheeks, leaving ghostly runnels in their wake.

And it was in this state that her mother found her.

"Where is Leviathan?" Haya said in fear and disorientation. "How did you get in here?"

"He gave me the key, but that's all he gave me," Chynna said. She was on her knees, weeping at the sight of her child made prisoner but also alive. Gloriously alive. "He is gone, I know not where or for how long."

Haya's eyes lit up, and for the first time since they had been swept off their boat, felt hope warming her chest. "Then if we can free me we can escape from this awful place."

"I'm afraid not, my daughter. We are both prisoners of this house. Every door and window is sealed with a spell I cannot defeat. And the window glass—if, in fact, it is glass, is utterly unbreakable." She put her hands against the curved shell of Haya's cage. "But you are alive and, I trust, well. What did he do to you when he was in this cell with you?"

"I . . . I don't really know," Haya said. "But he hurt me. He was very angry."

"Oh, my darling girl!" Chynna's head sunk onto her chest. "I'm so sorry. It's said that with age comes wisdom, but with Leviathan I've been selfish, and very foolish." She looked up, tears magnifying her eyes. "Please, Haya, don't hate me."

Something tender tugged at Haya's heartstrings, and she felt a rush of love for her mother. "It's not your fault," she said, more like a wise adult than a naïve child. "He has a glamour that's difficult to resist."

"A glamour?" Chynna's eyes opened wide. "Where did you hear such a word?'

Haya shrugged. "It came to me. It seems to fit, doesn't it?"

Chynna nodded. "Sadly, it does. But that glamour has faded, that flush of . . . physical . . . emotion is ebbing away from me."

"You have returned then." Again, Haya was inhabiting the role of adult to her mother's child. "This makes me happy."

"It makes us both happy," Chynna said through her astonishment, for this daughter of hers had grown in so many ways while Leviathan had blinded her to it, to how special she was.

"I want to know something," Haya said.

"Anything, my darling. You have but to ask and if it's in my power I will tell you."

"Is he really my father?"

"Leviathan?"

"Yes."

Chynna rested her forehead against the sorcerous eggshell. "The only good thing in this situation is that he is not," she said softly, as if the wall might have ears. But Haya, having searched, had already determined that there were no flies anywhere to be seen or heard. She had already learned as well what it took others a lifetime, many lifetimes to learn: one should never underestimate a Seraph.

And so she, too, lowered her voice. "Who, then, is my father?"

Chynna closed her eyes for a moment. "The truth is I do not know. Whether it was the man I married, whose name I cannot even remember, or a fisherman, a warrior, a drunkard, I cannot say. But when Leviathan asked I said you were his. I should not have, I understand that now, but I was a victim of his glamour and I felt compelled to say it. I think there was a time I even believed it."

"But now you don't."

Chynna pushed herself away from the cell in order to better see her daughter. "No, I do not."

Even though she felt a wave of relief wash over her, still she had to ask: "How can you be sure?"

At this, Chynna smiled, and Haya realized that it had been a very long time, possibly years, since she had seen that smile of pure happiness wreath her mother's face.

"It's simple," Chynna said. "I can be sure, darling girl, because you are so good. You're all good, and you could not be if his venom flowed through your veins. Not a drop of his blood infects you. You are pure light."

WHEN MOLLY and Lilith crossed the membrane into the world of the twin mountains, Lilith felt a shiver race down her spine.

"What is it?" Molly asked, turning to her.

"I don't know. I felt as if I'd placed one foot in my own grave."

Molly took her hand. "You can turn back, you know."

Lilith's laugh was half-sob. "I don't think so."

The two stood still for some time, staring out at the vista. Gradually, it came to them that there was no birdsong, no stirring of the leaves on the trees beneath a sky that was obscured by unvarying cloud cover, for want of another term. No creatures scurried in the forest on the edge of which they stood, and the scents of the underbrush were strangely muted, as if they weren't there at all. But they were. Lilith confirmed this by bending down to touch the low spreading plants. Other than the fact that they were paper thin, they seemed real enough.

"What is this place?" she asked rhetorically.

But Molly had an answer: "It's very much like the place where I was born."

"Are you kidding?"

"I'm perfectly serious." Molly pointed. "There are the twin peaks, there is the house on the hill." Her expression clouded over. "Though this house doesn't seem quite the same."

"Aha!" her sister declared, relieved.

"But only in the little things." Molly continued to direct her attention. "We didn't have so many windows, I think, and the ones on the second floor were dormers. The color isn't quite right, either."

"Maybe we're in the wrong place, after all," Lilith said hopefully.

But Molly showed her the light-sucking medallion, trembling in the center of her open palm. "I don't think so. Maybe there've been renovations after I left. But this tells me that house is home." She held onto her sister's hand more tightly, tugging on it now.

Lilith acquiesced. "We've come this far. We might as well find out if your intuition and that trinket are right."

BUT AS it turned out, the medallion was dead wrong—and *dead* seemed the operative word.

"This isn't where I was born," Molly said, hands cupped on either side of her eyes as she peered into a window. "I don't see anything I remember. The configuration of the rooms I can see are wrong, and the furniture is completely alien to me."

She pulled her head back as if bitten on the nose by a viper. "I don't understand." Tears shimmered in her eyes, enlarging them, electrifying their color. She turned to her sister. "Lilith . . ."

"It was a good idea." Lilith had no clue whether or not that was true, but it was what Molly needed to hear. "We tried." She took Molly's hand. "Perhaps it's best if we go now. Try another avenue."

"There is no other avenue." Molly flared. She broke contact with Lilith, tears of anger and frustration flying in either direction. "Don't you understand?" She held up the medallion. "This was . . ." She shook her head. "Beyond this there's nothing!"

So saying, she flung the medallion square at the window that had disappointed her. To their astonishment, a spiderweb of cracks radiated out from the central point where the medallion had struck the window. Against all expectations, it had stuck to the glass. The two of them watched, mesmerized, as its vibrations expanded the spiderweb, widening the cracks until, with a sharp *crack!* not unlike a pistol being discharged, the entire window shattered, raining shards of glass down the side of the house.

Instinctively, Molly leaned in and caught the medallion before it fell. As she did so, as her fingers closed over it, as the continuing vibrations began to fill every nook and cranny of her body, she looked up and there, standing in the center of the newly exposed room, was a woman who made her heart turn over, a woman her daughter's soul recognized.

And to Chynna Sikar she whispered: "Mother, I've come home."

21

THE DOOR WAS OLD—CENTURIES, EONS OLD. IT HAD NOT BEEN made by the hands of humans, but who had manufactured it and by what mystical processes was impossible to say, and Omega wasn't talking. At that moment, Emma didn't care. She was fully concentrated on getting through the door, finding out what—and who—lay beyond. But it was not without a good deal of trepidation that she followed Omega over the threshold.

As she did so, she felt her consciousness stretched and distorted in a way both exhilarating and terrifying: like an intense acid trip, only real. She tried to call out but her throat felt constricted, as if someone were trying to strangle her. Her hands came up but nothing was there. Gingerly, she palpated her throat and neck, but the feeling only increased in intensity. Belatedly, she sensed she should have invoked the blue fire before stepping through, but now it was too late; she couldn't find the inner path to it.

Now, at last, she was well and truly afraid, not only for her life, but for her soul. She felt helpless, naked to whatever sorcerous or cosmic forces had her in their grip. All at once, she felt that she was not alone. Instinctively, she reached out, grasped a hand, dry as sand, horny as a rhino, taloned, with ungodly strength.

In this manner—blind, on the brink of panic—she was pulled through to the far side of the door. Had she come through a membrane or, she thought wildly, was it the breach into the place where the Fallen were eternally imprisoned?

"It's not," Omega said.

It was the creature's hand she was holding. He was still gripping her so tightly the needle-sharp point of his talons had bitten into her skin, drawing tiny droplets of blood.

He loosed her, glanced at the welling red pinpoints with an odd expression Emma took to be sorrow, but really might have been anything at all. There was no sense of getting to understand Omega whatsoever. Whatever he was, his brain worked in ways beyond her comprehension. The best she could hope for was to make informed guesses, which still put her more or less in the dark about what motivated him or how he might respond.

"It's not what?" she asked.

"The Fissure." The way he emphasized the word she was sure it started with a capital *F*. "I would never be allowed near it."

"Where is it?"

His eyes opened wide, a viscid yellow all around the irises. "You didn't come here to steal the gold?"

Emma almost said *What gold?* but an eerie sensation running down her spine stopped her. Gold. Could Omega mean Solomon's hidden gold, the hoard adventurers had been searching for over the course of nearly three thousand years?

"I'm an archeologist," she said, which was more or less true. "Solomon's gold, if it exists, is of interest to me as a historical find of unimaginable proportions. Finding it would answer so many archeological debates my mind grows dizzy."

At once, Omega's hand reached out again, this time in a gentle embrace of her wrist, careful not to touch the scimitar-shaped string of wounds on her palm. "You will not fall here," Omega assured her. "You have me to hold on to."

He had mistaken the metaphorical for the actual. This was information she could use. Omega interpreted every sentence she uttered as literal. She resolved to keep the creature talking as much as she could. The more they interacted the better she would come to understand him. Above all, what she was desperate to know was whether Omega was capable of deception, whether he even knew what dishonesty was. Not every creature did, though, sadly, to humans that seemed almost impossible to believe.

Emma lit her blue fire, and Omega stepped instantly away, even though he was now convinced that she would not harm him; it was in his blood, this fear, Emma thought, and it set her to wondering at the fear's origin, whether it could tell her something important about her enemies. Holding the flame on high she saw that they were in a narrow antechamber, whose ceiling was so high the darkness above seemed to eat the light whole. Most interesting of all: the floor consisted of hand-hewn slabs of rock, making it clear they had left the natural cavern behind.

"Where are we?" she whispered.

Omega, beckoning, led her onward, through a slip of a doorway and into another, larger chamber. This one was lit by a sorcerous means invisible to Emma. Like the antechamber before it, this chamber appeared to have no ceiling, or else it was lost in the high-up web of shadows. However, here the floor slabs consisted of a form of schist, flecks of mica winking back at her like stars beneath her feet.

"Omega, who made this place?"

The creature seemed genuinely bewildered. "Why, the Phoenicians in the employ of King Solomon, of course."

Emma turned slowly, eyes wide and staring. *I'm so close to King Solomon's mine!* Her heart beat like a triphammer in her chest and she found her breath coming hot and hard, so that she had to consciously deepen her breaths to slow them down.

Watching her reaction, Omega said, "I will take you to the gold. Solomon's gold, which no human has set eyes on since it was entombed by Solomon's cadre of alchemists. They were a mischievous lot, those alchemists, and hardly above betrayal. A number of them chose to do Solomon's son's bidding even before the monarch died, certainly afterward, even though they foresaw that the son wished only for self-aggrandizement, that such actions would undo many if not all of his father's good deeds. It is well-known that alchemists care nothing for everyday matters; their laboratory experiments occupy their minds completely.

"That the son was interested only in himself, in becoming the greater king, more feared than his father, mattered to them not at all. He knew not how to be great, and the greedy alchemists who followed him did so for the remuneration he promised them, remuneration that would fund their ongoing experiments in areas forbidden to humans."

"And did the son keep his word to them?"

Omega produced what she, shuddering inwardly, could only imagine was a sardonic smile. "What do you think? He killed them, one by one, after they taught him their dark arts. Thus, Solomon's kingdom fell to ruins, assaulted on all sides by enemies emboldened by the king's death and the son who demonstrated no head for leadership or matters of state."

"So the gold has a dark and sordid history," Emma said.

"Many have tried to find it; some have tried to claim it," Omega affirmed. "None have survived." His watery eyes roved over her. "Which is as it should be. If Solomon wanted it used he would not have ordered the Phoenicians to build him the vault to contain it, for *this* gold is unlike any other. *This* gold was mutated by his cadre of alchemists."

"Why did the king want it mutated?"

"It is not known by me," Omega said without a trace of guile or perfidy.

God in Heaven, he doesn't know! Emma thought, almost beside herself with excitement. *He isn't aware that the texts we have come across claim that the gold was infused by his alchemists with the Quintessence, the life force of the universe. Anyone who came into possession of the gold, therefore, would have their life extended far beyond normal human understanding.*

Emma showed none of her excitement, however, keeping her face glum. "That's too bad, Omega. I'd dearly like to know the reason the king chose to secrete it so thoroughly."

He shrugged, seemingly uninterested in the answer. Beckoning her on, he led her to the far side of this second chamber.

"Now," Omega continued, "the gold belongs to Lucifer."

"And you," Emma said, "are Lucifer's creature."

"No. I am Emma's creature until the moment of my death."

"I don't want you to die, Omega."

The creature peered at her, seemingly concerned. "Do you fear death, Emma?"

"I . . . I don't know."

"I think you do," Omega said with astonishing perspicacity. "What you are afraid to admit to yourself, you are afraid to give voice to."

Emma wondered again how much she could trust Omega, or if she could trust him at all. True, she had freed him, but he had been loyal as a dog to his Creator. Why, she thought, should anything or anyone change that? But tasting freedom after being held captive—and for such a long time!—was a heady experience, its psychological effects not to be taken lightly. And so she found herself in something of a conundrum. To trust Omega or not to trust him, that was the question. But could she even go on without his guidance? Unless he was leading her into a trap. But if that were so how would he get around the blue fire and the incantation that invoked it that terrified him so? Weighing these questions in her mind led her back to the same inescapable conclusion.

She nodded. "All right, let's go."

With a nod, Omega let her directly toward a wall. At the very last instant, he slipped through what looked like a vertical shadow, but which turned out to be a narrow gap between two sections of rock, cleverly hidden unless, like Omega, you knew it was there.

Again, Emma felt herself traveling through a place whose laws were undefinable. The floor fell away from her feet, while, simultaneously, the walls moved inward, threatening to crush her.

"Look neither to the left or right." Omega's voice came to her as if from another time, another place. "Keep your eyes focused on what is ahead." Her head began to pound, a weight seemed to be crushing her skull from either side, and it took all her willpower not to look. "Do this," Omega said, "and you will survive."

Survive? What kind of place is Omega taking me to?

She found out soon enough. Out she popped like a cork from a bottle of Champagne, into a hall the color of honey. A six-sided space in the shape of the Star of David: two equilateral triangles, opposed, one on top of the other. Each of the six walls was carefully hand-hewn and painstakingly polished to bring out the flecks of mica gleaming like myriad stars in a midnight sky. Each of the six sides contained a niche—a seat, really—on each of which sat a shadowy figure armed and armored in the Phoenician style. All had deep-set eyes, long noses, thick, curling beards. On closer inspection, these statues appeared identical, as if they were sculpted using a single model. The floor was strewn with carpets of astounding patterns of silk interwoven with gold and silver thread. The ceiling was domed, constructed of a magnificent arabesque of hand-painted tiles that stunned her since, if this chamber truly was Solomon's mine, it was far older than the Islamic religion and its art. *How then was the tessellation of tiles possible?* she asked herself.

But that question and any others that clamored for her attention were wiped away by what she saw in the center of the chamber: a throne of solid black basalt, immense, the back rising perhaps twenty feet. The seat itself was surely eight feet off the floor.

But as for the treasure of King Solomon . . .

"Where is it?" Emma said, her patience nearing its end. "Where is the gold?"

All she heard in response was a brief gurgle, as if Omega had passed wind. Then there was the thud of a melon knocked off the back of a truck, and Omega's head rolled between her legs.

She whirled to see a creature she had never before confronted in the flesh. Nevertheless she knew what it was: it stood eight feet tall, had two sets of wings, the lower set folded around its body. Its face was blurred—one moment human, the next leonine—and it gave her a headache to look directly at its head. It carried a flaming sword that rose toward the tesselated dome.

When it spoke it was as the rumble of approaching thunder. The atmosphere immediately cracked open, charged with a painful electricity.

"I am Azazel."

Cherubim, she thought, and her blood ran cold.

22

THE GREAT LIBRARY AT ALEXANDRIA WAS NOT WHAT IT ONCE was even five years ago, let alone in ancient times when it was the glorious repository of all Western knowledge. Then, scholars from all over the known world traveled to the edge of Egypt to immerse themselves in learning or, quite often, to bring scrolls, hand-lettered books, and charts to add to the wisdoms at the navel of the world.

It had been reduced to something of a shambles five years earlier after the brazen attack by the Knights of St. Clement, which had also claimed a number of lives close to Bravo's heart. In the years since, Bravo had dispatched teams of the Order's finest minds—scholars, historians, art restorers, philosophers—to set the library back on its feet, and, if possible, to make it more complete and more up to date than it had been before the assault.

Now there were armed guards on the front door and, sadly, a metal detector to be passed through before Bravo and Ayla came to the high banc, from where Steward, the new librarian, oversaw both the analog and the digital log of visitors, in and out, volumes submitted for inclusion, the most read tomes, and the like. The title of curator had been changed from the time of Aither, the betrayer, the murderer. Behind Steward, also now sadly required, were CCTV monitors of all the stacks, reading rooms, and laboratories where fragments were still being painstakingly reassembled by the Order's experts.

"Always a pleasure to see you," Steward said as he unseated himself, came around the banc to shake Bravo's hand in the ancient Roman manner, both men grasping each other's forearms. Steward had wiry reddish hair, a thick beard, and exophthalmic blue eyes. He also possessed a ready smile, which he now turned on Ayla as Bravo introduced them. Bravo had been careful not to bring Ayla here until now, when the library had resumed functioning more or less normally; there was no point in subjecting her to the chaos here when she had already been through so much with the deaths of her parents.

"Very pleased to meet you," Ayla said, initiating the Roman handshake herself.

Steward nodded, seeming both amused and impressed by the gesture. "I've heard stories about you, Ayla Tusik." He cocked his head. "Or are you using Ahirom, your mother's family name?"

"I have both my mother and father in me," Ayla said, slightly surprised Steward knew that much about her background. But then, she thought, why shouldn't he? "I answer to both."

Steward showed his pleasure. "As it should be." He gestured. "Shall I show you around?"

"I'm afraid our mission is too pressing for a tour," Bravo said. "We'll just make our own way."

"Of course," the librarian said. "As you wish." His eyes twinkled. "Some other time then, yes?"

"Of course," Ayla said, mirroring his friendly demeanor.

When Steward climbed back up behind his banc, Bravo said, "Off."

Without a word, the librarian flipped a switch and all the TV monitors behind him went black.

ALMOST IMMEDIATELY after they left the entrance behind, Ayla lost all track of where they were inside the library. She was about to comment on this when she realized that was precisely the point. Content, she followed in Bravo's wake as they proceeded at a brisk pace.

At length, after innumerable turnings, two flights of stairs up, three down, they entered a room so small that, apart from its circular shape and domed ceiling, it might have been a large closet. In a place where before there had been no windows, one had been carved out of the ceiling, an oriel, and only the center of the room was lit by the oval of light streaming down. Ayla noticed there wasn't even a lamp to be lit. In fact, the room was bare of any furniture, save, now that Bravo had moved and she could see them, a table and a wood-and-glass breakfront that stood against the wall opposite the doorway. As she followed him she realized that the breakfront was empty.

Reaching the center of the room, she stood for a moment, transfixed. As if sensing her change in mood, Bravo turned back to face her.

"What is it?" he asked in a perfectly neutral tone.

Ayla was silent for some time, and Bravo did not seek to prompt her. Instead, he let her be, watching closely, silent as the abandoned breakfront at his back.

"Voices," Ayla said, after quite some time lost deep in concentration. "There was death here. Violent death."

"My mentor, Fra Leoni, was betrayed by the former curator in this room," Bravo said quietly. "He was beheaded."

"There was more."

"Yes, but it's not important now."

"This was a sacred place," she said, ignoring him. Her eyes were blank and glowing eerily as she made contact with events past. "It still is, even though it was violated by a darkness, a shadow so evil . . ." Her voice trailed off as she shuddered.

All at once, her eyes cleared, she was herself again. "What was here once upon a time?"

Bravo was exceedingly pleased with her, but hardly surprised. She was, after all, an Ahirom, her mother's daughter. "This used to be the Order's reliquary."

"Ah." Ayla stared around her. "I sense what used to be housed here. But they were destroyed, weren't they?"

"Yes," Bravo said solemnly. "They were burned. All we have left is their ashes. But that's all in the past. We must go downstairs."

But Ayla refused to move. She shook her head. "Why?"

"We have kept safe the bones of the eagle Antiphon."

Ayla's eyes opened wide. "St. John's constant companion? *That* Antiphon?"

"His familiar." Bravo spread his hands. "To understand, we must go back to the poet William Butler Yeats. He and Conrad were friends. Together, they traveled to Ethiopia just after the First World War. Conrad recognized Yeats for what he was: a diviner of the future." And Bravo quoted from Yeats's poem "The Second Coming."

"'. . . everywhere/The ceremony of innocence is drowned/The best lack all conviction, while the worst/Are full of passionate intensity.' My grandfather, your father, understood this was a prophecy of what was to come in future generations. Now the time of Yeats's Second Coming has begun. 'The blood-dimmed tide is loosed . . . Surely some revelation is at hand.'"

"Yeats's philosophy of the two opposing gyres," Ayla said slowly, thoughtfully.

Bravo nodded. "And in that widening gyre, the falcon can no longer hear the falconer. The old gyre—Yeats's spiral—is ending. Mankind's trajectory along the widening gyre of science, democracy, and heterogeneity has been failing since the millennium. The next one—the opposite gyre—will be one not of science and democracy, but of the primal power of mysticism, the rise of tribalism, the resurrection of what Yeats called the 'rough beast.'"

"And you're saying that Antiphon, St. John's familiar, is that falcon?"

"Conrad told me that Yeats possessed Farsight. He saw that bird of prey and used 'falcon,' because it sounded better in the context of the poem." Bravo fixed her in his intense gaze. "But, yes, that's precisely what I'm saying."

"If anyone can find Conrad it's Antiphon. Our mission here is to call her back from the highest level of the gyre. I am telling you that if we don't, if we fail, we will never find Conrad and free him from whatever hellhole he's imprisoned in."

He held out his hand. "Come, let me show you."

She shuddered. "If we do what you ask, we'll be doomed to fail." She turned to him, anxiety distorting her face. "Before we go any further this room requires exorcism. The darkness is still here, still lurking in the shadowed corners. It must be rooted out, taken apart, and reconstructed into light. Otherwise, it will defeat all our efforts to call Antiphon back."

Bravo stared at her. She was most certainly Conrad's daughter. His power flowed deeply and truly through her. And, her mother, Dilara, was an Ahirom—one of the four ancient Phoenician families that founded Arwad. Who knew what she had inherited from Dilara? After all, her mother was an immortal, whose murder only had been effected by beheading.

She was perfectly serious, and he had no reason to doubt her.

"All right. What do you suggest?"

"Suggestions are irrelevant," Ayla said in a voice a full tone deeper than the one he was used to. "It's what must be done."

He recognized that look in her eyes; he'd seen just such a look on her mother's face when she had warned him about going to Tannourine, when she had insisted Ayla go with him to protect him. He felt such a situation had come upon him once again.

Ayla pointed at the wood table and he went to fetch it. It was a Japanese scholar's writing table made of paulownia wood, small and low with beautifully scrolled ends. He set it down in the center of the room, as she directed.

Then she looked at him, her gaze steady. "We must make a *tophet,* a Phoenician sacred precinct impervious to the dark."

Bravo nodded. "For prayer, sacrifice, and burial."

Her voice was still in that lower register. "Dark sorcery was used to defile the holy artifacts. Normal fire would not have harmed them, Bravo. You understand that."

"I do."

"A sacrifice, therefore, is required to overcome the darkness, to transmute it into light."

She knelt and then he, too, at her side. She took out a knife she kept in a sheath inside her right boot, but before she could do anything, Bravo snatched it out of her hand.

"Bravo—"

"I understand, Ayla." Pressing his hand onto the scholar's table, he spread his fingers, dropped the knife's point into the wood between his pinky and fourth finger.

Ayla made no move, no sound, merely watched him from half-lidded eyes, as if she were in a trance.

The blade came down like a guillotine, severing the pinky finger. At once, she took a cloth from her pocket, wound it tightly around the stump, tying it off at his wrist. Bravo's face was white, beads of sweat forming on his forehead and upper lip. Ayla wiped them tenderly away.

When she produced a lighter, Bravo wondered dimly whether she had foreseen this necessity even before they had left Malta. It was something Dilara would have known; that was one of her abilities. She wasn't a

Farsighter like Conrad's friend, the poet W. B. Yeats, but shorter forays into the future were hardly beyond her. Possibly this was true of her daughter, as well.

Ayla lit the flame, touched it to Bravo's severed finger. At the same time, her lips formed words that fell on Bravo's ears like music: "You will not fear the arrow that flies by day, nor those that stalk the darkness. A thousand may fall at your side, but the darkness will not come near you. And you will see the punishment of the wicked."

Through the pain that was coming on, he recognized an idiosyncratic version of the ninety-first psalm, though she spoke it neither in English nor in Latin, but in Tamazight, the language of the Phoenicians. Up until this moment, he'd had no idea that Ayla knew ancient Tamazight, a form of which was still spoken in the Central Atlas Mountains of Morocco. What else did she know?

But this question, and others, were erased from his mind by the blinding light of the supernal flames that engulfed his finger. The heat was as intense as that of a crematorium. Then, all at once, she lifted the flame. The finger had not crisped, only blackened. Ayla wrapped the finger up and pocketed it.

Half-turning to him, she gripped his wrist, touched the flame to the bloodred cloth. It evaporated as if it had never existed and before Bravo could reflexively whip his hand away, she had cauterized the wound so completely it was possible to believe he had been born with only four fingers on his left hand. The flame burned away the blood on her knife blade, then she snuffed it out, and pocketed the lighter.

Ayla placed a hand on his shoulder. "Are you all right?"

"I'm fine."

"The pain will be minimal, I promise."

"Ayla, it's okay." He smiled. "Really." But his head pounded and his hand felt as big as a football. There was an air of unreality, as if suddenly they had been plunged into the depths of the ocean, as if he was breathing water instead of air. A throb went through his hand, and he groaned, his head coming down. He felt her cradling him, her hands at the nape of his neck, stroking gently, while she kissed the top of his head.

"It *is* okay," she whispered. "Just give it a moment."

They continued to kneel like that until the world began reforming around him. He found himself instinctually drawing strength from the light the ritual had poured into the room, and was doubly grateful for the sacrifice he had made.

At last, he disengaged himself. Ayla was staring into his face.

"Now we are bonded by more than blood." Her whisper was like a reed in a rising wind, its true strength brought out by adversity.

Bravo watched his procedure as if through a scrim of smoke. He was in shock, his body and mind grappling with the trauma. He thought he had been prepared for what was to come, but for the time being reality had flown away from him like a bird freed from its cage.

They rose and she helped him open the breakfront—they both could use only one hand. The left side swung away from the wall, revealing a stone staircase leading down. The stairs themselves weren't lit but whatever lay down below was, and the glow rose up to them like the sun breaking above the horizon.

The stairs debouched onto a large rectangular space. Parts of it were walled off with tall folding screens. The walls were bare, unpainted rock. The floor was paved in granite slabs forming a black-and-white spiral pattern at the center of which were five vitrines. They were waist-high, made of magnificently hand-worked African hardwood. All had glass tops; all were empty.

As Bravo led her to one after another, he narrated: "Once the partial skull of St. John resided here, and here the forefinger of St. Paul. This third vitrine held the skeletal foot of St. Peter, the fourth, here, the shriveled ear of St. Matthew."

Ayla took this all in before she said: "Show me the bones of the eagle, Antiphon."

He took her over to a chest, opened it with a small key. Lifting the lid, he revealed the bones. They were massive, larger than any eagle's bones had any right to be.

Ayla stared silently down at the bones for some time. She took each one up in her left hand, feeling the surface, weighing them as if she were the Egyptian god Ma'at, who weighed the human heart to determine if that person was worthy to enter the afterlife.

"As I told you," she said, "if we had simply come down here, whatever incantations you had planned to use to call Antiphon back from the highest gyre would have proved fruitless."

"And now?" Bravo said.

Ayla smiled. "Watch."

And then everything changed.

23

WHEN LUCIFER SPEAKS, LEVIATHAN THOUGHT, ***ALL OF US*** *Fallen listen. Well, I'm fed up. He's been infected with a God complex. Lucifer called for the rebellion, because we were all sick to death of God ordering us around, the endless fawning over . . . well, there was no language pronoun that was appropriate, as God was genderless—God simply* was—*so* they *would have to do, the endless fetching that was required of us. We rallied around Lucifer, listened to him. Greedy, we drank at the font of his plan. And what happened? God raised their right arm and that suck-up archangel, St. Michael, led an army against us. And God, calling us* wicked, evil, anathema, *cast us down to mill around in blackness like common curs for all eternity. Us! Angels!* Leviathan had never quite gotten over the indignity of his fate. *One never forgets an indignity,* he thought in high ire, *not* this *one anyway.*

It was enough to make his blood boil. If Leviathan had blood, which he didn't. Ichor was more like it, a substance so disgusting he couldn't tolerate the sight of it. Or the smell. Cloying. Sickening. It stank like roses in full bloom.

Leviathan had taken the form of a kraken—a monstrous creature he'd concocted numerous times, ages ago before the Fall, when he felt particularly depressed, scaring the living daylights out of whalers.

Look at me, look at what I'm reduced to, he thought. *Slithering on my stomach across the floor of a sea so dead there isn't even the hope of life left in it.*

And yet here he was, obeying his Lord and Master's order to find the Regent and convince him to abandon his legendary Medius neutrality, to join the assault on God in Heaven.

How he despised an existence that was less than life and more than death. In following Lucifer, he had become a nullity, a being without anything of his own. Oh, he had Chynna, of course, but for how long? He knew that insidious child of hers was undermining him with every breath she took. He also knew, much to his dismay, that she was no ordinary child, not even a typical Sikar. There was something quite special about her, a vital spark he had never encountered before, and this disturbed him greatly, because it was proof positive that she was not his child. Who, then, was Haya's father? Certainly not that dimwit Chynna had married on Arwad. But what *was* she?

None of this would bother him overly if it hadn't been for Chynna herself. Over the millennia he had had so many human women he could recall none of their faces. Except for Chynna. Just as he knew he had entrapped her by his glamour, so had he been entrapped by her ethereal beauty, her lush body, her earthy sensuality; she possessed a glamour of her own. The appalling truth was that he couldn't get enough of her. Her inventiveness, her hunger, her acrobatics, her stamina during their hours-long bouts of congress stunned even him. He'd experienced nothing remotely like her.

And he was losing her. He was between Scylla and Charybdis: Haya was poisoning Chynna against him, but if he got rid of the daughter he would surely lose the mother, and this he could not abide.

While he fretted over this bewildering conundrum, he had almost completely traversed the dead sea. The water was grayish, so laced with salt and human ash nothing could survive its embrace. Not that there were creatures other than his like hereabouts, but it would be heartening, he mused, to have the company of living entities, as he did at the house he had conjured for Chynna and Haya. Only, sadly and perhaps inevitably, they weren't company anymore, if they ever had been. Possibly, he had blinded himself to the truth: he was alone, he always would be alone. This was his cross to bear, but if he were being honest with himself, difficult and distasteful though that was, he had made his bed of nails when he had thrown in his lot with Lucifer. He had only himself to blame for his eons-long predicament. But strangely, like humans, it was not in the nature of Fallen angels to blame themselves. Far less painful to drive the blade into another's breast.

He was almost on the far shore, and he thought of how much easier it would have been if he were a great bird of prey, flying over the ocean at five times the speed the kraken could swim through the viscous murk.

Two things prevented this transformation. First, it was far better to reach this far shore unseen and unheralded. Second, and most crucially, a bird was the one shape he could not attain. Over the millennia he had tried numerous times, without success. Why this was so he could not fathom, and if his Lord and Master knew he wasn't sharing that knowledge. What did he have three pairs of wings for anyway! But he knew, of course. The use of his—and all of the Fallen's wings—had been rendered useless when they had been defeated by God and St. Michael, and cast out of Heaven. *And, really,* he thought, *if Oq Ajdar can take the form of any avian she desires, why can't I? She's a chimera, for hell's sake! Just a chimera.* But of course she was a Medius, a Neutral. She hadn't Fallen. She was clean as a fawn's soul.

Such is my sulfurous lot, Leviathan thought evilly for the thousandth time since he had crawled into the dead sea. Far behind him, the shore, now out of all cognition.

As a lowly sand crab he scuttled up onto the strand, but soon enough transformed himself into one of those feared sea snakes from whose bite nothing living could survive.

"Oh, no." He heard the deep booming croak coming from above him. "No, no, no."

"Ah, Ayeleye," he replied, "thank you for such a warm welcome!"

Ayeleye raised the carved wooden walking stick he always carried, indoors and out. "Get the hell out of here!" he yelled, then started laughing at the inadvertent joke he had made.

Leviathan grew legs, then wings—his many useless wings. And with them came the flies, humming a tuneless ditty that made Ayeleye shudder visibly.

Dressed in riding boots, leggings, a waistcoat, and a checked wool hunting jacket, he was a peculiar creature. Immensely tall, barrel-chested, standing on short, bandy legs. With buggy eyes, nostrils where a nose should be, no chin to speak of, a lipless mouth as wide as his face, and bare earholes, he was far from a pretty sight. But Leviathan was not gulled by outward appearances; Ayeleye was both smart and clever, a fairly rare combination that made him someone the Seraph admired. What an ally he would make! But, of course, all Medius were bound to their oath of neutrality. Which made his mission somewhat of a conundrum; what did his Lord and Master know about the Regent that Leviathan himself did not? What made him believe that the Regent could be lured off his lofty perch of nonalignment? But at the moment Leviathan had a more pressing problem to deal with.

"Hold on, old boy. No cause for alarm," he said, trying to mollify the Medius.

"Don't 'old boy' us. The last time you said there was no cause for alarm three of the Fallen got strung up by their private parts for, what, a hundred years."

"Five times that, more like." Leviathan shrugged. "They transgressed; they lay with human females. Which is why you told me."

Ayeleye shot him a skeptical—almost, perhaps, a contemptuous—look. Did he know about Leviathan's own transgressions? About Chynna? Leviathan was well aware of this Medius's talent for winkling out secrets and spotting trouble before it began to brew.

Behind him the dead sea lapped listlessly at the gray shingle. Where sand crabs and shorebirds should have been was only a stony, immutable silence: no wind, no gulls, no sea wrack. Nothing.

Ayeleye gestured, and Leviathan trudged up the steep side of the strand onto the shore proper. Ten minutes later, they were standing in front of a large double door leading into a two-story sandstone manor house Ayeleye insisted on calling "The Hall." But that was perfectly in keeping with his other affectations.

Ornate oversized key in hand, the creature turned back to Leviathan. "Don't think you will darken our doorstep. Not like that." A glare. "And get rid of those disgusting flies of yours."

Grunting, Leviathan transformed into the human form with which he had seduced Chynna. No possibility of that with this base thing.

With a curt nod, Ayeleye unlocked his door and led the Seraph into the interior, large and dim as a cathedral. They proceeded through an oval entryway, down a short, wood-paneled hallway.

"Why d'you bother to lock your door?" Leviathan asked. "There isn't a soul anywhere in the vicinity."

"There's you now, isn't there?"

Ayeleye led him into a perfect replica of an English country drawing room, complete with immense stone fireplace, oversized sofas, a high-backed leather chair, carved oaken tables, and tapestries on the walls of humans hunting stag and wild boar.

"What? No Agassian lying by the hearth?" Leviathan was referencing the prized hunting dogs of ancient Briton, endowed with powerful claws for rending flesh from bone and a mouth sharp with close-set venomous teeth. But above all else Agassian were valued most highly for their supernal tracking skills. He lifted a hand, waved it. "I could conjure one for you, if you like."

"No living beings allowed." Ayeleye sniffed. "We play by the rules, which is more than you can say."

"I'm a First Order Seraph. I do whatever I want."

"Then why are you here?" Ayeleye said slyly as he settled himself into a comfy-looking leather chair.

Patience already wearing thin, Leviathan perched on a facing pew-like affair. It made him uncomfortable, which, he supposed, was the point. Acutely aware of the time he had been away from the house, he decided to get down to it.

"It's important I find someone," he said.

"It's always important, what *you* want," Ayeleye muttered. "What about what *we* want?"

Leviathan sighed. "Give me what I want and we'll see."

"Not good enough." The creature shook its wide, flat head. "Not nearly."

"How do you propose we proceed then?"

"Ha! Not by your usual mode of persuasion, we can tell you that." Ayeleye glared at him in defiance. "We are Medius. Like our brother and sisters, nonaligned. You cannot lay an extremity on us."

"The thought never entered my mind." He was right, of course, Leviathan thought bitterly. Another aspect of his existence where his hands were tied. *What is the point of being a First Sphere Seraph,* he asked himself, *if I can't have what I want most—which, paradoxically, is everything I can't have?*

Sensing his black mood, Ayeleye said, "Here is some advice we shall provide for free. Wherever you go from here, you had better get your head on straight, or you're quite likely to lose it."

Once again, the Medius was correct. While it was true that the Medius had an ability to see through façades, he could not afford to have his roiling emotions so transparent. This state of affairs forced him to realize how close to the surface he had allowed his discontent to rise. If his Lord and Master ever caught even a whiff of that particular stink he would lose his head, and much more.

Ayeleye, aware of his guest's ruminations, crossed his hands over his rotund belly. He only lacked a briar pipe to suck on. "So what can we do for you?"

"I fear we have gotten off on the wrong hoof."

Ayeleye threw his head back and laughed, which was the response Leviathan was hoping for.

"Shall we start again?" Leviathan said.

"I believe we already have."

Leviathan nodded, grateful for the new beginning. "I am seeking your brother."

Ayeleye goggled at him, which was quite the sight considering the natural state of his eyes. "You want to speak with the Regent?"

Leviathan chose not to answer what he considered a rhetorical question.

"What about, if we may ask?"

On firmer ground here, Leviathan said, "My assignment comes directly from my Lord and Master."

"Huh. Now he has dragooned you into being his emissary. Well, we must say there has never been a better time to be Medius."

Leviathan had tried being nice and what had it gotten him? Ayeleye was all too maddening, his contempt all too clear. If Leviathan's cheeks could have reddened they would have. "I may not be able to touch you, old boy, but I can take all this from you, this ersatz fantasyland you've created for yourself." He lifted a hand once more. "With the wave of a hand I can—"

"Desist!" Ayeleye cried. "We will have no more talk of that."

"Then . . ." Leviathan deliberately left the sentence unfinished.

"Very well." Ayeleye sighed. "But the fact is I have not the faintest idea where my darling brother might be. We haven't spoken in, oh, I don't know, it must be millennia."

Leviathan leapt up, eyes narrowed. "This place reeks of unfulfilled dreams and thwarted ambitions. But mostly it's you who makes me sick. You with all your abominable affectations!"

Ayeleye regarded him from deep in his cushions. His hands had not budged from their position bisecting the impressive arc of his belly. "And what about your own ambitions, *old boy*? Do not for an instant delude yourself into believing that we don't know what you crave most." A smile so genuine it rocked Leviathan. "Frankly, we cannot fathom why you have waited so long to come to us."

It was a sunny day in the underworld when Leviathan was struck dumb, but against all laws sunshine must be somewhere warming the dead sea. Ayeleye's mercurial moods were dizzying, but then Leviathan recalled the Medius's love of game-playing. What precisely was this one on about? He determined to keep his mouth firmly shut until Ayeleye made himself clear.

That sly aspect had returned to Ayeleye's pancake face. "You may be here under the auspices of your Lord and Master, but we very much doubt that is the sum and substance of this visit."

He was altogether cannier than Leviathan remembered. He was right, as far as it went. How much more did the wretched creature suspect? And that sly look was something Leviathan needed to keep under close surveillance.

"You came to us for advice." Ayeleye stroked his chin as if he had a beard. "We admire your intelligence, Leviathan." He grunted, as if pieces of a puzzle were falling into place. "You wish to talk to our brother—and doubtless our sisters as well—about abandoning our pledge of neutrality. You want us to join with you when you move against your Lord and Master." Ayeleye nodded. "A clever plan, we grant you. And daring. Possibly *too* daring, might we be so bold as to venture."

"Might *we* indeed," Leviathan said, because, now that Leviathan thought about it, it was highly likely the Medius understood him better than he imagined. As such, they would make even better allies than he had suspected. He had prepared a veritable laundry list of reasons why they should throw their lot in with him, starting with this being the advent of the End Times, when neutrality was no longer of use to anyone. He laughed to himself. This encounter was going far better than he had dared hope. "Are you up for a dare?"

Ayeleye's gaze turned toward the coffered ceiling. "Much as we love our Hall, we must admit it is too quiet, too lonely." His eyes lowered, alighting on the Seraph. "We are overfed with lifelessness. We crave something more. We crave sunlight, moonlight, starlight. The wind on our face, clouds scudding across blue sky. Above all, we crave *life*."

At once, Leviathan's spirit lifted. "Does that mean we crave the same things?"

Ayeleye levered himself out of his cushy seat. "Well, you have your women." He crossed to the fireplace. "Where is our Agassian?"

24

CHYNNA'S EYES NARROWED. "WHO ARE YOU?"

"I'm Molly. Your daughter."

Chynna regarded the young woman and her older companion through the shattered window. She waved a hand. "How did you manage this?"

"This." Molly opened her hand, showed Chynna the octagonal medallion that sucked light out of the air. "You gave me this before you let my father take me away from you."

"I have no idea what you're talking about." She was tall, slender, dark-haired, her exotic face almost Arabic in aspect. Too, she projected a smoldering sexual heat. She wore a white robe over which was wound a voluminous white cloak that covered her head like a Muslim woman. "You must be delusional, child."

"I'm neither delusional nor a child." Molly stepped through the window opening, Lilith just behind, ready to defend her if necessary. "I know what I know." She held up the medallion. "You gave me this. None other."

Chynna's frown had been known to strike terror into the hearts of children young and old, but Molly was impervious. Undaunted, she stepped toward her mother.

"Why don't you greet me?" Her arm swept out. "This is Lilith, my sister. Well, my cousin. Whatever. It's complicated. The important thing is that she knows who her mother is; I don't. As I said, I was taken away from her when I was an infant."

"A sad story, is that what you want me to say? But it has nothing to do with me."

"Molly has come here looking for her mother," Lilith said pointedly.

Chynna's gaze moved just enough to take her in. "It's possible I can help."

"Well, so far you've been singularly unhelpful." A typical Molly comeback. Lilith put a hand on her arm, which Molly shook off. "Don't," she said without looking at Lilith. "Just don't."

Lilith settled back. She thought it best now to keep her hands to herself and her mouth shut.

"First of all," Chynna said, "I would never name a child of mine Molly." Her gaze flickered, alighting nowhere and everywhere at once. "And in any event, I already have a daughter." The edge of her hand cut through the air between them. "I am, therefore, sympathetic to your quest. As I said, I might be able to help you find your mother, Molly."

"Ah." Molly nodded. "Here it comes, the quid pro quo."

"For such a relatively young thing," Chynna replied, "you do seem to have an excellent grasp of how the world works."

Molly took a step toward her, an icy glare in her eyes. "I'd rather rule than be ruled. Do you understand me?"

A right eyelid fluttered, but other than that Chynna was still and silent.

Molly waited and, beside her, Lilith began weighing this contest of wills.

"Currently, Haya, my daughter—my *real* daughter—is imprisoned in this house." Chynna indicated with her head. "Your medallion shattered the window when I could not open it or break it. I'm hoping it can do the same with Haya's cell."

"Who imprisoned her?" Lilith asked. "Who imprisoned both of you in this house?"

Chynna was trying to move them along, into the maze of hallways leading to the room where Haya was imprisoned, but Molly held up a hand.

Chynna turned back to her. "Please. My daughter—"

"We're not going anywhere until you answer Lilith's questions."

Chynna projected her hardest glare, but when this didn't faze Molly in the least, she sighed inwardly. "You've made it this far, so what I have to say shouldn't shock you overly. Haya and I have been imprisoned by a First Sphere Seraph."

"Not Leviathan," Lilith said, who with Emma's help had studied both the Shaw family tree and the legions of the Fallen. "Don't tell us it's Leviathan."

"It is," Chynna affirmed.

"And what are you doing with him," Molly demanded, "let alone allowing your daughter anywhere near him?"

Chynna put her hands together, fingers laced. "It's a long story." She looked at Molly meaningfully. "A very long story."

"It seems we have more time than you do," Lilith said, catching Molly's steely mood. She sensed this was the only way to deal with this imposing woman.

"I am very old. Older than either of you can imagine."

"How is that possible?" Molly asked. "You appear to be in the prime of your life."

At this, Chynna produced an enigmatic smile, which looked to them more like a scimitar blade. "Leviathan came to me, swept me off my feet. There is no other way to put it: he seduced me."

Lilith's eyes narrowed. "Exactly how long ago was this?"

There was no point now, Chynna thought, in dissembling. She needed to free Haya before Leviathan returned, and she could see that the only way to do that was by telling the truth.

"My name is Chynna Sikar," she began.

"Wait!" Lilith felt her heart constrict. "Chynna Shaw, nee Sikar, established the Shaw family name. Chynna Shaw was Bravo's great-great-grandmother. You cannot be her. It's impossible."

"Improbable, yes," Chynna said, not unkindly. "Impossible, no." She lifted her arms, as if in benediction. "Not in this world."

"Go on," Molly said. "We'll decide whether your history is improbable or impossible."

Chynna lowered her head slightly as if accepting their judgement. "I was born on the island of Arvad, now known as Arwad."

"I've been there," Lilith said.

Chynna nodded. "I can tell. The island changes everyone who sets foot on it." She shifted on her feet, a sure sign of her discomfort at confession. "I transgressed against the other main families and was forced to flee to the mainland. Since they came after me, I was forced to change my name, to create not only a name, but a family all my own."

"Hence the Shaws sprang into being," Lilith said.

"Precisely." Chynna nodded. "However, I died relatively young by modern day's standards. I was sixty-two. But I wasn't dead long. Leviathan brought me back, selfish prick that he is . . ." Here she faltered, her eyelids flickered. "Only it wasn't to life—not the life I'd had, not the life you two know. Something was missing; something essential."

"You're hálf-dauður," Lilith said in a shocked whisper.

"Hálf-dauður." Molly turned to her. "What is that?"

"The half-dead," Lilith told her. "I've read about them but I thought they were myth."

"So much of myth is a form of the history humans can tolerate." Chynna's eyes clouded over. "Possibly I was always this way. I was very selfish; I was amoral; I did whatever I wished without regard for whatever consequences might occur. But now I am hollowed out inside. I'm not the same as I was when I gave birth to Gideon, Bravo and Emma's great-grandfather. I exist, but I have come to believe that I am alive only in the way Leviathan requires."

Silence enfolded them for a time, until they became aware of a soft buzzing.

"Oh, God," Chynna cried. "The flies!" And when she saw the bewilderment of the two young women, she added: "They're his spies. We can't let them—"

But Molly had already raised a hand, extending it toward the flies with the black medallion gripped in it. At once, the flies—like the light near the medallion—were sucked into it, vanishing as if they never existed.

Chynna stared, her mouth half-open. "How . . . ?"

But Molly was as shocked as Chynna. As when she had thrown the medallion at the supposedly unbreakable window, she had acted by instinct alone, as if somewhere inside her she already knew the powers of the medallion. But that was impossible, wasn't it? And then she heard the echo of Chynna's voice: *"Improbable, yes. Impossible, no. Not in this world."*

Stunned as well by what had just happened, Lilith's mind was nonetheless speeding down a different track. Now she said, "Gideon was Nephilim, wasn't he?"

"Nephilim," Molly said. "What's that?"

"Someone who is half-human, half-seraphim," Chynna replied. And to Lilith, "That's right, he was."

Molly made a face. "That's . . . that's just disgusting."

Chynna tried to ignore the insult. "Can we make our pilgrimage now? My daughter is waiting. Even though she exhibits more patience than I ever have, it's past time she was freed." She stepped toward the interior doorway, when Lilith spoke:

"One more thing. If you've been resurrected, as you claim, and if, again as you claim, a piece of you was missing when Leviathan brought you back into existence, and now you're living, what, half a life—hollowed out, as you put it—how is it you were able to get pregnant with Haya?"

At this, Chynna's regal façade, turning from steel to glass, shattered completely, as if Molly had thrown the dark medallion at her as she had done with the window. The jagged stress lines shot out from a central point, and Chynna, all at once exposed as she never had been before, dropped to her knees, face in her hands, weeping like a lost child.

EMMA, PARAPHRASING Genesis 3:24 silently: *God drove Adam out of Eden; and at the east of the garden, as Adam made to turn back, he stationed the Cherubim, Azazel, whose flaming sword, from every direction guarded the way to the tree of life.*

This was what stood before her now: the monstrous Azazel.

Azazel, who swept his flaming sword across Omega's neck, beheading the creature as if he were a sacrificial bullock. And perhaps he was, Emma thought now. The innocent bullock to lead her here to the place where, doubtless on the orders of Lucifer himself, the Cherubim awaited her.

Hadn't Bravo warned her of the peril of her decision to find a Fallen? Wouldn't Lilith have talked her out of coming here? And yet, deliberately, almost mulishly, she had turned away from both of them. Now she understood her terrible mood swings, the bubbling up of her jealousy and resentment to the point where the harder her brother tried to stop her, the more determined she became to defy him. Now, too late, with Omega's head at her feet, with the Cherubim Azazel grinning greedily at her, she recognized the trap the Sum of All Shadows had carefully and calculatedly laid for her.

She felt like a fox caught in a forest trap. *What a fool he's made of me!* she silently lamented, and though she was right, a part of her urged her to take a figurative step back, put aside blame and self-recrimination, and figure out how she was going to escape.

To keep herself from falling apart, she said in her lightest voice, "How the mighty have been laid low. What once was beloved of God, now is reviled by that same deity, expelled in the same breath as Lucifer, Leviathan, and the other Fallen."

"I'm in good company then."

Azazel merely touched the tip of his fiery blade to Omega's headless body, collapsing it like a pricked balloon. There was a violent stench of rotting lilies coming from the charred neck, where the sword had sliced through it. But no blood; of course, no blood, just a soft ooze the peachy-orange color of embalming fluid.

"Et ignis ibi est!" Let there be fire! Emma cried, and, holding out her hand, spread her fingers like a flower opening to sunlight. The blue fire, cold as ice, sprang from the center of her palm.

Azazel halted momentarily. "Where did you . . . ?" Then he shook his head, and came at her sword-first.

Emma backed up to avoid the initial swipe of the blade. At the same moment, she flung her hand out. The blue flames were loosed like arrows from a bow directly at Azazel's head. He brought the sword up, crimson devouring blue, but her assault staggered him, and she was heartened. Her fear for the moment banked, she stepped up, flinging more cold fire at him.

His blade flicked this way and that, absorbing her weapon's barrage, but he was down on one knee now and she came forward again, seeking to press her advantage. But so intent on her target was she that her lead foot came down on Omega's head, and with all her weight upon it, squirted to one side. Her ankle turned, and she felt a sharp pain like an electric shock run up her leg all the way to her hip.

Crying out as she canted over, she sought to regain her balance, but her forward momentum pitched her over and down. She fell heavily on her right shoulder, her hand curling up in reflex. The cold fire was extinguished.

Azazel had regained his feet, was shaking off the effects of her last fusillade. With a grim smile, he came at her.

Half-stunned, she was nevertheless able to summon her courage. *"Et ignis ibi est!"* she cried again and, as he brought the flaming blade down to split her skull in two, she caught it between her hands.

Heat against cold. Fire against fire. Azazel bore down with all the power in his torso. She could no longer feel her hands, could no longer distinguish between fire and ice. Her hands began to tremble, the sword came closer, the flames flickering like an adder's forked tongue. The tremors passed through her wrists into her forearms, continuing to climb, despite her best efforts to head it off. When it reached her injured shoulder, she screamed. The agony was so great she felt herself falling into a gaping abyss.

No, she thought frantically. *No!* But her world was reduced to the circumference of a tunnel, then a tube, which narrowed so quickly she never knew when she tumbled from consciousness into blackness.

25

ONE BY ONE, AYLA TOOK THE BONES OF THE EAGLE ANTIPHON from the chest and laid them on the floor where there was plenty of space around them. Using the knowledge he had gleaned from the books he had been studying before they left Malta, Bravo incanted in English. "For in him all things—"

He paused at Ayla's raised hand, watched as she unwrapped his blackened finger, held it over the bones, and again, it became an offering. She nodded, and Bravo began again:

"For in him all things are created: things in Heaven and on earth and in between, visible and invisible, whether thrones or powers or regents or authorities; all things have been created through him and will be now. Rise up, Antiphon. Return to the rage of thine enemies. Awake to the judgement that has been commanded."

Bravo took hold of Ayla's right hand. "Move back," he said softly. "Stand with me."

The atmosphere in the room began to shift—to waver, as if they were beholding a mirage in the middle of the Sahara. But what rose from the floor was no mirage. Bit by bit, with bone, sinew, feather, beak, claw, and eye the great sacred eagle of St. John arose from its long, lonely flight at the end of the final gyre, returning to the earth, to Alexandria, where some said she was born, to the cellars deep beneath the library.

To Bravo.

"Antiphon."

At the sound of her name, the eagle turned her head, one eye, bright and golden as the sun, taking him in—all of him, inside and out, and she spread her immense wings and shook herself in a gesture of the greatest pleasure.

Despite Ayla's promise, Bravo had begun to tremble. His legs felt like rubber bands, his left hand felt like a boxing glove. And then he went down, collapsing to his knees. Ayla bent to tend to him, but Antiphon, wings folded, made a sound that though not an intelligible word, was clearly a warning. Ayla froze, then slowly and carefully stepped back without taking her eyes off the avian.

Bravo, oblivious to everything but his pain, was bent over, hair hanging over his face. His shoulders were hunched and his breathing was stentorian, as if something sharp were caught in his windpipe. Ayla might have thought the eagle would hop, but it didn't. It walked, not clumsily like most grounded avians, but with an uncommon grace. When it was close enough it spread one wing over Bravo. The feathers covered him completely. Then it climbed onto one of his thighs, pressed its breast against him, and stayed like that, until both of them began to breathe in tandem, until Bravo's right hand came up, stroking Antiphon's head.

The bonding between the two both exhilarated Ayla and caused a tendril of jealousy to unfurl like a sail inside her. She fought against it; jealousy was a failing in others and she hated it in herself. Besides, she told herself, there was no reason for her to be jealous. Except, of course, she wanted to be the one to comfort Bravo in his pain and suffering. And she was ashamed that she had lied to him, telling him the pain would loosen its grip on him shortly. No, not shortly. It would be his close companion for some time. This was the way of sacrifice, otherwise what would be the point. Bravo knew this—he'd known it the moment she had brought out the knife. He had accepted the burden instantly, unquestioningly. But they were together in creating the *tophet*; by all rights they should be together now. But how, she asked herself, could she be jealous of a bird, no matter how intelligent? Antiphon, for all her power, was not family. Conrad was her father; he was Bravo's grandfather. Only in a family like the Shaws could such an anomaly occur.

As if sensing the swirl of her emotions, Antiphon swiveled her head, her gaze falling on Ayla, and Ayla, with a laugh, would have sworn on the Qur'an that the eagle smiled at her. At this, Bravo lifted his head, Antiphon withdrew her wing, and Ayla came to kneel beside him.

"I think we need to get you some rest."

But Bravo shook his head. "I can rest when I'm dead." He lifted his maimed left hand. "Thanks to you, the wound is cauterized. Thanks to Antiphon, most of the pain has been leached out of me." He gave her a reassuring smile. "I'm a bit tired, but we can put that down to the flight and lack of food. I'm starving, are you?"

Both Ayla and Antiphon nodded at once, and Bravo laughed both at the gesture and in relief of the terrible tension he'd been under from the moment they set foot in the library, a place of such horrific memories.

But as they gathered themselves to ascend the stairs into what had been the reliquary, the ground beneath their feet trembled and shook so hard that several of the walls collapsed with the horrific noise and percussion of a bomb detonating.

Amid the hail of debris and dust, a crevasse appeared, the floor cracked open, spilling them headlong into a red-tinged superheated darkness.

FOR LONG moments, Molly and Lilith stared in bafflement at Chynna's emotional collapse. She knelt, much as Bravo in the chamber below the library, had bent over. Her tears overflowed the hands pressed to her face, rolling down her wrists, staining her long cream-colored wrap dress. She was without jewelry but there was the gleam of gold scrollwork on her sandals.

Lilith was the first to respond, stepping closer, hunkering down in front of Chynna. "I think it's time you told the truth," she said gently, deliberately leave out the "us," as it might trigger a negative recoil.

But that recoil came from just behind her. "Why would you believe anything this woman has to say?" Molly said with an all too obvious sneer. "She hasn't told us a word of truth since we came upon her."

"Hush," Lilith admonished her. "Keep still." She touched Chynna briefly. "There's a truth that's burning a hole in you. If you can't let it go, it will surely eat you up from the inside out."

Molly rolled her eyes at this, but thankfully neither of the other women was aware of it. Still, she curbed her anger and frustration, observing Lilith's command. In a relatively short time, her feelings toward her sister had turned 180 degrees. The love, the admiration she'd had for her older sister came flooding back to her now. And she liked this adult Lilith, strong and commanding. More importantly, she trusted her, even in a charged situation like this when she was itching to grab Chynna and choke the truth out of her. She knew Lilith wanted the same thing, and it began to dawn on her that, in this case, her way might bear more fruit.

Lilith took Chynna's hands off her face, lifted Chynna's chin until their gazes met. "Now," she said. "We're here to listen. You have only to tell us." When she noticed Chynna's eyes flick toward Molly, she added: "Just look at me now. Molly won't say a word, I promise."

And she was right, Molly thought with some astonishment. Once Chynna began she would not interrupt her. She had the presence of mind to recognize that the flow of information, once it began, was a delicate thing. Any interruption, no matter how brief, could bring it to an abrupt and abortive end. So she crossed her arms over her chest and prepared to watch the next few minutes unfold.

And yet they refused to unfold along anticipated lines. Instead, without even the smallest move to wipe her eyes, Chynna rose, resuming her former icy regal mien. "Must I remind you once more that my daughter, Haya, is still imprisoned. If either of you possesses a shred of humanity you will do your best to free her instead of seeking to weasel a bargain."

This imperious speech was too much for Molly, who, with fists clenched, took a run at Chynna. Lilith rose just in time to catch her around the waist and swing her around.

"What the fuck are you doing?" Molly cried. "What this queen bitch needs is a swift kick in the teeth."

Over Molly's head, Lilith stared into Chynna's face, as if to say, *Here but for my intervention is your fate.* "Take us to her, then," she said in a not altogether friendly tone. "This Haya of yours."

Chynna turned then, leading the way down corridors that appeared to stretch or contract, to turn in on themselves, to change shape, like a child's game of Chutes and Ladders; past rooms from which wafted eddies of odors, by turns sweet, exotic, acrid, and deeply revolting, as if the structure was both hothouse and abattoir.

Lilith's progress was slowed by her efforts to contain Molly's struggles. They both heard the high shriek from just ahead of them at the same time. Lilith let Molly go, rushed on into the room into which Chynna had disappeared. She was halfway to where Chynna stood, clawed fingers scraping down the convex wall of an egg-shaped enclosure, when Molly entered behind her.

The enclosure was clearly the cell in which Haya had been incarcerated. Its sides were translucent, and as she came up beside Chynna, Lilith could see that the prison enclosure was empty. No one was inside.

"She's gone! Where is she?" Chynna's cries were anguished, desperate. Her fingernails dug into the walls of the translucent egg again and again until they were half-flayed off and her fingertips began to bleed. She whipped around to stare at Molly. Her fingers were curled now into the hollows of her palms. "What's happened to her?"

"How the fuck should I know? But I know what's happened to *you,*" Molly shot back, impervious to Chynna's despair. "You got that swift kick in the teeth I was talking about."

"How can you?" Chynna's voice was thick, clotted with emotion. "How can you be so cruel?"

"You're the cruel one. You got Haya into this mess." The cords on Molly's neck were standing out like the cables on a bridge. "You've got no one to blame but yourself."

Lilith understood Molly's rage, but saw no benefit in her keeping up the hectoring. After all, Chynna, no matter her attitude, had just lost a daughter. She stepped between the two women, but the animosity between them was at such a pitch that she was almost literally tossed aside. Planting her feet and squaring her hips she resolved to keep them from ripping each other's face off.

Chynna's eyes were blazing. "Don't you understand what's happened, you cretin? Use your medallion to get me inside Haya's cell."

"Why bother?" Molly retorted. "We can all see she's not there." And then because she couldn't stop herself from twisting the knife, "If she was there at all. I mean, maybe she's a figment of your imagination."

Chynna's face turned white as death. "You have no idea who you're dealing with." But with a supreme effort she controlled herself, pointing. "Just get that *thing* open."

Molly's face was taunting, an expression at which she excelled. "Say please, queen bitch."

"All right." Lilith whirled to face her sister. "Enough is enough."

"Is it?" Molly's eyes were fairly sparking. "Is it really?"

"Go on," Lilith urged under her breath. "For God's sake, just do it!"

With a little cry, Molly moved her out of the way, threw the dark medallion at the egg-shaped mass. The instant it struck, there was a soft hissing as the entire structure collapsed in on itself, evaporating so quickly it might never have been there.

While Molly went to pick up the medallion, Chynna rushed by her. "Where are you?" She was weeping. "Haya, speak to me! Where are you?" But there was no one to respond. No trace of Haya remained. It was as if she had evaporated like her prison cell.

She turned on her heel. "Where could she have gone?" Was she speaking to Lilith or to herself? Possibly it was both.

"Maybe she escaped."

Chynna was wild-eyed, her torso bent forward, rigid as a steel girder. "Don't you understand? There was no escape, no hope until you came along with that *thing*." She pointed to the medallion. "What if someone's taken her? What if she's . . . *dead*." The last word came out in a hiss. Her extended finger shook. "It's your fault. If you'd come with me right away . . . but no, you had to strike a bargain. You took your time when I *told* you—I told you *expressly*—we had no time to wait!"

Molly's eyes narrowed. "I had a mother once—or rather someone who birthed me. But she sure as hell wasn't a mother; she allowed me to be taken. She threw me away like trash. She didn't want me. Well, fuck her, and fuck you, too!"

Chynna rushed at her with such passion Lilith had no hope of restraining her. She tossed Lilith aside as if she were a handful of feathers. She and Molly grabbed each other, teeth clenched, muscles bunched and straining. Molly got a heel behind Chynna's ankle, and brought her down. Chynna struck her in the face with her leading elbow and Molly got in a nasty knuckler to Chynna's kidneys. But Chynna evinced no outward manifestation of pain. Instead, she snatched Molly's wrist, twisted the arm until it was behind her back. Then she rose, straddled the girl.

As soon as Lilith saw her elbow cocked, her fingers held rigid as boards, she was on the move. She registered Chynna aiming at the soft spot directly beneath Molly's sternum, a blow that if delivered with the sorcery of the hálf-dauður would certainly kill Molly.

Oblivious to the extreme danger to her, she wrapped her hand around Chynna's weaponized fingers. "No," she said softly and calmly. "You don't want her blood on your hands."

Once again, words triggered an unexpected alteration in Chynna's demeanor. The fire in her eyes was banked to embers. Her muscles relaxed. Her fingers slipped from Lilith's, and she swung off Molly. She sat next to her, knees drawn, feet beneath her, pressed hard into the floor, as if it was important now for her to feel grounded.

"It will never be all right," she whispered hoarsely. "Possibly it never was." Again, who was she speaking to besides herself? "Maybe everything that came before was a dream." Her eyes were vacant, as if focused on something or somewhere visible to neither Molly nor Lilith.

Molly, risen to her elbows, stared at Chynna. "What is she on about?"

"I'll tell you." Chynna's voice was a straw in the wind, pale and insubstantial. "I'll tell you everything. Why not?" Her eyes, pale and insubstantial as her voice, nevertheless caught them in a web. "What have I to lose now? I've lost everything; I cannot sink lower."

Her head turned and she gazed at where the egg prison had been. "Haya is real," she began. "As real as I could make her."

"What . . . ?" Lilith's heart turned over and her breath caught in her throat. "What does that mean?"

The ghost of a smile passed across Chynna's lips. "I am attempting to answer your question: How could a hálf-dauður—not living, yet not dead—give birth? The short answer is she cannot. The long answer is I did."

She paused, but neither Lilith nor Molly felt inclined to speak. The silence of a graveyard, where confessions are whispered but never heard, settled over them, and Lilith felt the blood pounding in her temples, a berg of ice congealing in the pit of her stomach. The terrified part of her didn't want Chynna to go on, as the rational part of her sought comfort.

"The man I married on Arwad thought Haya was his child. Leviathan was convinced she was his. I never told them otherwise. Deliberately."

The tip of her tongue emerged between her sharp white teeth to moisten her lips. "I birthed Haya in this way: I created her out of sugar and spice and everything nice. So the children's rhyme goes, but there is a kernel of truth in those words. I am, as I told you, less than I was before Leviathan resurrected me. Once upon a time, I was grateful to him. I was so sure that this was what I wanted, to live again. But be careful what you wish for. But to live again—not like this, never like this.

"The truth is I couldn't bear it. I had never been so alone, so isolated from everything and everyone. I needed a companion. I needed a child."

Chynna's head tilted back, her eyes on the ceiling, though what she was seeing there God alone knew, and perhaps not even them. Because it seemed to Lilith that Chynna had passed beyond God's sight, and was no longer worthy of their help or succor. This, truly, was what being immortal meant. A deep-seated shiver passed through her.

"But if I, a hálf-dauður, am less than human, I am also more. I am able to perform feats beyond human ken. Not on the level of the Seraphim or even the Cherubim, but so what? What I *can* do I do better than they can. Because I am female, because I have the will, because the drive to have a child is woven into the strands of my DNA. And this drive is so powerful, so undeniable that it survived both my death and my resurrection.

"What does this mean? I imagine you're asking yourself this question. I would too if I were in your shoes. I went down to a river on Arwad, a deserted place overhung thickly by trees twisted by the violent storms off the sea. Lilith, you said you were on Arwad, so you may know that it is a special island, pregnant with Phoenician sorcery. There is a gateway to the Hidden Lands on Arwad, yes? Only one of four in the world of humans. Arwad is, in short, a power spot."

Her gaze descended to her hands in her lap. She stared at her open palms, as if trying to divine the future in those lines that crisscrossed them. Either that, or hoping to somehow change the past.

"At the edge of the river I shed my clothes," she continued. "Naked, I slipped into the shallows. It was cold, but of a single mind, a sole intent, I scarcely noticed. Like a waterfowl, I stalked my prey. Presently, I found what I was hunting for: a tadpole. Scooping it up into my cupped palm, I bit into the finger of my other hand, deep enough that drops of my blood fell, mixing with the river water. More and more of my blood fell, until all the water had been displaced."

Her fingers twined and retwined in her lap. Her breathing was short and quick, a sure sign of her inner turmoil.

"I spoke to the tadpole then. I called it by name. 'Haya, *habibti,*' I said, 'I have come for you. I am your mother and I will keep you safe now and forever. This I swear if you will come to me from the nameless land I can see but dimly.'"

She displayed her left hand, and they both saw the pair of scimitar scars on the pad at the base of her thumb, a remembrance of how she helped bring Haya to life.

"And so she did. A child. A daughter. She rose from that tadpole, that bit of life, and infused it with her own form of sorcery. I had no control over that part, I admit. Whatever she brought from that nameless land is all her own—a mystery—all of her a mystery. And the more beloved because of it."

Her voice had grown hoarse with the telling of a tale she had expected to share with no one. And she looked around, blinking heavily, as if only now emerging from a dream-state.

"So you see." Her voice like metal scraping against metal. "Now you know what Haya means to me. What her disappearance means to me." She clutched a fist to her breast. "It's like my heart has been ripped from my body. I'll find her or die trying."

Molly was mute. She felt wrung out, as if she had just run a marathon. Every time she thought she knew what was going in inside this insane asylum of a house, it turned out to be a false image, a reflection not of what was happening, but of herself. And so it was hardly surprising when she reversed course and said:

"We'll help you find her, Chynna."

26

"DON'T LOOK SO SURPRISED," LEVIATHAN SAID. "THE TIME FOR keeping you inside the egg has passed." He held her by the nape of the neck. "It's time you were hatched, don't you think."

It wasn't a question, and Haya did not take it as such. Anyway, she was too busy looking around her, taking in her richly embroidered and wood-paneled surroundings.

"Where am I?" she asked.

"Is this her?"

She turned to see a tall, stoop-shouldered individual with a frog's face. He was dressed in the style of rich country gentlemen she'd seen in illustrated historical novels of nineteenth-century England. It was not only his incongruous mien but also the way he peered at her with his goggle eyes that caused her giggle to escape the hands she had clapped over her mouth. Despite her fear, or possibly because of it, she could not control her giggling, which continued over Ayeleye's annoyed, "What is the child doing?"

"She's laughing," Leviathan said equably.

"At what, pray tell?"

"At you, Medius. Look at yourself. You're an object of foolishness to the child."

"Us? Why?"

Leviathan grunted. "If I have to explain it, there's no point." He turned Haya around to face him, then let her go, and her hands came away from her mouth. "You are in a wondrous place, Haya. This is the great Hall of Ayeleye, the person who makes you giggle. Ayeleye is one of the Four Medius. They are neutral, pledged not to interfere in the dealings of humans or angels or demons."

Haya's eyes narrowed. "Then why are you here?"

Now it was Ayeleye's turn. He threw his head back and laughed deep and long, his ample belly rising and falling like a juggled ball. He clapped his long-fingered hands together. "Yes, by all means tell the child why you're here."

"Don't call me 'the child,'" Haya snapped. "My name is Haya."

Now Ayeleye peered at her more closely. "How old are you, anyway?"

Haya, crossing her arms over her chest in defiance said, "Old enough to know I'm being held against my will."

"Well." The Medius looked over her head to where Leviathan stood. "What should we make of this?"

"Haya is . . . different," Leviathan said.

"Then let us by all means render unto her that which is due her." Ayeleye pursed his lips, bending forward in something resembling a bow. "How would you like a cuppa, Haya?"

She frowned. "A what?"

"Tea, my dear," Leviathan said. "He's offering you a cup of tea."

Haya wrinkled her nose. "Why would I want that?"

"We have found," Ayeleye told her, "that tea calms the nerves and soothes the spirit in troubled circumstances."

Haya cocked her head. "You talk funny."

The Medius smiled benignly. "All part of our charm."

"Well, whatever charm you have is certainly more than Leviathan can muster," she said in the manner of all children who can cut through the fog of adult words to get at the heart of the matter.

Ayeleye stood up straight, fists on hips. "We like this girl," he said. "She says what she means and means what she says." Again he took a quick glance over Haya's head. "As opposed to you who spews out lies with every breath you take."

Haya took a step closer to the Medius, then turned to address Leviathan. "How did I get here?"

Leviathan regarded her with an unreadable expression. "My egg, my rules."

Ayeleye smirked. "Egomaniac."

"Isn't that what you count on?" Leviathan sniffed.

And in that seemingly simple exchange, Haya caught the complex nature of their relationship. But then one of the attributes she had brought with her was a sharply honed empathy. She was able to glean from both words and tones the layers of meaning, like translucent pages stacked one atop the other. These two were frenemies, who disliked but needed each other, she concluded. How that relationship could be exploited she had yet to determine, but she harbored little doubt that by hook or by crook she would.

And so she smiled sunnily and, taking Ayeleye's oddly shaped hand in hers, said, "Where to next?"

RISING FROM the bottom of a well is no easy task, even for one such as Emma. And so her journey from darkness to light seemed a long and arduous one, and by the time she reached the top of the well and, metaphorically speaking, pulled herself out, she was exhausted.

She was also disoriented. It took her some time, lying face up on the chilly floor, to recall what had happened to her: her firefight with Azazel, her sense of gaining the upper hand, just before he destroyed her defenses. He could have killed her then and there, but instead had chosen to keep her alive.

Why?

She sat up, her head spinning, and wondered what had happened to her after she lost consciousness. She had been at the Cherub's mercy. Now here she was in a nearly lightless room with no inkling of where she had been taken or how long she had been unconscious.

All her limbs were intact and functioning. Apart from some aches and bruises she appeared to be unharmed, the fierce headache behind her eyes notwithstanding. But then, clutching her chest, she discovered that the necklace with Beleth's talon was gone, and, eyes burning, tears overflowed her eyes, plopped silently into her lap.

It took some minutes for her to recover her equilibrium and to even want to go on with her inventory, but at length she managed it. Now, her surroundings: dirty gray light filtered through a single window, too high up for her to see out of, too small for her to crawl through. It was barred with a material she could not immediately identify. Clearly, she was in some sort of prison cell. The floor was a solid sheet of stone, the walls blocks of the same material. As for the ceiling, it seemed to be made of a crystalline material formed into triangles. Impossible to tell whether they were transparent or opaque, as they were a uniform dense black.

It was fiercely cold in the cell. She began to lever herself off the floor, but had to stumble to a wall for support as dizziness swept over her like a tide, and then like a tide receded. She made her way to the door. It had a slot in it. It was locked. She thought she heard voices or echoes of voices and she pressed her ear against the rough wood-grain of the door.

It was difficult to tell whether what she was hearing were indeed faint voices or the groaning of machinery. But she was sure she had a way out: her cold fire. She opened her mouth to shout the words that would bring the fire: *Et ignis ibi est!* but nothing came out. Not only did she have no voice, she had no sensation of even being able to open her mouth.

Abruptly terrified, her hands flew up to her face. Where lips and teeth and gums and a tongue should be only smooth flesh. She tried to scream.

But, of course, she was greeted only by silence.

27

THEY FELL. AND KEPT FALLING FOR, IT SEEMED TO BRAVO, forever. The heat was overwhelming. Cinders flew into their eyes and singed their clothes. Above them, Antiphon was struggling to stay aloft in the vicious downdraft, dipping and swooping, and once or twice, almost losing altitude entirely, her wings starting to fold in on themselves from the pressure. Below them, Ayla, close enough for him to touch, was face up, her eyes wide and staring at him, terrified. Her mouth opened and closed but he could not hear a word she said over the shriek of the hellish wind that rose from far below.

He heard Antiphon calling, though, and he understood what she meant, because now, somehow, defying the laws of human physics, they had begun to fall at a faster rate. It should have been impossible. It *was* impossible, and yet it was happening, and he knew that whatever fate awaited them below was bound to end in their deaths.

Locking eyes with Ayla, he reached down. She raised one arm toward his outstretched hand, which kept being battered back by the ferocious updraft. The heat was becoming unbearable, making it difficult to breathe, and with the heat came carbon dioxide and other toxic fumes that made their eyes water and burned the backs of their throats. He calculated that they could not survive in this atmosphere longer than a matter of minutes.

Desperate now, he reached down even farther. Fighting the wind with all his strength, he caught the tips of her fingers for seconds before the tenuous grip was whipped away. He tried again, extending himself to the very limit of his ability, and this time his fingers wrapped around hers.

She held on tight, refused to let go, though the updraft tried its best to sever their connection.

The moment he had Ayla in his grasp, Bravo felt Antiphon's talons penetrate his shirt, dig into the flesh of his back. The pain was excruciating, but both he and the great eagle knew there was no other way to safety.

And even this was no sure thing, for now the burning wind shrieked and clawed at them like a soul in torment. Antiphon continued to struggle, especially now with the added weight of Bravo and Ayla. But she was no ordinary avian, and was used to riding heat thermals even in the midst of violent storms.

When Bravo felt the arresting of their freefall, his heart leapt with elation despite the agony racking him. Gradually, ever so gradually, the pace of their violent descent slowed until, finally, it ceased. For what seemed a long time, they remained in stasis, neither falling nor rising. But what a victory that was! Below him, Ayla took advantage of the respite to grab his wrist with her free hand, her fingers curled securely. The ghost of a smile lit her face.

And then Antiphon, her wings spread to their fullest, began to haul them upward. Now the updraft was a boon, aiding them, pushing them from below, so that once her herculean effort had overcome their inertia their momentum built naturally, and they began to rise, gaining speed until the ascent became positively dizzying.

But then, all at once, the updraft disappeared. They fell. Hard. Bravo almost lost his grip on Ayla. One of her hands swung away. She gripped him only by one wrist, and this was the wounded hand, whose insistent throbbing had been pushed to the background by the eagle's talons digging deeply into his back.

Antiphon recovered, regained control, but Bravo was fast approaching unconsciousness. The pain had become all but unbearable. Blood streaked out of his ripped skin, and his muscles, pulled taut, were stretched past all reasonable limits. Black spots danced before his eyes, everything was going out of focus. He no longer knew whether they were rising or falling. His lids fluttered as his eyes began to roll up.

Ayla, seeing this, began to swing her body back and forth like a pendulum. The strain on her arm and shoulder where she gripped Bravo's wrist made her cry out. But just as she felt as if her shoulder would dislocate, she built up enough momentum. Back and then up her hips and legs went. She scissored open her legs, clamped them tight around Bravo's waist.

Letting go of his wrist, she climbed onto him, reached up with both her hands and grabbed on to Antiphon's sturdy legs. The rough skin bit into her palms as she tightened her grip, but now she had taken some of the weight off and, closer to the eagle, the agonizing stretch in Bravo's back eased somewhat. Moments later, as Antiphon pulled her talons free, it was gone completely. Now it was up to Ayla to keep herself and Bravo connected to the great eagle as she flew upward.

Mesmerized by the rhythmic flapping of her wings, Ayla soon forgot her own pain, the taxing of every muscle in her body, tensed to the utmost.

And then Antiphon was lowering them onto—what exactly? Ayla looked around. The eagle had found a broad ledge. How far they had come, how much farther they had to go to get out of this hellhole she had no idea, since, looking up, she saw no helpful landmark.

But at last she could let go, roll onto her side, let go of Bravo. She could not tell which ached more deeply, her legs or her arms. Not that it mattered; the pain was all-consuming. At least, they had ascended far enough so that she could breathe fairly normally without feeling as if with each breath she was inhaling poison. Bravo lay beside her, all but insensate. His breathing was shallow and rapid. Weary as she was, she rose, turned him face up.

"Bravo," she said. And then more loudly, "Bravo."

She slapped one cheek, then the other. His head rolled from side to side. She lifted her gaze to where the eagle perched, looking on, expressionless.

"Antiphon," she said hoarsely. "I don't know what to do. I think he's dying."

The eagle's golden eye fixed her in its gaze. Her beak opened and closed but no sound emerged.

Tearing herself away from that terrible gaze, Ayla pinched Bravo's nose with one hand, opened his mouth with the other, took a deep breath and, placing her lips over his, gave him her breath. Over and over, she repeated this procedure, until, dizzy and disoriented, she was forced to stop. Tears of frustration and fear overran her eyes, but almost immediately she wiped them away with a grimy sleeve. *Giving in to despair will do him no good,* she told herself sternly. *You either.*

She needed help, but in their present situation she had no idea how to get any. Then her gaze once again settled on the great eagle.

She rose. "Antiphon," she said firmly and clearly, "Bravo is gravely wounded. Can you help him?"

"I can," Antiphon said, startling her so much she stumbled backward, almost toppling off the ledge.

"What? W-what did you say?"

"You heard me." Antiphon's voice was that of the wind in the willows, fluttery and ephemeral.

She swallowed hard. "All right. Then I'll put him on your back and climb on. You'll fly us out of here. There are people in the library who can get him to a hospital."

The great eagle stepped forward and Ayla moved back to get out of her way. Near Bravo, she spread her right wing, passed it over him, then, folding it, retreated.

"Bravo will never survive the flight," Antiphon said with implacable logic. "He cannot be moved."

"But . . ." She glanced back at Bravo. "We can't just leave him here."

"We must," Antiphon said. "It is his only chance."

"No." She shook her head. "You go. I'll stay here with him."

"Ayla, you yourself are in no shape to help Bravo. And, also, how shall I speak to humans who are not of the Four Phoenician families?" Antiphon said. "Please tell me."

"I . . ." Her heart flipped over in her chest and she felt a hideous pressure grip her head in a vise. "I can't. I don't know."

"Then . . ." There was no point in Antiphon completing the sentence.

She took a halting step toward the great eagle. "I know, but how can I make this decision?"

"It must be done, Ayla," Antiphon said.

"No, I—"

"Be brave. The bravest you have ever been."

Tears flooding her eyes, she returned to Bravo, knelt, and kissed him on the forehead. "I'll be back as soon as I can," she whispered. Her lips brushed both his cheeks, wet with her tears. "Above all, Bravo, hold on to life."

Then she rose and with strides as painful as they were purposeful, launched herself onto Antiphon's back. The instant she did so, the great eagle took off, spiraling up and up in an ever widening gyre.

FOR SOME time, then, nothing stirred. The broiling wind from below did not return, which was a blessing. The silence was oppressive. Bravo lay unmoving. He breathed shallowly. His racked body kept his mind from understanding what was happening. He was beyond understanding where he was; all unknowing, he had stumbled into the twilight world between wakefulness and sleep.

But something else knew where he was. Even now, it was climbing the craggy fissure it had opened up. One hand over the other, fingertips gripping the sheer rock, hauling a thick, misshapen body higher, she drew ever closer.

28

LATER, MUCH LATER, THEY CAME TO GET EMMA. WITH BLOOD streaming down her face, she never did get a look at who it was who opened the door, calling, or at the people who lifted her out of the cell. They were mere shadows, and she was not thinking clearly, having scraped her nails down her face, leaving bloody bits of her skin embedded beneath the nails' tips.

While she lay on a soft bed, floating through consciousness on a calm sea of drugs, the thought came to her, unbidden, that they must have been watching her the entire time she was in the cell. They had come so quickly, moments after the blood began to flow, that they must have had eyes on her constantly.

Whoever "they" were.

She wondered why she wasn't thirsty or hungry, and even if she were, how would she drink and eat? Rolling her head to one side, she saw the metal stand with the bags of fluids running via tubes into her, and thought, *Oh, that's why and that's how.*

Later, much later she was still alone. But there were less drugs eddying through her system, and she became aware that her wrists and ankles were strapped to the bed. She was as much a prisoner here in this white, bright room as she had been in the cell into which she had awakened. It was windowless, but it wasn't icy, and she wasn't lying on a hard, unforgiving floor, so that was something.

Later, much later a door she couldn't see opened and closed. She had the impression of someone standing by the head of the bed, just out of the range of her vision. She tried to ask who was there, and couldn't, and somewhere inside her the screaming began again. This was worse than having been blind. In the two years she had spent as a sightless person she had learned to be mobile, to navigate on her own, allowing her the independence she had had when she was sighted. But this—this abomination—was intolerable. And if she could find no way to reverse whatever sorcery had been worked on her, she would be tied to sacs of nutrients until the day she died. Which might only be a matter of months; hadn't she read somewhere that conscious humans could only subsist on liquids for a limited amount of time before wasting away?

Movement behind her, the presence of a strong aura, a shadow falling across her face and shoulders, and the panic expanded from her belly into her chest, constricting her breathing. She thrashed mutely against her bonds, twisting her head back and forth as she lost control of her body. Just as she felt her bladder about to give way, a hand clasped her shoulder.

"Calm yourself." A voice deep and low, with a hint of mountain rumble. "Emma, please."

Releasing her shoulder, the hand hovered above her face, and to her horror she saw the curved talons and her panic ratcheted up another notch. But before she could void herself the forefinger bent, the tip of the talon traced a line across the new skin. It peeled back, then vanished, leaving her lips, gums, teeth, and tongue just as they had been before she was taken prisoner.

She felt around her palate with her tongue. She opened her mouth and, with tears streaming down her cheeks, tried to speak. Only a frog-like croak sounded, but she was grateful even for that.

A hand slid behind her head, lifted it slightly so she could drink out of a glass. Water, cold, clear, sweet. She closed her eyes in ecstasy. She had to force herself not to gulp it all down. Sipping slowly, she remoistened her mouth and filled herself. When the glass was at last empty it was taken away somewhere beyond her vision. Another pillow was slipped behind her head, and the hand that had been supporting her was removed.

Lips moving as if controlled by a stranger's muscles, she struggled like a child speaking her first word: "Who?"

"Ah, well. Before I tell you *who,* I must tell you *why*—specifically why your wrists and ankles are bound. I assure you that it's for your own protection."

Anguish struck her in the solar plexus. She had forgotten about the flayed flesh of her face, what she had been forced to do to herself.

"I have healed your wounds, Emma, but I don't want you to reinjure yourself."

She willed her body to relax. Her eyes closed. "I'm calmer now," she said, forming each word carefully. Her tongue felt swollen to twice its size though she doubted that was true. "I have my mouth. I can speak."

When no response was forthcoming, she said, "Why was I a prisoner?"

"A prisoner?"

"That cell."

"Ah, that. To be honest that never should have happened. You were treated quite poorly, and I apologize most profusely."

"Why did you . . . ?" She had to stop, to swallow. Her mouth was still in recovery from its abrupt winter's sleep. "Why did you . . . mmm . . . do what you did to my mouth?" Even saying it sent chills through her, and the dread started up again in her belly.

"I asked you to calm yourself," the voice said. "No harm will come to you so long as I am looking after you."

"Why . . . why do I need looking after?"

"Ah, well, that is another matter entirely."

She tried to make sense of her situation, of what this creature was saying, but with no success. "If I'm not a prisoner, as you c-c . . ." Her mouth had trouble forming the "cl" combination. "If I'm not, as you claim, a prisoner, then unbuckle my restraints."

"Will you promise not to harm yourself?"

"You have my word." There was absolutely no chance of that happening again.

The hands, returning to her field of vision, unbuckled the straps restraining her wrists. With a cry of relief, she lifted her arms, rubbed her wrists. Her hands were cold, her fingers tingling pins-and-needles.

"Better," she said, rising up on her elbows. "Now my ankles."

"Not quite yet."

Because, Emma surmised, that necessitated the owner of the voice moving into her line of sight. She desperately wanted to turn her head in order to catch a glimpse, but sensed that she was on thin ice when it came to their relationship, such as it was. So, with an effort of will, she occupied herself with disengaging the tubes from the back of her left hand, sliding out the needle, pressing the tape back over the tiny hole before it could start to bleed. These little bits of housekeeping exhausted her, and she lay back down on her pillows.

Staring up at the ceiling, which was as white as everything else in the room, she said, "What did I do to my face?"

"You caused yourself harm." The comment was as neutral as the tone of voice.

"What did I look like?"

"Do you feel any pain in your face?"

"I don't," she said.

"That is good news. The healing is complete."

"My ankles are still in restraints."

"Yes."

If that didn't do the trick, then perhaps a more direct approach was required. "I want to see you," she said.

"Of course you do."

With that, the shadow was in motion. It entered Emma's field of view. The shadow was female, and a beautiful one she was. At first glance, she seemed human, but as she undid Emma's ankle restraints, there was something about the manner in which she bent that was anything but human. And when she turned to Emma, the sight of her face elicited a gasp. Her brow was wide and high, with a sharp widow's peak of glossy red hair. An aggressive nose and pronounced jaw, arresting in themselves, were still overshadowed by large green eyes with a reptile's vertical pupils.

"Try not to gape, Emma," this not-quite-human said with a degree of amusement. "Though your reaction is hardly unique."

Sitting up again on her elbows, Emma swallowed her astonishment. "You know my name. I'd like to know yours."

"Would you now." The redhead came and perched on the side of Emma's bed. She seemed to make no indentation at all, as if she weighed nothing more than a passing cloud. She smiled, revealing very sharp teeth that bore no resemblance to Emma's or any human's.

"I'm very glad to meet you." She extended a hand. Emma took it; it was as cold as her former cell. "My name is Surah. I am one of the Regent's sisters."

29

"BUT WHAT IF SHE DOESN'T WANT TO BE FOUND?" CHYNNA said.

"Why wouldn't Haya want her mother to find her?" Molly replied.

"If I were her," Chynna said, "I wouldn't want any part of me."

The three of them—Chynna, Lilith, and Molly—sat around the dining table, trying to draw up a coherent plan for finding Haya. Lilith had made them tea—a variety she had never tasted before. Now, as they sipped at the strange-tasting brew, Chynna went on. "The truth of it is I was never cut out to be a mother. My son, Gideon, was a horror. I understand that now, but it took me a hundred years to figure it out." She shrugged. "Blinded by love, I imagine."

She took another sip of tea, and neither Lilith nor Molly spoke. "After that catastrophe I took a solemn vow never to be blinded by love again."

"But you stayed with Leviathan," Molly pointed out.

Chynna gave her a sharp look, but also a rueful smile with lips compressed by tension. "That wasn't love; it never was. That was lust, but also the effect of his intense glamour."

"You understand you've used the past tense," Lilith pointed out.

"I know." Rather than sad, her voice was defiant. "I'm quits with him."

"That may not be so easy to do," Lilith countered, "from his side."

"You let me worry about that," Chynna told her. "Right now, our focus has to be on Haya, and only Haya."

Molly looked around the table. "Any ideas?"

Lilith was silent. But Chynna was not. "I have one, but I hesitate—"

"No time for hesitation." Pushing her cup aside, Molly rose. "Let's get on with it."

"WE ARE going to see a wondrous creature," Ayeleye said.

"Who?" Haya asked with a child's directness.

"Why, our sister, of course!" Ayeleye replied.

He seemed in a jolly mood, though that was more than could be said of Leviathan who, displeased with Haya's attachment to the Medius, was in a fouler mood than usual. The trio had left the Hall behind, and now were descending a steep packed-earth track that led from the landward side of the Hall down to a winding river. The track was strewn with rocks and loose pebbles, which clattered, dispersing as they made their way.

"What makes her wondrous?" Haya asked.

"When you meet her you will see," Ayeleye promised. "She's beautiful, unlike us."

"I like the way you look," Haya said, again with the directness of youth.

"Why, thank you, dear." The Medius smiled. "We rarely hear such a compliment."

"If ever," Leviathan added from just behind them.

Ayeleye was still holding Haya's hand, which annoyed Leviathan no end. He himself had never touched the child, save in high dudgeon, and then the experience was one that was distinctly unpleasant. He had been brooding over this singularity ever since he had punished her. He had showed none of his discomfort to the child, of course, aware that such knowledge would only embolden her already rebellious spirit. Try as he might he could not fathom her. What had Chynna done? he wondered. In what way had she gifted her daughter? He knew better than anyone that his attraction to Chynna was toxic. If he possessed a better nature he would have cut her out of his existence, but he had not, and so he returned to her again and again, to snuffle at the center of her like a wild animal in rut.

Up ahead was the embankment and, along it, a sailboat. When Haya caught sight of it, she let go of Ayeleye's hand and, running down to it, clapped her hands and laughed in a joy so pure Ayeleye was abashed and Leviathan felt wounded.

Clambering aboard, she turned back to them and beckoned impatiently. "Come on!" she called gaily. "What's taking you so long?"

Once Ayeleye and Leviathan were aboard, the Medius untied the ropes, flinging them back onto the wooden pilings to which the sailboat had been moored. While he did this, Haya unfurled the sail, swung the boom. Leviathan did not help; he stood in the stern, arms crossed. His face seemed bloodred.

Haya came away from the boom as Ayeleye thanked her and took the wheel, steering them out into the current. The sail caught the following wind and the boat leapt ahead at speed.

"You look like you're about to explode." Haya cocked her head "What's wrong with you?"

Leviathan kept his gaze fixed on the river's course they were following with Ayeleye's customary precision. He could not understand why the child was addressing him after the way he had been treating her. He despised what made him feel stupid or inadequate.

"Nothing is wrong with me," he replied gruffly.

Haya, hands on hips, said, "I don't believe you."

Why does the child keep querying me? he asked himself. She was like a mosquito that once it smells blood cannot be gotten rid of. *Doesn't she know I took her here to punish her mother? Or doesn't she care?* Now *that* was something he could understand.

"I don't much care for Ayeleye's sister." He had realized belatedly that with this child the truth mattered. She could sniff out a fiction with terrifying accuracy.

"Huh," Haya said, "I don't think you care for Ayeleye either." When he made no reply, she added, "Why is that?"

I should kill her now, he thought. *But I won't, at least not until I find out what makes her tick.* Besides, he intuited her death would discommode Ayeleye, who had taken quite a liking to her. And at this precise moment in time he could not afford to antagonize Ayeleye, or any of the Medius for that matter. They were far too important to his plan. He needed them as allies.

So he bared his teeth in what for him constituted a smile, but for anyone who didn't know him would cause them to run away, screaming. "Ayeleye and his sisters are . . . different," he said carefully. "And sometimes—often, actually, in my experience—we form an antipathy toward that which is different." He grunted. "You know what 'antipathy' means, yes?"

"Hatred," Haya responded, unblinking.

"Not quite that far," Leviathan said, somewhat startled. "But perhaps I misspoke. I think that 'wariness' might be a better word for it."

Leviathan pried his gaze off the way ahead to at last look her in the eye. "Are you wary of me?"

"I am."

"Do you feel antipathy toward me?"

"I don't think so, no. Not anymore."

Once more a sense of being in uncharted waters suffused him. "Something's changed in you. I imprisoned you. I hurt you."

"I think you're misguided," Haya said in her direct way. "Being near you makes me sad."

From behind the wheel, Leviathan heard Ayeleye's soft peal of laughter.

"HOW DO you know my name?" Emma asked.

When Surah smiled she looked something like a crocodile, but an adorable crocodile. Until now Emma hadn't thought that possible.

"I think you'll want this back." Surah handed over the necklace Emma had fashioned to hold Beleth's talon.

Emma's hand closed around it tightly, feeling its shape and contours impress themselves into her palm. She took several deep breaths, then put on the necklace. Feeling the familiar weight on her breastbone both calmed and comforted her.

"That means a lot to you," Surah said. It wasn't a question, but a statement of fact.

"Beleth meant a lot to me," Emma blurted out, and immediately wondered why. She knew nothing about this creature, and just hours ago she was a prisoner here. For all she knew, though she was free of all restraints, she still was.

"To me, as well." Surah nodded in response to the look of astonishment on Emma's face, and produced that oddly adorable smile again. "It was through Beleth that I came to know your name. To know you, as well."

Emma shook her head. A mistake, as her headache made a swift foray out of the back of her brain where it had been lurking. She winced, her eyes squeezing shut for a moment.

"I must apologize again for the discomfort you're feeling. But it is a fact that Azazel is difficult to control, even for me. His tendency to rash behavior is well documented, and to try to tame him would, I'm afraid, only lead to catastrophe."

Emma took some time to digest those words, before she said, "Am I a prisoner?"

Surah appeared offended. "Certainly not!" She stood up, swept her hand toward the door. "You may walk out of here anytime you wish."

Throwing back the sheets, Emma swung her legs over the side of the bed. "Now?"

"As you wish," Surah said. "But I wouldn't advise it."

"So I am still a prisoner."

Surah sighed. "Take my advice. Have a shower—it's through that door over there. Fresh clothes are folded on the small table in there. Afterward you'll have something to drink and eat, if you like—tea and crumpets and clotted cream might do you. And then we'll go for a stroll. Does that sound agreeable?"

"I could do with a shower," Emma said. "I am a bit ripe."

Surah laughed, showing three rows of terrifying teeth. "Then by all means be my guest!"

TWENTY MINUTES later, Emma emerged from the steamy bathroom dressed in the loose-fitting indigo clothes that Surah had provided. They were not unlike a dojo *gi*. Her hair was still damp, slicked back from her forehead.

"You look like a different person," Surah said, clearly delighted. "Now come on over here so I can change your bandage."

She projected such a positive aura that Emma didn't hesitate, though she was wary of Surah's reptilian nails. And now that she was more herself and therefore more observant of the little things, she noted that the fingers were webbed at their base. But she needn't have been worried as Surah was especially gentle peeling off the tape Emma had used when she pulled out the needle. Like any professional nurse, Surah cleaned the puncture, applied a dab of antibiotic cream, and covered it with a bit of sticking plaster.

"Now," she said, "for a bite to eat and then, if you feel up to it, our little stroll."

She led Emma out of the surgery, down a wide stone hallway lit with lamps within niches that gave off an oddly cool light.

"Naphtha," Surah said, as if reading Emma's thoughts. "There is no—what do you humans call it?—electricity here. But we have other means of light and locomotion that make electricity, oil, and natural gas irrelevant."

They sat at a table of burnished burlwood, set with plates and glasses, a pitcher of water, and a full tea service in a porcelain pattern of lotus water lilies. Suddenly famished, Emma ate and drank until sated. It was only after she pushed her crumb-littered and cream-smeared plate away that she realized Surah had no plate or cup of her own.

"Aren't you eating?" she asked.

"I have no need of food or of drink," Surah replied.

When Emma looked at her oddly, she laughed. "Never mind." And pushing her chair back, she stood. "Come. Now that you're refreshed we will have the stroll I promised you."

Because she could think of no good reason to refuse and because for the moment her stomach was full she rose and followed Surah. Also, and this was probably the most compelling reason, she was curious. Where was she? And who was this creature, Surah? What relationship did she have with Beleth, the Second Sphere Power who had Transpositioned himself into Emma last year?

They exited the structure which, upon turning around, bore no resemblance to anything Emma had seen before, but perhaps most closely fit the description of a palace. She had imagined herself inside something along the lines of a medieval castle, or possibly a prison out of the French Revolution. But Surah's home looked like nothing so much as a layer cake. It was circular. Tier upon tier, each one smaller than the one below, rose up into the night-dark sky. And that sky! It was starless and moonless, unlike any night sky Emma had ever encountered, even in the Hollow Lands.

"Where are we?" she said as they set off down the winding dirt road that led up to Surah's abode from a deep valley below.

"First, I should introduce myself formally. I am one of the Four Medius." And she explained briefly the circumstance of a Medius.

"So you and the others are a version of the four fates of myth."

Surah nodded. "In a manner of speaking, yes. But in many ways we are more, and in others, less. For instance, we are not Farsighters; we cannot see the future."

The way now steepened, and as they moved farther and farther from Surah's naphtha-lighted home Emma found herself wondering how it was they could still see the road ahead of them. Then she turned her head and discovered that the land on either side of the winding road was pitch-black, featureless, impenetrable.

"But to answer your question," Surah said, "we are somewhere between Heaven and hell."

"I thought that was where I come from."

"Possibly. But we are in another Sphere. There is no life here, only existence."

"Then how am I—?"

"Beleth's talon protects you here, where you have no business being."

"But you brought me here."

"That I did," Surah acknowledged. "But only because you had waded out into perilous waters and were about to get in over your head."

"What d'you mean?"

The road ahead afforded a view down into the valley, where naphtha lights flickered, hinting at a small village.

"Penetrating the cavern behind the cataract in Tannourine on your own was foolish, Emma. There are too many unknowns for you to be able to navigate them successfully."

"I thought I was doing very well," Emma replied. "I thought I had made friends with Omega."

"Who?"

"The guard chained in front of the door."

Surah's face darkened. "Emma, there was no guard."

"Yes, there was," Emma insisted. "He told me—"

"No chains, sad tales of woe, none of that."

"Then . . ."

"Yes. It was all in your head."

"But Omega unlocked the door. I saw him do it."

"No, you did not."

"Then how did I get through the door?"

"There was no door," Surah said grimly. "You were *allowed* to pass through the membrane."

Still baffled, Emma said, "But he led me into the chamber where King Solomon's gold—I was right there, about to uncover it, see it, touch it until the Cherub appeared."

"Mm, that's just what I mean." Surah took Emma's elbow. "I saved you, I stopped Azazel from making sure you *did* touch it—for it would have annihilated you."

"Annihilated me? You mean the gold . . ." But there seemed no point in continuing along this line if it was all a fantasy, one fabricated especially for her. But by who? Leviathan hated her. He was the most likely candidate. She took a breath, let it out. "I wasn't going to find the gold there, was I?"

"Indeed, not." Surah let go of Emma's elbow, indicated the way forward with her head, and they continued on toward the village below. "I know you have many questions, Emma, and please believe me when I tell you that they will be answered, but in their own time and place, all right?"

"Do I have a choice?"

"With me, you always have a choice," Surah said. "I thought I made myself clear."

She had, Emma thought. Distinctly. But her mind was boiling over, the questions coming so fast and furiously they tumbled over each other.

"I understand what a bewildering experience this must be," Surah said. "Perhaps it would be best to begin at the beginning—or as close to it as I can get. Beleth and I had what you might call an intimate relationship."

"You had *sex* with Beleth?"

Surah laughed. "Ah, no. My grasp of human languages is possibly not all it should be. No, Beleth and I were . . . allies. You must understand why I say this is intimate. As a Medius, we are not allowed to interfere with the doings of either angels or humans. However, recent events—and by recent, I mean the last thousand years—have forced our hand. The rising tide lifts all vessels—isn't that what you say?"

"Something like that."

Surah nodded. "In this case, we must discuss the impending assault on Heaven that the Sum of All Shadows is preparing to mount. It is in its final stages. This extreme bellicose action has tipped a balance we Medius were meant to keep. You must understand that balance is everything to us. When it is disturbed we must act to return it to equilibrium."

The road was flattening out as they approached the village. By the naphtha lights Emma could make out the shapes of houses, streets, shops, ateliers. But so far no people.

"My decision to recruit Beleth was done in this light," Surah continued. "I chose carefully, and it took me quite some time to find the right member of the Fallen. I required someone from the lower ranks, someone who would never be under the close scrutiny of either Seraphim or Cherubim. Someone who was smarter and cleverer than his station."

"That was Beleth, all right," Emma affirmed.

Surah glanced at her. "He loved you, you know. In his own way, he loved you."

"And I him." Emma clutched the talon at her breastbone. "I miss him." It was a relief to admit this to someone who understood in a way her brother never could.

"Ah, yes, we both do."

For some time, Surah seemed lost in contemplation. And all the while they drew closer to the village—close enough that Emma began to sense something strange and ominous about it. The night was eerily still. No bird sounds, no insects whirring past her ear or biting the back of her neck. Whatever Sphere they were in, Emma thought, this was a profoundly sad place, one in which she most definitely did not belong. With mounting certainty she knew that if she stayed too long Surah's world eventually would suck all the life out of her, despite the protection Beleth's talon afforded her.

"Surah," she said. "I'm suffocating here. I can't stay. I can't."

"Be brave now, darling. The bravest you have ever been." Surah took Emma in her arms. "I would never have brought you here if it wasn't absolutely necessary."

Emma scarcely heard her, she was weeping so profusely. Over the past several minutes her heart seemed to have shattered. She felt bereft. She had never been so alone, not even when she had been blind. There was always family around her, friends—people who loved her. And now, what? She was God alone knew where, with no direction home, and in imminent danger of drowning in this Sphere of nothingness.

"This is absolutely necessary." She heard this whispered in her ear, but whether it was from Surah or from some other even more mysterious source she could not tell. This level of unknowing frightened her all the more. She knew what she had to do.

Tearing herself away from Surah, she staggered back, held out her hands, palms up, and said through gritted teeth, *"Et ignis ibi est!"*

"Don't!" Surah cried. "Emma, don't bring the light!"

But she ignored the Medius. This she must do for herself. She stared at her palms. No blue fire. Nothing. *Why won't it work?* she wondered.

And again: *This is absolutely necessary.* But this time in the center of her mind. She stared at Surah, stunned, and then through her. And it came to her.

"Djat had'ar!" she cried. *He is present.*

"I never should have given you back your mouth." Surah took a step toward her, her arm outstretched, and in a louder, more plaintive voice: "Emma, I beg of you. Stop!"

And then as with a detonation like a cannon shot, the sky cracked open. Emma intoned again, *"Et ignis ibi est!"*

And the blue fire leapt into her hands. She held them high over her head, illuminating the village, revealing it as nothing more than uninhabited hollow shells that vanished in smoke with the coming of her light.

But then out of the vapor, a form was made manifest.

"Oh, no!" Surah cried. "No, no, no!"

The form took shape as it strode through the swirls of smoke.

"I told you," Surah said, her voice now subdued with sorrow. "I warned you."

Emma saw the figure emerge, the last of the vapor trailing off him as if, like an evil djinn, he was made of smoke and fire. The sight of him made her tremble. Her heart sank.

30

"WHAT IS THAT?" LILITH SAID. "A MIRROR?"

"Not a mirror," Chynna told her. "At least not exactly."

"What then?" Molly was one pace ahead of them in the room that Haya had found on the morning that Chynna had followed her. She turned. "And, anyway, why are you standing in the doorway? Why aren't you coming in?"

"I will try to answer your questions to the extent of my knowledge," Chynna said. "But at this remove and not a step closer."

"And what about us?" Lilith asked. "Is it safe for us to be so close to whatever this is?"

"Perfectly," Chynna replied without missing a beat.

"Meaning there's something about you, or something about this mirror-thing that you don't want to confront."

Chynna ran a hand over her face. "Listen to me, I've been in hiding ever since I stole the golden apple from Arvad. I fled to the mainland, changed my name from Sikar to Shaw, buried myself in a nunnery on the outskirts of Jerusalem, and had my baby there. Gideon. The monster, so like his father, Leviathan." She shuddered. "It was this golden apple I stole that was the cause of every dreadful event that happened afterward.

"It was Conrad, my grandson, who chose to go after the apple, to find it, and return it to its rightful place. From there everything unraveled, leading to the breach in the realms being opened."

Molly's eyes narrowed. "You want us to believe that your coupling with a First Sphere Seraph had nothing to do with it?"

"It was Leviathan who tricked Conrad into opening the breach," Lilith added.

Chynna stood silent and sad, still on the threshold. She had gone too far with these two women to begin lying to them now; they knew too much.

Lilith shook her head, then pointed. "So back to this mirror-thing."

Several moments passed before Chynna was able to rouse herself from her vast array of sins. "As I said, it only looks like a mirror. Deliberately. So that if anyone should stumble on it by accident they would pass it by without a second thought."

"So what is it, really?" Molly said.

Chynna hesitated long enough for the other women to put her under their scrutiny. "It's a prison," she said so softly they could scarcely make out her words. "A very special kind of prison."

"Sorcerous," Lilith said. It wasn't a question.

Chynna nodded.

Lilith had turned to look fully at Chynna, to press her if necessary for a full disclosure. "Whose sorcery?"

Chynna passed her hand over her face again, as if she could wish herself away—anywhere but here. "The ultimate sorcerer." And Lilith had to strain to hear her. "You must promise me that if . . . all is lost . . . if the center falls apart . . ." She held her breath, let it out slowly, reluctantly. "Lilith, you must promise me you will sever my head from my body. It's the only way to ensure my death." Chynna's eyes seemed to radiate her anxiety so palpably Lilith could feel it on her skin, like an army of ants. "Will you do this for me, Lilith?"

"It will never come to that," Lilith said with a conviction strange to her. "The center will hold, we'll see to that."

Molly wasn't listening; she was no longer interested in what Chynna had to say. The mirror-prison had captured her full attention; the dark medallion in her pocket had begun to vibrate so strongly that it became almost painful. She took several steps toward the prison. She was less than an arm's length from it.

Chynna's intensity forced her to lean slightly toward Lilith. "But if it doesn't . . ."

Lilith nodded. "Then, yes. You have my word."

Chynna visibly relaxed.

"The prison." Lilith fixed Chynna in her hawk-like gaze. "Empty or not?"

"It's not empty." Chynna's whisper sent a chill down Lilith's spine.

Meanwhile, Molly reached out with her forefinger, touched the bronze surface. It gave like soft taffy. And then the tip of her finger vanished.

Lilith was determined to drag all the answers out of Chynna. "So who is—?"

"My grandson," Chynna whispered.

And it was at that precise moment that Molly stepped out of the room and into the Elsewhere imprisoning Conrad Shaw, vanishing from their sight.

THE HAZE across the river had thickened, rolling, as if a ghostly ocean had risen from the depths of the river to assert its hold on the gray and forbidding afternoon.

The rain started before they reached the elaborately constructed dock, the wood carved and lacquered, the metal incised with incomprehensible runes. Ayeleye guided the boat expertly toward the slip while Haya furled the sail. Leviathan had moved to the bow, stood with arms still folded across his chest, head up, looking as if he, not Ayeleye, were the captain of this modest vessel.

He was the first off, too, his back to the other two as they made the boat fast. On the dock Ayeleye gave Haya a hand up.

"I think it would be better if I led the way," Ayeleye said.

Leviathan merely grunted, but allowed the Medius to step past him. Haya, her hand in Ayeleye's, paid him no mind, which did not sit well with him. He had tried every way he knew to break her, to find out who she was and where she came from—Chynna's womb, of course, but before that. His questions about her origin had mounted with every moment he spent with her. The mystery was an itch he could not scratch, and it was driving him to distraction. He had never failed at anything, ever—apart from coercing Bravo Shaw to abandon humankind to partake of the pleasure of immortality. He could not fathom why this had proven so difficult, given that Bravo felt such kinship with beings who were nasty, jealous, grasping, and petty, with thin skins and a lovely penchant for sadism. It was true that the Shaws were almost as mysterious to him as Haya, and therefore, by definition, dangerous. Which is why he had really come to see Ayeleye, as the Medius had correctly interpreted: to move the needle, and to ensure Leviathan surviving the war that any day now would break out. Unlike the Sum of All Shadows and his legions, Leviathan saw the possibility of utter annihilation for everyone and everything, including his Lord and Master. In the process he feared that all the Spheres would be laid to waste at once, that nothing would be left. Nothing at all.

It was with these dark, disturbing thoughts that he followed Ayeleye and the girl who had somehow become his charge, off the dock and up a winding path shouldered with wisteria and other climbing vines that seemed to reach out and cling to them as they steadily ascended.

Soon enough the way grew steeper, necessitating a set of stone stairs. Their deep risers made it apparent they had been built for beings of a larger size than any of them. This fact only increased Leviathan's uneasiness. Of the Four Medius, Ayeleye was the only one he had encountered. Truth be told, he wasn't eager to meet any of the others, for they were bound by laws and conventions altogether different than those of either angel or human.

As they rose, the mist parted in sections, like veils being drawn back one by one. When they reached the stairs' top step and were standing on a high ridge below which the river twisted and twined as complexly as the wisteria, the home where Oq Ajdar dwelled was revealed.

To say Leviathan didn't care for it would be a vast understatement. In fact, it gave him a repugnant feeling, as if a worm, having hatched, was now crawling around inside him. The structure looked like nothing so much as a female's sexual organ. It held the faintest of pinkish hues, with a shiny, almost slippery surface that seemed to move as he stared at it, as if it were alive. But that might simply have heralded the Medius. Oq Ajdar appeared through the curved opening that served as the front door.

She changed shape and form as she approached them, as befitted a chimera, becoming first a reptile, then an avian, then a human female, then, as if mocking Leviathan, a kraken. But when that seemed to alarm the child, she quickly reverted to human form. For this, she chose the figure of Artemis, mistress of the hunt. Flowing white robes over her body, golden sandals on her feet, a silver ring in her nose. An emerald band held her thick red-gold locks off her face. Her eyes were cornflower-blue, her cheeks pink as tea roses. A wooden longbow was slung diagonally across her back, along with a quiver of long-tipped arrows. She smiled as she neared them, but that smile was solely for the child who, having forgotten the forbidding aspect of the kraken, returned the chimera's smile.

Oq Ajdar clapped her hands. "My dear brother! Under what circumstances do you find yourself in the company of such a delightful child?" She ignored Leviathan's presence entirely.

Dropping Ayeleye's hand and stepping forward, Haya said, "Hello! My name is Haya." She extended a hand.

The chimera laughed and, sinking fluidly onto her hams, took the child's hand in hers. "My name is Oq Ajdar."

"If you're Ayeleye's sister than you must be a Medius, too," Haya said with her accustomed directness. She cocked her head. "But you're also a chimera."

"Indeed, I am!" she exclaimed. "What a clever child you are."

"You have no idea," Leviathan muttered darkly. He was about to say more when Ayeleye shot him a venomous look.

Neither Oq Ajdar nor Haya took the slightest notice of the byplay. They were already in their own world.

"You have come a long way to see me, I think," the chimera said.

"Yes," Haya replied in all seriousness. "A *very* long way."

"May I ask why you have made this tiring journey?"

Haya pursed her lips. "I left my mother behind," she said. As always, there formed a seesaw battle between the child and the adult inside her, but this time the adult seemed stronger, most assured. "I don't know where she is."

"Hmm." Oq Ajdar rubbed her chin with a tentacle that appeared from behind her back. This had the hoped-for response: Haya giggled. "Well, now, why exactly did you leave her behind?"

Haya gave no vocal answer. Instead, her eyes slid toward the side where Leviathan stood with growing impatience, kept in check both by Ayeleye and his trepidation in approaching the chimera.

Only in her eyes did Oq Ajdar reveal that she understood Haya's signal, but when she spoke it was not only to Haya. "Perhaps that wasn't the wisest thing to do. You're terribly young to be without your mother."

"I know," Haya piped. "Right?"

The chimera plucked the bow and quiver of arrows off her back. "It seems to me that for a child of your age life is often like a rowboat on an angry sea, tossed this way and that, its oars rendered useless. You understand?" She peered at Haya. "You are surrounded by forces bigger and stronger than you. Does that sound familiar?"

Haya nodded wordlessly, all at once acutely aware of the gathering darkness off her starboard flank.

"Well then," Oq Ajdar said, "what do you say we do something to level the playing field?" She held out the bow for Haya to take. "Go on," she urged, and Haya took it.

"Now," she continued, "is there anyone here besides you who knows where your mother is?"

"Yes," Haya replied, fingers running over the bow's smooth finish.

When she did not continue, the chimera took an arrow from her quiver and handed it to her. But before she could nock the arrow to the bowstring, Leviathan stepped in and snatched them out of her hands.

"No weapons for the kiddies," the Seraph said sternly.

Behind him, Ayeleye rolled his eyes, shaking his head. Leviathan, despite the Medius's warning, had stepped into it. Ayeleye was not going to intervene for him; he knew his sister far too well.

Oq Ajdar rose up off the squat where she had been engaging Haya in congenial conversation, and as she did so, her form changed into a mirror image of Leviathan in every way. Haya rose with her, turning to face the Seraph.

"This is my house," Oq Ajdar said in an exact duplicate of Leviathan's voice. "You are in Medius territory, and you are not to interfere."

"Interfere?" the real Leviathan spat scornfully. "Why is it a Medius wastes her time talking to a child?"

Oq Ajdar was about to cut a caustic reply, when she felt Haya's left hand touch the back of her hand discreetly, stilling her.

Haya's eyes blazed brightly as twin suns, her adult side shouldering itself to the fore, protecting the fearful child. "You would do well to heed Oq Ajdar's advice," she said.

Leviathan laughed. It sounded like a pack of hyenas braying.

"This is meant," Haya said. "Truly, deeply. Unequivocally."

Leviathan's frown deepened until it seemed, like a cyclops, he had one eyebrow.

Leviathan shook his head, swept his free hand across the space between them. "Enough of this child's play," he bellowed, and cracked the bow in half across his raised knee. A pace behind him and to his right Ayeleye squeezed his eyes tight shut, anticipating the cataclysm. Leviathan took one step, but that was all he needed.

Grabbing Haya by her shirtfront, he pulled her to him, took a handful of hair, jerked her head back.

Oq Ajdar raised her hand in warning and her brother's eyes popped open. "You don't want to do that, Seraph," Ayeleye said.

"I've had enough of her." Leviathan's voice was like thunder rolling off the jagged sides of mountains—if there had been any mountains. "And I've had enough of the two of you. I came her seeking an alliance against the Sum of All Shadows. But what do I get instead? Both of you are fixated on this child, for reasons I can't understand."

"And don't want to," Oq Ajdar said. "That is clear enough." She morphed into Athena, the powerful goddess of wisdom, daughter of Zeus. "Aren't you afraid?"

"Afraid?" Leviathan looked puzzled. "Of what? This child?"

"Of what she is," Oq Ajdar said. "Of what she will become."

"Not in the least," he snapped. "And why should I be?"

"Because—"

But she was cut short as Leviathan drove her own arrow into Haya's chest, piercing her heart.

Eyes rolling up, Haya collapsed in his arms.

31

WHEN BRAVO RETURNED TO FULL CONSCIOUSNESS, HE found himself staring directly across the ledge, his attention drawn there by movement. At first he thought the ledge itself was crumbling, then as the movement became more localized, he realized that he was seeing something altogether different.

The figure rose up to crouch at the lip. He could not understand what had happened: Why had he been abandoned by Ayla and Antiphon? He knew there must be a good reason, but whatever it was he was here now alone with this unknown being that had climbed its way out of the fiery depth that had opened up beneath them.

And then the thing began to edge toward him, but on a diagonal vector, as a crab would. In fact, it was hunched over like some inhuman creature, larger than the largest crab but somewhat smaller than Bravo. He tried to move, but found himself virtually paralyzed. All he could do was lie there, helpless and in pain, while the creature approached him. A female, he could now make out, her body grotesquely malformed, as if put together by some deranged creator. In shocking contrast, its face was that of a very young Madonna—oval, porcelain-skinned, breathtakingly beautiful.

The closer she came the more beautiful she seemed, and the stranger. When she was only a step or two from him, she stood, and he could see that she was indeed human. Reaching out toward him, she meant to poke him with her forefinger, but at the last instant she snatched it away. Sucking on her finger as if it had been burned. What had she encountered? Bravo asked himself vaguely.

He watched as she sat cross-legged in front of him. “Can you speak?” she said in Hebrew. “No? I didn’t think so.” Bravo knew the language intimately, as he did every ancient language, learned during his years of study with the Gnostic Observatines. "You must be severely wounded," she went on. "You wouldn't be so well-protected otherwise." She shrugged shoulders sharp as knives. "No matter. I know who you are, darling. Bravo Shaw. I'm not wrong, am I?"

She put her finger by the side of her nose. "I know this because it was you who answered the call. What call, you wish to ask. I know. I can see the question in your eyes, darling. No words necessary." She giggled a bit before continuing. "The bleeding at *The Last Supper*. You remember that, yes? But how could you forget it? The blood. Where did it come from, you might ask. You *are* asking, aren't you, darling?"

Her head tilted to one side and her cupid's bow lips pushed out in a moue, as if she were preparing to plant a big wet one on his lips. "I imagine you must be thinking, oh yes, the blood. Oq Ajdar made it appear somehow." Her head wagged from side to side. "But where would a Medius obtain human blood? No, no, darling. But no need to guess again." She turned her head so that he had a full view of the side of her neck, where two points the color of oxblood stained her skin directly over her carotid artery.

She licked her lips. "That's right, darling. That was my blood seeping from *The Last Supper* painting." The tip of her tongue flickered between her half-open lips. "And why would I do that, give of myself? Well, the answer is both simple and complex." Her eyes twinkled. "Quite a conundrum, yes, darling? But only for now, I promise."

She switched the positions of her legs, moving a hair closer to him at the same time. "So, first things first. My name is Mary." Laughing now. "No, not Magdalene, though I knew her, if only briefly. No, I am the Mary that served the principals at the Last Supper—the real Last Supper, darling, yes, indeed. All the plates, platters, goblets, pitchers of wine and water passed through these hands."

Her brows knit together. "But, of course, you do not believe me. Why would you, darling? I wouldn't if I were in your place. Yes, well, good thing I anticipated that." And now she recited from the Bible's chapter on Mark:

"'On the first day of Unleavened Bread, when the Passover lamb is sacrificed, his disciples said to him, "Where do you want us to go and make the preparations for you to eat the Passover?" So he sent two of his disciples, saying to them, "Go into the city, and a man carrying a jar of water will meet you; follow him, and wherever he enters, say to the owner of the house, 'The Teacher asks, Where is my guest room where I may eat the Passover with my disciples?' He will show you a large room upstairs, furnished and ready. Make preparations for us there." So the disciples set out and went to the city, and found everything as he had told them; and they prepared the Passover meal.'"

She looked at Bravo with a strange intensity. "You know this passage, darling? Yes, I see by your eyes that you do. So. Let us continue with the narrative not as it is written but as I observed it:

"'Attend well to me: one of you will tonight betray me.' This was what Jesus said to his disciples. As you can imagine this pronouncement did not sit well with them. By this time, they were used to his pronouncements, but this one hit them where they lived. They were only human, after all, and, let's face it, they were mainly at this particular Passover in order to curry favor. It's only natural, right?

"Jesus knew this, of course, and he had set about dropping a fox into the henhouse, as it were." She shrugged. "In any event, one of his disciples—the one whom Jesus loved best, the owner of this house, the one the others knew not at all—reclined next to him and watched slit-eyed as Peter piped up on cue: 'Lord, who is it?' Jesus tore off a piece of the unleavened bread and told him that it might be the one to whom he gave the bread when he had dipped. 'Or perhaps not,' he added, to keep them all on edge. Well, all except the disciple he loved the best, the only one who had not raised his voice to ask, 'Lord, who is it?' Why? Because he already knew who it was who would betray Jesus that night. In fact, he had been planning this moment from the time the two of them were very small children." Her head bobbed up and down. "That's right, darling. Even then.

"Jesus dipped the piece of bread, and handed it to Judas, the son of Simon Iscariot. Then Jesus said, 'Do quickly what you are going to do.' But he did not direct those words to Judas Iscariot, but to the disciple he loved best, who, obedient to this command because it chimed with his plan, rose and left the table, the room, his house, even the street in which his house was situated."

Mary licked her lips to wet them after her long discourse. Her eyes never left Bravo's. "Now, being a smart fellow and, even better, a clever one, you must know of whom I am speaking."

She smiled. "I see by the look in your eyes that you do. Good." Her sharp shoulders lifted and fell again. "Attend well to me. I was there. I saw everything. I heard everything." She reached a hand out, letting it hover just above whatever it was that had burned her before. "So, darling, now that I have told you a secret—a very valuable secret, there is no denying—we are bonded together, you and I. But that is as it should be."

She placed her other hand next to the first, as if she were by a hearth, warming herself. "Do you know what comes next, darling? Ah, your eyes are so sweet. Expressive, too. I'm quite sure you know, darling."

She kissed the air in front of his mouth. "You are coming with me, darling."

SOMETIME AFTERWARD—it was impossible to calculate how long, precisely—the air began to stir, then swirl. Loose rock and pebbles were swept up into conical dust devils. Not long afterward, the soft sounds of Antiphon's beating wings filled the air above the ledge.

The great eagle alit on the ledge with Ayla on her back, and clutched in Ayla's hand a leather case bulging with medicines, bandages, syringes, powerful antibiotics, and a range of sedatives, all to care for Bravo, to heal him sufficiently so that he could make the return journey to the surface without endangering his life.

But Bravo was nowhere to be seen.

"No!" Ayla was in a panic. "This can't be! We left him right here. In his condition where could he have gone?"

"This is the real problem," Antiphon said.

She put her head in her hands. "I never should have left him."

"Recriminations are unwarranted. You had no other choice."

"That's of no help." Ayla voice was anguished. Her hands curled into fists. "What I need to know is where he has gone."

"He was too gravely wounded to climb either up or down," Antiphon observed with an inhuman sangfroid.

"Oh my God!" Ayla ran to the edge, knelt down. "What if he rolled off?"

"Impossible," the eagle replied.

"Impossible?" She turned to stare at Antiphon, in this moment hating her because who else could she hate for what happened? "How can you know?"

"Before we left I spread a protective cocoon around him. He couldn't move even if he regained consciousness."

Ayla remembered her wing passing over Bravo before they left. She rose. "I don't know whether to kiss you or kill you."

"Neither would be an appropriate response," Antiphon said. "Neither would it bring us closer to discovering where Bravo has been taken."

Ayla frowned. "Taken?"

"Exactly." The eagle stepped toward her. "If it was impossible for him to emerge from the cocoon, if it was impossible for him to move, and he is not here, by process of elimination someone or something must have taken him."

Ayla thought her head would split open. All these desperate hours she had lived with the prospect of a reunion, reviving Bravo, healing him, saving him. These were the only things that allowed her to keep self-recrimination at bay. And now *this*. A reality that had never been on her radar.

She staggered, and the eagle spread one of her wings to keep her from falling.

"This is no time for weakness, Ayla," Antiphon told her. "We need to find Bravo, and quickly before whatever abducted him finds a way through his protective cocoon. Right now, his energies are at their lowest ebb. He will not be able to fight. He is utterly helpless."

32

THE DEMON OF FATE, THE LORD OF LIMBO, KNOWN MORE IN-formally as the Regent, stepped out of the last swirl of smoke. He was a male human of dapper mien—at least he was at the moment—dressed in striped trousers, a velvet smoking jacket of a deep and delicious claret color. His feet were clad in formal patent-leather slip-ons, and he wore something like a cravat around his neck. He had eyes as black as his slippers and very pale skin. As a consequence, his eyes seemed to glow. His hands were slender, with unnaturally long fingers. He was of regal bearing, his face composed of noble features: wide-apart eyes, an aquiline nose, lips neither thin nor thick. In all, he cut quite a dashing figure, which, Emma decided, was the idea. And yet something about his face disconcerted her. It was as if he had chosen each feature from an assembly line, placing them on a tabula rasa one by one until this whole was achieved.

"So sister, what have you brought me?" His voice was thin, almost strangled, as if speech was not native to him.

"My name is Emma," Emma said before Surah could utter a word.

He lifted his arms wide. "And what brings you to our fair land? Not as a tourist, surely. We get so few tourists here." His voice held a sardonic edge as he shot Surah a glance. "And when we do they never leave."

"I'll bet," Emma said.

"They wished they had never come." He suddenly looked very dangerous. He rushed her, a blur accomplished so quickly that before Emma could draw another breath he had stretched her to her tiptoes with his hand clamped around her throat. The fingers were so long they ran right around to the nape of her neck to meet his thumb. "I tell them to sue their travel agent." His face was so close their noses nearly touched. His breath smelled of cedar oil and bitumen. "That makes them laugh, but believe me soon enough they're weeping like babies and calling for their mother."

"Don't hurt her," Surah said, coming to stand beside them. "We were on our way to find the path to bring her back home."

"You know that was never going to happen."

Surah tossed her head. "I know nothing of the sort."

The Regent snorted. "You always say that about these human trespassers when you know full well how abominable they are." His lips pulled back from lupine teeth. "Especially this one." His fingers dug into Emma's throat, causing her to cough and choke. He had lost all semblance of civility and politesse. "You brought the cold fire. Didn't you, dear?"

"My . . . name," she managed to get out, "is Emma—"

"You told me that already." The Regent's glowing eyes transfixed her as if they were dagger blades.

"Emma Shaw."

The Regent slammed his forehead into hers, bringing stars to her eyes and then tears. He loomed over her, casting a shadow as thick as asphalt. "You fucking Shaws." He began to shake her as if she were a tree full of ripe apples. "You're the reason for this war—you know that, don't you?" He shook her harder. "Don't you!"

Emma stared at him, unable or unwilling to utter a word.

"It was Conrad Shaw, gulled by Leviathan, who caused the breach between realms. It was his grandmother, Chynna, who had the misfortune to mate with that insatiable satyr. Again Leviathan! Out popped Gideon, Conrad's father. A Nephilim. Filled with Leviathan's evil ichor."

He raised his arm until Emma's feet dangled off the ground, until, with the noose of his hand around her neck, she was in the process of being hung.

"Now all of you Shaws are tainted with that same foul ichor. You are abominations. You sicken me to the point of violence."

"Brother, please!" Surah clawed at his arm, trying to bring it back down, and Emma with it.

The Regent shook her off. "What is it with you and humans, Surah? What exactly is the attraction?"

"They are complicated creatures, brother. More complicated than we are."

"Which is why they are continually enmeshed in trouble."

"Their complications—"

"Enough!"

Still Surah persisted. She felt something for the human woman, it was true. "She is not responsible for the sins of her great-grandmother and her grandfather."

"Irrelevant. She is spawn of Nephilim."

"Brother, we are Medius," Surah said, trying one more time. "We are pledged to neutrality. This action violates the Compact of the Medius."

"You violate the Compact every time you interact with humans."

"I don't kill them or even harm them," Surah said, thoroughly indignant. "I would never even contemplate such a thing!"

"I am Regent!" he roared. "I bend the knee to no one. Not them!" With his free hand he pointed over his head. "And certainly not *him*!" He pointed at the ground beneath them.

"But you are still Medius, brother. We are wed to reason."

He glared at her. "Reason—"

"Put her down, brother, while we talk. I implore you." She placed a hand on his cheek, said softly, "Leviathan would surely treat her violently. But not you. Not you."

At last she had moved him, if only a fraction, but it was enough, and he lowered Emma until her feet were once more on the ground.

Surah kept her eyes on him. "And . . ."

Immediately as he loosened his grip Emma began to gag, sucking air through her bruised windpipe, into her oxygen-starved lungs. Her legs were like rubber, and Surah snaked an arm around her waist to keep her from collapsing against her brother's hand.

"Reason you say." The Regent took out a great gold pocket watch, snapped its lid open. Daring to look down, Emma could see nothing on its face; it was blank as a stone wall.

The Regent looked up. "When Conrad Shaw's love for his mother caused him to lose all reason, to step into the trap Leviathan had laid for him, the breach opened, all reason was drowned. A blood-dimmed tide arose and slowly, slowly it began to slither out of the dark prison of God's imagining."

He snapped the watch closed, returned it to an inside pocket. "Hear me, Surah. As if I don't have enough on my platter with this war almost upon us, I have *this*"—he tilted his head toward Emma—"to contend with."

"She isn't what you—"

"Silence, sister! Allow me to elucidate the truth of Emma Shaw and her cursed line. Witness the cataclysmic moment when myth and history entwine, and because of that moment history becomes stranger and more disastrous than ever the myth was."

"Wh-what myth?" Emma's voice was as slurred as her mind was muzzy. Yet still she had sense enough to understand the final mystery of her bloodline was likely about to be revealed to her.

"What myth, she asks?" The Regent sneered. "A myth you should know by heart, a myth you should have taken in with your mother's milk, but I see by your expression that isn't the case. And don't you for a moment confuse ignorance with innocence. You are anything but innocent, Emma Shaw, despite what my softhearted sister falsely claims."

His face settled in to the look of a professor about to distribute a final exam. "When Zeus looked upon the human Leda he lost all reason. Assuming the shape of a swan he dropped from the sky, fell upon her, and raped her. The issue from that rape was the impossibly beautiful Helen—Helen of Troy. Do you see? Do you understand? That single moment of lost reason—that act of rape—caused the Trojan War. A decade of death and destruction on the plains of Asia Minor."

He looked from his sister to Emma. "Have the scales fallen from your eyes? Leviathan's illicit congress with the human Chynna caused the issue of Gideon. From this one act came all the rest: the breach, the eternal enmity between Leviathan and the Shaws, and, worst of all, the war on Heaven, engineered by Leviathan on orders from his Lord and Master, abetted by the Shaws."

"All unwittingly," Emma managed to choke out.

The look of contempt on the Regent's face fell on her like hard rain. "Please. Conrad's mother warned him. She begged him not to try to save her—but, as I told you, all reason had been trampled under Leviathan's hooves. All that was left Conrad in his frenzy was that most despicable of human traits: hubris. Continually baited by Leviathan, he still thought he could save her, still considered himself smarter than the First Sphere Seraph. He had his mind locked on an unreachable goal he should have known better than to try for. And what happened? His mother died and Conrad accomplished what neither Leviathan nor the Sum of All

Shadows could ever have done: he caused the breach between the realms of humans and the Fallen.

"Now all sorts of vermin who live in the crevasses between Spheres are creeping and crawling out to where they—like you, Shaw—do not belong, wreaking all manner of mischief and havoc, upending the delicate balance of the Spheres.

"Now there is nothing for it but, like Agamemnon and his army, to go to war."

The uncanny silence of the place, where not a single sound common to Emma's home could be heard, closed around them. She was abruptly aware that, should the Regent get his way, she might never hear them again. The thought that she might never again see Bravo or Lilith was intolerable to her. She refused to accept the possibility that her life ended here in what appeared to be Limbo.

Gathering her wits about her, she said, "I can dispute little of what you've said, Regent. I have never before considered the confluence of the myth of Zeus and Leda with the reality of Leviathan and Chynna. Although one was a rape and the other probably was not—"

The Regent's eyebrows lifted. "No? You think not? Was Chynna's charismatic seduction any different than a physical rape? I think not."

Something snapped inside Emma. The artifice of this conversation, that it was anything but a brutal browbeating leading to either her death or her torture at the Regent's hands, had become unacceptable to her.

"I am not interested in ancient history, you pompous prick!" Her cheeks were as flaming as her throat, but for a different reason. "I am interested in the here and now. I'm not responsible for the actions of Chynna or of Conrad. They made their own decisions, for better or worse. Now is *my* time! *Mine!* Emma Shaw's moment!"

Momentarily taken aback, the Regent said, "I don't know what you think—"

"A Shaw, sister to Bravo, granddaughter to Conrad—whatever else you may brand me doesn't count for a dropped penny. I am Aqqibari. I am one of the Protectors against the Darkness to Come." She shoved both hands against his chest. "Now get off me!"

"I will not—"

"Djat had'ar!" Emma cried. And then, in almost the same breath: *"Et ignis ibi est!"*

At once, the blue flames ignited from the center of her palms, sending the Regent reeling back. His smoking jacket was on fire—cool, smokeless flames that nevertheless ate away at the jacket's front so that in moments it slid off him, fell onto his patent-leather slip-ons, curling as it crisped, as if it were made of paper.

With irritating fastidiousness, the Regent brushed the ashes off his shirt. "Is this really the way you want to play this, Emma Shaw?"

"It's the only way I know how to play," she shot back.

"Consider yourself warned." With that proclamation the Regent unwound the ascot from around his neck.

Surah rushed at him. "This isn't right, and you know it!"

"I know no such thing." Her brother's neck was bare now, and they both could see the red line that went straight around it, as if he had been beheaded and his head placed back on the bleeding stump of his neck. He wound the ends of the ascot around his fingers and stretched it between his hands. As he did so, the ascot commenced to alter its form and shape. But before Emma could see what it was becoming, Surah stepped between them, blocking her line of sight.

"I won't let you."

"Step aside, sister."

"I will not allow you to harm her."

He shook his head. "I will ask as kindly as possible: How d'you propose to stop me?"

"You know full well how." Her hands did something at her breast that Emma couldn't see.

The Regent's eyes opened wide. "Wait, what?" He shook his head. "No, you can't!"

"Watch me." Surah's voice was calm and steady and, above all, determined.

This her brother heard. Fear came into his eyes. "Sister—Surah—surely she's not worth—"

"An Aqqibari? Of course she is, brother. And even if she were not, even if she were simply a human female . . ." Her words drifted off, replaced by her brother's exclamation.

Emma had moved enough so that she had an angle of view that allowed her to see that Surah had reached into her own chest and was now holding her heart in her cupped palms.

"What are you . . . ?" The Regent's face was pale as ice.

"Do it," Surah commanded. "Do it, brother."

"But—"

"There is no other way," Surah said.

"If you are found wanting . . ."

Her head tilted. "Yes?"

"You will . . . you will die."

Surah smiled. "This is what I choose to do for her, for Emma Shaw. Brother, I know that you cannot comprehend the bond between us. Nonetheless, here is my heart. You must comply."

The Regent looked at her as if he had never truly seen her before. "I fear I have misjudged you, Surah." And, swirling the ascot-thing back around his neck, he drew from his back trouser pocket a scale, which grew in size and weight. The Regent set it on the ground before him.

"Emma," Surah said softly. "My brother has many titles, but only one name."

"Osiris," the Regent said, his gaze fixed on the scale.

"God of the Dead." Surah smiled to ease Emma's distress, for it was a gentle smile, filled with love. "Another of his titles."

"One not much used in this day and age," the Regent grumbled. He looked at his sister. "I want it known and duly inscribed that I perform this ritual under duress."

"Noted." Surah looked at Emma, held out the bundle cradled in her hands. "Now you must place my heart on the scales."

"What? No! I can't."

"But you must," Surah said, "for I cannot."

"The ancient Egyptians believed that the heart was the font of both intellect and emotion."

"They were not wrong." Surah took a step toward Emma.

"This ritual," Emma said. "You will be judged."

"Against the feather plucked from Antiphon, the eagle-goddess of truth."

Surah tilted her head, and Emma saw that the Regent was holding a very long, very beautiful feather in both his hands, cradling it in precisely the same manner as his sister held her heart.

"Now, Emma, take my heart and place it on the scales."

Frightened nearly out of her mind, Emma did as Surah bade. The organ seemed light as air, almost as if it did not exist. There was no blood, either around the heart or in the hole in Surah's chest, just darkness there, as if the cavity defied logic, as if it could be as deep as the cavern at the top of the Baatara Gorge waterfall in Tannourine.

Emma turned to face Osiris and the scales, but now a new fear struck her. "Into which pan should I place it?" she asked. "The left or the right?"

"That is entirely up to you," Surah replied. "That is why I cannot do it myself."

"So it matters which side I decide on," Emma said.

"It does," Surah confirmed.

The Regent looked up, straight into Emma's eyes. "Choose!" he commanded.

Emma closed her eyes for a moment, then stepped to the scales, bent down, and without another thought, placed Surah's heart onto the left-hand pan. The scales moved; of course they did, the left side now lower than the empty pan on her right.

"So be it," the Regent said, and placed the feather onto the right-hand pan. The scales shuddered, wobbled, then down went the pan holding the feather.

Surah came and plucked up her heart, returning it to her chest. That done, she held Emma at arm's length. "Now he can never harm you."

"But," said Osiris's voice from behind her.

Surah's expression grew grave indeed. "But now you must do the same."

"What?" Emma was stricken. Her heart turned over in her chest and her throat closed up.

"Your heart must be weighed," Osiris said.

"No, what? I can't," Emma said, panic-stricken. "I won't."

Surah's eyes were filled with an emotion Emma could not decode. "I'm afraid you must, Emma. This is your one path back. Otherwise—"

"Otherwise," Osiris said, "you will remain here forever, cut off from everyone and everything you know and love."

Then, before Emma could make a move or even think clearly, Surah placed her hands on Emma's chest.

Emma began to scream.

PART THREE

WAR FOOTING

33

DOWN AMONG THE BURGEONING RANKS OF HIS ARMY, BIVouacked on the bottom of the nameless, waterless sea, the Principal Resident strode through the divisions. The one hundred Fallen folded their wings and bowed their heads as he passed. As for the damned, who made up the bulk of the host, they stood stock still, slack jawed, and glassy-eyed. Some of them drooled. Those, the Principal Resident called out, directing his Cherubim to the ragged line they formed. As he passed, the Cherubim disemboweled the droolers, one by one, before beheading them, ensuring there was nowhere for their souls to go.

Their job finished, they shrieked at the damned to return to their preparations.

The Principal Resident paid the scene no mind; his thoughts were elsewhere. In a perfect world he'd want Leviathan by his side, but this was far from a perfect world; it hadn't been for a long time. It was even far from an imperfect world. It was a prison. But the time of his incarceration was coming to an end, without the unspeakable humiliation of repentance. The blitzkrieg on the world of the humans was about to begin. With their enslavement, with them joining the ranks of his Fallen, the assault on Heaven would commence.

The stench of war footing was unique unto itself. Nothing like it had ever existed, even during the uprising in Heaven before the Fall. There was no scent in Heaven, by decree of the Chief Autocrat, another rule that stuck in his craw, one of many. Countless, actually. It was a miracle the uprising took so long to coalesce.

The Principal Resident had learned from the Fall. His nemesis was not only God, but that damnable cadre of Angels of Sanctification. In all, there were five, led by the Archangel St. Michael, who had commanded God's army against the Fallen, defeating them. The other four were Metatron, Suriel, Phanuel, and Zagzagael. For the assault to succeed the Principal Resident knew these five needed to be neutralized, if not exterminated. On this subject he had thought long and hard. Over the centuries, he had devised schemes simple to complex, in the end, finding fatal flaws in all of them.

Until he had come across the illustration of the blackest of black spikes with directions on how to make it, how to bring it to life, and how to empower it. This he had done, and the spike had temporarily imprisoned the spirit of Conrad Shaw until, perfect, it had conjured the impregnable cage behind the bronze mirror. It was Conrad whom Leviathan had tricked into cracking open the fissure between the realms. For this alone the Principal Resident owed the First Sphere Seraph a debt of gratitude—or he would have if he were human or had a shred of decency in him. But he had disavowed decency the moment he had fulminated against God's autocratic rule of Heaven. He had abandoned everything and everyone for the chance to usurp God and their sycophantic Angels of Sanctification.

At the stables, he paused to admire the mounts his dark sorcery had created: six-legged steeds with clawed paws instead of hooves and stout necks to support their tigers' heads. Nostrils flared, they scented him and responded as the Fallen did, bowing their heads as he briefly stroked their thick manes before passing on.

Conrad Shaw, the Principal Resident thought now. Conrad was the key to the Principal Resident's long-coveted ultimate victory. Now that he had Conrad Shaw imprisoned with no chance of escape, he could not return with the help of his grandson and granddaughter to the Rift to close it. Once sealed the Principal Resident and the army of the Fallen would be trapped in their prison for eternity. Once resealed by Conrad Shaw, the breach could never again be reopened.

The war was now or never.

He came upon a strategy session, a semicircle of Seraphs that by rights Leviathan should have been leading. Then again, perhaps it was just as well that he was elsewhere. For several moments the Principal Resident joined the discussion as the Seraphs parsed out the shock troops of the first blitz, circling out from there in a widening gyre.

"Planning is all well and good, but once in the field the situation is fluid," he reminded them. "Account for all possibilities, and remember there will be at least one that you haven't planned for, so leave one or two cadres of your best in reserve to deal with surprises."

Amid somber nods and murmurs, he moved on. He knew all too well about surprises on the field of battle. He had made the mistake of trying to suborn Emma Shaw with Beleth, one of his best Second Sphere Powers. When that didn't work he had sent Leviathan to annihilate Bravo Shaw. That tactic failed as well. Which is why he had settled on the imprisonment of Conrad Shaw.

Conrad had been in hiding ever since the Principal Resident had tried to snatch his soul at the moment of his body's death. He had made the mistake of thinking it would be easy, that by going after Conrad when he was at his weakest, his corporeal form broken and disintegrating into ash and dust, he could just reach out and snatch him.

But Conrad had learned from his encounter with Leviathan, and he had been ready. More than ready. Not only had he evaded the attack, but at the same moment he had vanished absolutely from the Principal Resident's sight.

His nose lifted. The air stank of hot metal and sparks from the host of armorers who were finishing their work on the sorcerous weaponry he had designed. Taking a brief detour, he stepped into the armory, a vast shed, a mile long. In it, uncounted specialists were bent over their naphtha forges, creating weapons that detonated phosphorus missiles—ever bright, ever burning—that blinded, charred flesh, and ate their way through the thickest armor or bunker. Just for fun, he took one that had just been loaded, squeezed off a round that immediately immolated three of the assemblers before they could even let out a shriek. Laughing, he tossed the weapon back to the armorer who had made it, before resuming his stroll.

It took him a long time to work out where Conrad Shaw had secreted himself. As to how Conrad accomplished this sleight of hand he was vexingly still at a loss to understand. The first place he looked was inside the statue of the Orus—the horse/lion/serpent hybrid: the war-mounts of the Four Thrones. Not finding Conrad there, he moved on to the Four Sphinxes of Dawn. No joy there either. He moved on to the dark side—his side. Working off the idea that Conrad would hide in plain sight he checked in on the remaining three Thrones—the fourth one had been killed last year in the battle beneath Arwad. Finally, the Four Dominions. No sign of Conrad there, either, though Azazel, his prime Cherub, had nosed out the scent of Conrad in Paimon. But that spoor was faded, and Conrad was long gone, if he had ever been there in the first place. It would be just like Conrad to seed false trails to put himself beyond the reach of the Principal Resident.

For some time thereafter, the Principal Resident had proceeded under the assumption that he had been correct in thinking that Conrad would choose a hiding place in plain sight—meaning someone close to the Principal Resident. He had even sniffed around Azazel, but this was before the Cherub had picked up Conrad's scent. Thereafter, as Azazel had proved himself, the Principal Resident left him alone to train the advance cadres of the army of the Fallen.

It wasn't until he had dispatched Azazel through the Rift he himself could not yet fit through to the Shaw's ancestral home, that, using the Cherub's eyes, he had discovered Conrad Shaw's hidey-hole—and it was in plain sight. He had merely been looking in the wrong direction.

But now he'd found him: Conrad's spirit was sleeping soundly inside the heart of the apple tree that grew on the hillock behind the manor house. The place where his corpus was buried. What better place to hide, the Principal Resident had thought. *What a splendid mind Conrad Shaw has. A great pity he's not one of mine.*

So he trusted Azazel, and a good thing too, since he and his flaming sword would be put to good use when the time came, cutting down St. Michael, for the Principal Resident knew that once he took out their leader in battle, the other angels—even the cadre of archangels—would bend their knee to him, pledging eternal fealty, ushering in the Principal Resident's longed-for endless night.

But trust was a tricky animal, with its own masks and traitorous elements. When it came to Leviathan, his trust had eroded to the point where he felt it imperative to test him. The mission he had sent him on, to find and recruit the Regent, was this test. Either Leviathan would obey his marching orders or he would use his time away from his Lord and Master's side to promote an agenda of his own. For his strong right arm's growing restlessness had not been lost on the Principal Resident. Outwardly, he ignored it, wanting to capture not the bud, but the blossom.

It was not only Leviathan the Principal Resident wanted to catch but also those foolish enough to be recruited by his honeyed words. Only the Principal Resident knew that Leviathan's vaunted charisma was merely a reflection of his Lord and Master's own dark glamour. But as with all reflections, the simulacrum was weaker, paler, less dominant. Lacking in self-examination, Leviathan could hardly be aware of his faulty power. If he had been he would make a much more difficult entity with which to deal.

The Principal Resident, smirking among his army, busy as ants on their war footing, knew he had no cause for concern. Not as long as Leviathan was besotted with the most recent human female in a long string of female lovers. Disgusting trait—repellent, actually. The only reason the Principal Resident allowed such deviant behavior was that it kept Leviathan in line and out of real trouble so that he would do the Principal Resident's bidding expeditiously and unquestioningly. Only too well he knew the urgency of Leviathan's desires. To forbid them would only engender anger, resentment, and rebellion.

Miles from his island fortress, he had finished his tour. He turned and headed back, threading his way through alternate sections of the army, until up ahead, the spiderweb tower on the pinnacle of black rock loomed before him, ripping the gray sky to shreds.

Time to work his dark sorcery so foolishly skimmed by King Solomon's cadre of alchemists. It was they who had created the cache of gold—the gold they had altered. Where Solomon had them stash it was a riddle he had been trying to solve for hundreds of years. Well, he would just have to begin without knowledge of the gold's whereabouts.

Almost time for him and the host of the Fallen to move out.

Almost time to ascend.

WITH A grunt of contempt, Leviathan tossed Haya's limp body into Oq Ajdar's waiting arms. "Now the adults can get down to hammering out an alliance that will benefit all of us."

Into the ensuing shocked silence, Ayeleye croaked, "A child. A child! How could you?"

Leviathan turned on him. "What d'you mean? It's what I do. As for what *you* do, it's anyone's guess."

With a cutting gesture, Ayeleye seemed to fling away the Seraph's words. "You kill a child in front of our eyes and then talk about an *alliance*? An alliance of *adults*? We'd sooner slit our wrists."

"That can be arranged," the Seraph said blandly. "But maybe I was being overly optimistic. Maybe some of us aren't adults." His face was a mask, a fortress. It was anyone's guess what lay within. "Listen, Ayeleye, war is nearly upon us, and blood is going to be shed—rivers of it, lakes of it, a sea of it. And a good deal of it will be from children, whether you like it or not."

"Well, we do not fucking like it," Ayeleye snapped. Unusually mild-mannered, it was not like him to use curse worlds.

"Too *fucking* bad. This is what our existence has come to, so grow up already and face it."

"There are consequences," Oq Ajdar said from behind him. "To everything."

At the sound of her voice, Leviathan whirled, ready for a nasty rejoinder. But even though he opened his mouth, his words stuck in his throat like a fistful of stinging nettles.

Haya's eyes had opened. They burned again like twin suns.

"You see, Seraph. Here are consequences," Oq Ajdar said, astoundingly without a trace of malice. "You cannot kill her."

"But I *did* kill her. I saw it, you saw it, even this little frog-man Ayeleye saw it. My aim was true. The arrow pierced her heart." Leviathan was almost shouting. "No human could survive that. She died."

"And yet," Oq Ajdar said in her quiet, methodical manner, "here she is. Alive."

The almost feral glow emanating from Haya expanded, until it encompassed her entire being.

"I warned you, but you chose not to listen. You have eyes yet you cannot see." Oq Ajdar was unruffled by what was happening. It was almost as if she expected the resurrection. "Haya is made of light. Pure light."

Then Haya's feet rose above the ground. Oq Ajdar let go of her, and Haya, arms spread wide, levitated into the air, a wingless avian.

"Who are you?" Leviathan asked. "*What* are you?"

And Haya answered him: "Your salvation."

34

WHEN NEXT BRAVO OPENED HIS EYES THE INVISIBLE COCOON was gone. He was without pain or numbness. Relief rolled over him. He had been healed.

Then he cried out. Like the roaring of a river in spate, the recent past came rushing back, engulfing him in bewilderment.

So this was neither a dream, nor a hallucination. Ayla and Antiphon must have come back for him after he passed out. But then where was Mary? And, more importantly, why couldn't he move? Dumbly, he looked down, then to his left. The blackened stump of the little finger of his left hand stared back. However, the hand was no longer angry red and swollen.

He was bound in place, on a roughly hewn wooden cross that had been pounded into the dun-colored ground. So then outside. Unlike the crucifixions inflicted by the ancient Romans, his feet were on the ground, bound at the ankles with a chain, just as his wrists were.

He looked around. In every direction, for as far as he could see, there was nothing but an endless mist so thick he could not distinguish even a single landmark.

Calling out, he turned his head this way and that, but, apart from his own echo, shouldering its way through the mist, there was no response. Raising his voice again, he waited for the echo, transposing the length of the delay into an inexact calculation as to distance. It seemed that he was in a vast place, mountainous, judging by the echo's repeats, and he must be high up on one of the peaks, for a wind whipped his face and clothes.

As if this knowledge were a trigger, the mist slowly began to lift, revealing the place where he was imprisoned. He was confronted with a dizzying expanse of sheer cliffs. What lay between them were gorges so deep he could not in his present state see their bottoms.

With the light streaming in from above the shredding mist came Mary, even more striking, her Madonna's face glowing, her body as bent and gnarled as a seaside pine tree. How she walked was a mystery, but, Bravo supposed, she had adapted, like all creatures whose will to survive triumphed over their circumstances.

"How are we feeling today, darling?" Mary said as cheerfully as if they had just sat down for a nice tea and a chat. She was still speaking to him in Hebrew.

"I'd feel better if you unchained me," he replied in the same language.

Looking disappointed, Mary made a clucking sound with her tongue. "I healed all the terrible wounds that had been inflicted on you by your so-called friends, and what thanks do I get?" She shook her head ruefully. "I have to be honest. You are an ungrateful wretch, darling."

Approaching him, she peered up into his face. "Now that you are healed—"

"What do you want, Mary?" He shoved his words at her. "What is it you hope to gain by these chains?"

Mary's eyes narrowed. "I thought my purpose would be self-evident, darling. No?" She sighed, clearly disappointed. "I am seeking to ascertain the limits of your powers."

"You want to see if I can free myself, then."

Her eyebrows rose as a smile wreathed her lips. "That is it entirely!"

"You're insane," Bravo said.

"That's as may be," Mary replied without hesitation. "But it's not for you to decide, darling, is it." It was a statement of fact, not a question.

She rubbed her hands together, and Bravo noticed that they were nearly as beautiful as her face. What a conundrum of a character she was.

"Now, let's see what you can do."

"I'm not a zoo animal," Bravo said. "I don't perform tricks for my keeper."

"Mm, I thought as much." Mary's expression was as enigmatic as those of the figures depicted in *The Last Supper.* "Perhaps what you require is an incentive."

"Perhaps," Bravo said sardonically. "But you've already as much as told me who's missing from all versions of the painting."

Mary's expression turned crafty. "I've as much as told you *a bit* of what you would like to know. I've saved the best for last, darling. It's the key to everything, trust me."

Bravo shook his head. "Get yourself another guinea pig."

"But, you see, there *is* no other, darling. There is only you. Lovely, beautiful you." She sighed deeply. "But now comes the unpleasant part. *Most* unpleasant."

Something grave came over her, a shadow cast from a cloud that smothers the sunlight, and she stepped away, quickly and nimbly, until Bravo could no longer see her.

"Time for you to have this stage all to yourself," she said. "Well, *almost*."

One moment all was clear and open before him. But a heartbeat later the atmosphere turned dark and out of the darkness appeared something he had never conceived of even in his worst nightmare: a magnificently stunning woman, without a stitch of clothes. She was perfectly proportioned, and she wasn't a woman. In fact, she wasn't even human.

Mary had somehow summoned a Liderc. Bravo had read about these mythical creatures in a tome at the Library in Alexandria, when he was idly going through the European Myths section. The Liderc had its origins in Hungary, and now here one was standing in front of him. So much for myths, Bravo thought. As the Liderc stepped toward him, he tried to steel himself for what was to come, even knowing it was useless.

Reaching out her hand, the Liderc made to touch her forefinger to the place between and just above his eyes. When he twisted his head away, she took his jaw in a viselike grip, held his head steady. Her fingertip pressed into his forehead and he felt something leave him. For a moment his knees grew weak. The sensation vanished.

Then the true horror began, for this was when the Liderc went to work. Before his eyes, she became someone else, guided by the image she had drawn out of Bravo's mind. Standing not a pace away was his sister, Emma.

Then the Liderc spoke and a shiver went down Bravo's spine, for she spoke in Emma's voice, used Emma's cadences, used Emma's favorite phrases. To all intents and purposes she was Emma. And now as she pressed her naked body against his, she began to writhe. Her hips bucked, began the age-old rhythm of erotic seduction—for this was what a Liderc was, a succubus that invaded your memory and took the form of the female family member you loved the most.

True horror was defined not by the defilement or maiming of the body, but by the invasion of the mind. Mary had sent the Liderc to drive him insane. Emma ripped open his shirt, pressed her breasts against his chest. Her nipples were hard, the rest of her hot as if with a fever. And the most horrifying part was that she was so clever in her ministrations, in what she whispered salaciously in his ear, that completely against his will he felt himself responding.

And yet it was this very response that tore him free of his mental bondage, and this in turn stoked something buried deep inside him, something Conrad had hinted at when he was a boy pushing his grandfather in his wheelchair to his spot beneath the spreading branches of his beloved apple tree. He was too young to understand, and possibly this was deliberate on Conrad's part. He buried a trigger deep within Bravo's memory, to be awakened at the proper time, in the proper place.

This was the time. This was the place.

Like a magic box, the trigger popped a word into Bravo's mind: *Aqqibari*. It was the term Emma had come across in a distant, dusty corner of the Order's archives in Addis, but had had no time to bring up to Bravo. But Conrad had gifted him with more, much more: the Aqqibari terminology, the powers bequeathed to the Aqqibari by God himself, when he anointed their ancestors, when he anticipated their future, the need for protection that even St. Michael and his cadre of archangels could not give, bound as they were to the precincts of Heaven. The cold blue fire that Emma had accessed was only one of these powers.

There now emanated from Bravo's body an enormous heat, concentrated in his wrists and ankles. The chains binding them turned jellylike, as if they were only a desert mirage. They lay at his feet, sizzling, turned a grayish-black.

He was free of the cross, but not of the Liderc, who seemed unaffected by the heat he had generated. Her nails grew as long and as sharp as an old mandarin's. They tore into his remaining clothes, shredding them to get at his sex.

Emma's fingers closed around him, stroking him gently but insistently. No, not Emma, he told himself furiously. The Liderc. But such was the succubus's talent for mimicry, he, her own brother, could not tell the difference. He had to trust his Aqqibari mind, which remained free from the Liderc's uncanny genius for driving her victims insane.

Dizzy with a mounting lust he struggled mightily to crush, he willed himself to return to the Aqqibari mind. This was not a retreat but a strategic retrenchment from which to strike back. But the Emma-Liderc was spreading her legs. Her thighs trembled, the muscles on their insides taut. Her nipples scraped against his chest. Her hands were guiding him into her, and he knew that if she effected that ultimate connection, that intimacy, he was lost. Aqqibari mind or not, she would take him down, shred his mind as easily as she had shredded his clothes.

Only seconds left now. She had not responded to fire. Of course, she hadn't, he realized now. She was a creature of sexual heat. Then this might stop her. And yet here again he faltered. She had him, the most delicate part of him about to be absorbed inside a cavern that would clamp him tight and never let go until he was driven insane.

He closed his eyes, on the verge of being transported to that place of ecstasy she had created especially for him. What man could resist his own personal bliss? From the deepest part of him where Aqqibari had been born, incubated throughout his formative years, and now finally, matured, emerged the sorcerous ice-blade the temperature of dry ice. The time for thought had ended. He shoved it into the core of her.

When he heard her sharp cry—like that of an animal caught in a trap—his eyes snapped open. His gaze met hers. He cringed, expecting to see Emma dying, but his sister was no longer there. Only the Liderc—but the Liderc as she really was, stripped of all her powers. An old woman who stood before him now, her face deeply lined, scarred from the immense number of years she had lived. Her body was thin to the point of emaciation, and where her bones were visible, they seemed brittle, about to break apart.

Staring blankly into his eyes, she sighed once, a long exhalation that spoke of many lifetimes, many deaths delivered, many souls stolen. They all came rushing out of her now, these souls, freed at last.

Bravo let go of the ice-blade and the Liderc collapsed. As she sank to the ground the ice-blade dissolved, and the Liderc with it. But the memory of what she had become, the fact that she had almost caused the annihilation of his body and his soul, still lurked, a demon in the remains of the day.

35

EMMA SANK TO HER KNEES. SURAH HELD HER HEART IN HER cupped palms. *Thub-thump, thub-thump, thub-thump.* The sound of kettle drums rhythmically struck. The cadence of Emma's heart was precisely the same as the pulse in her wrists, in her carotid artery. She felt no pain, only wonder and bewilderment.

"How?" she asked.

"How do you explain the sun setting, the moon rising, the stars burning," Osiris said.

It's a simple statement, Emma thought. *Or not simple at all. It depends on your point of view.*

She stared at her hands for a moment, then moved them toward her chest, only to be halted by Surah.

"Don't touch the vacant part of you," the Medius ordered, "or the ritual will be invalidated, your heart can't be returned to your body. Without your heart you will die within minutes."

"And now?" Emma asked.

"You know what comes next." Osiris had not budged from his position behind the scales. He nodded to Surah, who turned, brought Emma's heart to the midway point between the pans. "Which one?" he said. "Choose."

Never hesitating, Surah placed Emma's heart in the pan on her right. The pan dipped down. Solemnly, Osiris placed the feather in the pan on the opposite side. The pan with Emma's heart rose, dipped, then steadied, as if it was of equal weight with the feather.

Emma watched, breath caught in her throat. From somewhere deep inside her a fierce pounding started up, making her limbs quiver and her head throb. A headache blossomed behind her eyes, like a terrible night-time flower.

The pan holding her heart dipped slightly.

"No." Her voice was a reedy whisper. "Please, God, no."

Perhaps he heard her, perhaps she really was worthy. Whatever the case, the pan with the feather laid across it dipped, this time decisively. Emma's heart rose, and with it her spirit. She commenced to breathe again. Her headache receded, her limbs stilled their quaking, and her pulse slowed with the inflation of her lungs.

Taking up Emma's heart, Surah returned it to her chest. At once, Emma felt a wave of velvety blackness overwhelm her. Her eyes rolled up in her head, and she fell backward, where the Regent caught her, held her gently while his sister completed her complex task.

"All right, I admit it." He watched with all the care of a gemstone cutter. "She surprised me."

"In what way?" Surah, aware of his close scrutiny of her, nevertheless kept her concentration on the labyrinth of connections required for the human heart to begin functioning normally again within its cavity.

"In every way." The Regent grunted. "My dear sister, we may not see each other overmuch, nevertheless I am well aware of your incomprehensible affinity toward humans." He gestured with his chin. "Your intimate knowledge of their anatomy is just a single example."

"My interest is not so incomprehensible," she said, continuing with her delicate work. "In a very real sense, we Medius are torn. Humans have abominable traits, it cannot be refuted. Their treatment of each other is disgraceful."

"They are blighted with fear, envy, and greed. They are covetous, and they are sadistic. Everything they covet they eventually kill." His lips turned down in a sign of disgust. "Invidious creatures."

"And yet," Surah replied, unruffled by his venom toward humans, "the Fallen and their Lord and Master are so much worse. They are solipsistic and inveterately lustful. The case of Leviathan is proof enough that they transgress against their own laws at will. And when it comes to sadism they put humans to shame."

The Regent gestured with his chin toward Emma. "It never occurred to me that she would be found worthy."

"I imagine not," Surah said. She put a great deal of meaning into those three words.

"She is a Shaw," the Regent said, contriving to ignore her. "I need not remind you that all Shaws are polluted by the vile impregnation of the Seraph."

"It cannot be denied," Surah answered, closing up Emma's chest. There was a vertical line, white as snow, not quite a scar but something akin, which would stay with her for the rest of her days. "Turning the card over, however, we find that both Emma Shaw and her brother, Bravo, are Aqqibari."

"Beloveds of God. Yes, I know." The Regent's face darkened. "A paradox I cannot explain."

"Is that not the nature of paradoxes?"

Surah helped him lay Emma down. The Regent, still in his guise as Osiris, covered Emma with the blue-green Silk of the Dead, a wrap used only for those whom the scales had rendered worthy. Unlike Emma, those humans were already dead.

"In that manner, they are like us," Surah went on. "Held in the balance until the End Times come."

"I refute that analogy," her brother said tersely. "The Shaws are not like us at all."

Surah's reply was a simple smile, whether sad or mocking or both he could not tell. Nonetheless, her words caused a wrenching at the core of him that made for a disquieting moment. In order to reestablish his equilibrium, he said, "If I am not mistaken there are four Aqqibari. So far I am aware of only two." He searched her face for an answer.

"I, as well," she acknowledged. "At present, the third and fourth Aqqibari are unknown."

The Regent's disquiet returned, stronger this time. "But they cannot mobilize until the other two are found."

Surah looked down at Emma. "Perhaps she knows. Perhaps when she wakes she will tell us."

"HOW ARE we ever going to find him?" Ayla lamented.

"Bravo wasn't taken up," Antiphon pointed out with her unerring logic, "so he must be below us. There is no sideways here."

"All right," she responded, "but how *far* down, and who even might know if this fissure widens out at some point far below?"

"We don't." The great eagle walked to the edge of the ledge. "And yet it doesn't matter."

"How can you say that?" Ayla was nearly beside herself. Despite the eagle's sage advice, she still held her own feet to the fire, blaming herself for leaving Bravo.

"Give me his little finger."

Ayla's head snapped around so fast she heard her vertebrae crack. "What?"

"Bravo's finger," Antiphon said patiently.

"Why?"

"It will guide me to him, Ayla." The eagle turned her head. "This I know. This will happen." Her golden eye caught Ayla in its glare. "If you please."

Hesitantly, she dug up the finger in its soiled cloth wrapping. It was black with charcoal, yet underneath she knew the flesh was as pink as when it was on Bravo's hand. Reluctantly, she revealed it, held it out for Antiphon's inspection.

"You won't harm it in any way, will you?"

The great eagle's head shot forward, with her beak she plucked the finger from its wrapping, and, without a sound, gobbled it down.

Ayla screamed.

"Trust me," Antiphon said, calm as ever. "This was the only way."

"You . . ." She gulped, her stomach queasy. "Did it work? Do you know where he is now?"

The eagle tossed her head. "Climb on, Ayla. Bravo has encountered a Liderc."

A terrible fear rose into Ayla's throat. "What's a Liderc?"

"Bad. Very bad," Antiphon muttered.

The fear inside Ayla grew. "What d'you mean, 'very bad'?"

Antiphon blew air through her nostrils. "The Liderc took Emma's shape."

"What? How—?"

"Now come," Antiphon commanded, and then to herself, "The Liderc, the Liderc." Her body shuddered.

Deeply troubled, Ayla climbed upon the eagle's back, held on tight as they lofted into the center of the fissure, then plunged steeply downward into the abyss.

36

MOLLY THROUGH THE BRONZE LOOKING GLASS. SHE HAD MADE a bold step—possibly too bold. That was her first thought—or, more accurately, her single moment of regret. Then she felt the octagonal medallion burning her hand, and she understood that it was leading her—this was where she was meant to be, never mind why. She believed the *why* would come later. She had faith. And then she laughed. She couldn't help it, despite her current circumstance.

She stood in a place of nothingness. Looking down, she could not even discern a floor or ground. And yet she stood on *something*. Stamping her foot proved fruitless. She stood on something hard, but when struck it made no sound. No echo resounded through a silence so absolute it quickly took on a curious three-dimensional quality, like smoke from a burning building.

Faith. She continued to laugh. She had no faith in God, in Scripture, in any organized religion, even Buddhism, which, strictly speaking, wasn't a religion at all, but a way of life. Molly had flatly rejected anyone or anything telling her how to live her life.

And yet because she harbored a desperation to find her mother, to find out who she was, why she had abandoned her, she had cobbled together a form of faith true to her inner self. And when she did find her mother, what then? How would she feel? Relief at looking into her face and perhaps seeing the ghost of herself? Anger for having been abandoned? Insistent that her mother provide answers to all the questions she'd stored up over the years growing up without her? Likely all three, and surely other emotions she could not yet grasp.

Taking out the medallion, she saw that it had changed color. No longer black, it was instead a beautiful pearlescent gray. She took this as a sign that there had been a material change in her circumstance. The medallion her mother had given her had been altered when she had stepped through the bronze looking glass.

Looking around, she called out into the atmosphere that was neither dark nor bright. Odder still was that she could not make out whether what light there was was natural or artificial. She turned a full 360 degrees. Hadn't Chynna told them this was a prison meant to contain Conrad Shaw, in whatever form he now existed? But then, Molly was absolutely convinced that Chynna was a lying bitch—as dangerous as a spitting cobra beneath the dark, smoldering exterior she presented. She might miss her daughter, but in all other matters Molly felt she was eminently untrustworthy.

Which way was she to go? There were no landmarks, nothing to distinguish one direction from another. But her medallion had successfully led her here. Why should it stop now? She turned again, more slowly this time, watching the pearlescent face.

However, as it turned out, the face was the wrong place on the medallion to look. As she rotated around to a certain spot the triangle on one of its edges turned a pure white that glowed as if it were the beam of a searchlight.

Molly turned the medallion on edge so she could see the burning triangle. She held it out in front of her. Then she set off into the nothingness. For several minutes, her path proceeded straight as a ruler. Then, quite without warning, the white triangle ceased to glow. At once, she stopped. She looked from one of the eight edges to the next, until she found the triangle that was glowing. She turned in this direction—to her right and on an approximately 45-degree angle, and set off again.

Not long thereafter, she came upon a wall. It was colorless but it shimmered in the light of the unknown source. She pushed against it, but it was hard, like the cell in which, Chynna claimed, her daughter Haya had been imprisoned.

She looked down at the medallion. It had not changed color. All the triangles were quiescent. Now what? she wondered. It did not seem possible that, after guiding her unerringly to this place, the medallion would now cease to work.

Closing her eyes for a moment, she allowed her mind to drift. She snatched at the first image that surfaced: the image of her hurling the medallion at the spell-crafted window in the house where they found Chynna.

She opened her eyes, stood back, and threw the medallion at the wall. It hit and dropped, landing in an awkward spot at the wall's base. Nothing. Retrieving it brought Molly almost smack up against the wall and she stumbled as she picked it up. As she felt herself slipping to one knee, she pushed her hand with the medallion in it against the wall to support herself.

Instantly, the medallion turned scarlet. Molly snatched her hand away. Lucky for her. The wall around the medallion was melting away in what seemed to her a perfect circle. The medallion returned to its pearlescent hue, fell away into Molly's waiting hand. She looked up to see that the circle was not only perfect but also, if she bent low, just the right size for her to step through.

And when she did, she found herself in a kind of drawing room, windowless, yet filled with glass and mirrors so that her image was repeated endlessly, into infinity. A domed ceiling, a tiled floor that was no more than a three-foot band around the edges of the room. In the center was a pond complete with pink waterlilies, yellow lotus, water-spiders, and here and there a loose-boned frog or two.

Curious, she moved around to a corbeled archway through which she passed into a wide corridor. Running down either side were stepped sluiceways along which water, which presumably fed the pond, flowed, gurgling like a contented infant.

Up ahead, voices floated to her like the water-spiders skating across the surface of the pond. Presently, she came to the end of the corridor, which debouched onto a series of connected rooms. All contained water in some form or other: a stone fountain; another, smaller pond in which what looked like white-and-orange koi swam in perfect peace.

Soon enough, she came upon a knot of people—young men and women, all of whom looked odd in a vague sort of way. They turned their heads away from her as she passed, apart from one who, becoming aware of her, ran off with astonishing alacrity. She paused, speaking to them several times: Who are you? Where am I? What is this place? Who owns it? But either they did not understand her or they were purposefully ignoring her. Or was it that they found her hideous in some way? She was different from them, of that she felt certain, though she could not pinpoint why; it was a feeling without hard evidence, but strong enough.

She heard the hubbub raised in her wake, but when she looked back, she caught the gossips turning their heads away again. Apparently, it was permissible to talk about her, just not look at her.

Her curiosity building exponentially, Molly set off through the front rooms of the building, noting that all of them were deserted, a few completely empty, as if awaiting instructions on their future use. This part of the house was like a house into which new tenants had just moved and were awaiting delivery of their furniture. Some of these rooms were small, others quite large. None of them had a water feature. *Tabula rasa,* Molly thought as she reached the front door.

There were two males guarding the double doors. They were made of thick slabs of a hardwood Molly didn't recognize, and were bound in solid bronze bands affixed with studs of the same material. When she stepped toward the doors, the two males blocked her way. She spoke to them, in all seven languages in which she was fluent, but her words fell on deaf ears. She made one abortive run at the doors, but stopped abruptly when the guards drew weapons of some kind. They weren't firearms, but neither were they swords. They looked dangerous, however, and Molly decided that the best course of action was to back off, at least for the time being.

In the meantime, she took a moment to study their faces because these two weren't afraid to look her in the eye. With a start, she realized that their eyes were reptilian, with vertical pupils and nictitating membranes. At once, she thought of the pond, all the water features.

She backed away, a bit frightened of what these creatures might be. More and more she was feeling like Alice, falling through the bronze looking glass. What next? she wondered. A bottle marked DRINK ME? A white rabbit with a pocket watch he pulled from his waistcoat? A mad tea party perhaps?

Resettling herself, she turned on her heel, determined to find another way out that wasn't barred. But just as she was setting off, the front door flew open. She felt a breeze on her back, and a vaguely familiar voice saying, "At last! You've come home!"

37

AFTER WAITING FOR WHAT BY LILITH'S ESTIMATION WAS thirty minutes or so, she gave Chynna a meaningful glance, then stepped toward the bronze mirror.

"Wait!" Chynna cried, clutching at the sleeve of Lilith's jacket. "What are you doing?"

"Going after my sister." Lilith snatched her sleeve away. "D'you think I'm going to leave her there?"

"You can't! You—"

But Lilith had already passed through, and now Chynna was alone in the vast house that Leviathan had claimed would be their home. But Chynna knew it was only a prison, albeit a comfortable one. So what did she have to lose? If she stepped through the mirror she would be exchanging one prison for another—most likely an eminently disagreeable one. But if that got her closer to recovering Haya, how could she stand still? She would not be able to forgive herself. Anyway, waiting for Leviathan to return was no option.

So, following Lilith's lead, she plunged through the bronze face into the yawning void of the world beyond.

THE PRINCIPAL Resident in female form had left his spiderweb eyrie behind for what she believed would be the last time. She wore a full suit of armor she had forged herself with small bits of conjuring, constructing it a scale at a time. These scales were overlapping, made of a metal that caused light to be annihilated, making her almost impossible to discern with the naked eye. She was mounted on an immense black-and-white Orus, the war-mount with the body of a horse, the head of a lion, and the tail of a serpent. Normal-sized Orus were the war-mounts of the Four Thrones, but in anticipation of the final battle, the Principal Resident had created Orus for all the First Sphere Fallen angels.

As she rode out into the assembled host, she was acutely aware that Leviathan should be riding at her side. But Leviathan was lost—lost to his aberrant lust for human females, for Chynna Sikar in particular. The Principal Resident was not particularly surprised, just disappointed.

But she had lived with disappointment so long that all bitterness had been burned out of her. In its stead was a void. It was the same with Leviathan. The difference was that he could not bear his own personal void, sought to fill it up with his necklace of human females. Each one was found wanting. Of course; it could not be otherwise: they were human and he was Other. Which was why Chynna Sikar had lasted so long, why for the first time in his existence Leviathan had been beguiled. The Principal Resident was familiar with Chynna. Though, unlike Leviathan, she had not been intimate with her (the very thought caused her to shudder), she was nevertheless acquainted with her story. From the moment she had stolen the golden apple, fleeing Arvad in the process, she had laid herself bare to the Principal Resident. Chynna's powers were formidable and she had, after all, founded the Shaw family line, an immense achievement in itself, especially considering the monster she had birthed.

She rode through the ranks, picking up all her mounted troops as she passed. They spread out on either side of her, in arrowhead formation. The sky was gray—always and forever gray. No clouds, no birds, but winds and storms aplenty.

I've been here too long, the Principal Resident thought. *No more. No more, this I swear on the body of my disgraceful brother.*

And as for the Regent, the Medius she had sent Leviathan to recruit, she knew there was no chance of success. No one—not even Leviathan with his legendary silver tongue—could persuade the Medius to abdicate their neutrality. After all, neutrality was all they had, poor things. Without it, their existence had no meaning.

She laughed as she rode on, her army marching double time in her wake. The waterless, nameless sea was immense, their journey was long, but it had begun.

LEVIATHAN FACED someone—some*thing* for which he had no ready explanation. He was a creature of the dark; he always had been. Even before the Fall he had buried deep within himself a heart of darkness to which he clung in the moments when he wasn't running to and fro, attending to God's errands, when he wasn't praying to God, when he wasn't praising God as the holiest of holies. God's smugness was like a needle beneath his skin, being plunged deeper and deeper until he had no choice but to make Lucifer his Lord and Master. Did he regret it now? Regret was one of many emotions inaccessible to him.

Haya, letting herself flow back down to the ground, said again, "Salvation."

Leviathan snorted in derision, the better to hide his consternation. "That word means nothing to me."

"What about love?"

The light coming off her kept Leviathan's eyes half-closed. He felt as if his skin was curling off him in charred strips, which was odd, since his body had an unnatural affinity for fire.

"No one has ever loved me," he said with curiosity but without a trace of self-pity, another emotion of which he had no knowledge.

"*I* love you," Haya said.

Leviathan shook his head. "I don't understand."

Reaching out to take his hand, she said, "That's the problem, isn't it?"

FROM THE distance he had maintained, Ayeleye was about to say something, but his sister shot him a look, beckoned him over to her. "Let's leave them to it, don't you think," she said softly.

"What? No!" Ayeleye was irate. "Leave the girl with him? Not a chance."

Oq Ajdar shot him a piercing look. "In case you haven't noticed, she's no longer a girl."

"No? What is she then?"

"Something new," his sister told him. "Something we have never seen before."

"We don't—"

"Something that could only exist at the advent of the End Times."

Ayeleye risked a quick glance at Haya. "We do not want her harmed."

Oq Ajdar's wide lips curled upward into the hint of a smile. "Your kindness is showing, my good brother. However, I wouldn't worry about that."

"But it's been clear from the first that Leviathan has evil plans for her."

"He may have done," his sister acknowledged. "But everything has changed now."

"Evil cannot change," Ayeleye declared firmly. "Evil is monolithic, dumb, vicious, incapable of either empathy or remorse."

Oq Ajdar took him by the shoulders, turned him. "Look at Leviathan, brother, and tell me nothing has changed."

Ayeleye watched the couple, becoming increasingly fascinated, and his sister whispered in his ear, "Either Leviathan is not truly evil, or the received wisdom concerning the nature of evil is incorrect."

"Which one is it?" her brother croaked in a dry whisper.

"That is something we are about to find out."

"**MY EYES** hurt," Leviathan said, while thinking, *What is happening to me?*

"Yes," Haya acknowledged, "I imagine they do." Her fingertips stroked his curved talons. "But that will change."

Her eyes opened wide as she saw him beginning to transform into the human form he had shown to her back at the house overlooking the enchanted river where she had encountered Conrad Shaw in his boat with its spirit sail.

"No! Don't!" she said. "You need to be seen as you really are." She tossed her head. "I will see you that way now no matter what shape you choose to take."

To his surprise, Leviathan did as she bade. "You were born from Chynna's womb."

"Yes."

"Who is your father?"

"Chynna is not my mother," Haya said. "Not really."

Leviathan digested this bit of confounding information. "So you are not of her body."

"That's right."

"So where—?"

"I believe I told you. Did you forget? I am from another Sphere."

"Not the Sphere of humankind."

"No."

"If you were from the Sphere of us angels I would know." His eyes narrowed. "What Sphere then?"

"I am the resurrection," Haya said, "and the light."

Leviathan shook his head, once more lost within the mesmeric spell she cast.

"I am a vessel of light."

He asked the question again, and this time she answered:

"I am from God's Sphere."

Leviathan almost laughed. "God doesn't have a Sphere."

"That you know of."

At once, an icy terror overtook him, and he shuddered. "What else don't I know?"

"The light," she said. "You don't know about the light." She stepped closer to him. "Tell me what it is you want—really want."

He could have lied to her, he wanted to lie to her, to protect himself, but also because deceit was what he knew best. And yet he didn't. "I am as tired of Lucifer's yoke as I was with God's," he said resignedly. "I want to cut him down. I want to take his place."

Without hesitation, she answered him. "You have been thinking this for the longest time."

"Yes."

"And each time you think it, you reinforce the thought."

"It's more than a thought."

"No, it isn't," she said. "It's the way you have deceived yourself."

"What?" Now he did laugh. "Why would I want to deceive myself?"

"It's the only way you know to deny your real self." She laid the flat of her hand against his chest. "You have lied for so long that you can no longer separate it from the truth. *That* was your objective all along."

She smiled up into his forbidding face, which no longer frightened her; she had come to discern its beauty. "The truth, Leviathan—*your* truth—is that, like me, you are of the light. You alone of all the dissident angels carried a shard of it with you when you fell. And now here you are—different, apart . . ."

"Alone."

"But, you see," Haya said, "you are not alone." When she looked around at Oq Ajdar and Ayeleye, he followed her gaze. "Far from it."

"I don't believe you."

"I shouldn't wonder," she said equably. "You don't believe yourself."

"Start making sense."

"I asked you what it was you really wanted."

"And I told you."

"You told me what you thought I wanted to hear. Because it's what *you* want to hear."

As he started to turn away, she said, "What you really want, Leviathan, is the only thing that makes sense. The only thing that will make you whole." As he remained silent, she concluded: "You want to return to the light."

38

EMMA AWOKE TO THE BEATING OF HER HEART. IT FELT LIKE drumbeats. Part of something wild, untamed. Wagner's "The Ride of the Valkyries," for instance. Emma recalled her heart in Surah's hands, on Osiris's scale, and, breathless, she felt animal panic seize her.

The Regent's face bent over her. He was doing his best not to look forbidding. She thought that it must take a great deal of effort, and this made her laugh out loud.

"I'm pleased to see that you're feeling better," the Regent said through his quizzical look.

Emma sat up slowly, but not slowly enough. As a wave of vertigo overcame her, her fall backward was arrested by the Regent's strong arm. Still, the room swam around her and when she said, "Where am I?" her voice was thick and muzzy, as if she were still asleep.

The Regent offered her a hot liquid, thick with an edge that briefly burned her throat before warming her insides like a wood fire easing winter's chill. She felt almost instantly better, as her body absorbed its sustenance.

Seeing that she was more herself, the Regent said, "My sister and I were worried about you."

"I didn't think anything worried you."

The Regent, a dour being by nature, did his best to smile.

"And speaking of your sister," Emma said, looking around, "where is Surah?"

"Tending to family matters."

"That tells me exactly nothing," Emma told him.

The Regent guided her as she stood up, held on until she nodded, assuring him that her equilibrium had returned. Still, her fingertips gently probed the area between her breasts.

"Just a small white line remains," the Regent reassured her.

"Will it fade?"

"You won't want it to," he said, not unkindly. "It will serve as a reminder that you are what you are."

"I don't need—"

"In times of extreme duress it will serve you well."

She looked at him curiously. "What a strange creature you are!"

"I think, Emma, that we are strange creatures to each other." That ghostly smile returned. "I do not believe that should be a bad thing."

She took a deep breath, let it out slowly. "I feel . . ."

"Disoriented," the Regent proffered.

"Yes. Exactly. Disoriented." She looked around again. They were in a perfectly square white room with nothing in it save the bed she had woken up in, a nightstand with a naphtha lamp and the empty vessel from which she had drunk the fiery elixir the Regent had given her on it, and a wooden chair with a woven rush seat. The walls were bare. A single window provided a vista across the valley. There were two doors, one on either side of the room. "Am I back in Surah's home?"

He nodded. "I carried you here after you collapsed."

"It seems rather—"

"Austere?"

"Antiseptic. More so even than the surgery where I was taken earlier."

"This is where I sleep."

Emma's curiosity increased elevenfold. "You don't have your own home? I imagined the Regent would live in a magnificent palace or a stone castle surrounded by a moat filled with hungry crocodiles."

"That would be cruel," the Regent said. "To the crocodiles."

"You were cruel to me."

"No, Emma. Just severe." He paused, seemingly unsure in which way to steer the conversation. "I admit that I misjudged you. I did you and my sister a disservice."

"I accept your apology." It was raining outside, or whatever passed for rain in this Sphere. The valley was veiled in mist. The weather mirrored the mood that had taken hold of her. "Tell me, Regent, do you ever eat?"

He gestured. "As you can see, I have no appetites."

"That is a great pity." Emma turned away from the window. "My appetites are great, and right now I'm starving."

THE INSTANT he took her out of the white room, color took over. Surah's colors. Emma thought she loved Surah. Not as she loved Lilith, of course—whose absence sent a pang of longing through her core—but as someone with whom she could share feelings and dreams. Someone Lilith would love as well.

They passed through a room with a pond. Frogs rose from the water to sit on lily pads. A jeweled dragonfly poked through the water lilies, searching for tiny insects. A pair of water-spiders skated across the other side of the pond, keeping well away from the dragonfly. The air was sweet, heavy with oxygen exhaled by the plants.

In the vast kitchen, they sat together at a long table, while others cooked and served. Eggs whose yolks held a greenish cast, toast, smoked fish, a pyramid of glistening gray fish roe. Emma ate greedily, her hunger needing to be assuaged. The Regent did not partake, but given what he had said this was no surprise.

"You have no appetites," Emma said, during a lull in her eating while she allowed her stomach to catch its breath, "but it seems Surah does."

Again, he appeared to consider how to answer. "My sister is different," he told her at length. "She harbors a great affinity for humans."

"I can feel that."

"I'm sure you can." He studied her for some time as she resumed eating. "What does that do for you?"

"What? Eating? It satisfies me." She put down her spoon with its mouthful of roe. "You don't understand."

"I confess I do not."

She picked up the spoon, held it out to him. When he hesitated, she said, "Surah eats this. It won't kill you." Then: "You might even like it."

"I very much doubt that." But he took the spoon, stared at its contents for a moment, then with an almost convulsive gesture, put it in his mouth. He handed the spoon back to her as he chewed and swallowed.

Scooping up a second spoonful, she said, "Another?"

After that, they ate together. Emma could see that as the strangeness of the tastes and textures faded he began to enjoy the food.

When at last they were done, he turned away and was sick. The kitchen staff immediately scuttled over to clean up.

"I'm sorry," Emma said, distressed. "I guess being close to humans isn't that easy."

He wiped his lips and said, "Next time it will be better." What he meant was if Surah can do it so can I.

By mutual consent, they rose. He guided her to a room with a smaller pond, the shallow water alive with koi. She could see the flashing reds and golds of the fish, their amusing way of shimmying through the water.

"I must ask you a question."

"Anything," Emma said. She was surprised at how much she had enjoyed his company at breakfast, not counting the moment of unpleasantness, for which she blamed herself.

"You and your brother are Aqqibari."

"As I have said."

"You know there are destined to be four."

"I didn't." Emma was momentarily surprised. "But then I know so little about being an Aqqibari. I am sorely lacking in details."

His face fell. "So you don't know the identities of the other two."

"I'm sorry, I don't." She peered at him. "Why is this important?"

"You understand that you are a vital part of God's defense against the Sum of All Shadows."

"That much I do know."

"Whatever your function, as war between the Fallen and the human Sphere breaks out prior to Lucifer's assault on Heaven, it cannot be effected until the four of you are united. And, unfortunately, the Sum of All Shadows and his army are at this moment marching toward the Rift between his realm and yours."

Emma felt a stab of panic. "But that task seems impossible. I don't even know where my brother is. How are we to find him and the other two Aqqibari in time?"

THROUGH THE pearling mist, Chynna could just make out glimpses of Lilith, flickering as if they were in a dense forest. She did not know where they were. She did not like where they were. This was Conrad's prison, devised for him, she imagined, by Leviathan himself. But, if so, where was Conrad? Lost within the labyrinth as she and Lilith seemed to be.

But Lilith did not appear lost. She moved as if she knew more or less where she was headed. How she could have picked up any clue in this fog-bound land was beyond Chynna. She was more than a little put out that Lilith could do something she couldn't. From the moment she left Arwad with the golden apple and forged a new life for herself, she was used to being the queen bee, having more power than anyone else around her—apart from Leviathan, that is. Now Lilith was front-running her and she did not like that at all. She picked up her pace, determined to press any and all advantage she could muster.

IN THE presence of her mother, Molly became a child again. She wept tears of bitterness and joy. She fought the intimacy of her mother, who sought to hug her; it was too much and not enough. Her mind became a battlefield with conflicting emotions fighting for supremacy.

I hate you, she thought. *I love you,* she thought. And then: *I have nowhere to go in between,* and the tears spilled onto her cheeks again.

"Molly."

The sound of her mother's voice both soothed her and infuriated her. The tones touched her in the deepest, most protected part of her brain where primitive memories cluster. She slapped her mother across her face—her beautiful face, like looking in a mirror. Was she punishing her mother, or herself? Both, maybe.

"I'm lost," she whispered. "I've always been lost." Tears shivered in her eyes. "You made me lost." Her hand balled into fists. "You, you, you."

"Molly." Surah's hair flowed around her like a halo, first deep red, then the color of copper, melting.

Only later would Molly truly register the oddity of her mother's green eyes. For the time being there was an overload of sensory information muddled with her reopened emotional wounds.

"You let them take me away." Molly was shaking in her rage. "Why didn't you want me?"

Her anguish was like an arrow piercing Surah's flesh. Her daughter's loneliness wrenched her heart, and she heard again her brother's admonition, *"You're a fool for believing in humans. You're doubly a fool for getting too close."* As he had stared pointedly at her bulging stomach. *"Now look at what you've done!" "It's what I wanted from the start,"* she'd said. *"Triply a fool, then."* And he had walked away, washing his hands of her folly.

Now here was the product of her exploration of humankind, hurt and rageful, and Surah, having no experience with children, did not know how to comfort her. For a breathless instant, she wondered whether her brother was right. Was her coupling with a human an act of hubris, her desire for a child an act of selfishness?

No, no. Ten thousand times no!

"Molly, please. . . ." With sorrow and doubt laying waste to her elation, she stumbled over the words. And then something deep inside her kicked in, pushing all rational thought aside, fighting its way to the surface. "Molly, I love you," she whispered. "I've loved you from the moment you were conceived."

Her daughter stared at her with red-rimmed eyes. "How . . . ?" Molly began. "How can I trust anything you say?"

Again without thought, with only instinct to guide her, Surah produced her own octagon. "Do you have yours?" A mother's instinct.

Eyes wide and staring, Molly pulled hers out, displayed it in the palm of her hand. It had turned a gorgeous shade of blue-green, the precise color of the one Surah held. They were twinned.

"I left that with you," Surah said, "so that you would know I loved you, even though I could not be with you."

Molly stared at her, standing on the knife-edge of indecision.

"The medallion brought you to me," Surah said. "Across the years, across all the Spheres, it guided you home."

Molly clasped the medallion. It was as hot as her palm. "Why? Why did you let them take me away from you?" she wailed.

Surah sighed. The ice had been broken, if only on the surface. She had no illusions; there were many miles to go before the thaw. If it ever came. *Don't think like that!* she admonished herself.

They were still in the entryway. "I will try to explain it all, Molly." She lifted an arm. "Will you accompany me to a more comfortable venue?"

After some hesitation, Molly followed her down a wide corridor. Water tumbled and gurgled in a waist-high sluiceway down one side. She dipped her fingertips, trailing them along as she went. The water felt good, momentarily calming her wildly thumping heart. Sadly, it didn't last.

"Your journey was long," Surah said. "Are you thirsty? Hungry?"

Molly shook her head. Her bitterness ascended from the pit of her stomach, burning her throat. She swallowed hard, and again, but the lump in it wouldn't go away. The truth was she could use a glass of water—a whole pitcherful!—but she was not yet ready to accept a kindness from her mother, let alone break bread with her.

As she passed the open doorway into the kitchen, she caught a fleeting glimpse of two people eating at the far end of a long table, but was too preoccupied to pay them any mind. They moved deeper into the interior, until at last, passing through two sets of heavy hardwood doors, they entered a suite of rooms that, by their intimate aspect, Molly guessed were her mother's private quarters. The rooms had an aqueous air about them, from the colors of the walls to the sinuous nature of the upholstered sofas and settees. The low tables were made from found wood, sanded, polished, and sealed without in any way changing their original shapes.

The third room, larger than the first two, was taken up by yet another pool, fed by water arcing from the mouths of a pair of carved stone carp. Around the perimeter a forest of leafy plants and flowering shrubs displayed themselves like bathing beauties. Surah stood on the edge of the pool facing Molly. Molly caught a flash of what appeared to be scales running along either side of Surah's neck, dimly refracting the gray daylight filtering down through an immense skylight. Rain pattered against the triangular panels, running like Molly's tears.

She watched as Surah waved a hand. Above them, the panels folded back, letting the rain in, falling on them both. Now her mother's eyes took her breath away. Her mother regarded her evenly. A smile wreathed her face. It took a bit for Molly to realize the smile was a step toward reconciliation.

No. Just no. She crossed her arms over her chest. "So." Her voice was cool, distant, but underneath her emotions were running wild.

"I have a weakness for—"

"Stop," Molly said. "Your eyes. The pupils are vertical. And they have nictitating membranes."

"You have nictitating membranes, as well." Surah's expression was most beguiling. "We're part crocodile."

Jesus, no, Molly thought, even as her heart thundered in her ears. "Open your mouth wide," she said, giving away nothing of the wildness building inside her.

Surah did not respond to her request. "You do want to know what happened."

"Yes." Molly nodded. "Of course."

"As I was saying, I have a weakness for humans, one that my brother does not share."

"Did you love my father?" Molly broke in.

"Certainly not."

Molly felt a quick stab in her belly. "Yet you fucked him." Her voice was harsh, another storm rapidly building.

"Out of curiosity, yes. Please don't look so shocked, I'm being honest."

"So I'm a product of your curiosity," Molly said acidly.

Surah sighed again. "Obviously, I'm not good at this. I'm getting it all wrong." She licked her lips, started over again. "I didn't want your father, Molly. I wanted *you*. I wanted a child."

Molly's eyes narrowed. She could scarcely breathe. "But not with your own kind."

"Please understand, I am one of the Four Medius. Two sisters, two brothers. We cannot breed; my brothers do not manufacture sperm."

"You are Medius! You are Surah! I met your sister."

"Oq Ajdar—you two have met."

"The chimera." A peculiar shiver went through Molly as she recalled the chimera's piercing gaze, so powerful it had dizzied her. "I have."

"How did she impress you?"

"Favorably." Oq Ajdar had laughed. *Was it at me, as I had thought? No! It was because she recognized me. Her niece.* "A bit forbidding, but I liked her. She helped Bravo."

"I see."

Molly's eyes narrowed again. "What does that mean?"

"I was the first, but it seems that now all of the Four Medius have become involved in the affairs of humankind."

"The specter of war has changed everyone and everything."

"I agree completely." Surah nodded gravely. "And it will soon consume us, Medius and humans alike. Which means I was right to move closer to humans, to have a baby with one."

Molly felt another wave of resentment. Her emotions, ugly and raw, recommenced bleeding. "Now you're saying that I'm a child of convenience."

"Not at all." Surah's lips pursed. "Forgive me, Molly. As I have said, when it comes to my child my communication skills are sadly inadequate. But I am learning." She smiled. "You are teaching me."

"It's 'I'm' and 'you're.'" Molly's voice was still harsh, quick to judge.

Her mother regarded her quizzically.

"Instead of 'I am,' say 'I'm.' Instead of 'you are,' say 'you're.' Contractions make your speech less formal," Molly explained.

Surah absorbed this lesson at once. "A mother shouldn't speak to her daughter formally, is that correct?"

"It is."

"It's?"

This brought a sound bubbling out of Molly. "Not in this case. English is a complicated language."

"Puzzling, too, I think."

Molly could think of nothing in response. She was torn between again striking the woman who had abandoned her or fleeing, forgetting she had ever been here.

"But then my own brother is a puzzlement to me," Surah went on. "He seems to have been born with no empathy for anyone or anything."

"A perfect personality for a neutral, don't you think?" Molly honing the edge to her voice.

"If that is so, then I'm happily imperfect."

With battlements raised, Molly leaned forward, her expression dark, her heart still stormy. "We're still dancing around the elephant in the room."

Surah shook her head. "I don't understand."

"Did you put up a struggle when my father took me away from you?"

When Surah declined to answer, Molly pressed on: "Why not? You claim to love me. If you did, how could you let it happen?"

"My brother said it was the best thing for you. You're half-human, after all. He said there were no facilities here to provide for you. No friends, for instance."

"From what you've told me about him, of course he would say that. He just wanted to get rid of me."

"He said you were better off in the company of your own kind."

"My father—what you call 'my own kind'—raped my cousin, my sister, Lilith. Every night. Until she outgrew his depraved tastes. Then he set his sights on me."

Surah, eyes wide and staring, clapped her hands over her ears.

"That's not going to help. The truth is the truth. You can't shut it out."

Surah tried to take her daughter in her arms, but Molly evaded her embrace.

"But how . . ." Surah, defeated, began in a faint voice, ". . . how was I to know?"

"A mother—a *real* mother—wouldn't have taken the chance by giving away her child."

Into the charged silence, Surah finally said, "And your adoptive mother? What did she do?"

Molly felt as if Surah had thrown ice water into her face. *What* had *Lilith's mother done?* Molly asked herself. *What if she knew, and did nothing? What if she was too weak to . . .*

Their house was not so big. How could she not *know?*

Oh, God! Oh, Christ!

"*You* are my own kind," Molly blurted. And shoved her mother backward into the pool.

Floored by what she had just done, Molly looked down at Surah, who stared back at her unblinkingly. Head out of the water, bobbing. She seemed to have taken Molly's outburst with equanimity. Neither of them moved. Neither of them said a word.

Molly's breath came hard and fast. Her heart seemed to be living in her throat, paining her with each double-beat. Diamond tears trembled in the corners of her eyes, but she refused to give vent to them; she had already revealed too much weakness.

Not again, she thought. *Never again.*

A curious thing happened at that moment. Having vomited up the bolus of rage she had carried inside her for so long, she felt suddenly drained of the poison she had been husbanding for years. A chunk of her iciness calved away into the pool, where it melted by Surah's side.

She peered down at Surah with a newfound curiosity, and something else besides. Time passed; perhaps a great deal of it. Gradually, the rhythm of the two women's breathing coalesced, like those of a mother and the infant she cradles against her chest.

Something passed between them, then, though neither of them could say just what.

"Molly, I'm so, so sorry. From the moment I birthed you I've done everything wrong."

"Don't expect sympathy." And yet Molly's voice was without spite or even a hard edge.

"I don't expect anything." Surah lifted a hand out of the water. "I do love you. More than I can ever articulate. You are of me. You *are* me. It was a long time coming, but the scales have fallen from my eyes."

Thoughts flew through Molly's head like birds scattering before a burst of emotion. Quite deliberately, she removed her boots and socks, her toes wriggling in their freedom. She lowered her feet into the pool. How delicious. How soothing. As the cool water rose to just above her ankles, she stared down. Through the lens of the water her feet were white, thin, and delicate as a fish's fins.

"What a woman you've become," Surah whispered in awe. She laughed softly as a crimson-and-gold dragonfly alighted on the back of Molly's hand.

Molly felt a stillness wash away the last crust of anger that had hardened her heart. Lifting her hand, she examined the dragonfly. Was it her imagination or was the insect examining her? It lifted off, alighted upon Surah's shoulder, seemingly comfortable there. Still, it seemed to be regarding her with its many-faceted eyes. What did it see? Who did it think Molly was?

Smiling, her mother backpedaled as smoothly as a seal. Or a crocodile. "Won't you join me? I would love to see your beautiful nictitating membranes again."

At last, someone to show them to, someone who will understand and not consider me a freak. She recalled Lilith intruding while she was showering, scaring her silly, and how she felt compelled to turn away so her sister would not see, and think her weird.

Yes, yes, she thought. *Yes. Now.* Her heart leapt like an excited fish as she slipped into the water, and thought, *I'm home.*

39

"YOU WILL BE DIFFERENT," MARY SAID, "NOW THAT THE LIDERC has touched you."

"Different how?" Bravo asked.

"You will see for yourself." There was no guile in Mary's face, nor an iota of triumph.

They remained standing on the windswept mountain arête where, moments before, Bravo had struggled with the Liderc. A dark oval on the uneven rock was the only physical evidence that the succubus had existed.

"Don't worry, darling." She smiled. "It is the way of things."

Bravo was irked. "Is that why you brought me here, a test of strength with the Liderc?"

"I did not summon the Liderc. I have not the ability. No one has. I did not know who or what would come. The Liderc arrived of her own accord."

"Because of me?"

"Partly," Mary confessed. "But also because this is a place of sacrifice, like Gulgoleth." Gulgoleth was the Hebrew form of Golgotha, the hill outside the walls of ancient Jerusalem where Christ, along with two common thieves, was crucified.

The wind had shifted, the temperature dropped, and now rain as hard as buckshot stung them hard enough so that they retreated inside Mary's residence. It was like stepping back into the time of the Crucifixion. The living quarters beside the manger. Crude wooden furniture was scattered about a soot-and-creosote-encrusted hearth, where a fire crackled beneath an iron pot hung on a hook attached to a crossbar. Rough-hewn shelves held leather-bound books, much paged-through, small statuettes, presumably of Mary's bevy of patron saints. A small kitchen, a square table with a pair of rickety chairs. A large carved image of Christ on the cross, brown and gold and bloodred, hung on one wall. Opposite, a tapestry of Christ rising from the dead, amid a flurry of angels and Cherubim. In all, the room exuded a suffocating atmosphere, burdened with reminders of the wages of sin, sacrifice, the promise of resurrection. To the extent Bravo expected to see any trace of how Mary had effected his healing he was disappointed; there was none. Nor were there any photos, any means of communication, nothing whatsoever from the modern world at large.

Bravo took all this in with a single, sweeping glance, as he stripped off what was left of his clothes and donned the pants, shirt, and waist-length jacket Mary had made for him, folded on a wooden stool.

"So," he said, when he was once again fully clothed, "the Liderc . . ."

"The Liderc never met a male she didn't love." Mary settled herself into the depths of a cushioned rocking chair that had the look of her favorite indoor perch. "When she parts the curtain and peers into her prey's mind she falls deeply, irrevocably in love."

The clothes were of hand-spun cotton, rough against his skin. "And yet she kills him."

"It's a paradox, you see, darling. It's in the Liderc's nature to torture and kill the thing she loves the most. A sorrowful existence, don't you think?"

"I think she nearly did me in." He stepped to the square soapstone sink, drew himself a cup of water.

"But she didn't." Mary watched him swallow the water down. "And she knew she wouldn't the moment she touched you."

"What d'you mean?" Bravo put the cup down, came over to the hearth. It smelled of burnt wood and stewed meat. The warmth of the flames felt good on his back. "She came at me. She crawled all over me."

"Because she loved you the most of all her victims, darling."

"Why?"

Mary rose and, stooping, stirred the iron pot with a large wooden spoon. "She knew that you would kill her."

"She couldn't have known."

Mary nodded, stood back up, glistening spoon in hand. "It's true, darling. And there was pleasure for her in that knowledge. To be killed as she killed." She cocked her head. "Poetic justice, don't you think? Along with a kind of release."

Bravo turned away, stared out across the abyss toward the farther mountain peaks, but there was nothing to see there. The sill was unfinished, leaking air like a sieve. There were a handful of long, slender nails in one corner; she had obviously left off work when she had brought him back. He took one up, studying it to see what kind of metal it was made of. It was black; not of his world, but of this one. "I'll only ask this one more time," he said. "Why have you brought me here?"

"You don't know? You haven't figured it out yet?"

"What I know—" He swung back to face her. "What I know is that I've been here too long. There are people—friends of mine, colleagues—who are looking for me."

"There are others who want you dead—or worse." She jerked her chin in the direction of his maimed left hand. "I see they have already started."

"That was my decision," he said with a distinct edge.

"Ah, so you're not above sacrifice." Mary nodded. "Like the apostles, except, unlike you, they were cowards." Her voice turned bitter. "It was the apostles-to-be who insisted that the artist leave Lucifer out of the painting, to leave a gap where he sat."

"I suppose it's obvious why."

"They were shrewd ones, darling. They were considering their legacy. And how would it look if he appeared in the painting—of an event they would ensure would be portrayed, copied, and repeated endlessly in the centuries to come?" She began stirring her brew again, slowly and with great deliberation. "No, the four of them were protecting themselves, their spotless images. They did not like Lucifer; they did not trust him."

"They trusted Judas," Bravo pointed out.

Mary laughed. "Proof that they were fallible."

"Unlike God."

"Well . . ." Mary turned away to sip the contents of the spoon, blowing across it first. She nodded to herself, satisfied. "Lucifer never forgave them, you know. It was a bad start—very bad. The incident coughed up the evil hiding inside him like smoker's blood."

Bravo studied her, mulling over the implications of what she'd just said.

"According to you the incident at the Last Supper was the start of it all. The enmity—"

Coming away from the hearth, she shrugged. "That enmity is primordial. It existed long before, but the Last Supper was an acorn that, over time, and with the proper incentives, turned into an immense oak." She gestured as she sat back down. "But come. Sit with me. Have no fear or trepidation. Here you are protected from your enemies and their plans for you."

"But not from the Liderc, clearly."

Mary shook her head emphatically. "Ah, that encounter was something different. It was a trial you had to go through."

"Why?"

"I told you. The Liderc's touch changed you. It was a necessary change to help prepare you for what is to come."

"Then, if I am prepared, allow me to leave." Despite her invitation he had remained standing.

"I advise against it in the strongest possible terms." Mary lifted her hands from her lap. "But if that is your choice I will not stand in your way."

"I'm not leaving until you tell me the final piece of the secret of the missing place in *The Last Supper.*"

"I have told you why he wasn't painted in, why there is only a blank space at Christ's right hand."

"Honestly," Bravo said, "I don't believe that Lucifer was at the Last Supper. Why would he be there? Those who would become the apostles—Christ himself—wouldn't have allowed it."

"As I have said I was an eyewitness, darling. I saw it all."

"So you say." Bravo's voice was edged in skepticism. "But if you're telling the truth, you'll tell me why Christ tolerated him at that Passover seder."

"Well. He had no choice, really, darling. Lucifer is his brother."

40

MAROU, EATER OF CHILDREN, FIRST SPHERE CHERUBIM, RODE a steed's length behind and to the left of Lucifer, in the first rank of the Fallen army and its acolyte-slaves.

If he had a reaction to Lucifer's female guise he gave no sign of it. At his left was Astoreth, his own personal acolyte. Astoreth was a Third Sphere angel, but that didn't bother Marou one bit. He was not a stickler for the separation of the Spheres of the Fallen—the ranking system put in place for as long as he could remember. Besides, it was his very private opinion that the three Spheres of the Fallen were the product of humankind's Catholic Church, an artificial entity constantly bound and determined to categorize and catalog everything, even the things, like Marou and Astoreth, which were impossible to categorize. But that was humankind for you, always trying to keep their terror of the unknown in recognizable boxes. As if that would save them!

Marou laughed, a rich, dark sound like the striking of hollow ebony instruments. It would feel very good indeed to help put them all under Lucifer's thumb. He had been aching for this day to dawn, and now that it had he was filled with an elation he could scarcely contain.

"Azazel is not with us," Astoreth said over the noise of the steeds' hooves, the jangling of Lucifer's armor, and the grunting of the Fallen behind them. "Have you seen him?"

Astoreth's question pulled the Eater of Children back from his musing. "I haven't." When had he become so philosophical? Perhaps it was a product of the End Times, when all things changed.

"If he isn't here," Astoreth wondered, "where is he?"

"He was summoned to the Baatara Gorge cavern, but he should have been back in plenty of time to saddle up."

"Then . . ."

Marou shifted in his saddle. "Something has delayed him." First Leviathan, now Azazel. The End Times were a mystery, it seemed, to everyone save the Sum of All Shadows.

A half mile later, Azazel appeared, riding past them, galloping full out astride Turael, the bloodred Orus he himself had bred and raised from a whelp. That animal would follow him to the ends of the Spheres, give its life for his.

Azazel gave Marou a curt nod as he passed. When he came up level with Lucifer, he leaned in and said something neither Marou nor Astoreth could hear. Nodding, the Sum of All Shadows spurred his war-mount, Azazel by his side, putting some distance between them and the others. Astoreth glanced at Marou, who shrugged, maintaining his steady pace. But his eyes did not leave the two, already deep in discussion.

"AND EMMA Shaw?" Lucifer asked.

"She is precisely where you said she would be," Azazel replied.

"Excellent."

Azazel shook his head. "I don't know how you managed it."

"And that is the way it will remain."

Sensing that the gap between them and Marou had shrunk, the Sum of All Shadows dug his spurs into his Orus's muscular flanks. The dry seabed across which the chargers' hooves thundered was brittle as battle-scarred bones. He had changed genders at Azazel's approach. Now his lambent eyes blazed through the slots in his helmet. "She still believes that she was close to Solomon's gold."

Azazel nodded. "Absolutely."

Lucifer clenched one gauntleted fist. *With the Shaws there is always a need for subterfuge and misdirection,* he thought. *Keeps them chasing their tails instead of being where they ought to be.*

"And further."

"I engaged her in combat," Azazel said, though he had hoped to avoid recounting these details. "Wielding the cold fire, she is a formidable opponent. Nevertheless, I prevailed. She fell, semiconscious. I would have slaughtered her where she lay, but—"

Without warning, Lucifer's hand shot out, grabbed Azazel's tunic in his gauntlet, nearly dragging him off his Orus. "What did I tell you about acting extemporaneously?"

"You told me to follow your orders to the letter."

"And yet you raised your sword."

"The Medius prevented me from striking Emma Shaw's head from her body."

"Just as she was meant to."

"I thought—"

"You weren't made for thinking." Lucifer spat. "Follow, don't lead."

"Yes, Lord."

Lucifer shook Azazel so hard Turael bucked and whinnied, turning its leonine head in Lucifer's direction.

"You had better direct your beloved prince to settle down before I put you both out of your misery."

Bending low over Turael's snorting head, Azazel whispered into its ear. At once, the Orus calmed, and Azazel sat up in the saddle with exaggerated military precision.

It is as I predicted, Lucifer thought. *The Medius are involved with the affairs of humans and angels. Those hundzarim. They have abrogated their brief of neutrality. Yet more proof as if any were needed that the Shaws are marshalling their family. Well, that plan will arrive stillborn. Finally, I have found the way to neutralize Bravo Shaw.*

His eyes cut toward Azazel, he relinquished his grip. He felt only contempt for all of them—all of the Fallen. How they lacked for anything and everything! With a violent spasm, his hatred of them burst forth, sickening him. Was there no one with whom he could converse, no one in whom he could confide? *This* was his true prison, not this dreary place where God had seen fit to mete out their punishment, far from their sight.

He glanced behind him. Pestilence, as far as his eye could see. He was ashamed of these things, these Fallen angels who had so ineptly lost the first uprising for him. He had been a fool to count on them in a firefight against St. Michael and his Angels of Sanctification. But he had learned his lesson. Millennia of scheming had provided him with the answer at last. It had taken him all this time to figure out where King Solomon had secreted his cache of gold. In his wisdom, Solomon had done what Lucifer liked to do. Employing a magician's misdirection, he had his Phoenician architects draw up plans for the caverns in Tannourine to his alchemists' specifications. That was where he would stash his gold, yes? That was what the king's cadre of alchemists and his greedy son surmised, anyway. But they were wrong; they found only the barest number of bars. Solomon knew full well the myriad failings of his one male progeny. Other kings and queens coming after Solomon would have murdered a son so weak-willed and grasping. But Solomon was not like them, not at all. And yet, he knew he needed to do something to protect the bulk of the gold after he was gone.

He waved his magician's wand, hiding the gold in another place, another direction, far away from the maze of caverns he had ordered his Phoenicians to build. For so long this misdirection had led Lucifer, like all others who studied the arcane histories, to chase his tail, and always, like them, his hands came up empty. Then, after the breach had been widened, he had chosen a Second Sphere Power by the name of Beleth to look into the place where King Solomon was buried. He chose Beleth because he was a nothing, beneath everyone's notice. In fact, Lucifer had to look three times before he saw him the first time. Far beneath the sepulcher where clever looters were drawn, where even more clever archeologists followed in their wake, Beleth journeyed at his Lord and Master's orders.

The body of the king had not been found in the sepulcher, but neither had Beleth found it in the place far beneath. *So, then, where had Solomon been buried?* Lucifer asked himself. *Where would this mighty magician have his corpse placed, if not alongside that which was most precious to him—his cache of alchemical gold?*

Another century passed while Lucifer made lists of the king's favorite places, while he sent out this Beleth to each one. Once, he was sure Beleth had found Solomon's final resting place, beneath the ancient stone temples of Lalibela in Ethiopia. In fact, it was to this very spot that Conrad Shaw, having dedicated much of his adult life to the study of King Solomon, brought W. B. Yeats just after the end of the First World War. But he, like trusty Beleth, had failed to find any trace of either Solomon or his gold.

What had stuck in Lucifer's ever restless mind was Solomon's obsession with trade and trade routes. The king understood, long before any of his peers, that the key to fortune and influence in the ancient world was dominating the local trade routes. This could not be accomplished without mastery of the desert—immense swaths of blinding sunlight and baking sand dunes. For this, Solomon looked to the Nabateans, who inhabited the area now known as Jordan. Early on in his reign, he forged a treaty with this powerful, nomadic tribe. In exchange for their expertise, Solomon provided them access to areas of his magic.

Solomon visited Petra, the seat of Nabatean civilization, many times, but always in secret, traveling by night, cloaked and disguised, in the company of a special Nabatean caravan of protectors. At Petra, Beleth had learned, the king had built a sorcerous place of serenity and repose for Aretas II, the Nabatean king: a large open plaza with only a modest-sized structure for Aretas II to take a break from the complexities of reigning over an entire civilization. No one save the two mighty kings knew of it, let alone was invited there. In this secret place, the two monarchs spent many pleasant hours in discourse on various subjects of interest to them both. Often, Solomon would bring scrolls and manuscripts already ancient even in that time and Aretas II the most precious of Nabatean writings and maps. Together, the kings pored over these artifacts, absorbing arcane wisdom otherwise lost to time.

With this knowledge, Lucifer was certain he knew where Solomon's final resting place was, where he had secreted his golden cache. The answer to the riddle that had perplexed thousands over the centuries was a simple one, as all such answers tended to be. Once in possession of the key, even the Gordian knot could be unraveled.

The hidden plaza deep below Petra would be Lucifer's first destination after emerging into the realm of humankind. There, he would grind the gold to dust, feed it to the one hundred Fallen. They would become invincible, even to St. Michael, even to the Shaws, who were even now learning more than they should about being Aqqibari. He needed to stop them before all four were united. For this, he turned to Azazel, whose flaming sword had already defeated Emma Shaw once, and would now do so again.

"I want you to go to Surah's home. Take Marou and whomever else you deem necessary. Find Emma Shaw and the Medius, and deal with them both."

"By what means shall I deal with them?" Azazel inquired.

"By any and all means necessary," Lucifer replied. "Let your sword annihilate everyone in your path."

Azazel's choices of his raiding party were Lucifer's, though, of course, he did not know that. As Lucifer watched them ride off, he already knew the outcome of the confrontation Azazel would lead them into, and he was satisfied. All was going to plan.

CHYNNA, HURRYING on through the mist, reached Lilith just as the young woman was heading through the circular aperture.

"Wait," she called. "Look."

Pulling back, Lilith shook her head. "What?" She was clearly annoyed by the interruption.

Chynna pointed. "A perfect circle. That octagonal medallion your sister carries broke through the membrane as it did the window of the house."

"You're right," Lilith replied. "I'll be sure to thank her." Ducking, she went through the membrane.

"Don't you see?" Chynna called after her. "The medallion led her here. It must have. It knocked down all the barriers that stood in her way."

"What d'you care?" Lilith said over her shoulder. "Molly's not your daughter."

Climbing through the circle, Chynna caught up to Lilith, which was easy enough; Lilith had stopped short, and now Chynna could see why.

They were in someone's home—a large, many-roomed, high-ceilinged palace. Whoever lived here, she thought as they moved quickly from chamber to chamber, loved water above all other elements. And then her heart skipped a beat. She had heard tales about a creature who loved water above all other elements. A creature who, it was whispered, was half-reptile. A creature who was sister to the Regent himself. Is this where they found themselves now, she wondered, in Surah's palace?

She paused, quailing at the thought. Lilith had moved on, and Chynna had lost sight of her, but now she didn't care. The energy here was all wrong; she felt as if she was on the edge of a giant spiderweb. If she took one more step forward she was certain she'd become enmeshed in something that would drag her down, that would destroy her utterly. Besides, staying here would not get her any closer to finding her daughter. Haya was all Chynna cared about. Molly and Lilith had gotten her through the membrane into the sphere where she surmised Leviathan had taken Haya. They had served their purpose. Now they could burn in hell for all she cared.

She heard her name being called. Lilith had discovered that she wasn't right behind her. Chynna could have answered her, could have responded: "I'm coming!" or "Be there in a minute!" or "Go on without me!"

She did none of those things. She turned tail and, as she always did, ran.

THE BEATING of immense wings announced Antiphon's imminent arrival. Bravo glanced at Mary. Despite her assurances that no one would find him here, the great eagle had somehow spied him out. His heart lifted. He wanted no more to do with Mary; the imprint of the Liderc's assault was still deeply upon him, and she with it.

"They're here," he said, and stepped across the threshold of the front door. Mary emerged a pace behind him.

"Who?" she said in a querulous voice. "Who is here?"

Bravo, on the verge of telling her, stopped. Something in her tone—like sudden sunlight revealing the trapper's invisible wire—gave him pause, caused him to rethink his time with her. He used the cold fire in a way she couldn't detect to view her in a new light. Icy, pitiless, the light cast shadows off her, sharp as butcher's knives.

"Whoever you're most afraid of," Bravo said.

Mary shot him a look, and in this new light he saw what he had not before: her eyes were ruby red. He knew what that meant. At that moment, Antiphon, in full flight, soared into view. And there was Ayla, bent over, clutching the eagle's feathers. Seeing his expression, Mary turned. Recognizing Antiphon, she raised her hands. In the new light, Bravo understood immediately that this gesture wasn't defensive—not at all.

She had cast a spell over him while he was still unconscious. The blue fire had boiled it away. He could feel the energy she was generating from deep inside her, could sense the dark bedlam working its way outward toward Mary's hands. Except that she wasn't who she said she was. In the new light, he saw her real identity, though it was unknown to him. Something new, something dark, something very, very evil.

The sorcerous energy reached her hands. They were outstretched toward Antiphon and Ayla.

Before he could bring forth the full power of the cold fire, she turned on him. And now, even without the new light, she was revealed—and what a grotesquery she was: hideous, feral, jaws like a jackal, teeth like a wolf, eyes like a vulture. Her hair was a long, tangled mass the color and texture of charred skin; strands of it kept falling away, spiraling as they floated down.

This was what Ayla saw as Antiphon reared back, talons outstretched for a landing. But in the new light, Bravo saw even beyond this second guise, to the inner being, the servant of the Sum of All Shadows, a Fallen angel so far beyond redemption its wings had been amputated. There were the stubs between its sharp shoulder blades. Somehow, through a dark spell, they had grown claws of their own, which contracted spastically, as if trying to rend the air itself. And now Bravo recognized the monstrous creature from his extensive readings in Asian myths and folklore. This was a Churel, another form of succubus. Originating in Persia, Churel migrated to India and thence to Pakistan, as well. They were born of women who had died in childbirth. Their rage and desire to revenge themselves on all males was legendary.

And now the Churel opened its maw, its tongue emerged, gray as rotting flesh, and Bravo felt the terrible pain returning to his back, his left hand, his entire body as all the healing "Mary" had effected was reversed. Or maybe it had never been done, maybe it was part of the spell the Churel had put him under while he was still unconscious.

His back arched, his face froze in a grimace of agony. Ayla saw this and spoke to Antiphon, trying to get her to pull up, to delay her landing, but it was too late. The snare the Churel had set was triggered. A sorcerous net swept around the great eagle, capturing her. Antiphon struggled against it, but the more vociferously she fought the tighter the net became.

Bravo could hear Ayla calling his name, but there was a blackness throbbing at the periphery of his vision. Spots danced before his eyes, and his breathing was ragged, as if he could no longer take in enough oxygen. Falling to his knees, he looked up to see the Churel standing in front of him. His neck hurt, as if he had been choked or strangled. A sudden flash of the succubus sitting astride him as she cast her spell bloomed behind his eyes. He tried to conjure up the pages of the ancient texts he had read on Churels.

"What . . . what is it you want?" he managed to get out.

The Churel grinned down at him. "I have what I want."

"Take what you want from me," he told her. "Let them go."

The Churel crouched down so they were on the same level. Its charnel-house stench made him want to gag, caused another memory flash: the Churel bent over him, the noxious fumes from its half-open mouth, filthy hands around his neck, squeezing, squeezing while it chanted in some long-forgotten language. The very sound of the syllables raked his memory with the force of teeth crunching through sinew and bones.

"You poor fool." She took his jaw in her hand, pulled it and his torso toward her. "I've already gotten what I want from you. You are garbage to me now." The Churel's eyes were burning with a zealot's fever. "I brought you here as bait. I wanted the bird—and now I have her." A bubble of saliva appeared at the corner of its mouth. "Tonight I will kill it. I will hang it upside down, slit its neck, and drink its blood. Then I will feast on its raw flesh."

Bravo's stomach churned. "Freak," he said, and spat at her.

"I'm not a freak, darling," the Churel sang to him. "I'm a visionary . . . Ah, the look of horror on your face! Poor thing! You have yet to grasp that I and my kind are in the vanguard of the new order the End Times has established. The hegemony of humankind is over, darling, of this I can assure you. I and others like me will take your place, hour by hour, day by day, until, having served your purpose, you will be annihilated, cast aside and burned in pyres that will turn the skies black and ashen."

He swayed suddenly, as if about to lose consciousness. Grasping the Churel's shoulder to steady himself brought him momentarily closer, and he fought down the urge to vomit. Instead, he palmed the nail he had taken from the windowsill and, with all his strength, pierced the spot where her neck met the base of her skull. He angled it sharply up, buried it in her spinal cord.

The Churel stared at him, eyes almost popping from her head. "How?" she asked. "How did you—?" She keeled over, dead before her head struck the ground.

"IF YOU don't stay still," Ayla said, "I can't help you."

"Where were you when I needed you?" Bravo said, lying on his stomach. "And where is that damn eagle?"

"Right over there." Ayla, keeling beside Bravo, was working on the wounds on his back.

"You both left me on that ledge."

Ayla sighed. “I know. You have a right to be angry.”

“Angry doesn’t even begin to cover it,” he snapped. “First the bird gouges me to within an inch of my life, then the both of you take off.”

“You wouldn’t have survived the flight,” Antiphon told him. “And grabbing you as I did was the only way to save you from falling.” She made a sound in the back of her throat. “You’re welcome. And, by the way, I would appreciate it if you use my name when referring to me.”

After that, Bravo settled down, keeping his peace while Ayla cleaned, disinfected, and stitched up the wounds.

“Thank for getting us out of that snare,” the eagle said softly.

Bravo nodded. “How did you find me, anyway?”

“Your finger,” Antiphon said.

“What about it?”

“I ate it.”

Bravo began to laugh. He laughed so hard tears welled up in his eyes. After all he had been through, all he had endured, to be saved by his own amputated finger caused dissonance in his head, a chord in both a major and a minor key.

“I’ll be damned,” he said, sitting up at last, the pain in his back reduced to a deep ache.

“You almost were,” Antiphon pointed out.

Alarmed, Ayla paused in packing up her medical equipment. “What d’you mean?”

“I told you that a confrontation with a Liderc was very, very bad.” She turned her beady eye on Bravo. “Did she touch you?”

“She did more than that,” Bravo said. “She assaulted me, stripped off my clothes.”

The eagle shook her head. “Not what I meant. Did she *touch* you?”

“Her finger pressed right here,” Bravo said, pointing to the center of his forehead just above the bridge of his nose.

“Ah, ah, ah . . .” Antiphon paced back and forth in a clear state of agitation.

“What’s happening?” Ayla asked, spooked by the eagle’s behavior.

“We did not get here in time,” Antiphon said. “It has happened.”

Bravo scrambled to his feet. In his mind he heard the echo of the Churel’s voice when she still presented herself as Mary: *“You will be different, now that the Liderc has touched you.”*

"How?" he said, his voice thick. "How am I different now?"

"Who did the Liderc appear as after she touched you?"

"My sister, Emma."

Antiphon's agitation increased tenfold. "Then you must not see her," the eagle said. "Ever."

"Not possible," Bravo said. "Brother and sister. We're tied at the hip."

"Not anymore."

Bravo shook his head. "Impossible."

Antiphon said, "If you do see her, you will kill her."

41

"I REJECT CATEGORICALLY EVERYTHING YOU'VE SAID." LEVI-athan glared at Haya. "What you're spouting is no more than a fistful of human psychological jargon. Oh, yes, I am quite familiar with the ways of humans—the darker ways, especially." He laughed, a singularly unpleasant sound, like the wailing of souls in torment.

Oq Ajdar stepped forward. "If that is what you believe then you are both deaf and blind."

"You!" Leviathan jabbed a taloned finger at the chimera. "I will oblige you to keep your opinions to yourself. I've heard enough from all of you"—his finger traced an arc from Oq Ajdar to Haya to Ayeleye—"to last me multiple lifetimes."

His eyes narrowed as he fixed Haya in his implacable gaze. "I may not know what you are, but I know with certainty where you gestated. The fact is your mother's womb is tainted—by what I do not know. But anything that comes out of it is a freak, an abomination." He leaned forward. "You are a freak, Haya. An abomination. You had better face it." The sweeping forefinger again, like sand running through an hourglass. "All of you."

He grunted. "If you won't join me—if you are content to sit back and do nothing while Lucifer changes the balance of things—be my guest. You will have failed in your duty to keep the balance between angels and humans. Isn't that why you were created? Isn't that your one and only purpose?" He looked from one Medius to the other. "Well, isn't it?"

"It is," Oq Ajdar and her brother said simultaneously.

"Then tell me, if you can, how it is that you have allowed yourself to be swayed by the yammering of this child?"

"Every word I say is truth," Haya told him. "The light is within you, Leviathan."

"Light, light! What is this light you speak of?" Leviathan raged. "Foolishness. An inconsequential nothing. Ashes I crush under the heel of my cloven hoof." His finger swung toward her. "I will do these poor Medius a favor and answer my own question. You, Haya, possess a glamour—almost as powerful as mine. Even I can feel its magnetic pull. But rather than allow myself to be sucked into its orbit as Oq Ajdar and Ayeleye have, I reject it outright."

"'I reject.' You have said those words before." Haya appeared curiously unperturbed by his rant. "They hold as much meaning now as they did previously."

"Every word I say is truth," Leviathan answered, deliberately mocking her.

"You would not know the truth if it was a house landing on your head." It was Ayeleye who suddenly piped up. He moved so that he was closer to his sister. "You are a First Sphere Seraph. You live by lies; they are what sustain you. Only Lucifer stands above you."

"Or below," Oq Ajdar interjected. "Depending on your point of view."

"The language of semantics suits you." Leviathan sneered. "Another unhealthy human trait. You have been infected by them—the humans. They have crawled under your skin, and now make their nest in your brains, softening them."

"It's clear enough," Ayeleye said, "that one side doesn't believe the other."

"But why have you taken the side of the child, when I tell you that I will restore the balance between angels and humans?"

"You never said any such thing," Oq Ajdar snapped.

"Well, I'm saying it now," Leviathan told her.

Ayeleye pulled a face. "Please. You would say anything, do anything, spin any number of lies in order to get what you want most—the downfall of Lucifer."

"And how would that be a bad thing?" Leviathan's black lips drew away from his teeth. "I swear that I will restore order, return the balance to what it once was. I will do what needs to be done."

"You," Oq Ajdar said, "who freely transgresses with human females, you who craves only power, who desires more than anything else to be out from under Lucifer's thumb."

"You see? That proves I'm telling the truth."

"And out from God's thumb, as well," the chimera continued. "You, who continually flout rules and regulations, would have us believe that you will happily reinstate them once you overthrow Lucifer?"

"Precisely."

"Do you hear yourself?" Ayeleye's serene demeanor was well-known; it was why Leviathan had mistaken his foppish mien as clownish. But now he was agitated to his core, and this change in his emotional state brought out an awareness and sensitivity that had lain dormant for millennia while he wallowed in the hollowness of his beloved Hall. "God and Lucifer demand the same two things from you: obedience and commitment. But you are incapable of either. This we know firsthand."

"Sometimes," Leviathan said, "in order for things to remain the same, there needs to be change."

"The Medius could not agree more," Oq Ajdar replied, "but one must choose the form of change carefully, lest it arrive in the form of catastrophe."

"I am not that. I am not catastrophe." Leviathan held out a hand. "Look, you know what is coming. Lucifer's host is almost upon us. As Medius, you see it. The time for decision is now. There can be no hesitation, no second-guessing either."

Silence, electric, tense, unsettling.

"It seems," Oq Ajdar said at length, "that we are at something of a standoff."

"Fuck that!" The edge of Leviathan's hand scythed through the air between them. "I want nothing more to do with any of you." He grunted. "It was a mistake to come to you, Ayeleye, I see that now. And following you here with the child was worse."

Haya had been conspicuously silent through the increasingly bitter debate. But as he turned to go, she said, "You cannot leave."

Leviathan's brows rose, all three sets of wings unfolded. His armada of flies returned, black and buzzing like a lumber factory. "Don't be ridiculous. There is nothing you can possibly do to stop me."

"I won't, and neither will the Medius. You will stop of your own accord."

Leviathan laughed; glass shattered somewhere nearby. "You are delusional if for one minute you think—"

"There is a third way." Haya's uncanny eyes bored into the Seraph. "If, as you say, you can be the agent of the change that will reset the balance, you will embrace the light inside you. Otherwise, you are no better than your Lord and Master."

Leviathan's wings worked like bellows: in, out, in, out. His flies hovered, angry, greedy as ever. "And I told you—"

"If, as the Medius expect, you are pure evil, like your Lord and Master, then you're right—you cannot embrace the light. I will be wrong. There is no spark of light inside you." Her voice, her demeanor were relentless, a thoroughly disturbing ability in one so young. And yet, she was an old soul. She must be; there was no other explanation for her mastery of thought and language. "But, hear me, Leviathan, if that is the case—if there is no light within you—then you are not the agent of change you claim to be. You're just another despot, grasping for power."

"Quite a conundrum for you," Ayeleye said. "We are frankly astonished that your mind hasn't exploded with this decision. Continue to lie, and you lose everything. Tell the truth—the objective truth if you are even able—and you may acquire the allies you so desperately need."

Leviathan frowned. "Scylla or Charybdis."

"Here is your essential problem," Haya said. "There is only Charybdis in your choice—the whirlpool in which you will drown. The cliffs opposite the whirlpool hold no many-headed monster."

Leviathan was silent a long time. His mind was in a muddle. At some point he realized that he was frightened. He had seen fright—terror, really—in others often enough, felt the emanations like sweat breaking out on their skin. He came to the reluctant conclusion this was what gripped him now. He was on the edge of Charybdis's undertow, tugged by the insistent surge that threatened to pull him under. Just as the child had said.

He grit his teeth; somewhere outside a tree lost its life. "I . . . I don't know what to do." A tremendously difficult admission, a sign of weakness delivered gift-wrapped to his enemies. But was it? For so long he had believed it so, a hard and fast rule never to be broken or even bent. But that was when he was alone, before he required allies.

"No one can tell you what to do," Haya said. "The first steps are yours to make. I can only meet you halfway."

Self-interest was what always motivated him; that was the eternal way of evil. There had never been a sense in him that what others felt or believed mattered a whit. He was safely locked away in his ironbound tower of certainty. The sacrifice of one for the sake of the many? Never heard of it, or if he had he had laughed in the face of it. How absurd!

But now for things to remain the same, there needed to be change. That much was clear enough. He had boasted that he could be that agent of change. The child intimated this could be so. Was that actually possible? Or was she running a long-game con on him? Studying her with renewed interest he saw something beneath her surface he hadn't noticed before: there was great guile in her, but its nature was one wholly unknown to him. It was not the guile that was second nature to him—to all the Fallen, especially his Lord and Master. It was clear as spring water, not clouded with evil intent.

"The light," he said. "What is it?"

"Acceptance of the greater good," Haya said without hesitation. "Something that you have already categorically rejected."

"Did I?"

Ayeleye made a derisive croak.

"We all need to make up our minds," Oq Ajdar said. "I believe Haya; I believe she—and the Aqqibari—need us to help them restore the balance. There are four. The Shaw siblings are two, and I strongly suspect Haya is the third. The four must act as one in order to triumph over Lucifer and his army."

"I agree, sister," Ayeleye said. "I put my trust in Haya almost from the moment we met. That, for us, is a singular experience."

"And what of me?" Leviathan asked.

"That is the wrong question," Haya said. "That is the question that will send you into the abyss of Charybdis."

"So if I say yes. If I join you. What happens afterward? If the balance is restored I will remained consigned to the dark exile into which God sent us Fallen."

"Perhaps," Haya said. "But perhaps not. There has never been a spark of light in your exile dominion. What do you imagine would happen if you brought that light into your eternal darkness?"

"I don't know."

"Exactly," Haya said. "None of us know. That is where faith comes in. You must have faith that the spark of light exists within you, Leviathan. You must have faith that you will effect change by helping to restore the balance."

"He lost faith when he joined Lucifer's rebellion," Ayeleye pointed out.

"No," Leviathan said. "I lost faith when I could no longer tolerate being yoked to God."

Haya remained placid. "Then you must regain your faith."

Leviathan snorted. "In God? Impossible."

"In God? No," Haya said. "In yourself."

42

CHYNNA RAN. BUT SHE DIDN'T RUN FAR. HER FIRST PANICKED thought had been to return through the opening in the membrane, back to the house, but like a bird on the wing that idea passed soon enough. What was left for her there? Which led to her wondering what had ever been there, save a clever illusion conjured from Leviathan's glamour.

Making a hard right turn just before she reached the circular opening, she tore off into Surah's palace, the membrane vibrating with the speed of her passage. Dodging several of the household staff, she at last found a small room, bare, windowless, shadowed with reflections from a stream running through it, but nothing more. Curled into a corner farthest from the water, she set her shoulder blades against the fastness of the walls and shivered.

She did not like being here, it was true. There was something inimical to her in the very air she breathed. But gradually, as her pulse settled, her resurrected heart stilled in her breast, and she was able to think clearly again.

Being in such a hideaway reminded her of her earliest days, after she had stolen aboard a boat bound for the mainland. In the hold, surrounded by creaking wood, the salt and damp, the minerals of the sea, the bright pink pinpoints of rats' suspicious eyes, she was at last free to be herself. Clutching the golden apple to her as, months later, she would the baby gestating in her belly, she did not feel alone; well hidden, she felt triumphant.

She tried to conjure that same feeling now. No one knew she was here. As far as Lilith knew, she had retreated back into the world of the bronze mirror. At the moment, she was safe. Neither hungry nor thirsty, she wanted for nothing—nothing except Haya. She felt the loss of her daughter as she would the loss of a limb or a lung. Without Haya she was diminished, different, done for. Haya was as different from her first child as day from night. Gideon was hell-spawn, rotten with Leviathan's seed even before his birth. She had loved him because she had needed to love him: he was, at that time, her entire family. Only he had made the long, arduous journey out of Arvad to Jerusalem with her. Though she had protected him all the way, she felt as if it was he who had protected her, that as long as he was in her belly nothing untoward would befall her. But now, belatedly, she realized that it was Leviathan who was protecting her—and Gideon. Now, belatedly, she wished she had smothered him with the thin, meagre pillow the nuns had given her when they had taken her in.

But she had not, and now the entire star-crossed line of Shaws, the name she had given herself to hide from the Sikars and the others who had come after her to bring her and the golden apple back to the island, stretched across the ages, generation after generation, each one more extraordinary than the one before.

Why couldn't she derive solace from that? But no. It wasn't her due at all. It had been effected by those who came after her, those who had the courage and strength to throw off the pernicious effects of her son, born solely out of selfishness, to assuage the loneliness of her exile from Arwad.

But, oh, this child was different! No taint of Leviathan had entered her blood. Her bones were pure, carved from light. A wonderment, she only recognized now that she was away from the Seraph's malign influence. He hated Haya, hated that he did not understand her, that she took Chynna's attention away from him. Chynna understood now how he had worked his glamour to turn her against her own daughter. How she hated him then. Fists clenched, heart hardened. Never again would his dark glamour entrap her. Never again would he penetrate her. Never again would he imprison Haya. And let him just try to hurt her again. She felt forces inside her erupting like lava from a volcano's maw. All directed at him.

Abruptly, her thoughts switched from darkness to the light.

How she missed Haya! She rocked back and forth, her arms wrapped tightly around herself. Without Haya she was nothing. Without Haya she was only Leviathan's concubine. Now, belatedly, she understood what a horror Leviathan was. Then again she was a horror herself: she had failed the primary responsibility of motherhood; she hadn't protected her child from Leviathan's depredations.

She beat the side of her head against the wall at the thought of having him on top of her, inside her. And all the while her child was in that dreadful egg-prison he had devised for her. If she could vomit, she would have, but other than her heart the walls of her organs had turned to petrified amber, hollow chambers, dead. When she ate, for appearance's sake, the food and drink passed through her without being digested. This, also, was what his resurrection had done to her. How she could have allowed it, how she had exulted in it was now a mystery to her. Sorrow overflowed her like a river at the height of a hurricane, and she had to bite down on her knuckle in order not to scream. If she had, she would have woken the dead.

UNLIKE MOLLY, who was too preoccupied with her mother to pay any attention to the couple sitting at the table in the kitchen, Lilith stopped at the kitchen doorway. With a whoop of sheer pleasure she charged in.

The Regent stood up so abruptly his chair crashed over backward, and at once he assumed the aspect of Osiris, high magisterial hat, long black beard jutting from his chin. His eyes were long, heavily kohled, and he held the crook of his office out like a weapon.

But Emma had already turned, saw Lilith, and letting out an answering whoop, ran to her.

The Regent, despite his talk with Emma, watched the two women embrace, kiss, and weep, and had no inkling as to how to feel. Were they injured? Were they sad? It never occurred to him that humans could weep for joy.

"It seems like forever since I've touched you," Lilith whispered huskily.

Emma kissed her again. "I'm sorry I bugged out on you."

Lilith stared into her eyes, her lips curved upward.

"You should be angry," Emma said. "Are you angry? You *are* angry."

Lilith laughed softly. "No, Emma, I'm not."

Anxiety clouded Emma's eyes. "But you were."

"Of course I was!" Lilith exclaimed. "Wouldn't you be?"

"Sure, but I . . ."

"I know. You did it to protect me." Lilith took hold of Emma's shoulders.

"But, come on, you couldn't have imagined that I would just hang around and wait for you to return. You must have realized that I would move Heaven and Earth to follow you."

"I'd hoped you wouldn't."

"Really?" Lilith shook her gently. "Really?"

"I'm just happy you found me," Emma said. "Really."

Lilith kissed her again. "That's better."

"But come to that, how *did* you find me?"

"Maybe you should sit down for this."

Lilith led her back to the kitchen table. The Regent, returning to his dapper form, accepted Emma's introductions with perfect sangfroid, but stepped back, standing as someone apart, content to be a bystander at this feast of human emotion, which, he had to admit, was more to his taste than human food.

Sitting beside her lover, Lilith took her hands in hers. "The way I found you is through your great-grandmother Chynna."

"No." Emma felt all the breath go out of her. "You must be mistaken. She's long dead."

Feeling Emma's hands grow cold, Lilith rubbed them between hers. "She died maybe a century ago, but was resurrected by her lover."

"By Leviathan?" Emma choked, scarcely able to get out the words.

Lilith nodded. She told Emma about the house on the hill above the twisting river. "Molly had glimpsed it when Bravo took her and Ayla to meet Oq Ajdar, one of the Four Medius."

Lilith took a longer look at the Regent. Dutifully, he nodded to her in the way of all human gentlemen. It was curious that, like his brother Ayel-eye, he had adopted the outward accoutrements of humans while having only the most cursory knowledge of them.

"Molly is how I got here," Lilith said. She explained about the bronze mirror in the house Leviathan had built for Chynna. "And Haya," she concluded. "Haya is Chynna's daughter. Well, we think she is, though Molly has had her doubts from the beginning."

She looked around. "And where is Molly? I followed her here. The whole venture was her idea. She's obsessed with finding her mother."

Emma glanced at the Regent. "I have a strong suspicion you know where she is."

He regarded both women for several moments. He found them a curious pair. He did not know what to make of them. Hardly surprising. But his talk with Emma had convinced him that she could be trusted—as his sister had said. He hated when Surah was right, but the simple fact was she was always right, which compelled him to fight against her. Otherwise, he feared she would get a swelled head.

"Stay here," he said. "I will return shortly."

When they were alone, Emma took Lilith's face between her hands, kissed her long and hard. "I won't leave you ever again," she whispered. "I promise."

Lilith smiled. "As you can see, I don't need protecting."

"I do see that. I do."

A rustling at the doorway directed their attention to Molly and a beautiful stately redheaded female.

Emma rose. "Surah." And to her brother: "So this was the 'family business' you said she was on."

"I did not lie," the Regent pointed out, in a brief but rather touching round of self-justification.

"My brother has told me about your beloved, Emma. Your happiness is also mine."

"Thank you. It's a relief to have her by my side again."

"Most excellent." A sly smile wreathed Surah's face as she put her hands on Molly's shoulders. "It is my honor and pleasure to present my daughter."

"You found her!" Lilith was on her feet. "Molly, you found your mother."

"Another Medius," Emma said, rising and coming toward them. "Lilith, this is Surah."

"Look," Molly said, blinking her eyes rapidly. "I'm part crocodile."

Peering at her sister's nictitating membranes, Lilith said, "Why so you are! How is it I failed to notice them before?"

Molly grinned. "I can be rather devious when I have to be."

The two sisters embraced.

"I'm so happy for you," Lilith said, squeezing Molly hard.

Molly briefly rested her forehead against the hollow of Lilith's shoulder, before pulling back. "Now that we're all together—"

"Where is Bravo?" Emma asked.

Surah turned to the Regent. "Brother?"

But he shook his head. "I cannot see him."

"We must find him," Emma persisted. "The three of us aren't strong enough."

"I understand." The Regent's expression darkened. "And this lack makes the conundrum with which we are presented even more urgent. Lucifer is on his way to the Rift. I know what he is after, but I have no idea how to prevent him from obtaining it."

A RAIDING party of powerful Fallen angels was fast approaching Surah's land. Azazel had chosen Marou, despite their enmity, but not Marou's shadow the Third Sphere angel, Astoreth. That was too much risk even for him; with both of them in the raiding party, the possibility of a mutiny was too great.

Instead, he'd added Marchosias, Nilaihah, and Oeillett, Dominions all. The Dominions were an odd lot, tribal, jealous of the lands over which they held sway—as if one parcel of the grayness to which God had consigned them was any better than another. But that was the nature of Dominions. Many were the times when Azazael stood upon this height or that, observing the petty squabbles over territory so blank and barren it made Earth's deserts seem like paradise. It took him a while to understand that it was these squabbles that nourished the Dominions as food nourished humans. And, once known, their weakness was revealed to him. They thrived on discord, discontent, the friction of enmity; they existed as uneasy neighbors, as likely to welcome one another to their table as clash over boundaries.

Marou rode up to him now. He was a glowering presence, dark of mien, heavy of brow, thick of body. A malodorous aura pursued him like an avid pet. His chin thrust forward, his jaws snapped with each word uttered. He took some getting used to, inclined to seek out Astoreth overly much, as if they were siblings. But he was a brave Cherub, for all that, which was why he had chosen him. Though they had clashed numerous times—a power struggle that had yet to be resolved—Azazel had determined that his raiding party be composed of the best and most powerful of the Fallen.

"You know our prey?" Marou's voice was as thick and rough as a highland Scottish laird.

"Some," Azazel replied. "You will leave the human female, Emma Shaw, to me. I have a score to settle with her."

"And the rest?"

"There almost certainly will be a Medius."

"The Regent?" Marou inquired.

"Not the Regent, no. His sister, Surah, though." Azazel's visage twisted. "Can you imagine the horror of being trapped for all eternity as part-crocodile? What a shit existence that must be!"

"Then I will be doing her a favor by ending it."

Azazel laughed.

"What has amused you now?" Marou asked.

"The thought of you ending someone's misery is a jest I never imagined I would witness."

"Then I will ensure her end is as slow and painful as I can devise."

"On that, I trust you, brother."

And the two Cherubim laughed as one.

43

BRAVO'S RETURN TO THE LIBRARY AT ALEXANDRIA SIGNALED both relief and loss. It was good to be back in the world of the living, and as quickly as possible he made his way up to the ground floor, and out into the blinding Egyptian sunshine. The heat hit him like an anvil, but that blow never felt so good, for there'd been moments when he suspected that he might never see this white-hot sun again. And yet, strikingly, there was a distinct sense of loss, as if the world of the living, the one that had birthed him, in which he'd been raised and educated, lacked a vital element—a color or scent—he had become used to in the area of the underworld into which he had strayed.

Ayla stood by his side, silent, watchful, and Antiphon perched above them in the shadow of the building's wide eaves. Though Ayla said not a word, he could feel her extreme concern for him just as if she were voicing it inside his head.

"I'll be all right," he murmured to her. "Everything will be fine."

"Nevertheless," she replied, "I will not leave your side, even for a moment."

He turned to her, smiling. "Your parents would be so proud of you."

"You loved them both, didn't you?"

Bravo looked out at the busy streets, choked with hurrying pedestrians, hawkers of charcoaled food, leather sandals, Persian slippers, silk scarves, fake gold baubles waiting to ensnare unwary tourists busy snapping selfies. All as yet unsuspecting how close they were to Armageddon. What would they do if they knew they very well could be living in the twilight of the human race? He shivered, turning his thoughts away from the possibility.

"Your father was a good friend to me. For years, he was my most reliable set of eyes and ears in Istanbul. As for your mother, I knew her less well, but in the end, more intimately than her husband. I only wish I could have saved her."

"No one could, Bravo. Not even me."

He nodded, for it was true. Dilara Tusik had her own destiny to fulfill. It was through her that Bravo learned about the cavern behind the cataract in Baatara Gorge, where the true history of the Shaws began to reveal itself to him.

"Bravo." The squawk came from above them, and a moment later, a wind arose as Antiphon dropped down beside them. All around them, shocked people yelled and ran helter-skelter until it became clear that the great eagle was no threat to any of them. In fact, the avian ignored them as if they didn't exist.

"There are people searching for you."

"My enemies."

"On the contrary," Antiphon said. "These folk are desperate to join up with you."

"Can you take us to them?"

"I cannot," the eagle said. "They are in a land that would annihilate me were I to wing into it."

Ayla pushed her hair off her face. "Then we'll journey there without you."

"You will not," Antiphon said in a tone of voice that chilled them both. "Bravo, you spoke just now about destiny being fulfilled. It is your destiny to be elsewhere, at least for the time being."

"Nothing could be more important than meeting up with those searching for me."

"One of them is your sister, Emma; you have become her poison. More importantly, there is something far more pressing." Antiphon moved from one taloned foot to another, a clear sign of her distress. "The Sum of All Shadows knows where King Solomon hid his cache of alchemical gold. He means to use it to ensure that each member of his army is invincible, even against Aqqibari, even against St. Michael and his Angels of Sanctification. Even against God."

Bravo was staggered, but wisely kept the consternation off his face. He did not want Ayla more worried than she already was. Any weakness or hesitation now would undermine her faith in him, and that faith was a major part of what was holding them together in the face of what increasingly seemed like insurmountable odds.

"You must stop him at all costs."

"Do you know where the gold is?"

"I do not. Nor can I understand how Lucifer discovered its whereabouts."

"Then how am I to stop him?"

"There is only one way," Antiphon said. "You must shadow him all the way to the cache. And then you must find a way to strike him down."

"Do you know where he is now?"

"I always know where he is. Being tied to him in this manner is part of my own destiny," the eagle said with unprecedented gravity. "He is on the march with his army of the Fallen."

"He will take the Fallen through the Rift?"

"Not yet. He will lead them to it. He will go through himself first."

"To find the gold."

Antiphon nodded. "With good reason, he does not trust anyone."

"Would you?"

The eagle made a peculiar sound that Bravo figured must have been a laugh.

"You say shadow him as if that will be a simple matter to accomplish."

"Not simple. Nothing is ever simple when it involves the Sum of All Shadows. He is a grandmaster when it comes to existence played as chess moves. And his long incarceration has had an unintended consequence: he has learned infinite patience, a trait he never had before the Fall, else he would never have engineered a failed uprising."

"Then how will I shadow him without his knowledge?"

"You still do not understand your place in the world." Antiphon's wings rustled. "You are what your grandfather Conrad knew you to be. This was why he insisted on your physical training, even in the face of your parents' protests. It was why he was adamant that you begin that training from a very early age."

Bravo felt another shock race through his system. "My mother knew? I thought my father kept my training secret from her?"

"Your mother was a singularly clever woman, Bravo. She understood more than her husband ever did."

"He didn't want to know," Bravo said bitterly.

"Indeed," Antiphon said without a trace of empathy. "But you are what you are, your parents' preferences meant nothing. Bravo, you are now what you were meant to be, what Conrad recognized in you the moment you were born.

"You are Aqqibari. You are a weapon."

Bravo was taken aback. "I must be more than simply a weapon."

"Well, that is up to you, of course. But as for this moment in time, a weapon you are, a weapon that must be deployed now or all is lost. The Sum of All Shadows comes, slouching toward Bethlehem. The Farsighter, Yeats's, vision is about to be fulfilled. Only you have a chance to stem the bloodred tide. For if you fail, it will drown us all."

This was precisely what Oq Ajdar had told him. Bravo stood rooted to the spot, while the hurly-burly of Alexandria continued its race all around him. All at once, his vision clouded over. The heat of the day, the cacophony of car horns, truck backfires, shouts, imprecations, curses, raucous laughter struck him a physical blow. He staggered, fell back against the library's wall.

"Bravo!" Ayla shouted, but he did not respond.

She caught him before he collapsed entirely, held on to him tightly as she called for help.

PART FOUR

RACING TO BETHLEHEM

44

"TAKE HIM TO THE RELIQUARY . . . NO, THE OLD ONE. IT'S BEEN resanctified and is the best place for him."

Bravo heard these orders as if from a house next door, through a scrim of fabric, vibrating along the glass pane of a closed window. But who spoke them? He was scarcely aware of being lifted by brawny arms, brought inside the library, transported along labyrinthine corridors, past innumerable stacks of books, manuscripts, scrolls, temperature- and humidity-controlled cabinets that preserved the oldest and most precious of the Gnostic Observatine documents.

Up stairs, down stairs, then up again, and at last he was brought to the old reliquary room resanctified by a combination of Ayla's ritual and his own sacrifice. This journey, hazed and juddering, came back to him much later, for he was all but unconscious by the time he was laid on a makeshift pallet of blankets and pillows.

At length, he opened his eyes. He lay on his stomach. Ayla's knees and thighs were the closest thing in his field of vision.

"Ayla," he began.

"Shh. Your wounds are deeper than I imagined."

He felt warm, immersed in water, rocked gently, and said so.

"I'm hardly surprised," she said. "It's the resanctification you feel, and thank God for that."

"What happened?"

"You passed out."

He could feel her fingers working on his back.

"You know, looking more closely at these wounds, it's almost as if you once had wings, which were clipped off where they met your body."

"That would make me an angel," he said. "Some kind of Fallen angel."

She laughed uneasily.

"That's what I feel like."

She drew back for a moment, her hands poised above him, perfectly still. She seemed to be holding her breath. "What d'you mean?"

"Antiphon told us that . . . Where is she, by the way?"

"Out front. Guarding the entrance."

"What from?"

"I was about to ask her, but then she gave me that look of hers."

"I've seen that look," Bravo said.

They were quiet for some time while Ayla resumed her work on his back.

Then he began again: "Antiphon told me—and, come to think of it, the false Mary, as well—that I had been changed by whatever the Liderc did to me. Antiphon said that if I saw Emma again I'd kill her. Do you think that's possible?"

"I don't believe that eagle is capable of lying."

"What if her information is wrong? What if she's mistaken?"

Ayla let the questions remain unanswered. Bravo hadn't actually thought she'd know. They were rhetorical questions.

"Ayla . . ."

"I'm here."

"I can't believe that my sole purpose in life is to be God's weapon against the Sum of All Shadows. Surely there's more to my life than that."

"Unless," she said quietly, "you were bred for it."

"Then the Shaws are breeding stock. No better than animals."

Ayla sighed. "There have been times I wished I *was* an animal, living for the day, with no foreknowledge of my death. What a relief that would be."

"But you'd miss out on so much."

"There are days when I think the trade-off would be worth it."

"Is this one of those days?"

She didn't answer, but then, he reflected, she didn't have to.

A shaft of sunlight fell across the floor, illuminating her hands and a slab of his bare back. Having taken out the original stitches, she reapplied disinfectant, then an antibiotic solution the Gnostic Observatines had given her, which she swabbed to a depth of a half inch into the wounds.

"This is only temporary, Bravo. You're going to have to see a proper surgeon, the sooner the better."

"I'll worry about that then."

She sighed, shaking her head. "You must be famished; I know I am," she said. "After I finish here I'll take you out to the best restaurant in Alexandria."

"Stop," he said.

She went still again, hands hovering over his wounds. "What?"

"Stop what you're doing." With great difficulty and pain he turned over onto his back.

"Bravo, your wounds are still open. They could become infected if you don't—"

He stilled her with a look. "Whatever the Liderc did to me is killing me."

Ayla seemed to choke on his words. "What . . . what are you saying?"

Bravo tried to blot out the growing terror behind her eyes. "Antiphon said I won't be the same. I think I still am, but I can't be sure. Whatever the case, I can't allow the process the Liderc started to progress any further. I won't allow myself to become a threat to Emma."

"I don't—"

"This has to stop. Now."

"What are you thinking of doing?" Her eyes were drawn to his hands, which were rapidly turning blue as he held them against his stomach. "Bravo, what are you—?" Seeing what appeared to be an ice-blade forming between his hands, she gasped. "I . . . Bravo, I don't understand."

Before she could utter another word, he rammed the sharp end of the ice-blade into the soft spot beneath his sternum.

Ayla screamed. "No! Oh, no!"

He arched up, his face in a rictus of agony as he angled the ice-blade upward toward his heart.

Ayla, still screaming, grabbed his hands, tried to pry them apart, but his strength was alarming, and she could do nothing to impede the weapon's progress. She saw his eyes open wide. They no longer focused on her, or on anything in the room. They seemed locked on the dust motes that danced in the thick slice of sunlight slanting in from above. His pupils were black as night, tiny pinpoints, as if at any moment they would wink out entirely, leaving only the blank whites.

Tears flowed freely down her cheeks. Her mind was paralyzed with terror.

She could not think what to do, only that she must do something. *Something* to save him.

She glanced upward into the same shaft of sunlight on which Bravo's gaze was fixed. She saw the dust motes shifting, as if in a dance. A pattern formed, and out of that pattern came a melody—the song-prayer her mother sang to her every night when she was a child, tucked into her bed but sleep still in another country.

The song, the prayer, spoke of great mountains sparked in sunlight, deep valleys bathed in moonlight, and the hidden spaces in between, from which all sorcery emanated. She had thought it was nothing more than a nursery rhyme, but what if it was something more? This was the song-prayer she sang to Bravo, bent over, her forehead pressed against the blunt end of the ice-blade, though it chilled her to the bone, turned her lips and nails blue, made her own pupils shrink to pinpoints.

She sang of burning deserts, djinns who traveled on whirlwinds of fire, of deepest seas, where great fish swam, fought, mated, and died.

"Heavenly Father, I ask you in the name of St. Michael and the Angels of Sanctification to whom I dedicated this once-abused reliquary, refuse eternally Lucifer and his acolytes this captive, who belongs to you."

Beneath her forehead, the ice-blade began to liquefy. It did so quickly, and with it the unnatural chill that had all but taken her over. Before it was completely gone, she pulled what was left out of him, held it against her forehead, as she completed the prayer:

"I ask you to surround Braverman Shaw with your white light and your everlasting strength so that the power of all those with evil influences wither as the wheat in winter, so they may withdraw empty-handed, yet with sure knowledge of your infinite love."

Then, bent double, she pressed her lips against Bravo's, breathing into him a warmth that came not only from the burning core of her, but from the essence of her mother, Dilara, an immortal versed in sorcery from both the East and the West.

45

"IF NOT FOR THE EVIL I DO, THERE WOULD BE NOTHING FOR me," Leviathan said. "I would be an empty shell."

"You already are an empty shell," Haya said. "Because that is what you believe."

"I believe in nothing," Leviathan retorted.

"Precisely."

"Therefore, I cannot be injured."

"Therefore, you cannot feel."

"I don't want to feel," the Seraph said. "It is too difficult."

Haya's eyes were filled with an ineffable sorrow. "Then you are of no use to me."

"We must go our separate ways, then."

Oq Ajdar and Ayeleye, watching from afar, glanced at each other. Neither was sure of how this debate was going to end, but it was clear that engaging Leviathan at close quarters made them supremely uneasy. Neither trusted the Seraph; they knew well his penchant for deceit and violence. Which was why neither could fathom why Haya would put her faith in attempting to teach him a lesson in decency.

Perhaps Haya was aware of their anxiety, their concern for her, but if so she did not give any sign of it. She was solely concentrated on Leviathan. Lifting a hand, she said, "Before you act irrevocably, you should know that God put you here, in this place, at this time, for a reason."

"Don't be absurd." Leviathan bared his formidable teeth. "I am no longer controlled by God. They lost sight of me after the Fall."

"In that, as in other matters, you're wrong." Haya held out her hand to him as if she were God's messenger. "God knows precisely where you are. They never let you go. After the Fall, God kept an even closer eye on you."

Leviathan pulled a face. "Why would God have anything to do with me?"

"You're part of their plan, Leviathan. God believes in you, even if you don't believe in yourself."

Once again, the edge of Leviathan's hand cut through the air. "You sound like an emissary of the church."

Just when the two Medius observers felt assured Haya and the Seraph had reached an impasse, that finally Haya would give up and they could be rid of the venomous adder that might turn on them at any moment, the girl stunned and terrified them.

"I have a proposition for you," Haya said, after several moments lost in thought.

Leviathan's eyes flared like struck matches. "Excellent." His black lips curled into a scimitar of a sneer. "I so love propositions." Clearly, he felt he had her now.

"But first I wish to show you something."

WAS *I* *ever a child?* Chynna wondered. She was still hiding out in Surah's palace, creeping like a horned beetle from empty room to empty room, drawing ever closer to a cluster of voices. And then she thought: *No. I was never a child. I do not remember childhood. I do not remember a mother. I do not remember a father. How then did I come into existence? Whose creation am I? Why was I created? What is my purpose?* But she knew her purpose; she had always known it. And it was so ironic, this purpose, for someone fixated on her own needs and pleasures.

What a waste she had been, a black widow in the center of her web, manipulating, when all the while it was she who was being manipulated by a force she had no hope of comprehending.

Nearing the voices, she wept in bitter frustration and disappointment. Wiping her eyes with the back of her hand, she began her search; she was no longer wandering Surah's palace aimlessly.

A short while later, when she had found what she had been looking for, when she had slunk close enough, those voices separated into individuals whom one by one she put a name to.

LEVIATHAN'S EYES narrowed, expecting a trick, but Haya did nothing untoward as she led him down to the bank of the river. Oq Ajdar and Ayeleye, silent observers of his fate, trailed behind like a Greek chorus waiting to find its voice.

Walking along the riverbank, Haya searched the purling water. At length, she found what she was looking for—an outcropping of rock. Wading in the shallows, she built on this with stones smoothed by centuries of swift current until she had created a miniature jetty. On the downriver side of this structure, the current was kept at bay. The water was all but still.

"Come," she beckoned. "Come closer."

Leviathan did as she bade, slowly, cautiously, for though he was comfortable in oceans, with rivers he was less so. Rivers—especially this one—reminded him of Styx, the river of the dead, whose waters were studded with reefs of skulls and skeletons, and, very occasionally, the hollow wing bones of angels who had drawn Lucifer's ire.

As he bent over, he watched, as Haya, crouching, passed her hands through the air. At once, the waters grew dark as iron. And then an image bloomed on the surface. An image of Lucifer. He was in full battle armor, riding his immense charger.

When he addressed Astoreth, the Fallen angel at his side, Leviathan heard his erstwhile Lord and Master use his name. He spoke of Leviathan as if he were already dead, drowned beneath Styx's black waters. He no longer trusted Leviathan. He knew the Seraph who had been his strong right hand was plotting against him. In fact, he said, he had sent him on his errand to give him enough rope to hang himself. And now all was made manifest to the Sum of All Shadows.

Leviathan strained to hear more, but the image was now no more than a ghost, the voice a shiver in the wind.

Rising up, Haya stepped back onto the bank. If she had been wet, she was no longer. Leviathan lurched backward, stumbling up the slope after her.

When they had gained the high ground, Haya turned and looked at him with perfect equanimity. "Here is my proposition: ask me for a favor. When I grant it you'll accept that everything I've told you is true."

Leviathan felt the urge to laugh, but the scene he had just witnessed lay heavy on his mind. Still, he found the wherewithal to say mordantly, "And when you can't?"

"You and I will go our separate ways," Haya said. "We'll never see each other again. You'll be free to negotiate a deal with the Medius without interference from me."

Ayeleye cried out his dissent. Oq Ajdar started as if she had been pinpricked. "I don't think we can—"

Haya raised a hand, stopping her in midsentence. She glanced from one Medius to the other. *Trust me,* the look said, and they did, if only reluctantly. "In fact, I'll recommend they join your rebellion."

Leviathan reared back. "Really?"

"Every word I speak is the truth."

The Seraph's eyes cut to the Medius, both of whom nodded. His smile returned, fainter than before, and more sincere. "I like that," he said to Haya. "I like that a lot."

"Then tell me what it is you want me to do."

"Locate Emma Shaw," he said, finding again the firm voice built on the innate glamour he used so often. "You *do* know who Emma Shaw is."

"I do."

"Why am I not surprised?" His mind was a seething cauldron of treacherous possibilities. "Furthermore, I want you to take me to her."

If Haya recognized those emotions in his face she gave no outward sign of it. "Those are two separate requests."

"Two sides of the same coin, that's all." He gazed at her skeptically. "Huh. As I expected. You default because of a technicality."

"Not in the least," Haya said. "But in return you will grant me the other side of my own coin."

46

BRAVO FELT DEATH'S VELVET CAPE CUTTING OFF ALL LIGHT, falling like ground-up bones against his naked flesh. It did not pain him; rather, it took all pain from him, until he wanted nothing more than to be swaddled in it, to give in to it, become one with it. This was part of Death's dark glamour: the peace. The utter peace.

Not yet now.

Whose voice was this, ringing in his ears like a pesky wasp? *Ignore it,* Death's frost-bound voice sang in his ear. *Annoying, isn't it? Bat it away.*

But the voice would not be denied, not by him, not by Death:

Not yet now.

His lips moved, or he thought they moved: *Grandfather.*

Come, Bravo. The final battle will be engaged at any moment. There is much yet to accomplish.

Grandfather, where have you been? I've missed you.

I've missed you. Was that a response or an echo of his own inner voice?

The pressure of Ayla's lips on his, her soft breath moving into him, surrounding his ice-blade-pierced heart brought him all the way back to the land of the living.

"Bravo," she whispered, lifting her lips from his.

"The ice-blade . . ."

". . . is gone." She smiled. "I have your heart."

"Your mother knew that the moment she and I met."

A vertical line appeared above the bridge of Ayla's nose. "What d'you mean?"

"You know what I mean."

Pretending she didn't hear or understand him, she said, "How are you feeling?"

"Myself. More or less."

"How . . . ? I mean, what did you do? I was sure you were bent on killing yourself."

He held out his hand. "Help me up."

She took it, and they stood close together in the center of the old reliquary. The shaft of sunlight was long gone. Gunmetal light bathed them, then came a patter of rain, but not much, a minute or two and it was gone, as if it had never happened. Moonlight descended, blue, delicate, more transparent than the sunlight, which had been thick as clotted cream.

For a moment pain transfigured Bravo's face, shadows chased across an open field. Ayla studied his eyes, trying to work out what powerful sorcery he had invoked. All of a sudden she was frightened of what he had become, just as frightened as when he had used the ice-blade on himself. She tried to swallow the lump in her throat. "Will you answer my question?"

"I am Aqqibari," he said. "You understand."

She shook her head. "I heard Antiphon call you that. She said you are a weapon."

Bravo nodded. "We are Aqqibari. The Protectors. The chosen of God's warriors against the Darkness-to-Come."

She blinked. "We?"

He held her by her upper arms. "Your mother being a Farsighter knew to send me to Tannourine with you." His eyes were entirely clear of the Liderc's influence. "It was why, years before, she took you there. Have you ever asked yourself why she would expose you to such a dangerous place?"

"I have tried to answer that question," Ayla said. "Many times."

"And?"

She shook her head.

"Your mother wasn't a reckless person, was she?"

"Far from it."

"And yet she took you to the red tent of shadows. Why? Because you were the only one who could destroy it and the evil it represented."

Ayla's face clouded over. "A rite of passage? But I was only a child."

"The moment you were born she knew what you were; she knew your fate. Just as she knew why Conrad had mated with her."

Now she thought she understood the meaning of their previous exchange that had so shocked her:

"I have your heart."

"Your mother knew that the moment she and I met."

But was she relieved or disappointed? Her mind said one thing, her heart something else entirely.

Bravo gazed deep into her eyes. "Like me, like Emma, you are Aqqibari."

LATER, THEY sat alone, backs against the wall. Moonlight covered their legs like a blanket. Food had been prepared for them, and water brought—lots of water, for they were both dehydrated as well as famished. The plates and platters and goblets were overlapping circles between their legs. They could have repaired to the refectory to sit on chairs, eat off the massive dark wooden table, but they both preferred this space, which was both sacred to them and intimate.

For some time, they ate and drank in companionable silence, neither finding the lack of conversation at all unusual.

At some point, Bravo chose to break the silence: "The thing I like best about you," he said, "is that you're a person who knows herself. You have a good deal of your mother in you, and I respected her very much."

"I remember the morning when she called me. I was at work, hating every minute of the fact that I had been passed over for senior manager. A male colleague five years younger got it. 'He's married,' my boss told me without a trace of irony, 'with a child on the way.' That plummy British accent. I watched his face. He had no idea the insult he had just delivered.

"'You have only yourself, Ayla. It's a question of need, you see.' That was the phrase that was in my mind when my mother called and said I was needed in Istanbul that very day." Her eyes regarded his, noting their intensity as well as their depth. Perhaps they were the same, she thought. They held her tightly, as if she were the only thing that mattered to him. "There were a fistful of reasons for me to come, but the overriding one was to meet you."

"Is that so?" He seemed genuinely surprised. "I didn't even know you knew about me."

Ayla laughed softly. "My mother never shut up about you."

"I apologize."

She laughed again, knowing he didn't mean it. "So you came into my life, as you had come into my father's life, then latterly, my mother's. She was quite taken with you. She said you were Hermes, the messenger—the harbinger. You brought the darkness to her doorstep—or rather you fulfilled the prophecy of her Farsight."

"Which you didn't believe in."

Ayla pursed her lips. "I did and I didn't. Her gift seemed crazy, impossible. And yet . . ."

"And yet, you had been a close observer of her prophecies."

"More than a close observer. As you said, it was I who burned down the red tent of shadows, something I think she had tried to do—possibly more than once—but failed."

The tonic of shared reminiscence acted like a balm, settling them into themselves, into each other. It opened a space that might have been there all along without them being consciously aware of it. Wordlessly, they stepped into that space, even though it might be fraught with peril. But the history of the Shaws was as gnarled and twisted as a seaside pine, lashed and torn by storms, silvered by salt, bent in terrible ways, but never broken. For in truth, the Shaws were something more than mortals. They were, perhaps, what humans had once been in the ages before time fully coalesced. In that sense, they were ancient as angels, but without their grace and their unquestioning yoke to God. In that sense, they were Outsiders, one-eyed observers in the country of the blind.

Bravo placed a forefinger in the center of her forehead. "This white mark—"

"I feel it, cool and steady. It's where I leaned against the ice-blade while I was praying."

"Thank you."

"No need."

"There is every need." He smiled. "It will never fade, you understand."

"I don't want it to." She took hold of his hand, pressed her lips to the base of his palm.

It was an acknowledgement, a pact, old as time, that had never changed, nor could it be changed by any known power under the sun or the moon, in Heaven or in the underworld.

MUCH LATER, after they had eaten their fill and rested briefly, while the moon waned in the sky, Bravo climbed onto Antiphon's back, Ayla just behind him. She wrapped her arms around him, holding on tight.

"What will happen to us?" she said in his ear.

He felt her breath, sensed her urgency to know, to parse the calculus of the darkness toward which they headed. He pretended he hadn't heard her; he had no ready answer for her.

"No matter. My mother told me you were a constant star." She held him tighter. "At last, I know what she meant."

In a rush and swirl of hot wind they rose, moonlit, rimed in chill cloud-shadows, spiraling higher and higher, flying headlong into their shared destiny.

47

"BROTHER," SURAH SAID. "YOU KNOW WHAT LUCIFER IS AFTER, and so do I: King Solomon's gold. You also said that you have no idea how to stop him, and nor do I. But it is just possible . . ." She turned to Emma. "Beleth was once Lucifer's emissary in the human Sphere. His master sent him to—"

"To find Solomon's gold." Excitement grabbed hold of Emma's heart and would not let go. "I know." Her hand closed around Beleth's talon. It was cold as marble, hard as a diamond, but there was only darkness surrounding it. She frowned. "Apart from its chill, I don't feel anything at all."

"And you won't," Surah said, "until you allow it to scratch you beneath the surface of your skin."

Emma moved the point of the talon toward the center of her palm, but Surah shook her head and pointed to the place above her heart. "Here."

Before Emma could change the talon's position, Lilith gripped her wrist. "No," she said, and looked at the Medius. "I don't know what this will do to her, and neither does Emma. I won't allow you to put her in harm's way."

In a neutral tone, Surah said, "I understand your resistance, but really, it is futile. First and foremost it is Emma's decision to make."

"But this talon comes from a Fallen angel," Lilith persisted. "Who's to say that it's not poisoned?"

"Emma," Surah replied, "you can answer that."

As Lilith turned to her, Emma nodded. "She's right. I knew Beleth better than almost anyone." She kept her gaze anchored on Lilith; she was not about to give away Surah's secret. What Surah had done with Beleth was her own business. "His talon isn't poisoned, or, if it is, it won't harm me."

"But how can you be sure?"

"Have you forgotten that he was inside me, a part of me? I know, Lilith. I know beyond a shadow of a doubt."

Though Lilith took a step backward mentally, still her hand clamped Emma's wrist. "And what will this experiment avail you? What will happen when Beleth's talon pricks your flesh?"

"Lilith," Emma said softly, "we shall find out together, yes?"

For another moment, Lilith hesitated, before her fingers loosened, freeing Emma's wrist.

Emma could see that Lilith remained unhappy. "Thank you, darling." So saying, she unbuttoned her tunic, pressed the point of Beleth's talon to the spot directly over her heart—the heart that Osiris had weighed and found worthy.

A flash of pain caused her to bite her lower lip. Blood welled, the bead running over the swell of her left breast. The world turned black. She saw stars as she lost her balance. As if from far away, she felt her lover's arms catch her. Her head lay back against Lilith's shoulder.

"Dammit," Lilith cried, "what has it done to her?"

Emma took a long, cleansing breath. The blackness dissipated like mist. In its place, she saw two worlds—the one in which she and Lilith and Surah and the Regent existed, and the world Beleth had found for his Lord and Master.

Her head came up. "It's all right." She smiled. "I'm okay." The concern in Lilith's face caused her to add: "Really. I am."

"And?" It was Surah's voice, interceding for the urgent present.

"And." Emma rose out of Lilith's embrace. "I know where King Solomon hid his gold."

In almost the same moment, Molly, who, along with the Regent had been a silent onlooker during this time, lifted her head. Her nostrils were dilated.

"What is it?" the Regent said. "What do you sense?"

Without replying, Molly rushed out of the kitchen. Down halls, chambers, and passageways unknown she went, unerring as an arrow, as if she, not her mother, were mistress of this palace.

When the woods go silent, she knew, when the birds cease to sing, when the insects' whirring fades, and not a single instance of padding paws can be discerned, something new has been introduced—something alien to the woods, something wicked.

Sounds came to her, muffled in their distress, and she picked up her pace, sprinting at top speed because the air had turned gray, shrouded with a stickiness that sought to slow resistance to a crawl.

Steps echoed behind her. The Regent drew forth Osiris's crook. He hurled it to the gleaming marble floor, and instantly it turned into a serpent—but not just a serpent: the mother of all Egyptian asps, the Empress asp. As quick as Molly was, the serpent was faster. It slithered between her churning feet, shot out in front of her. It lifted its triangular head, tasting the oncoming evil, and deployed its hood, baring its fangs.

As the Regent came around the last corner, he saw the front door on fire. With a resounding boom like a rifle shot, the door was cleaved in two. In stepped Azazel, brandishing his flaming sword. Behind him, shouldering their way in were four more of the Fallen—a Cherub and three Dominions. The Regent knew all the names of the Fallen, but at the moment he was so stunned by this unprecedented outrage he stopped dead in his tracks.

In all the ages he had been in existence, in all the time since the Medius had come into being, never had a Fallen angel, no matter how high up in the hierarchy, dared invade Medius territory, let alone enter its seat of power.

As the Fallen angels rushed in, he saw his sister's decapitated guards lying in pools of blood they had left in their wake. He thought, *This is a consequence of the End Times, of the center no longer being strong enough to hold.* But if the old laws were dead, he asked himself, what was to take their place? At this moment of breaching, it seemed chaos had been unleashed with the advent of the Sum of All Shadows.

It was a moment of weakness, this hesitation, and it proved fatal. First, Marou, the other Cherub, dispatched his Empress asp, her head spinning through the air like a hurled stone. Azazel set the serpent's magnificent black-and-cream-striped body aflame with a flick of his sword. The sickening stench of cooking meat filled the immense entryway.

The three Dominions, Marchosias, Nilaihah, and Oeillett had engaged more of Surah's guards. They were like triplets, ancient Assyrian warrior-priests, thick of body, dark of eye, with triangular beards of dense, black curling hair, which of course never grew. They swung their weapons, forged in Lucifer's ensorcelled workshops, wading through Surah's guards, who had been too slow or, like the Regent himself, too stunned to flee into the interior. Nevertheless, the guards fought with commendable valor. They used weapons whose blades were made of bronze, a composite metal whose unique composition could kill the Fallen, if you knew how. But, of course, they were not well trained in hand-to-hand combat, and certainly not against demonic angels. Why would they be, there having been no such occurrence in the Medius's lands?

Lambs to the slaughter, the Regent thought, using an all-too-common human saying.

Emma had once erroneously called the Regent the demon of fate. He was not a demon, and he was only one of the Four Medius. It was often said of him that he was the saddest and the most bloody-minded of the Medius, but these attributes were part of a smoke screen he himself had promulgated in the Spheres of both humankind and the Fallen. The truth was that he was neither. He was anything but bloody-minded, preferring his deep dives into the psyches of the occult gods of ancient Egypt. He had no idea what sadness meant. And now he was in the middle of a melee, the Dominions working their grisly way through the bloody thick of the entryway.

But it was Azazel himself who headed straight for the Regent. He had not taken his eyes off the Regent from the moment he burst through the door. The Regent had registered the shock in the Cherub's eyes subliminally, while taking in the harrowing chaos the Fallen angels were wreaking. He knew they had overstepped their bounds. Worse, they knew it and didn't care. In fact, they seemed to be having the time of their wretched afterlives, as if they were vegetarians who had suddenly developed an illicit craving for red meat.

"Emma Shaw." Azazel's voice whipped through the entryway like hot wind through a furnace. "Where is she?"

Even as Azazel strode toward him, he saw Molly out of the corner of his eye darting forward. Scooping up a sword from one of the decapitated guards, she advanced on Marou.

"No!" Reaching out, the Regent tried to grab her, but she twisted away. "Molly, don't! Get back!"

This byplay caused Azazel to grin, thick animal lips pulled back from teeth yellow as aged ivory. "You will bring the Shaw woman to me, or I will ensure you will become your own funeral pyre."

He thinks he's found my soft spot, the Regent thought, grinning himself.

He could not be more wrong. I warned my sister about getting involved with the humans, and now look at the chaos it has brought us.

But this was not the moment for recriminations, and he lost yet more time. Molly had already engaged Marou, a one-sided battle if ever he'd seen one. The human girl had no chance against a Cherub, and indeed, after Marou had allowed Molly to strike several blows with the unfamiliar weapon, he slapped the base of the blade she wielded with the flat of his sword. So powerful was the blow that Molly's weapon flew across the entryway, sparking as it skittered along the floor. Without missing a beat and with great glee, Marou thrust his sword into her side.

The Regent shouted in alarm, but curiously, Molly didn't. Instead of retreating, she lunged forward and, opening her mouth wide, went right for Marou's sword hand. She chomped down on the Cherub's wrist. With a snapping like branches breaking, her crocodile teeth ripped through skin and sinew, cracking the bones beneath. All angels' bones were hollow—marrow was for the quick, not those inhabiting the afterlife.

With a great twist of her head, Molly wrenched off Marou's entire hand. As he stood shocked and staring, she spat it onto the floor at his feet. Marou, who had never before endured such an indignity, though surely he had witnessed the maiming of others at his Lord and Master's command, howled like a creature on fire.

Leaping onto him, Molly climbed the tree of his body, bit hard into the side of his neck. Marou flailed out, trying to swat her away as if she were a gnat, but she came away with a significant chunk of him. Laying bare his vulnerable hollow bones, she snapped them in two. Unmindful of the Cherub's one-handed attempts to pry her off him, she bit again, this time severing his head, so that it flopped over, held by just a flap of skin. A moment later, it tore away under its own weight.

Molly caught it, held it in one hand, upside down as the torso collapsed onto the floor, where it flopped like a fish sucking air before it grew still and gray as the ash of a fire long dead.

Everyone froze, stupefied by what this young creature had done. Surah's remaining guards were the first to pull themselves together, swarming over Nilaihah, the Dominion, bringing him down beneath a welter of wounds, long enough for one to slice through his neck, ending his existence.

But their victory was a Pyrrhic one. His compatriots, enraged, redoubled their attack, slicing the last of the guards to shreds. Already wrong-footed at the unexpected presence of the Regent, confounded by a human laying waste to the Cherub on his right hand, Azazel was the last to come out of his shock. When he did, he bared his teeth. He was no longer grinning as he switched target, rushing headlong at Molly.

She threw Marou's head at him, but he batted it away as if it was a leaf torn from a book. He brandished his sword, sweeping it back and forth, preventing Molly from rushing him as she had done with Marou. And yet, he did not believe that, even if by some miracle she managed to insinuate herself inside his defenses, she could do much damage. He was not Marou; he was altogether greater, bristling with dark powers bestowed on him by Lucifer himself.

But as, leaning forward, he made to grab her, the Regent moved to block the Cherub's advance. "She is not for you, Azazel. She is my niece." At this, he saw Molly shooting him a bewildered look. "You cannot touch her. Not now, not ever."

Perhaps Azazel did not hear him, or more likely, he didn't care. This was the End Times. Rules, controls, and governing principles had collapsed. Order was in full retreat. Chaos was ascending.

Molly had fallen back, one arm pinned to the wound in her side. She staggered once, regained her footing, staggered again.

And Azazel swung his flaming sword once, twice, three times.

48

SURAH SCREAMED, FOR SHE HAD ARRIVED AT THE EDGE OF the debacle, Emma and Lilith at her side. Molly stumbled into her sister's arms. She was ghostly, sickly white. Blood ran down her left side. She gulped air as if it were water to slake an unending thirst.

"Molly—" Lilith began.

"Azazel," was all Molly could manage.

And then there was the terrifying Cherub, teeth bared, red-eyed, leading the two Dominions remaining from his raiding cadre. Held in front of him was his sword, whose flames licked and chewed on the Regent's decapitated head. The shocked expression on the Medius's face mirrored that of his sister, as if never in his life could this unthinkable and humiliating end occur.

Surah, eyes like torch flames, spoke a sentence in what Emma thought might be Tamazight. Overlapping shells of darkly gleaming armor sheathed her. A high curving helm, surmounted by what appeared to be a crest of crocodile skin, cured and polished to a high sheen, now covered her head.

Emma took hold of Lilith by her shoulders, drew her backward, and, along with Molly, they melted into the shadows. Then she took a step forward, standing on the edge where light and shadow met.

"What are you doing?" Lilith hissed.

"Stay there," Emma said without looking at her.

"And let you go to battle without me? Never!"

"You must think of Molly now. She's wounded. Take care of her.

"Djat had'ar," Emma intoned. *He is come.* And then: *"Et ignis ibi est!" Let there be fire!*

The cold blue fire erupted from the centers of her palms, shooting outward as she held them in front of her, the Aqqibari fire both a weapon and a shield.

Azazel stared fixedly at her. "I'm onto you now." The malice of his words ripped through the space between them. "Your circus tricks will no longer work on me." And seemingly in the space of a heartbeat he was standing not two paces in front of her.

Surah, transfigured from Medius to fearless warrior, rushed his left flank. "Here," he growled. "This is what you want, no?" And with the merest flick of his wrist, sent the Regent's head hurtling toward her chest. She caught it before it struck her, smothering the fire that had already destroyed his hair, turned his scalp to flaking yellow pulp.

She took two hammering blows to her right shoulder from one of the Dominions. She turned, and Emma lost sight of her. Her own crisis was upon her. Azazel hadn't lied. Between their first encounter and now he had found some way to nullify the blue fire. He went through it as if it did not exist. Terrified, she stumbled backward, just outside the sweeping arc of his flaming sword—a weapon that was meant to mete out justice, not annihilate innocent people. But he had chosen to follow Lucifer down past the depths of hell.

He opened his mouth and breathed on her, and she almost fainted—a toxic combination of methane and carbon monoxide devouring the oxygen around her. It was as if she were deep under water, her air tanks suddenly empty. Nothing to breathe, nothing even to keep her conscious for long. She fell to her knees, gripped her thighs to try and steady her swaying torso as he stood over her, gloating, ready to deliver the coup de grâce he so longed for.

She tried to rise, tried to counter his dizzying assault, failed at both. She could not even draw enough strength to raise her arms in an instinctive attempt of the body to protect itself. And so she closed her eyes, braced herself for what was to come. But when no blow fell on her, she looked up to see Azazel engaged in battle with what looked to be an immense frog, absurdly dressed in striped waistcoat, formal jacket, and trousers with a satin stripe down the legs. A jaunty silk ascot was knotted at his throat, kept in place by a diamond stickpin.

"Back away, my dear," he said to Emma in a throaty voice. "Give me room to fully engage with this blackguard."

He struck Azazel's sword with what looked like a simple wooden walking stick, but clearly it wasn't. Sparks flew in a white-hot rage where the two weapons met. Emma did as the creature ordered, retreating on her knees, working slowly backward, into the shadows where she had left Lilith and Molly. She called softly to them, and then again. No answer. She looked around, frantic now. They were no longer there.

Whirling, she glimpsed them, having returned to the field of battle. She set off after them, but her attention was so intensely focused on Lilith that she failed to see the blow come from her left side. Stars exploded behind her eyes. Without knowing how she got there, she was curled on the floor, unable to think clearly or move her limbs.

SURAH KNEW she was outnumbered. She had donned her armor for ceremonial occasions, when all of the Four Medius used to meet once a year, but that was a long time ago. She had never used it in hand-to-hand combat. It was fine for sitting and for short strolls, but now she found it heavy and hot. She longed for the cool water of her ponds, the soothing pastel colors of her water lilies, the soft croaking of the frogs, the silent skimming of the water-spiders.

No such luck. She understood, even while she was being battered to her knees by both Dominions, that she had brought this attack upon herself. In this sense her late brother had been correct: getting entangled with the humans brought with it their misery and pain. And now the unthinkable for a Medius: death. The Regent gone. Unimaginable!

Half-dazed, agonized, she still cradled his head in her hands and thought of the years of their estrangement rather than summoning the wits and strength to counterattack. Her sorcerous armor held, kept her safe, at least temporarily, but each moment that passed brought the demonic angels closer to finding the way through with their weapons.

Head bowed, eyes misted with tears, all Surah could do was mourn the loss of a brother who she had known not nearly well enough. Then a particularly vicious strike to her neck where it joined her shoulder shook her out of her daze. She remembered her daughter, recalled the blood running from her side, and placing her brother's head between her knees, she shook both hands. Five-inch spines appeared along the line of her knuckles.

Being on her knees gave her a certain advantage. What she lost in piledriver power she made up for by the low angle from which she was able to bury her spines into the right knee of Oeillett, the Dominion closest to her. He growled, his leg buckled. She raked the spines sideways, ripping out the knee itself, and the leg collapsed completely. As Oeillett went down, she drove the spines in her other hand into his neck, tearing through skin and sinew. The hollow bones snapped, disintegrating. Light went out of the Oeillett's eyes as the Dominion's head joined the Regent's on the floor between her knees.

She had no time to savor her victory, as Marchosias, the last remaining Dominion in Azazel's cadre, delivered a titanic blow to the back of her neck, dislodging her helm just enough for him to bury a stiletto-bladed dagger down through her neck. Her head arched back, her vision filled with his grinning face.

In terrible pain, she lifted her arms, grabbed the blade in her hands. Ignoring how the edge bit into her palms, she commenced a tug-of-war, bit by bit pulling the blade out, even though Marchosias bore down with all his might.

And yet she realized that it might be too little too late. An icy paralysis arose in her, snaking its way through her nervous system. She could feel her muscles losing strength, sense the world around her blurring, fading in and out, as her consciousness flickered like a guttering flame. She could scarcely catch her breath. She was losing her grip on the blade, her hands slipping in her own blood. Then with a vicious twist of the dagger, Marchosias sliced through her hands, and she was going, life leaching out of her, pooling around the head of her lost brother.

But it wasn't him she thought of in those last seconds: it was Molly. Her love for her daughter was immense—large as the moon, blinding as the sun, eternal as the stars. She harbored no regret for the affinity she felt for humans that had led her to birth a child, only a gratitude she had once assumed was beyond her—beyond all Medius—to experience. She loved Molly more than life itself, and if, as it appeared, she would lose her life, she was at peace with that. She would have loved to spend time with her daughter, grown now into a young woman, but they had had their reunion, they had swum in the pond together, watched jeweled dragonflies hang above their heads like diadems, felt silver-and-gold koi swim between their legs. They had spoken as mother and daughter. What greater experience could she have?

Just then a wave of inky fluid splashed her and, blinking through it, she saw Marchosias's headless torso quiver and spasm as it fountained more ichor from his severed neck, before sliding away from her sight.

***BRING HER** here.*

Lilith heard the voice in her mind as she held desperately on to her sister, who kept the flat of one hand pressed against the gash in her side still leaking blood.

Bring her to me.

Peeking out from the shadows, Lilith saw a commanding female figure who, with her longbow in hand and a quiver of arrows strapped across her back, looked like a classical portrayal of the goddess Artemis. The figure made eye contact, and Lilith heard her say, *I am the only one who can save her. Bring her now.*

And because she had no other viable choice amid the melee, Lilith did as the goddess Artemis bade her. When she got to her she saw a young girl by her side who stared at her with the oddest, oldest eyes she had ever encountered. The sight of the girl sent shivers down her spine.

"My name is Oq Ajdar," the goddess Artemis said. "This is Haya. Please give Molly over to me."

"How do you know my sister's name?" Lilith asked. "Where did you come from?"

"No time now," Oq Ajdar said, and took possession of Molly from Lilith's reluctant grip. At once, her shape changed, causing Lilith to take an involuntary step back. Soft tentacles wrapped tenderly around Molly's form until she was all but hidden. "Do not be afraid," Oq Ajdar said, and then, releasing Molly, continued, "There. Her wound is healed, her blood flow restored. She is well again."

But Molly, already craning her neck, sprinted away from all three of them, back toward her mother.

"Haya." That was all Oq Ajdar said, so quietly Lilith was unsure she had even heard the word, until Haya followed in Molly's wake.

"I have no weapons, no special powers," Lilith said. "I am entirely human, but you are a chimera—and a Medius, I would wager. Why aren't you fighting back against these murderers?"

"I am fighting back," Oq Ajdar said levelly.

"Really? I can't see it."

"Neither can anyone else," Oq Ajdar replied with a smile so sorrowful tears overflowed Lilith's eyes.

Lilith turned in time to see Molly spring like a tiger onto the last remaining Dominion's broad back. Without hesitation, she snapped her jaws shut on the nape of his neck. And again. The third time she bit right through, and he was done, collapsing to the floor in front of her mother.

Molly took Surah in her arms. "Mother," she whispered. "Mother."

Surah looked up into her daughter's face, noted how strong it was, how like her own. How had she not noticed that before? "Do you remember the dragonfly?"

"I do, Mother. So beautiful. Like a piece of jewelry."

"It landed on the back of your hand. My dragonfly. He knew you were my daughter. He loved you."

Molly, trying desperately to hold back tears, said, "I love that pool, Mother." Her voice was clotted with emotion. "I loved being in it with you. We'll be in it again."

"Yes."

Molly nodded. "It's home."

Surah sighed deeply, completely, as if she had been waiting all of her existence for this moment. Her eyes shone. "How I love you, my daughter. Forgive me."

Molly bent over, kissed her mother's cheeks. "There is nothing to forgive."

She felt Surah's uncertain breath on her cheek, and then it died, along with the rest of the Medius. Molly rocked her mother, sobbing.

Behind them, Azazel had no time for either of them. His attention was solely on Emma, still prostrate on the floor, and on the Medius Ayeleye, who was tiring at last, his walking stick charred and blackened by Azazel's fiery sword strikes. Cracks had appeared down its length; it was clear to both antagonists that the stick, powerful as it was, would not last much longer. And, in fact, in another two blows, it shattered, the fire having eaten clear through it.

Now Ayeleye was unarmed, completely unprepared for what must come next. Bending down, he tried to pull Emma away from Azazel, but the Cherub's next swing nearly sliced him in two. He leapt back, which was just what Azazel wanted. With a dismissive wave of his hand, he drew back his sword, arcing it downward toward Emma's unprotected head.

Ayeleye made to step in front of the blow, but Haya shoved him aside, stood with her feet braced, her arms outstretched. Looking up at the massive figure of the Cherub she shook her head. When he showed no signs of stopping, or even pausing, she caught his blade between her two hands.

Azazel jerked like a fish who'd been hooked. An almost seismic jolt raced through him, rattling his teeth and numbing the muscles of his arms. He stared at the girl, uncomprehending. And then, as she continued to imprison his sword, the flames ate into her. First, her hands blackened, then the skin peeled away from her forearms as they began to roast. So it went through her torso and legs, finally engulfing her head. Her face, the last to go, showed no pain, no surprise, nothing at all, in fact, save a faint and enigmatic smile.

Then the girl was gone, a curl of smoke rising slowly from her incinerated shell, rising to the ceiling, where it curled like a cat in the corner of a sofa. *Now, finally, I can annihilate the Shaw woman,* Azazel thought, and brought his weapon to bear, stabbing it directly downward, the point aimed at a spot between Emma's eyes.

49

OVER THE ROOFTOPS AND CHIMNEYPOTS, ABOVE THE SMOKE and the heat-haze, into the high place where the air was clear of the thick effluvia thrown off by human manufacturing, human living, human waste, they rose. Starshine only. The moon was already down.

"How are you feeling?" Ayla asked as they rode upon Antiphon's feathered back.

"I'd like to sleep for a year," Bravo said. "Maybe longer."

"But not yet, now."

"No." The echo of what Conrad had said. If it had been Conrad contacting him after so long a silence. Had he escaped his prison? "We've a long way to go, and our path becomes more perilous the narrower it gets."

They kept rising up and up, until they could see the curvature of the Earth as they winged their way east-southeast across the Nile Delta and out across the northern Sinai desert. As the oxygen thinned they took deeper and deeper breaths, and they settled deeper into Antiphon's feathers, huddling closer as the temperature dropped. The wind hummed and moaned all around them, taking their breath away, making it almost impossible to communicate.

As if intuiting their distress, Antiphon swooped down as she carved their path over the Negev desert, crossing the border into Jordan. Ahead of them loomed Jebel al-Madhbah, the altar mountain, beyond which lay the ancient city of Petra.

Down and down they went until the great eagle dug her claws into the rocky earth. They were in Wadi Musa, the Valley of Moses, below the foothills of the mountain chain that followed the Great Rift Valley, all the way down to the Gulf of Aqaba, thence to the Red Sea.

Jebel al-Madhbah was widely believed to be the biblical Mount Sinai. It fit the description perfectly; at its flat summit was a ceremonial plaza with benches around the sides, cisterns for ritual cleansing, and an altar at its center. Two immense obelisks rose from lower down. Thirty-three hundred feet below, where Antiphon set them to rest before the final leg of their journey, was Ain Musa, the Spring of Moses. Bravo had seen in the Gnostic Observatine library in Alexandria a manuscript wherein the thirteenth-century Arab chronicler Numairi wrote that Ain Musa matched several detailed accounts of Meribah, the location where Moses struck the ground with his wooden staff, bringing forth fresh water for the people of Israel.

It was clear that the great eagle needed to rest. Wings folded, she closed her eyes, and in the manner of birds everywhere, was instantly asleep. Taking Bravo's hand, Ayla drew him some distance away. They sat in the lee of a rock outcropping with only the eternal river of stars over them.

She took his hands in hers, looked directly into his eyes. "If we die today—"

"We won't die today," Bravo said softly.

"But if we do—listen to me, Bravo—if we do I want you to know that I love you. I've loved you from the moment I met you."

"You didn't act like it."

She tossed her head. "Of course I didn't. I was protecting myself. I had no idea who or what you were. I had only my mother's stories of you to go by. I had to see you for myself, spend time with you."

"And then you found out that you're my aunt."

"Conrad, my father, was your grandfather. He took my mother as a mistress late in life. A bizarre twist of fate if ever there was one."

He shook his head. "Par for the course for us Shaws. After all, Chynna and Conrad were our prime progenitors."

There was a certain stillness between them then. No birds called, no insects buzzed. Even the wind held its breath, as if waiting.

"Let me show you a couple of Aqqibari powers I've unlocked with Conrad's help."

They spent the next hour, virtually silent, working with their minds, until they both felt the onset of exhaustion.

"Aqqibari lessons are all well and good," Ayla said after they had rested side by side, "but you haven't responded to me." She gazed deep into his eyes. "I love you, Bravo." Her eyes were luminous in the starlight. "Do you love me?"

It was at this point that Bravo would have hesitated. If he had one fault, inherited from his father, it was a tendency to overthink situations. Conrad had made him aware of it without actually warning him or judging him, but his attention to it had stuck with Bravo, as had every word his grandfather ever said to him.

He leaned in and kissed her. "I do." Her soft lips opened like a flower against his, and he tasted her, musk and lemon and anise. "I need to tell you something."

She sighed, reluctant to let him go as he pulled back.

He had already told her all there was to know about the Liderc, but now he spoke to her of Mary, the Churel. "Since her death, I've been turning something she told me over and over in my mind. It was so crazy on the surface, I dismissed it the moment I discovered her true identity."

"Scarcely surprising," Ayla said. "All she knew was to tell lies to entrap unwary prey."

"True enough." Bravo nodded. "And yet, this one thing . . ." He took a breath, let it out slowly. "The longer I consider it the more sense it makes."

"What did she tell you?"

"That Lucifer is actually Jesus's brother."

Ayla reared back. "What? No, no. Impossible!"

"You know by now that when it comes to ancient history nothing is impossible." He waited for her to respond. When she didn't, he went on. "She told me that she was a server at the Last Supper. She said that it was Lucifer sitting at Jesus's right hand."

Ayla considered a moment, conjuring the painting of *The Last Supper* in her mind. "Then why isn't he depicted in the paintings?"

"The Disciples. They instructed the artist who painted the original—the one we found in the Knights of St. Clement's reliquary—not to. The artist obeyed, but kept the space there, where Lucifer had sat."

"And you believe in this one instance she was telling the truth?" Ayla asked. "Why?"

"Well, the bleeding on the painting came from the vacant spot on Jesus's right hand."

"That's hardly reason enough to—"

"There's more," Bravo said. "Ever since Conrad introduced me to the works of his friend, W. B. Yeats, what seemed like an anomaly stuck in my head. I asked Conrad about it once, but he had no answer. Neither has anyone else—at least no explanation I find satisfactory."

Ayla shook her head. "I still find the whole idea . . . I mean, if true it would be mind-blowing. If it became known, if it could be proved it would be a seismic event. It would blow up the entire Catholic Church, all of Christianity, for that matter. And all on the say-so of a congenital liar? No, Bravo. No. I cannot believe such a fanciful story."

"Then explain this to me," Bravo responded. "As you know, Yeats was a Farsighter. He predicted the End Times coming at this moment, and he was right. In his Farsighted poem, "The Second Coming," he writes at the end: 'That twenty centuries of stony sleep/Were vexed to nightmare by a rocking cradle/And what rough beast, its hour come round at last/ Slouches toward Bethlehem to be born?'"

Ayla shrugged. "So?"

"So when you read these stanzas carefully it seems that Yeats is conflating Jesus—the 'rocking cradle,' and 'Bethlehem,' with Lucifer—'stony sleep,' 'nightmare,' 'rough beast slouching toward Bethlehem to be born.' Jesus was born in Bethlehem; where was Lucifer born?" His stern visage caught Ayla in its web. "But what if they were *both* born in Bethlehem? What if they really are brothers? That would resolve the enigma of the poem."

Ayla was silent for some time, digesting his theory. It was crazy, she knew. It ran counter to all religious scholarship. And yet . . . And yet, there was something compelling, something—and she could scarcely believe it—that meshed, that felt right.

"But why would the Churel tell you the truth?"

"I wondered about that myself. I think she was taunting me. Telling me the truth when she knew she was going to kill me. Knowing that I knew the truth, that the secret would die with me, gave her a frisson too delicious to resist."

"Then you think Yeats . . ."

"I think Yeats couldn't help but tell the truth. His poems came from deep inside him, where the Farsighter dwelled. I think that part of him knew that Jesus and Lucifer were brothers, but that truth was something closed off from the rest of him. Recall that he was Irish, a devout Catholic.

The secret that the Farsighter part of himself saw was too terrible for the rest of him to embrace."

"But this is incredible."

"All the secrets buried in history are incredible, Ayla. They have been buried for good reasons."

She shivered. "So the thing we must stop today is the brother of Jesus."

He nodded. "I'm convinced it is."

Ayla passed a hand across her face. For a moment, she trembled, looked at him. "And if we die tomorrow . . ."

"If we die tomorrow, Ayla, we will know ourselves as well as each other."

She put her palm against his cheek. He had already started growing a beard, which she found she liked very much. "We will never know each other, Bravo. Not really. Not completely."

He nodded. "I stand corrected. But that's the way of humans, isn't it?"

"Humans and Shaws alike," she said with a mischievous curl to her mouth.

He laughed then, took her in his arms, held her tight while she kissed the side of his neck over and over.

"I wish we could stay here forever," she whispered.

"Unfortunately, that is impossible."

She jerked up and away from Bravo at the sound of Antiphon's voice.

"Let us be off," the great eagle said, looking down on them as if from a great height. "The time is now. A storm is heading our way. We must make haste."

They rose as one. Bravo swung onto her back and Ayla followed, looping her arms around his waist.

Without another word, Antiphon spread her wings wide and leapt into the night sky, heading toward the looming massif of Jebel al-Madhbah.

"I wish I knew more of what I inherited from my mother."

"Not only your mother," Bravo said. "Conrad, as well."

There were no longer any stars. The sky seemed to be rushing down onto them, wanting to crush them. The boom and crack of thunder and lightning came to them, closer than they had expected. The storm was rushing toward them at astonishing speed.

They passed over the summit, saw in the brief lurid light of a lightning spurt the outlines of the ceremonial theater rushing by. Antiphon ascended in an attempt to rise above the roiling clouds. An instant later, another spurt of lightning burst into Antiphon's belly. The impact nearly shook them loose from their perch. Feathers exploded everywhere, beaten down by the torrential rain.

"What happened?" Ayla cried.

"I don't know," Bravo said, but he was very much afraid that he did know. He felt the energy draining out of the great eagle, could feel her intense pain. Her consciousness flickered like flames caught in a storm front. "Hang on tight!"

Pitching over, they lost altitude at an alarming rate, plummeting toward the ancient desert city of Petra.

50

AZAZEL FELT A PECULIAR SENSATION, AS OF A RUNNEL OF water coursing down his spine from the back of his neck to his coccyx, and he hesitated, his weapon still poised over Emma's forehead. He whirled on his heel, to find himself confronting Leviathan. The Seraph's upper half was in the form of a wolf, the lower half that of a satyr—a powerful male goat.

He brandished no weapon.

"You! Where have you come from?"

"A place you will never find or see."

Then Azazel looked down, saw the gore-soaked head of Turael, Azazel's beloved Orus. It was the bloody muzzle of Turael's head that Leviathan had pressed down the Cherub's spine.

"What . . ." he cried. "What have you done!"

"Ended your steed's misery," Leviathan said easily. "You proved a frightful master."

"Liar!" Azazel screamed. "Traitor!" His face was flushed nearly black, his eyes opened wide, teeth protruding. "I will cut you to ribbons."

"You're welcome to try," Leviathan said equably.

In a rage, Azazel swung his flaming sword into Leviathan. It never got there. The edge cracked, the blade shattered like a dropped mirror. Leviathan gripped the flames in his fist, seized the Cherub's neck. The flames ate up skin, flesh. Leviathan splintered the vertebrae, and Azazel collapsed like a marionette whose strings had been cut. On his knees, he swayed drunkenly. Leviathan lifted one of his powerful caprine legs and contemptuously kicked what was left of him so hard the edge of his hoof split the ruined torso down the middle.

Leviathan looked up directly into Oq Ajdar's eyes. "I kept my promise," he rumbled. "I protected Emma Shaw." His eyes were alight with an infernal phosphorescence. "Now you must keep your end of the bargain. You and Ayeleye will join my rebellion." He raised his fist, still aflame from Azazel's sword. "It is unfortunate that two of you Medius have met their end, but it no longer matters. I have appropriated all of Azazel's power. It will be easier to bring down the Sum of All Shadows."

He saw the subtle shift in Oq Ajdar's gaze, but as he began to turn around, Chynna Shaw, who had appeared soundlessly from the place where she had been in hiding, quickly and adroitly severed his head from his torso. His body was still turning toward her, but without his head and neck, which were impaled on the six-inch spike at the apex of the war-axe she had found in Surah's small but well-equipped armory.

His eyes were open in astonishment. His mouth worked spastically as he sought to speak. He had, she guessed, two or three minutes at the outside before he was gone completely. Even he, a First Sphere Seraph, former right hand of Lucifer, had his limits, and Chynna Shaw, who had known him for hundreds of years, knew them all. The war-axe's double blade, now dripping Leviathan's black ichor, was made of bronze.

"Look at you," she said. "Poor thing, spitted like a hog." She spat in his face. Then with her free hand, she reached down, pulled Emma to her feet.

"*Azoul,* great-great-granddaughter. I celebrate you," she said in Tamazight formal greeting. "I am Chynna Shaw—Chynna Sikar, as I was born. Or I was, until I died."

Emma, still reeling from Azazel's assault, wanted to reply, but she could not find the proper thoughts, let alone words.

Chynna turned back to the Seraph's head. "There are things I need to say to you before you are truly dead, about what you have made me endure for nearly two centuries. You resurrected me without my permission. Had you ventured into the afterlife, I would have forbidden it. Unequivocally.

"But you couldn't be bothered. I was beneath that. And when you made me hálf-dauður, half-dead, I became a thing without choice."

"You never had a choice." Leviathan's voice, disembodied as his head, was like hail battering a tin roof.

"Oh, but I did," Chynna rejoined, ready for him, at last. She had stripped him of his glamour. "I simply never knew it, you made sure of that. Your glamour covered me, a snare through which I saw only what you wanted me to see."

"This is who I am, Chynna. This is *what* I am. I cannot be other."

"Yes. Of course you would think that. To change, to be other is such a human trait, and we all know how you feel about humans." Her upper lip curled. "But you could have, and that is the saddest part of us. Together, we both could have been better. We could have been other than we are."

"No, Chynna."

She spat in his face again.

"You see? All we are able to do is bring out the worst in each other."

Chynna began to respond, but the light faded from his eyes. They looked like stones in an abandoned quarry—hard, still. Lifeless.

THE LAST horrific moments seemed to its living participants to have occurred in slow motion. Now that the bloodletting had ended, the bones had crumbled, death and its consequences settled like a shroud over each of them. Now everything happened at once.

Lilith ran to her sister, who was still cradling Surah, talking to her as if she were still alive. Kneeling, Lilith wrapped her arms around Molly, laid her cheek upon the crown of her head. Ayeleye was crying at the loss of his brother and sister, but, curiously Oq Ajdar's face was devoid of emotion. Whatever she felt she was keeping locked inside.

Chynna grasped her great-great-granddaughter's shoulders. "My child. Where is my child?"

"What child?"

"Haya. Where is she?"

Emma shook her head, turned to look back at Oq Ajdar and Ayeleye. "Do either of you know—?"

"She is no longer," Oq Ajdar said.

"No, no . . . Oh, no." Chynna began to keen. "But where is she? I want to see her, I want to hold her."

"She is gone." Oq Ajdar seemed like a block of granite—hard, eternal, forbidding.

For once in her life Chynna was bewildered. "Gone where?"

"But then she was never really here."

"How can you say that?" Chynna blinked back tears. "I nurtured her in my womb."

"She nurtured herself."

Chynna shook her head, her bewilderment increasing. "I gave birth to her."

"She was a vessel," Oq Ajdar said.

"A vessel for what?"

"For that which had been pursued into the afterlife, for that which needed to be hidden from nearly omniscient eyes."

"I don't believe you."

"Nevertheless, it is true," Oq Ajdar told her. "Besides, I have no reason to lie."

"How . . ." Chynna took a breath, a step toward the chimera. Another breath, shuddering. "How do you know this?"

"I stashed Haya, and her secret, in your womb."

"But . . ." Another step forward, faltering this time. "How could you?"

"I am Fate, Progenitor Shaw." The chimera spread her arms. "My brothers and sister have assisted me from time to time, when I have called upon them. But unlike the Seraphs, Cherubs, Dominions, Furies, and all the rest, there can only be one Fate."

Chynna was trembling now. She had never in her life, death, or resurrection felt so ripped apart, so vulnerable, so filled with an agonizing disillusionment. "Tell me now, don't keep me in suspense a moment longer: What was my daughter's secret? What was she hiding?"

"Not what, Progenitor Shaw." Oq Ajdar smiled, not unkindly. "Who."

The swirl of smoke that had risen from Haya now began to coalesce. Darker it became. Denser. Slowly descending until it reached the floor. Chynna felt herself swooning, though she could scarcely credit it.

For there, standing tall and strong, his hair and beard turned white, was Conrad Shaw.

51

CONRAD SHAW'S APPEARANCE ASTONISHED EVERYONE. Apart, that is, from Oq Ajdar, who had orchestrated Conrad's escape from the mirror-prison and found the only way to successfully hide him from the Sum of All Shadows.

"Inside the daughter of Leviathan's hálf-dauður mistress you will be born again," she had told him six years ago, "inside a vessel of purest light."

He had balked, saying, "But I am thoroughly and completely hidden from Lucifer's sight."

"True. You have been. But it will not always be so."

"Then I will remove myself from this hiding place and find another."

"You may do that, but in six years he will find you."

"No matter where I am?"

"No matter where you are."

Oq Ajdar had smiled in that way of hers. "This vessel of purest light is the only thing that can save you now, Conrad. And you must survive. It is your fate."

"You know that better than anyone," he had said, acquiescing to trust her unconditionally, as he always knew he would.

And now here he was, seeing all the people Oq Ajdar promised him would be there when he was reborn: his granddaughter, Emma; Surah's daughter, lost no longer; Ayeleye; and Fate herself. It was a great sorrow to him that two of the Medius had been killed in the attack, but to have Azazel, three Dominions, and Leviathan himself dead was nothing short of a blessing. The lone surprise was Chynna exacting her revenge on her former lover. But he had resurrected her in the only manner he knew how.

To be hálf-dauður—to be simultaneously dead and alive—was a punishment beyond imagining.

As for himself, though he was more here than Haya had been, he too was a vessel of sorts, returned from the afterlife into which the Sum of All Shadows had consigned him to complete the circle that was his fate.

It was at that point he became aware of Emma, Lilith Swan, and Chynna staring at him in a kind of stupor. As for Molly, she was too consumed with grief over her mother's death to care much about him. But she would have to be brought out of her anguish soon enough. He had prepared her as best he could while still imprisoned when he managed to visit her on the river near the house Leviathan had conjured.

Understandably, it was Emma who found her voice first. "Grandfather," she said hoarsely, "is it really you?"

"Yes," he answered. "And no."

Oq Ajdar stepped forward. "Conrad has been kept in existence by forces far more powerful than those known to any Seraph." Even though she was addressing Emma, her words were clearly meant for Chynna, as well. "He is here for a very specific reason that includes you, Emma." She redirected her attention. "And you, Molly."

At the sound of her name, Molly looked up. Lilith knelt beside her, a supportive arm around her shoulders, Molly leaning into her older sister's strength. The fact that they were not truly sisters was meaningless to them forever more.

As Molly remained mute, Lilith felt compelled to speak for her. "What do you mean? What reason?"

"Molly," Conrad said, "you are one of the four Aqqibari."

Lilith sucked in her breath, held on to Molly all the tighter, as if she required protection from this news. In Lilith's mind, at least, she did.

"We have had a tragedy here, no question," Conrad said. "But it is time we left this place. The Sum of All Shadows is on the move. He has gone through the Rift. He is in your world, Emma and Molly."

Emma felt something slither through her. Her grandfather had said *your world,* not *our world.* This change in pronouns frightened her terribly.

"Grandfather—"

But he held up a hand, as if already divining what she would ask him. He had not yet looked at Chynna, let alone addressed a word to her. Still trying to absorb the shock of learning what her beloved child actually was, she remained as a statue, as if, following Conrad's appearance, she was unaware of everyone around her, everything that had been said. As if she had lost interest in anything but the loss of Haya, the child who had given meaning to her hálf-dauður existence. But now Haya was gone; the child Chynna loved beyond anything or anyone else.

What meaning has my existence now? she asked herself. *I lived too long in the first place, and I have been too long a hálf-dauðu, in the second.*

Looking up at Conrad, she said, "I no longer want this existence. Without Haya I am nothing. I live in a nightmare I can bear no longer. Please, Conrad, you of all people will understand. Quick and painless or slow and agonizing, I no longer care. I want an end."

Conrad stepped toward her. Everyone got out of his way. Even Emma and Molly were afraid of him, even, to a certain extent, Ayeleye, though Oq Ajdar seemed her usual imperturbable self. "You created us, Chynna, but through your endless machinations you were almost our undoing. You still may be the undoing of the world of humans and Heaven itself."

Chynna winced. She looked deathly white.

"But you have suffered for many years," Oq Ajdar, the Medius, the adjudicator, said. "You have suffered enough, I think. An end you shall have."

"But not yet, now," Conrad said.

"When?" Chynna, hands to her face, sobbed. "When will my torment end?"

"You will know," Oq Ajdar said, "when Death stares you in the face."

ANTIPHON LAY on her side, panting. Her underside was a hollowed-out black mass. She lay not far from the flight of steps carved into the mountain by which celebrants climbed onto the plaza to begin their religious rituals.

"There is nothing I can do for you, my friend," Bravo said.

"I know." The eagle's voice was scarcely a whisper.

He and Ayla crouched by her side in the waning of the night. Ayla stroked Antiphon's head.

"What happened?" Ayla asked.

Without taking his eyes off Antiphon, Bravo answered, "Two possibilities."

"Tell me."

"Either that storm was a freak of nature or it was conjured by the Sum of All Shadows."

She looked around. "If it's the latter, where is he then?"

"Waiting, I would surmise."

She tossed her head. She never stopped stroking the eagle. "His territory, his advantage."

Despite being mortally wounded, Antiphon had guided them unerringly to a glade within a dense copse of trees perhaps fifteen miles from the area's small town, near the spot that led down and down to the hidden Nabatean plaza where King Solomon had been buried with his hoard of alchemical gold.

"You knew this would happen," Bravo said to the great eagle. "And yet you brought us here."

"My death was foretold," Antiphon said. "I was the only one who could do it."

Ayla bent to kiss the top of the eagle's head. "We don't want to lose you."

"My death counts for nothing. Besides, I died long ago. You and Bravo brought me back from the afterlife for just this purpose."

"I didn't . . ." she spluttered. "I would never sacrifice you."

"We didn't know," Bravo said.

"Yes," Antiphon answered in a watery voice, "you did."

It was far from an accusation, simply a statement of fact. And with that she was gone.

The west wind shivered past them, whining through the dripping trees. One by one, the stars winked out as a faint blush came into the east. Then, in the space of a heartbeat, the stars vanished in fistfuls. The faint blush turned into a bloodred vein.

"Quickly now," Bravo said as he glanced at the sickly light. "There's no time to lose."

"But we can't just leave her here like this." Ayla's cheeks were tear-streaked.

"The desert will take her; it's right and proper." He took her hand, led her to the western edge of the glade where, behind a natural cairn of tumbledown rocks lay a hidden pool. It was a part of Wadi Musa of which neither the Jordanian authorities nor tourist guides were aware.

As they stood side by side on the steep, bare lip of the pool, Bravo said, "Ready?"

"What? Are we going for a swim?"

Bravo squeezed her hand. "Antiphon told me that the opening is in a small cave hidden behind the pool."

"And if it's not?"

"She never lied to me."

Skirting the waterline, they found themselves in a thicket of desert brambles higher than their heads. Pushing their way through resulted in scratches from long thorns, but at length they came out the other side.

There before them was the cave mouth. Pulling out the LED flashlights they had been given before they left the library, they entered, stooped over, backs curved like beetles. The cave was indeed small, the walls narrowing within eight or so feet of the entrance. They were squeezed together, then forced to proceed in single file.

"I can see the end of the cave," Ayla said. "It's solid rock." She played her beam of light over the floor just in front of the wall. That, too, was solid. "What d'you think?"

Bravo kept going, his light illuminating the walls. The farther they went the danker the air. There was no sign of the desert here; the walls were weeping, rivulets running down.

"We should be near the way down to the Nabatean ruins," Bravo said. "Antiphon told me it was at the rear of the cave."

Farther on, he stopped suddenly, bringing into prominence a familiar design incised into the left-hand wall near the back: the figure of a man sitting upon a throne, a circlet on his head.

"Look," Bravo said, as they approached. "The image of King Solomon we saw on the cave wall in Tannourine."

Ayla came closer still. "And that shadowy figure behind him, holding up a ceremonial platter."

"A royal disc," Bravo observed.

On it was incised a golden square. Within the square was a white-black triangle with bloodred trim. As in the cavern behind the Lebanese cataract, the sigil was depicted three-dimensionally, like an M. C. Escher drawing: a single uninterrupted surface over three dimensions.

"The sigil of the Unholy Trinity," Ayla breathed. "The Testament of

Lucifer, the *Nihilus Inusitatus,* written by Solomon's alchemists." She glanced back at Bravo. "And the third part?"

"We had no idea," he said, "until now, that is. That royal disc—do you see?"

She leaned in. "Could it be made of gold?"

"Indeed. I'm of the opinion that the third part of the Unholy Trinity is King Solomon's gold."

They continued on, until they reached the cave's end, but the entrance to the way down was blocked by a rockfall. It was impossible to get through.

Bravo put his hand out, moved it over the blockage. "This looks recent," he said. "Very recent."

Ayla put a hand on her hip. "Now what do we do?"

Neither of them had a ready answer.

52

THE FRIGATE WAS BLACK, SLEEK, ELEGANT. CONCEIVED BY Ayeleye in the British Empire manner, constructed of magnificent hardwood, built by master coopers, it was an extraordinary craft, which required neither captain nor crew. Its ebon sails, full out, caught the wind racing down the river. This wind, along with the strong current, kept them flying through the water, though the ship's origins might have had something to do with that. The high prow cleaved the river in two, as surely as Moses, infused with the hand of God, caused the Red Sea to part.

Aboard, Emma, Lilith, Molly, and Chynna were on their own. To whatever extent he could be, so was Conrad. Oq Ajdar and Ayeleye, the two Medius, had seen them off after Ayeleye had conjured the vessel for their journey back to the world of humans.

"We are forbidden to set foot on Earth," Oq Ajdar said when Emma queried her. "In any event, we cannot take part in what you are about to do. We have helped you to the limits allowed; possibly we may have gone a step or two over. But the possible consequences of that trespass is for us to worry about." She turned to Molly. "We will take special care of your mother."

"Of course," Ayeleye said, "she is our sister."

"But we would wait," they both said together, "if you choose to return, to pay our final respects."

"Yes," Molly said. "There's no question of that. I want to come back. Thank you."

Stepping closer to the chimera, Emma whispered, "Must we take Chynna? None of us are comfortable around her."

"Unsurprising," Oq Ajdar told her. "But necessary nonetheless. This journey is part of her fate also."

"But—"

The chimera held up a hand. "You will see," was all she said before she kissed her niece on both cheeks. "Return to us, Molly," she whispered. Then she and her brother stepped off the stone-and-wood dock, gaining the high bank.

"Chynna is an outcast, she exists nowhere," Conrad said to Emma out of earshot of the others. "She belongs with us."

Emma looked at him. "I don't have to like it."

Now the land of the Medius was far behind them. How long they had been sailing, how far they had come, none could say. But this was only to be expected. Theirs was a singular journey, perhaps the first one to leave from Surah's landing bound for the human world.

When Emma had asked Oq Ajdar how long their journey would take, the chimera had smiled grimly. "A very long time and no time at all."

Emma nodded in acceptance. "I do hope we will meet again."

That smile again, as enigmatic as the Sahara's dunes.

"IT'S THIS way." Bravo pointed the beam of light at the ceiling, in which there had been carved a shaft.

"So Antiphon didn't lie."

"Have faith, Ayla."

The shaft was big enough around to accommodate one person at a time. Peering up it, they could see hand- and footholds carved into the vertical stone.

"So we go up, not down," she said.

Bravo nodded. "I'm as surprised as you are. I was sure we'd have to descend to the Nabatean city beneath Petra."

"Instead, it seems we are to ascend into the mountain."

Not into the mountain, as it turned out. Up it. The niches, though difficult to climb, slippery with lichen and seeping mineralized water, only went a short way before they were gazing out onto a chamber large enough for a small party of five or six to stand comfortably. Spiraling upward from this was a stone staircase, with steep risers and shallow treads.

The staircase wound up and up above them. Even with their LED beams their flashlights could not find an end to it. Nevertheless, without hesitation they began their ascent.

The climb was arduous, not the least because the air felt heavy and stale, as if there was a distinct lack of oxygen. Before long they both developed headaches behind their eyes and in their temples. Still, they kept climbing, the darkness pierced only by two bobbing beams of blue-white light from their LED flashlights. After forty minutes of steady progress there was still no sign of an end to either the stairs or their labor.

And yet, something had changed. At first, with the pounding in their heads making it hard to think straight, they were at a loss as to what it might be. Then, as they climbed a little higher, a building pressure on their eardrums alerted them that a sound was building out of the blackness.

The sound split, split again as it increased in volume, until it seemed they were listening to the inchoate roar of an immense throng. The roaring lifted and fell arrhythmically. Each peak abraded their ears like a saw scraping through metal.

As they continued to spiral upward, the sound waves became almost overwhelming, and then when they crested another spiral they saw that the left-hand wall ended in a series of sharp points, ragged, their outer layers ripped off as if from some titanic force from deep within the earth. They had emerged onto a kind of promontory, raw, rugged, unmarked by the hand of humankind. In its center, most improbably, rose a stolid tree, ancient, beautifully vase-shaped—a pomegranate tree, if Bravo's eyes didn't deceive him, but without either leaves or fruit. Still, it abided, within a small oval of light coming in from far above. Though it was morning, the light was still wan and gray, barely visible.

When he told her what it was, Ayla said, "Just like in the Garden of Eden."

Bravo looked to their right, where the wall of rock kept going, up to the mountaintop, he supposed. Gouged into it was another set of stairs that turned sharply to the right within eight or nine steps, so that the staircase vanished into the rock face.

But it was what they saw beyond the tree that engaged their attention completely. It was an opening, a kind of shaft, lit by an infernal red-black light. The sound waves emanating from it were now so powerful it made even looking directly at it painful. They were obliged to blink rapidly to keep their eyes from drying out. They had difficulty catching their breath.

"What . . . what is that?" Ayla whispered.

"Your mother would know," Bravo said. "And so would Conrad. They'd both seen it before." He took her hand in his, squeezed it tightly. "It is a wound that never should have been inflicted: the gateway through which members of the Fallen have passed from their prison into our world. This is the breach Conrad inadvertently opened and your mother widened."

"PLEASE DON'T hate me."

"I don't think about you."

Chynna had come up to where Emma was standing in the prow of the black frigate.

"You didn't, I know," Chynna said. "But now . . ."

"I tolerate you, but just barely."

"Emma, I know—"

"You're not a person, you're a thing." Emma turned on her, teeth on edge. "You're a virus, infecting all of us Shaws. A fever we can't get rid of."

"Is that any way . . ." Chynna squeezed her eyes shut for a moment. It was not enough. Tears bloomed, spilling out, making runnels down her cheeks.

They had sailed into impenetrable fog. Waves lapped against the hull, as if they had entered a vast and unfathomable ocean. Likely they were no longer on the river at all.

Chynna began again, taking an unfortunate tack. "You wouldn't be here if it weren't for me."

Emma struck her then, her open hand slamming Chynna's cheek. It should have turned red, but it didn't.

"You see?" Emma snapped. "No blood rushing anywhere. No blood at all."

Lilith, who had been speaking with Conrad, turned abruptly and stepped between them, as if they were two boxers in a ring whose sparring had gotten out of hand.

Molly appeared beside them as if from out of nowhere. The last time Lilith had seen her, she was staring at the water, head down, brooding. Now she came at Chynna so quickly, Lilith barely had a chance to slow her.

Chynna's hands flew up as if to ward off a physical assault. "I can feel your contempt."

"You're unworthy even of that." Molly spat. Her eyes glittered and there was high color in her cheeks. "Why do you get to live and my mother doesn't?"

In the torturous silence that ensued, Lilith tried to fully restrain her sister, but Molly shrugged her off.

"No one can answer that, least of all me." Chynna's voice was a reedy whisper. "I'm so sorry, Molly. Please believe me, I am."

Their hatred for Chynna had scent, taste, and shape. It was an ugly thing. Nasty.

Conrad knew it, felt it strongly, but if he had any reaction to it he kept it to himself. He was unnaturally quiet, as if he, too, was an outcast who belonged to them. Nevertheless, he watched them with intense curiosity, as if at images in a kaleidoscope.

Lilith could feel her sister trembling. At least now that Chynna had backed away, melting into the fog-bound air, Molly let Lilith hold on to her. Her fury momentarily abated, she allowed herself to seek some solace in family.

"Don't let her get under your skin," Lilith said quietly to both of them.

"Too late for that," Emma replied. "She's in my blood."

Molly began to sob, caught herself, turned her face into Lilith's shoulder.

Around them a low moaning arose, as if from the deep, along with a sense of immense beasts gliding under their passage. No one spoke or moved as the ship raced onward into the eye of the fog, as the moaning resolved itself into the dissonance of souls in torment.

"THE HOWLING of souls in torment," Ayla said. "That's what it sounds like."

Curious, she started forward in an attempt to peer over the rim of one of the knife-sharp rock teeth rising high above them, but as she made to pass by the tree Bravo pulled her back. He shook his head. "Too dangerous."

"This is what has to heal," Ayla said. "Maybe we can find a way—"

"The two of us aren't knowledgeable or powerful enough."

He pointed, and they mounted the first steps of the second staircase carved into the right wall, leaving the howling pressure of chaos behind.

Wait, a voice said in the center of his mind. *Wait. We are coming.*

Bravo knew that voice as well as he knew his own, and he took Ayla back down to the promontory. *Grandfather! Where are you?*

Close now, Conrad said.

He was aware of Ayla staring at him. To her, it must look as if he had suddenly frozen in place. He put a finger against his lip to reassure her. *How close?*

We hear what you hear: the howling of souls in torment.

Ayla and I are on the promontory. We can see the Rift. And the tree.

What tree?

The old pomegranate tree, anchored in the rock. It's in the patch of light that—

Bravo, there is no patch of light. There is no outlet above you save for the second flight of stairs that lead out onto the Nabatean ceremonial plateau.

Bravo turned. *Then what . . . ?* But he knew. Now he knew what the tree was. Ayla's idle comment had been truer than she knew. This tree was, in fact, the very same one from which Eve had plucked the pomegranate at the serpent's behest.

And now here came the serpent at them, hissing and spitting venom.

53

THE FOG, LIFTING, REVEALED A SHORELINE OF SORTS. THEY had returned to the river, though it seemed unclear whether they had ever left it, such was the vertiginous nature of their journey. The river, it appeared to them now, was endless. Perhaps it circled all the world contained in the Spheres. This was the world myth at the heart of virtually every ancient culture's beliefs; and that was certainly Conrad's own surmise.

The shore was unlike any place they knew of where a vessel would dock or even drop anchor. Basalt-black cliffs, steep as to be almost vertical—a promontory of forbidding proportions that seemed inimical to any ship, even one as large and stout as their British frigate. And yet their vessel eased its way into a cove protected by gnashing basalt teeth on either side. A steep flight of steps that began precisely at deck level had been incised into the rock. There were no currents here, no eddies. The water was like a sheet of glass.

Conrad led them as they scrambled over the gunwale and began their climb. Soon enough, the river, the frigate itself were lost to view. Glancing back, it seemed as if they had never existed, that this was all a dream into which Oq Ajdar and Ayeleye had cast them.

And yet, everything felt real, and when Molly, running past Conrad, going too fast, scraped her shin, the blood she shed was real enough. It was Emma who noticed the change in Conrad's demeanor first. Though he continued his climb, his head and shoulders became unnaturally still, the atmosphere about him darkened considerably, and as she hurried along to ask if he was all right, she felt a chill coming off him in waves.

"Grandfather," she said, alarmed. "Grandfather."

But he did not answer, and when she passed him and turned back, she saw that his glassy eyes were fixed on something or someone she could not see, his gaze far, far away. She became agitated then. What if, now that he had left the protection Haya's shell provided, he had been recognized? What if he was being psychically attacked? What if, God forbid, he was being taken over by the Sum of All Shadows, who had been seeking him ever since his physical death?

Lilith, seeing the blood drain from her beloved's face, grabbed her forearm. "Darling, what is it?"

"Look," Emma said. "Look at him. I'm afraid he's been discovered."

Lilith shook her head. "No, I don't think so. I think by his own volition he's in contact with someone."

Emma stared at her, heart leaping. Was it possible that Conrad had reconnected with Bravo? "How could you know that?"

"I . . ." Lilith frowned. "I don't know. But ever since we disembarked I've been feeling . . ."

"Feeling what?"

"Different . . . I don't know, but the higher we climb the clearer the change becomes." She smiled. "For the time being, don't worry about your grandfather. I have a strong intuition that we are nearing the end. One way or another this conflict will be resolved. At this moment in time, Conrad cannot be touched or interfered with. All his power is now concentrated here, with us."

"So it's win or die."

"That's it precisely."

At that moment, they heard Molly shouting from up ahead. They could not see her, however, and they hurried on, Emma making sure that both Conrad and Chynna weren't being left behind.

Chynna had not uttered a word since the shipboard confrontation. Cocooned in her white cloak that covered her head, she had kept to herself, away from the others, her eyes averted, her head down. She looked for all the world like a penitent on a pilgrimage to the Holy Land.

Molly shouted again for them to hurry up. Emma and Lilith herded everyone around a sharp turn to the left. They found themselves inside what should have been the cliff itself, but was clearly not. For one thing, the character of the rock was completely different. The basalt was gone; in its place stone of a more sedimentary origin. For another, a spiral staircase lay before them, rising up a conical shaft that was clearly not a product of natural forces.

Too, there were glimmers of light coming from high above them, as if masses of fireflies had gathered for some unknowable conclave. Molly was already on the spiral, beckoning them upward.

"Come on! Come on!"

They needed no further urging. They raced ahead, up the spiral, faster and faster. Suddenly, they heard a deep, ominous rumbling and the entire staircase began to tremble and shudder. The firefly lights from above winked out, and the first rocks came hurtling down toward them.

THE SERPENT resolved itself. It grew hands and feet, then arms. When the legs appeared, he stood upright. Its triangular head morphed into that of the more recognizable face of Astoreth, the Third Sphere angel. He was clad in warrior's armor. The eyes, however, red as rubies, were the same as the serpent's.

He did not make a move toward either Bravo or Ayla. Instead, they came toward him in an attempt to hem him in against the tree and the Rift beyond. Drawing on his still dawning Aqqibari powers, Bravo created a sorcerous ice-spear while Ayla circled around to the other side of the angel.

Bravo, about to engage him, caught a movement out of the corner of his eye. At the same moment, Ayla shouted a warning. The next instant, a sturdy branch of the tree, acting unlike any other tree branch, whipped through the air. If he hadn't ducked back, it would have sliced right through him.

Astoreth took advantage of the distraction to swing his sword into the rock wall just above the top of the spiral stairs. Just before the sword made contact, Bravo threw his ice-lance. It struck Astoreth's sword hand, the blade slid sideways, scraping along the rock face instead of carving into it. The outermost sheet of rock exploded, crumbled, and collapsed down into the shaft around which the staircase wound.

THE HAIL of jagged rock and stones fell down the shaft. Conrad had shouted a warning, and they pressed as flat as they could against the outer wall of the staircase, shielding their eyes with their raised forearms. All but Molly, who had been in the forefront. She was still on the center of the treads, having been closer to the rockfall and thus having had less time to react. Although due to Bravo's intervention the main part of the avalanche of stone was hurtling down the shaft, bits and pieces were flying off, bouncing in every direction, including Molly's.

It was Chynna who, peeling herself off the wall, leapt up the stairs to grab Molly and rush her out of harm's way. A good-sized rock smashed into the tread precisely where Molly had stood just a moment before.

Molly, breathless and a bit shaken up, felt herself sheltered against Chynna's body, inside her cloak. She expected Chynna's body to be cold, but it wasn't, and she wondered at this, just as she wondered about the animus she had directed at Chynna. She had, after all, killed Leviathan, a pretty amazing feat, so far as Molly was concerned. Was it her fault that she was alive and Surah wasn't? Wasn't Molly just using her as a convenient whipping post on which to vent her anguish? But Emma despised her, as well.

"Thanks," she said softly, as the last of the rockfall swept past them.

"I wasn't going to let anything happen to you," Chynna said. "I'm not going to let anything happen to any of you."

Molly looked at her. "You don't—"

"That is my purpose. That is why I am here," Chynna said, as much to herself as to Molly.

Chynna's smile, when it appeared, made her look centuries younger, like a young woman. Molly saw herself in that smile, and this made her wonder if she was seeing Chynna as she had been when she was Molly's age, living on the island of Arwad—or Arvad, as it had been known then—innocent, before she had become a thief, a fugitive, the lover of a First Sphere Seraph. Before she had founded a dynasty.

"Everything was simpler then, wasn't it?" Molly said.

Chynna's eyes opened wide in surprise, and the smile appeared again, like sunlight at the ending of a storm. "I couldn't remember what I had once been," she said, "until I saw you. Then I remembered. At first, I was terribly sad. But then grateful to you for having brought my former life back to me." Her eyes shone. "You cannot imagine the gift you have given me."

"I wish I had known you then," Molly said. "We might have become friends."

Chynna regarded her carefully, possibly to find out whether Molly was making a fool of her. Coming to a decision, she answered, "And wouldn't that have been fun."

ASTORETH, ENRAGED, rushed Bravo, but in so doing he turned his back on Ayla. Following Bravo's instructions to the letter, she dove deep inside her mind, to the core where her Aqqibari self lay waiting for its moment. The ice-spear was in her hand and, without an instant's thought, she threw it. The point shattered Astoreth's armor, but penetrated only a bit farther. The moment he stopped, whirled to confront her, Bravo threw another ice-spear directly into the rent Ayla's had made in his armor.

This one ruptured sinew and muscle, shattered bones, as it pierced him to the core. Bravo stepped up, pulled out the ice-blade, and after Astoreth collapsed in a heap, severed his head from his neck.

If this was a victory, it proved Pyrrhic. In moving to where Astoreth stood, Bravo had put himself within close proximity to the tree. One of its sorcerous branches moved as if to circle Bravo's waist like a tentacle, but he was able to twist away at the last moment. In retaliation, the branch struck him across the back with such force he was propelled into the curving rock wall.

54

WHEN CONRAD AND HIS GROUP REACHED THE PROMONTORY they found it suffused with a ruby hue, as if the air itself were bleeding. The atmosphere was thick, had about it the stickiness of blood drying in the noonday sun.

Ayla was fully concentrated on Bravo, who had fallen, insensate, between the wall and the tree. She paid the newcomers no mind, was scarcely aware of them. She was attempting to insinuate herself past the branch that had struck him and was now guarding against him being dragged away from the tree. She launched herself forward, armed with an ice-spear, but was halted by a hand on her forearm. She whirled, expecting another Fallen angel, only to find herself face-to-face with her father.

Dumbstruck, she allowed him to bring her out of the radius of the tree's branches. She had seen Conrad only in the few photos her mother had of the two of them during the time of their passionate but short-lived affair.

She had so many questions, but no time even to ask them. Bravo was hurt, unconscious. Pulling away from Conrad, she cocked her arm and threw the ice-spear at the trunk of the tree. It shattered on impact. If the tree suffered any damage it wasn't immediately visible. She created another, thicker ice-spear, but Conrad, grasping her wrist, said, "It will do no good."

Fighting not to be overwhelmed by frustration and fear for Bravo, she snapped, "I can't just stand here doing nothing."

"Sometimes to do nothing is the only thing."

Her frustration burst like a lanced boil. "A homespun koan? Now? If you have something constructive to suggest, do it. Otherwise, get out of the way."

"I understand your exasperation."

"No," she said. "You don't."

"Oh, but I do." Conrad pulled on her, back to where the others were arrayed in a semicircle. "I have been in contact with my grandson. He will know what to do and when to do it. Please talk to Emma. She will explain everything."

Reluctantly, Ayla went to where Emma was. The two stood shoulder to shoulder, speaking in low tones, or rather, Emma spoke and Ayla listened.

In that space of time, Conrad stepped forward and, looking up, appeared to address the tree itself. "Your double-layered ploy with the Liderc and the Churel was clever, but not clever enough. My grandson wasn't compromised. He's more now; he is Aqqibari."

"I know who and what he is." The tree spoke in a voice like a buzzing of ten thousand flies feeding off maggoty meat; there was a greedy undertone that could not be hidden.

"Let him go," Conrad said. "It's me you've been searching for. It's me you want." He took another step forward. "Let him go and take me instead."

The tree shook, as if in laughter, but the sound emanating from it hurt everyone's eardrums and made their eyes shed droplets of blood.

"You old fool," the tree said—though everyone now knew that the tree was only the form, not the evil arch-demon beneath—"I desire you, him, and everyone you have conveniently brought here to the final resting place, the graveyard that once had been Eden."

Conrad ignored the taunt. "I am only an emissary," he said.

The tree tossed its limbs. "What nonsense. You—you could never be anyone's emissary."

"In a sense you're right," Conrad acknowledged. "There is only one for whom I would be emissary. It is he who sent me to you with a message."

The branches ceased all movement. The tree might as well have been carved from granite. "I do not listen to messages, no matter who—"

"Your brother," Conrad said in a clear, ringing voice, "wishes to speak with you."

"My brother?" The tree thundered. "I have no brother. I have no siblings whatsoever. I am an entity unto myself."

And yet the tree was dissolving, tossing off its knotty cloak, revealing what lurked beneath.

"And what if I did have a brother? He was the one who was chosen to be born again. Why not me? Are we not from the same flesh? The same hand fashioned us."

The dark helm rose above them. Red-rimmed black eyes glared out from within the war-helm.

"I should have been the one to be born in Bethlehem. I should have been the one to be venerated. I should have been the one to be turned into a deity. Instead, I was stuck kowtowing to the increasingly petty whims of God."

They could not see his face, which was possibly just as well, even a blessing; to look upon the face of Evil, it was said, was to be scarred even unto the afterlife.

"But nothing is fair in this Sphere or any other. That became my mantra."

Even the exoskeleton of his armor was difficult to look at for long stretches. It absorbed light, ate it up avidly as gluttons ate food. Dizzyingly, he radiated shadows in every direction at once: hence Lucifer's other name, the Sum of All Shadows.

BLOOD INCHING down from his hairline ushered Bravo into consciousness. Blood pounded through his head like a herd of stampeding bulls. Still, he kept his eyes closed, though it exacerbated the pain. He was listening, and from listening, learned that Conrad, Emma, Lilith, Molly, and Chynna had made it onto the promontory. The sense of his beloved sister being near him again was almost overwhelming, and this, above anything else, calmed him, for his grandfather's plan was so dangerous that one false move would mean annihilation for all of them, and following, all humankind. He learned, too, of the thorny negotiation between mortal enemies. It was as Conrad had predicted: there was no real negotiation, merely the appearance of one, a shell easily cracked through. The outcome, therefore, was inevitable. This also Conrad had predicted. Bravo waited for a break in the vitriol, then spoke to his grandfather. As in a dream, many things were passed back and forth between the dreamer and his subconscious, in the blink of an eye, for in this state time ceased to have meaning. The plan was repeated, now in its most minute detail. But like all man-made plans the way events unfolded made it moot, or, in any case, broke it to bits.

THE TREE. The pomegranate tree. Molly knew at once that it wasn't a tree they confronted. She knew who it was and what they were up against. She didn't care or, more accurately, she had more important things to do than fret over their horrid adversary. She had no time for terror or even hesitation.

The instant she saw the tree-that-was-no-tree freeze at Conrad's remark, she edged her way to her right, toward where Bravo lay, crumpled against the rock wall. His eyes were closed, and she supposed he was unconscious. No matter. She had made up her mind to get him out of there, whether or not the branch tried to stop her.

Apart from her wits and her speed she had no weapon, but these were enough, she figured. They would have to be. She stood stock-still as the tree began to transform into the Sum of All Shadows, lest he look over and spot movement. Out of the corner of her eye, she saw Chynna glance her way, shake her head imperceptibly but sternly. Set on her goal, she paid Chynna no mind.

When Conrad once more engaged verbally with the armored figure, she crouched down and ran, fast as she could. She reached Bravo, slapped his cheek twice in order to rouse him, then grabbed him by his jacket, and pulled at him. To her surprise, his eyes snapped open and he grinned at her. He scrambled to his feet with such alacrity that she realized he'd been simply laying low and she returned his grin in spades.

Together, they raced along the outer wall, heading for the edge of what had once been the extent of the tree's reach. But, of course, the tree was gone, and in its place stood the ultimate warrior of Evil.

"Go, go, go!" she hissed, pushing him forward. He made it past the perimeter, but she . . .

CONRAD SAW with mounting horror how even the cleverest of plans can go off the rails within the space of an unannounced heartbeat. Without even looking in her direction, one of Lucifer's shadows extended itself, flowing across the rock like molten lava. Forming itself into the shape of a long blade, it caught Molly in midflight, penetrating the meat of her right shoulder. She didn't cry out, and she didn't look for help. Instead, she stared directly into those black-and-red eyes. Conrad didn't know whether she was foolish, fearless, or just plain crazy. Whatever the case, with the plan blown, he had to help her. But before he could make a move . . .

THE MOMENT Lilith saw her sister was in trouble she was on the move. But to her astonishment, someone else brushed past her—the last person she would expect to help out in such dire straits. Chynna, her robe flying behind her like a cape, was already at Molly's side. *How the hell had she gotten there?* Lilith wondered, not pausing an instant, but speeding on toward her sister and the Shaw progenitor.

Chynna stepped in front so that the shadow-blade struck her instead of Molly. Or it would have if Lucifer hadn't spotted someone else. And in that unexpected moment when he forgot all about Molly, Chynna shepherded her back to where Conrad stood with Emma and Ayla, both of whom, under strict orders, and despite their human impulse to help, had not moved from the places to which Conrad had directed them. He was about to put his hands on Molly's shoulder to heal her when he saw that Chynna had already done that. For several seconds the two stared into each other's eyes as if no one and nothing else existed. What might have passed between them was a question that was destined never to be answered. Possibly it had no answer, or an adequate one, anyway.

FROM SEEMINGLY far away and close at hand at once, Lucifer said one word that chilled them all to their bones, not the least Conrad, who had made a desperate gamble the conflict would not come to this.

"Lilith.

"Lilith, the first wife of Adam," Lucifer thundered. "Come closer. Come to me."

As if in a trance, Lilith obeyed. She felt pulled by a force so strong it took her breath away. She felt like a fish, well hooked, being reeled in by the most violent of fishermen. At that moment, she saw her fate laid out before her: no Emma, no life, no happily ever after. Just death and whatever agony Lucifer had planned for her that went beyond death, that went on and on for all eternity. Did he want her as his bride, as his sacrificial lamb? Both? Or something far more dreadful, something so unthinkable it froze the very blood in her veins?

In that sense, she was already dead, already his. Floating outside her body, she was witness to the horror about to be executed, saw him, saw beyond the dark helm, to a visage no human being should be subjected to. Her mind screamed inside itself, the scream echoing on and on like a pinball ricocheting from bumper to bumper, and with each deflection instead of racking up points, he was being imprinted on her brain.

Riding the ruddy atmosphere, Lilith saw him take her body up in his gauntlet. She thought she felt the icy chill all the way through her clothes to her goose-bumped skin, but she could not be sure.

But she did hear his voice: "Lilith, first wife of Adam. Lilith, who knew of the fruits of Eden's tree. Lilith, who had partaken of the pomegranate of knowledge without any urging from my serpent. Smart Lilith, clever Lilith, brilliant Lilith, ostracized by God, destined to live outside the walls of Eden even after Adam and Eve were banished. Lilith, who never married, never bore children. Lilith, who died alone and unloved."

Lucifer's eyes glistered as if in sunlight. "You are here with me now. What a gift you have brought me, Conrad! I can undo everything that God did in the aftermath of Lilith's heartless expulsion." He drew Lilith closer to him, closer to the heart that beat or did not beat beneath the dark and abominable armor he himself had fashioned.

"You see how it is now, Conrad. How you chose to live your life and beyond it on the wrong side. You venerate a being who guards all knowledge so jealously that those who even attempt to learn are punished all the rest of their lives. Goaded on to imitation, human males took up that torch, punished females who wanted to learn just as their God punished Lilith and Eve. To my way of thinking there is no one crueler, no one more despicable, no one more wicked.

"But now that I have Lilith, I am able to wipe out everything they have done in their name. I will start all over, and this time it will be done right."

He pressed Lilith to his heart, beginning the process of completely bonding her to him.

55

CHYNNA TURNED TO CONRAD. "YOU MUST DO IT NOW."

Horrified, Emma said, "We can't. Not when he has Lilith. I won't allow it."

"You have no choice," Chynna told her firmly. "The time has come to do what must be done."

Emma beseeched Conrad. "Grandfather, please. She is the love of my life."

Afterward, no one understood why Conrad, man of action, hesitated, unless he knew, which seemed at once incredible and within his unknowable capabilities.

Whatever the case, Chynna flew by him, rushed at Lucifer with all the speed she could muster, and launched herself, propelled like the stone from David's slingshot.

"When will my torment end?" she had asked.

"You will know," Oq Ajdar had answered, *"when Death stares you in the face."*

And here was Death, in the form of Lucifer, staring her in the face, as she grasped his armor, clinging like a mountain climber to the sheerest cliff of the tallest mountain in all the Spheres.

Behind her, Conrad had taken his place, as she knew he would, in the center of the semicircle. He had trained his family well on their long river voyage and their climb up to the graveyard of Eden. The four Aqqibari were ranged around him, and now they began the inward journey he had made them practice over and over in the strange, enveloping fog, so that they could go deeper, ever deeper, into the dormant part of them, where the Aqqibari in them dwelled.

Chynna could see the torment on Lilith's face. What was being done to her was beyond human endurance; she knew that much from her long talks with Leviathan, who loved nothing better than to boast about his powers and those of his Lord and Master, which he coveted most.

Her heart, or whatever her heart had become, went out to Lilith, and she whispered, "Hold on. Hold on, now." Reassurance that applied to herself, as well.

Behind her, five voices had started up—the coordinated sounds similar to a Gregorian chant. The Aqqibari words rose up from the bellies, the stomachs, the throats, the mouths of Bravo, Emma, Ayla, Molly, and Conrad, their leader. He had told Emma that the ice-weapons were useless against Lucifer. Likewise fire, an element in which Lucifer regularly reveled.

But there was still light—the pure white light of faith.

As they continued, the atmosphere coalesced around them. Light sprang into being, grew until it was brighter than the moon, brighter than the stars. Brighter than the sun. The light blinded Lucifer, so that he was obliged to raise one gauntlet to protect his eyes. Still, the light grew, and he staggered back, the heel of one booted hoof at the edge of a valley between two saw-toothed rocks beyond which was the yowling maelstrom of the Rift. Chynna pushed at his chest, trying to help him stumble over backward into the abyss.

But then, at the height of the globe's blinding illumination, Lucifer swung his arm in an arc, and the light was snuffed out.

Conrad and his family stood stunned to silence. This had not been expected; this was not part of the plan. The plan lay in pieces at their feet. Certain defeat rose up, confronting them all with annihilation. They had trusted in Conrad, and he had failed them, failed all of humankind. Failed God.

Molly felt like a blow their collective faith in God falter, guttering like a flame at the end of its life. And without understanding why, the one who had never in her life believed in God yelled, "No! No, no, no! God would not desert us. Not now, not ever!"

They all heard her, of course, but it was Bravo who was spurred into action. The light had failed, so what was left them? He knew. He knew!

Stepping forward, he looked inward, at the place inside himself he had never dared look before. The dark place, the forbidden place, deep down at the bottom of the well he himself had made.

He felt again Ayla's fingers probing his bare back.

"You know, looking more closely at these wounds," she had said, *"it's almost as if you once had wings, which were clipped off where they met your body."*

"That would make me an angel," he had replied. *"Some kind of Fallen angel."*

Was that it? Was he some kind of angel, Fallen or otherwise? He didn't know; he didn't think he'd ever know, which was okay by him. Some things in life need to remain a mystery.

Light hadn't worked, but what about its reverse? And so he summoned the shadows. From deep inside him, he found the right incantations, the forbidden ones, to be used only in extremis, the furthest reaches, which is where they found themselves now.

The shadows grew exponentially, and as they grew they solidified. They became something for which no one had ever had a name, not even the earliest shamans of human history, when the world was young and the Spheres were more closely aligned.

All of Bravo's shadows had been summoned from the deep. The sum of them rushed at Lucifer with the force of a tidal wave. He tried to stop it, but his own shadows paled compared to this Sum of All Shadows, and he stumbled backward. One hoof slipped off the edge of the promontory, and he canted backward, arms flailing. On his chest, Chynna dug into Lilith's shoulders, ripped her off the armor, tossing her backward.

At the same moment Chynna and the Sum of All Shadows shoved Lucifer backward, Bravo caught Lilith. His knees bent under her falling weight, and then Emma, rushing to his side, took Lilith in her arms, kissing every part of her face.

Lucifer was gone, and Chynna with him. They realized that had been her plan all along. Her centuries with Leviathan had bound her fate to Lucifer's. It was her wish: not simply an end to her torment, but a victory as well, over Leviathan, over her worst nature.

Conrad strode to the lip of the abyss.

"Grandfather!" Emma cried, moving to follow him. But Bravo, who understood more than she did, held her back, kissed her cheek, said, "Only he can heal the wound he created. Leave him to it."

And they did, though by the time the Rift was sealed, healed for all time, there was nothing left of Conrad Shaw, apart from their memories of him.

EPILOGUE

In the Garden of Pomegranates

AS FOR THE REST, IT IS ALL HERE. BATTERED AND BRUISED, the small family group ended up in the Gnostic Observatines hospital/retreat, set in a lush oasis of date palms, fruit trees, and natural springs in an area between Marrakech and the Berber desert. From many of the rooms on the second floor of the facility could be seen the Atlas Mountains, the piercing blue sky, the occasional hawk or falcon, riding the thermals, circling, searching.

Each one reminded Bravo of Antiphon. He missed the great avian, her strength, her loving, sardonic wit. Certainly he did not regret resurrecting her, but he mourned the brevity of her second life. As for his grandfather, he felt only love, immense and abiding as the open sea. And, of course, gratitude for all the gifts and knowledge Conrad had given him. He did not miss his grandfather overly; he had mourned his physical death years ago. Besides, a part of Conrad was with him, would always be with him.

These were his thoughts as he lay on his stomach in his hospital bed following the surgery to repair his ripped-apart back. When the surgeon told him that he would have two scars between his shoulder blades and suggested Bravo consult with the on-site plastic surgeon, Bravo demurred. Though surprised, the surgeon had, of course, accepted his decision. To Bravo, those scars were a reminder of the many things he had survived; he did not want them skinned over. In the back of his mind lurked Ayla's observation that the scars looked like the stubs of wings, clipped off and discarded.

Ayla came and sat by his bedside every day. They held hands, mostly wordlessly, together watching the shadows of clouds race each other across the palm fronds and over the sand dunes, until they were far away. Once, thunder came to them, clear and trembling, along with a quick stab of lightning, blue-white and electric in the pewter sky.

Emma popped in twice or, sometimes, three times a day. As with Ayla, they didn't talk much. They didn't need to, and the truth was, Bravo was mentally exhausted. The summoning of the Sum of All Shadows had taken its toll on him; he suspected that its imprint would be with him to the end of his days. But each day was better, which was true for all of them.

It was Lilith who had taken the worst of it. To her horror and extreme distress, Emma had discovered marks on Lilith's chest, breasts, and stomach, as if suckers from a monstrous sea creature had been attached to her. The doctors assured her that they would fade in time, so they were hardly the worst of it. For the first week of their stay at the oasis, Lilith remained unconscious, sweating, gripped by a fever the doctors were at a loss to explain. Neither could they get it under control. Their mounting alarm terrified Emma. Once or twice, as they frantically pumped more and more liquids and increasingly exotic antibiotic cocktails into their patient, Emma was afraid she would lose Lilith.

But on the seventh day the fever broke, never to return. Afterward, Emma shooed the nurses away, bathed Lilith herself, sluicing away the sickly sweet stench of illness and near-death, tenderly kissing every part of her the sponge cleansed.

And it was a joyous day, indeed, for both women when Lilith opened her eyes. Emma was the first sight that swam into her vision, and she laughed and cried all at once, Emma joining her. Yet still, as Emma slept beside her beloved, she was awakened time and again by the violence of Lilith's nightmares. These persisted, even when she took the Ambien the doctors prescribed. Emma prayed for them to end, for Lilith awoke each morning exhausted, trembling and fearful, until, swaddled in Emma's embrace, she slowly calmed. Often, then and only then, she fell into a blessedly dreamless sleep for an hour or so. Sometimes Emma did, as well.

For Molly, the sight of her sister in such distress was too much. To consider the loss of her sister as well as her mother was insupportable. She wept every time she entered Lilith's room, and to witness Emma's anguish was terrible. Wonderful, as well. The fact that her sister had someone who adored her heart and soul was a balm against the ordeal they were going through.

Molly despised herself for not being of use to her sister, but there was Emma, and Molly didn't want to intrude on their intimate bond. Instead, she swam alone in the retreat's pool, wandered the perimeter of the oasis, ate and napped during the heat of the day, not only because there was nothing else to do but because she tossed and turned all night, fearing the worst would come to pass. Late in the afternoon, when the desert's nighttime chill crept down from the mountain, she lounged in the lush garden at the oasis's still center, beneath the dappled shade of a pomegranate tree. The irony of that pierced her like a knife, as did her guilt that she could not help either Bravo or her sister. She prayed for them both, but seeing as how she had no expertise in prayer, she had no idea if it would do any good. Still, something was better than nothing, right?

Apart from the health of her family, she had much weighing on her mind. She mourned the loss of her mother. So soon, so soon! Again and again, she returned to that glorious pool with its gentle koi, its bejeweled dragonfly, water-spiders skimming the glinting surface. And, above all, her mother, swimming with her, baring her crocodile teeth in a greeting that only a mother and child could share. Always, her eyes burned, swollen and red from weeping. She missed her mother desperately, missed her world almost as much. She felt torn, one foot here, the other there. She was calmer when she imagined herself there, no doubt about it.

And then there came a day, three weeks after they had arrived wounded and exhausted in body, mind, and spirit, when they all met at dusk under the pomegranate tree.

"I want to have a memorial," Molly declared, after they had all exchanged hugs and kisses.

"Conrad didn't want a memorial," Bravo said. "He was quite clear on the matter."

"I think," Ayla said softly, "she means for Surah."

"Actually, I don't mean either." Molly looked from one to the other, trying to gauge the temperature of each of the members of her strange and wonderful new family. She took a deep breath, let it out. "I'd like us to have a memorial for Chynna."

For a moment, a stunned silence reigned, until Emma said, "You're joking, right? Tell me you're joking."

"I'm not." Molly, expecting this resistance, stood firm. She had been pondering this idea for days, until it grew too strong for her to keep to herself. "Whatever she did in the past—"

Emma gave out an exasperated sound.

Molly began again. "Whatever she did in the past, it's on us to acknowledge what she did for us—for all of us. She saved me, twice. She saved Lilith. And her bravery with Lucifer—"

"Molly's correct," Bravo said. "It's the right thing to do."

They met at midnight in the garden, beside the pomegranate tree. Above them, a hundred million stars burned the black sky. Torches had been set; they saw each other as flickering images in an old-time movie, and Bravo was put in mind of Conrad's epic journey to Ethiopia with his friend, the Farsighter poet, William Butler Yeats.

Molly spoke first, of her intimate moments in Chynna's company, and then Bravo reminded them of the legacy Chynna had left them, the good she had done them in an attempt to atone for her past mistakes. And then, strangely, Emma asked to speak. They all turned to her expectantly; they could not imagine what she might say.

She started slowly, hesitantly, but soon enough her confidence returned, and her voice rang out through the garden. "When I look back on the events of the last weeks, I realize that I missed something crucial. Chynna lost the one thing in her long, dissolute life she cherished above anything else. I cannot imagine what it must be like to discover that the daughter you loved unconditionally never actually existed. What frightful anguish this must have caused her is unthinkable. That it didn't immediately tear her apart is a miracle. And now I'm sorry I fought with her when I should have given her solace."

And that was it; there was nothing more to say. They bid each other good night, drifted off in twos. Save for Molly. She went directly to the pool, lit a phosphorescent green, and, shedding her clothes, executed a perfect shallow dive. She swam laps until her arms ached and her legs grew tired. She longed for her mother to be beside her, delighting in the water as she did. Even the dragonfly would have sufficed.

Instead, she got something even better. She watched, wide-eyed, as her sister made her careful way along the concrete pathways that wound to the pool. She wore a one-piece bathing suit that covered most of the sucker marks. It was the first time Molly had seen her sister alone since they had arrived.

Lilith used the ladder to slip into the pool. Molly swam over to her and, wordlessly, they embraced. They held each other like that for a long time. Molly could feel hot tears on her bare shoulder, and kissed the side of Lilith's head.

"I'm so sorry," Molly said.

"I know."

"How are you?"

"How is any one of us?" Lilith sighed. "Damaged, but not beyond repair, I hope."

"You have Emma. I'm so happy for that."

"And you. I have you."

There was a silence then, causing Lilith to hold Molly at arm's length, the better to see her expression. "I do have you, don't I?"

Molly nodded. "But for just a little while longer."

Lilith's look of alarm spread over her face. "What d'you mean?"

"Sister, I'm going back to my mother's world. Oq Ajdar and Ayeleye are waiting for me." *And her beloved dragonfly,* she added silently, *which surely has a piece of my mother inside it.* "They're keeping my mother's body until my return. I promised them I would come."

"But—"

"This is my choice. I want to."

Lilith searched her sister's eyes. "But then you'll return. You'll come back to me."

Molly smiled. "You'll always be in my heart. But, no, when I go back I'll stay, take charge of my mother's lands, her house, the ponds." She smiled, trying to coax one out of Lilith. "I belong there, sister. I know that. I knew it the minute I slipped into the pool with my mother. I never felt such joy in my life. I want to feel that again, and every day of my life."

"But I don't know, your family is here."

"I have family there, as well. My aunt and uncle, and all the wonders they can show me. This is what I want, Lilith. This is what I need. Please give me your blessing."

"You'll go anyway, no matter what I say."

"Yes, but I want to leave without feeling ripped away from you. Please, sister. Give me this gift."

And, of course, Lilith did, for she had come to love her sister with all her heart, and though she would miss her, knowing she was happy and content was paramount.

As for King Solomon's gold, there was no sign of it. Lucifer had blocked the way down to the Nabatean plaza below Petra. It was clear he had not found it, or else he would have taken it back with him to distribute to the remaining Fallen. It was nowhere on or around the promontory. So the question remained: Where was it? Did it even exist? Beleth had claimed he had found it, but that might have been a ruse to placate his Lord and Master, for surely he would have been severely punished had he reported failure.

In the end, the family had more important matters on their minds than a cache of gold, alchemical or not, that might or might not exist. Their love for one another manifested itself as the days at the oasis grew to weeks, the weeks to a month.

After that, the gold was forgotten, as it had been so many times in the past, as it would be again in humankind's future.

Then Molly was gone, having said her farewells, and the four remaining—Bravo, Ayla, Emma, and Lilith boarded one of the Observatine jets. On the short flight back to Malta, they mostly slept.

At one point, however, Bravo awakened to see Ayla looking at him.

"What?" he whispered, his voice still clogged with sleep. "What is it?"

And Ayla smiled, even laughed softly. "Nothing," she said, and took his hand in hers. "Nothing at all."

ACKNOWLEDGMENTS

Many, many people were instrumental in the creation of *The Sum of All Shadows,* but I'd like to mention first and foremost my wonderful publishers, Tom Doherty and Linda Quinton, whose love of my work and unwavering belief in me has been, as always, of immeasurable value. My wife, Victoria, my first editor, with whom I am constantly consulting to make sure each scene works psychologically. Dan and Linda, my shepherds, who keep out the dark. Last, but surely not least, W. B. Yeats, whose collected works were inspirational, and continue to echo throughout the Testament series.

ABOUT THE AUTHOR

Eric Van Lustbader is the author of twenty-five international bestsellers, as well as twelve Jason Bourne novels, including *The Bourne Enigma* and *The Bourne Initiative*. His books have been translated into over twenty languages. He lives with his wife in New York City and Long Island.